Sara Paretsky
BREAKDOWN

HODDER &
STOUGHTON

First published in the United States of America in 2012 by The Penguin Group

First published in Great Britain in 2012 by Hodder & Stoughton
An Hachette UK company

1

A CIP catalogue record for this title is available from the British Library

Hardback ISBN 978 0 340 99413 9
Trade Paperback ISBN 978 0 340 99414 6

Printed and bound by CPI Group (UK) Ltd, Croydon, CR0 4YY

Hodder & Stoughton policy is to use papers that are natural, renewable and recyclable
products and made from wood grown in sustainable forests. The logging and manufacturing
processes are expected to conform to the environmental regulations of the country of origin.

Hodder & Stoughton Ltd
338 Euston Road
London NW1 3BH

www.hodder.co.uk

For Tom Owens, Bill Towner, Michael Flug, and the many other librarians who've helped me navigate the great sea of learning—including my mother, Mary E. Paretsky

"He who owns books and loves them is wise." —Roger Duvoisin

ACKNOWLEDGMENTS

Doctors Nancy and Ed Burke talked me through Leydon Ashford's mental illness. They also put great effort into helping me find someone who could give me inside information on the operation of a forensic wing of a state mental hospital. In the end, I relied on my imagination. Ruhetal State Mental Hospital is a completely fictitious facility. I invented all of its protocols, personnel, history, budget, and architecture. Aaltje Baumgart helped me select medications for Leydon, Xavier, and V. I.

Professor Mark Heyrman at the University of Chicago Law School persuaded me that it would be a terrible mistake to have V.I. go undercover as a patient in a mental hospital. He explained law and procedures that would give a lawyer access to someone charged with a crime but considered unfit to plead by reason of mental defect. All the errors in interpreting law and due process are mine alone, and shouldn't be imputed either to Professor Heyrman or to V.I. Warshawski.

Jonathan Paretsky stepped me through the different obligations of trustees, guardians, and those entrusted with durable powers of attorney. Again, all mistakes are mine alone.

Joanna Krotz read an early version of the manuscript and made many helpful comments. Sue Riter read a late version and was similarly helpful. Thanks to both friends for their insight and support.

Tampier Lake does exist in the southwest suburbs of Chicago, but Tampier Lake Township is a completely fictitious entity. Similarly, I have carved out a fictitious Area Six in the downtown area for the Chicago Police Department.

I am indebted to Dave Case, watch commander at the 018th District in Chicago, for letting me sit in on police briefing sessions and letting me ride with his team, who show exemplary patience and dedication in dealing with the public. V.I.'s contentious interactions with Chicago police officers are due to her fractious temper and the demands of the story, and don't reflect my own experience of the CPD.

I have taken liberties with the Marlboro Festival's schedule by extending their concert season to Labor Day. Thanks to Laura Shapiro for suggesting that Jake Thibaut be invited to be a musician in residence at Marlboro. Maybe next year, I'll get to go myself.

Louis Baggetto sketched out the dynamic between brother and sister that provides the linchpin for *Breakdown*'s plot.

When I started writing this novel, I imagined writing *Carmilla, Queen of the Night*, in tandem with it. I wrote a synopsis and several chapters of *Carmilla* before realizing that I couldn't complete *Breakdown* on schedule if I also included a shapeshifter novel. However, it's floating there at the back of my mind, along with my penname, Boadicea Jones.

CONTENTS

x CONTENTS

1. GRAVEYARD SHIFT

RAIN HAD TURNED THE STREETS A SHINY BLACK. IT COATED windshields with a film that cut visibility to inches, and turned potholes into lakes that trapped unwary drivers. All month long, Chicago had been hit by storms that put as much as three inches of water on the ground in an hour, but left the air as thick and heavy as a wet parka. Tonight's storm was one of the worst of the summer.

I'd come up empty in all the likely spots: bus stops, coffee shops, even the sleazier nightclubs that might not have carded a bunch of tweens. I was about to give up when I saw lights flashing in the cemetery to my right. I pulled over and rolled down my window. Above the rumble of rain on my rooftop I could hear high-pitched chatter and bursts of nervous laughter.

I zipped up my rain jacket and walked down the street, looking for the cemetery gates. They were padlocked. A notice board read that Mount Moriah was permanently closed. Trespassers would be violated, but if you had a grave to tend, you could call the number on the board.

I went back up Leavitt until I found a gap in the fence big enough for me to slip through. By then, the girls had disappeared.

Grass and weeds had taken over the grounds, obliterating paths, covering up the grave markers. The remains of the paths had turned to a mud that sucked at my running shoes. Bits of old gravel wedged themselves inside my socks. Water seeped under the hood of my rain jacket. I tripped over a marble slab that had fallen on its back, and landed hard on my tailbone. The only good thing about the weather was that it masked the sound of my fall, as well as the curse I couldn't hold back—I was in my favorite party dress, which was now smeared with mud underneath my jacket.

While I was on the ground I made out winking lights—cell phones, or flashlights—to my right. The rain stopped suddenly; I caught the girls' nervous laughter again and worked my way toward it.

As I got closer, I heard a stifled shriek. "Did you see? The vampire—he was here; I saw him going into the woods."

"Yeah, right, like we believe *you*, Tyler—you haven't even been initiated."

"I did too see him. Kira, didn't you? You grabbed my arm."

"That wasn't Kira, dummy, that was Arielle. She screamed louder than you."

"Did not. I'm not afraid of vampires, I've got an amulet from Carmilla!"

"But why do we have to do this in the middle of the rain, anyway? Why can't we stay in Kira's apartment?" a new speaker demanded.

An authoritative voice answered. "We have to be under the full moon for the power to work."

"But it's wet, you can't even see the moon." This was Tyler again, the one who'd seen the vampire.

"We tried to do it inside last time, but Kira's little sister saw us and freaked out. You could hear her scream all the way to Wisconsin."

"I think that was a sign from Carmilla," the girl with the authoritative voice said. "We need to be as brave as the girls in the book, when they went outside the town gates. See—we're outside the town gates, kind of—we went away from the city when we climbed over the cemetery gates, and that temple thingy, it's like Carmilla's cottage."

Vampires. In a way, it was refreshing that a bunch of tweens had sneaked out to see a vampire—when my cousin Petra called me, desperate for help, I'd assumed the kids had gone clubbing.

Petra told me she'd gotten a frantic call from Kira Dudek's little sister.

"Kira Dudek?" I'd repeated, bewildered.

"You know, Vic," my cousin said impatiently. "Kira's in one of my book groups, the ones I'm running for the Malina Foundation. Her and Lucy's mom works a night shift as a hotel maid, and little Lucy says all the big girls come over to their place, only tonight, they all went out in the rain and left Lucy by herself. She's only seven, Vic, she's hysterical, and I can't leave her here by herself. I know I said I wouldn't keep calling you for help, but, gosh, Kira and her friends, they're just twelve or thirteen, I can't let them just run around the city on their own."

In the two years my cousin has been in Chicago, she's had five jobs, if you count the three weeks she worked for me last winter. Most recently, she'd been taken on by the Malina Foundation, which serves immigrants and refugees. My old friend Lotty Herschel, who sits on Malina's board, had recommended Petra for the position. My cousin's boundless energy made her popular with the foundation's youth programs. I'd been impressed with the job Petra was doing, but teen curfew breakers were more than she could handle on her own.

I'd been at a particularly annoying event with Murray Ryerson and was just as happy for an excuse to leave—until, of course, I landed in the mud in my scarlet party frock. I'd changed from high heels into running shoes in my car, and I had my waterproof slicker, but I hadn't packed a backup outfit. I hadn't been expecting to go from black tie to black mud this evening.

The wind had picked up while I was listening to the girls. The full moon began to shine through the last thready shroud of clouds and I could make out the shapes of uncut shrubs and tombstones. My view of the girls was blocked by a big monument, the "temple thingy" one of them had mentioned. It had a bunch of columns supporting a dome, and a dark figure draped realistically on a slab in the middle. The whole structure was missing chunks of marble, as if a giant had chewed off slabs at random.

When I worked my way around to the front of the monument, I found the girls in a kind of clearing—at least, it was free of the tangling bushes that had overgrown most of the cemetery paths. The ground was marked with a concrete border that had crumbled, exposing pieces of rebar. Gravestones around the perimeter were tilted at drunken angles.

The girls had stopped arguing. They were passing around a bottle of something that made them laugh more raucously. I didn't know if they were drunk or just thought they ought to act that way, but their wildness was disturbing.

There were seven in all. Several were videoing one another with their cell phones. Tomorrow their friends and relations would be able to admire their antics on Facebook.

"We'd better get started." It was the girl with the authoritative voice. In the moonlight, she looked like a sprite, as if she herself had come out of elf land. She was shorter than the others, her silhouette topped by a mop of dark curls.

"Get your phones out and set and we'll go on three." She counted, and on "three," the girls all pressed the music buttons on their devices so that a kind of tinny rap concert began.

"Tyler, stand in the middle." This was the tallest girl in the group. "Everyone else get in a circle and hold hands. We'll feel the power while the moon is full."

"Yeah, before Kira's mother gets off work and we're all busted," someone else chimed in.

I was going to bust them myself, but I was curious enough about the ritual to let it run for another few minutes.

"Close your eyes," the tallest girl said. "Put the phones away and hold hands. Tyler, are you ready?"

"I guess so, Nia." Tyler's voice was a barely audible whisper.

The tallest and the shortest were running the show. They bowed to each other, then the tall one intoned, "Carmilla, bless Arielle so that her hand is guided right, and help me, so the ritual is chanted right. Amen."

"Amen!" The other girls tried to sound solemn, as if in church, but two were so excited that they giggled instead.

The tall girl pulled something from her pocket, an object too small for me to make out, and gave it to Arielle with another bow. Arielle took Tyler's hand and led her to the middle of the clearing, where the two knelt. The other five gathered around them in a tight circle, blocking my view.

The tall girl began a chant, which the rest of them joined. "Under the full moon, we call on Carmilla. Carmilla, give us power, and let us send your power into Tyler! Carmilla, give us wisdom, and let us send your wisdom into Tyler! Carmilla, give us immortality, and let us share it with Tyler!"

Tyler screamed. I broke through the circle of girls and pulled the sprite away from Tyler.

My abrupt arrival terrified all the girls. They shrieked and backed away from me, huddling in a frightened group at the edge of the clearing, clutching one another's hands—except for Tyler, the sacrifice in the middle of the circle, who cried, "I hate you, I hate all of you and your stupid club, I don't care if you don't speak to me for the next five years." She ran away from them, up the shallow steps of the miniature temple.

"Just what's going on here?" I demanded.

"Who are you?" the tall girl gasped. Her voice shook, but she was brave enough to step forward to look at me.

"I'm a detective, and, incidentally, Petra Warshawski's cousin. She called me to find you. All of you are in violation of curfew. Time for this party to break up. I'm going to take you home."

Like many U.S. cities, Chicago has a curfew for kids under seventeen. A group of shrieking twelve-year-olds would get police attention, maybe not a bad thing for this group's ringleaders, but not so good for any of the immigrant girls whose families might be here illegally.

Petra's name reassured them; they let go of one another's hands, their shoulders relaxing.

Arielle said, "This isn't a party, this is serious."

"I know it's serious: your friend Tyler didn't like it one bit."

"We told her it would hurt, but she wanted to do it anyway," Arielle said. "Everyone else did it, including me and Nia; we did it first to each other, so it's not like we were attacking her!"

The tall girl, Nia, apparently, nodded agreement. "She begged us to let—"

Tyler screamed again before Nia could finish her explanation, a cry of terror so horrible that everyone, even Arielle and Nia, shrank into silence and clustered near me. I ran back to the temple and joined Tyler at the top of the shallow set of steps. Her mouth was opening and shutting in a mime of horror. She didn't move, just pointed at the figure on the slab.

It wasn't a statue, as I'd idly thought when I'd glanced inside earlier, but a man. He was laid on the slab in a parody of a crucifixion, arms wide at his sides, feet together. In the dim light from my cell phone I saw something sticking out of his chest.

I stepped between Tyler and the figure and knelt to feel his neck. His skin was cool and the carotid pulses were still, but when I stuck a gingerly hand underneath his windbreaker, I could feel the wet flood of fresh blood. We must have arrived on the scene right after he died.

While I was kneeling I squinted at the stick in his chest. I couldn't tell much, but it looked like a metal rod, perhaps a foot long. Behind me I could hear Tyler starting to give way to sobs. I got up and guided her down the stairs. She was trembling and she clung to me convulsively.

The man had died a terrible death, but I had learned from years of experience with violence to suction off my feelings, to keep the outer shell of my self smooth and dry. A twelve-year-old didn't need this experience, and shouldn't have to acquire my patina.

The other girls were huddled at the foot of the steps. "What happened?" "What's up there?"

I started to say, "There's a dead man in that tomb," but that sounded ludicrous. "A man has been murdered up there. And not very long ago. I have to call the police. I'd like to protect you ladies from a police investigation, at least until you've gone home and talked to your parents about what you were doing here tonight. However, before I can let you go, you need to answer a few questions. You claimed that you saw someone right before you began your ritual. I believe it was Tyler who said there was a vampire nearby?"

The girls sucked in a collective breath and looked furtively into the thick shrubbery beyond the clearing.

"So she really did see one, even though she wasn't initiated?" one of the girls who hadn't spoken before said.

"No, she didn't see a vampire, she saw a person." I pushed Tyler shoulder distance from me so I could look into her eyes. "Was it the man on the tomb up there?"

"I don't know why I said what I did, about seeing a vampire, I mean. I didn't see anyone," Tyler whispered.

"What about the rest of you? Did any of you see someone in the shrubbery when you got here?"

They all stared at me dumbly. Finally, Nia said, "Tyler was really excited about the ceremony, so maybe she thought she saw something."

Lightning flashed in the eastern sky and clouds began to thicken across the moon again, a warning that Mother Nature hadn't finished with us for the night. I didn't want to stand arguing with these kids in a rainstorm, and I needed to call the cops to report the murder. I told the girls I would take them to the apartment where they'd met up, and leave them in my cousin Petra's charge while I talked to the police.

"You can call your folks from there, but none of you is to go home unless Petra sees who's escorting you."

Arielle started to object, but I overrode her. "You are not in charge of this expedition; I am. If you try to leave the Dudek apartment with anyone besides your parents or guardian, Petra will sit on you until I get back."

"They can't sleep there." A girl with long, pale hair spoke for the first time. "We only have three beds."

"You're Kira Dudek, right? Lucy's big sister? I don't care if your friends stand on their heads all night, as long as they don't leave without an adult. Let's get going."

"But my mother—" Kira started to say.

"This is known as education," I said. "You are learning, all seven of you, that actions have consequences."

I corralled them into an ungainly bundle and started pushing them toward Leavitt Street. As we got closer, blue lights flashed beyond the fence. Someone must have heard Tyler's screams and called the police.

"Cops on Leavitt," I said. "I want you girls to be with your parents before you have to deal with the police. We're going to turn around and try to find a way out on the street at the back of the cemetery. It's going to be rough going because I don't want to show a light, so stay close together, and close behind me."

I turned around, made sure my team—if that's what they were—was with me, and started picking my way back toward the clearing, the temple, the thicket of briars.

Tyler insisted on holding my hand. This made it harder for me to stay on a path, but I didn't have the heart to detach her. Behind us we heard the bullhorns: *This is the Chicago police; stay where you are; we know you're in there.* We could see the glow from their searchlights as the cops began to work their way into the cemetery. Tyler grabbed me more tightly and one of the girls whimpered in fear. The lightning intensified and thunder began to rumble among the clouds like a moody drummer.

"It's okay," I said softly, under the cover of the thunder. "They're just guessing; they don't really know we're here. The important thing is to keep as quiet as possible."

More than once the girls or I stumbled against a piece of broken marble as we threaded our way east. Rain began to fall again, fat, greasy drops that slipped through the tree branches and down our necks. The storm broke in earnest as we reached a wall that marked the cemetery's eastern edge.

As the rain swept down, I turned to Arielle, the sprite. "I'm going to give you a leg up to the top. Look over, and if there're no cops or prowlers on the street, you climb over and jump down. And all of you: go to Kira Dudek's apartment and stay there. I will join you as fast as I can, but I have to talk to the cops. And please don't imagine you can just run away: Petra will be able to give me all your names, and I will talk to all of your parents tomorrow."

Nia started to protest, but Arielle cut her short. "My mom will handle it; don't try arguing with *her*."

I decided to pretend I hadn't heard that and made a cup of my hands for Arielle. She sprang up lightly to grab the top of the wall, where she bent over and looked around before giving me an "all clear." I hoisted the others over as fast as I could, even Tyler, who said she'd rather stay with me.

"Right now, it doesn't matter what happened to you in the middle of that circle back there," I said. "Being with Arielle and the others is going to be way better than a police interrogation. Why were you out after curfew? Did you know the dead man? Did you and your friends put a spike through his chest?"

She gasped. "We didn't kill him; we didn't know he was there!"

"Those are the kinds of questions the police will ask, and they won't believe your answers. They'll keep talking to you all night long, until you say something they want to hear. So get over that wall."

She nodded bleakly and let me push her to the top. I waited a minute but didn't hear any sounds of pursuit from the other side.

As I stood there, rain pouring under the hood of my jacket, I wondered about the girls. Tyler and her friends were twelve and thirteen, but it didn't take much imagination to figure out how a girl that young could persuade a man to lie on his back, arms outstretched, waiting passively for a blow to the heart.

I didn't really believe these girls had killed the man in the temple. It was far more likely that they hadn't been aware of the violence taking place just steps from where they were dancing and preening. But why was Tyler unwilling to admit she'd seen someone earlier? She'd cried out that she'd seen a vampire—but perhaps, on reflection, she'd recognized the figure, and didn't want to identify him. Or her.

I'd have to talk to all the girls in depth, which sounded exhausting. Or turn them over to the police, which seemed callous. In the meantime, I needed to talk to the police myself. There were risks inherent in presenting myself to them, but there were bigger risks in staying away. I turned around and started working my way west again.

2. IN THE GARDEN OF BAD AND WORSE

IT WAS SEVERAL HOURS BEFORE I WAS ABLE TO JOIN THE GIRLS at the Dudek apartment. I hadn't been foolish enough to think the cops would let me show them the crime scene and take off, but they put me through a longer process than I'd expected.

By the time I'd retraced a path through the undergrowth to the Leavitt Street side of the cemetery, rain had pounded through my jacket and I was soaked to the skin. My scarlet frock was cut from silk faille; I sincerely hoped it would survive tonight's abuse.

I slithered through the hole in the fence I'd used to enter and walked down Leavitt to the cops. Four squad cars were parked there, their lights flashing so brightly that I could see the people in the apartments across the street peering at us through the cracks in their curtains. Most of the officers were already in the cemetery. I told the man left to watch the street that there was a dead body in one of the tombs.

"That doesn't seem too shocking, miss," he said and smirked. "It's a graveyard."

"Right." I grinned sourly. "A murdered body. Can you call your team and tell them? If they come back for me, I can show them the location."

He asked me—a thinly veiled order—to get into the back of his squad car and wait to talk to Sergeant Anstey. The sergeant arrived within a couple of minutes and moved me to his own car to hear my story.

"You want to phone your team, tell them to wait for me? It would make their lives easier if I went with them," I said. "I know where the victim is."

"They're big boys and girls; they can find that tomb thing on their own. Tell me again what you were doing in an abandoned graveyard in a thunderstorm."

I repeated my story. "I was on my way home when I thought I heard someone screaming inside the cemetery. I followed the sound, but then I tripped on a chunk of marble and landed in the mud. By the time I got back on my feet, the screams had stopped; I poked around and found the dead man, but whoever killed him managed to take off without my spotting him."

Anstey snorted. "You really expect me to believe a woman goes alone into an abandoned cemetery in the middle of a thunderstorm? Why didn't you call 911?"

"I know what kind of backlog this district has on Saturday nights— my dad used to work out of the Twelfth."

"This is about a lover who dissed you, isn't it. Or was it a drug deal gone bad?"

"Just a South Side street fighter who forgot for a minute that she was fifty, not fifteen." I rubbed my arms, hoping to get some blood moving in them. "If I'd known you were going to give me a hard time, I would have made an anonymous call about the vic to 911, but I thought you would appreciate help in locating the body."

Anstey phoned in to the station and got a report back on me. The CPD file said I was a private eye with a track record, both for results and for a chip on the shoulder. I couldn't argue with either claim. The file apparently also included a note that a senior officer, namely Captain Bobby Mallory, was a personal friend. And that my dad really had been a cop.

Anstey revealed that news with disgust—it meant he had to treat me like a person, not a criminal. Although the hostility of his questions lessened, his voice still sounded like he wished he could use his baton on my skull.

The person who lingers around a crime scene is a perpetrator more often than not. I'd known that was what the cops would think. But if I'd left a print at the crime scene, they'd have found me fast enough, and they'd have grounds for getting the state to suspend my license if I didn't report the crime.

I decided it was time to shift the ground. "What brought you here, Sergeant, on a night like this? Is Mount Moriah a regular part of your unit's beat?"

"That's right. We like driving around among the dead, cheers us up to think that we have peace and quiet to look forward to even if we'll never be able to afford to retire."

"Someone called you. I wonder why? Was it someone who wanted that body found, or had they heard me running through the grounds?"

Anstey paused, measuring me in the dark squad car. "Give Captain Mallory a call, see if he'll tell you, because I certainly won't."

After that, Anstey turned to his computer and began clearing incident reports. When I started to make bright conversation, he ignored me, so I tried to leave, but he'd locked the back doors. He kept me in the car until his troops phoned that they'd found the body.

"Okay. Your turn to shine, Warshawski. Lead me to my team."

Anstey unlocked the back door and pulled me out. His squad had used bolt cutters on the chain across the front gate, so at least we didn't have to sidle through a hole in the fence.

The police spots sent a bright glow through the cemetery, which made it easy to pick out the remnants of the gravel paths. The rain had stopped again, and Anstey and I didn't have any trouble getting to the crime scene.

Under the lights, the little temple looked like part of a movie set, maybe for something like *In the Garden of Bad and Worse.* It was an elaborate tomb, resembling an Italian cathedral. A carved frieze swung from the dome that had been planted on top of the columns. Like the columns and the shallow steps leading to the tomb, the dome and frieze were badly cracked and covered with lichen. The Saloman family, whose name was on the mausoleum, had put a lot of money into interring their dead, but now there was no one to care for the dead or the tomb, or even the graveyard.

The lights made it easy to see the space where the girls had performed their ritual. It wasn't actually a clearing, just an area where tombstones had been placed flat into the ground rather than set at right angles to it. At one side, I saw a bottle of alcopop and hoped that wasn't what the girls had been passing around. I didn't call attention to it—plenty of drunks hang out in cemeteries, after all. People without a lot of options make love in them, too. Empties are a cemetery commonplace.

Sergeant Anstey dragged me up the shallow steps to look at the dead man. "This the guy you want me to believe was screaming in here? You put a spike through his chest as payback for dragging you through the mud?"

I didn't respond to the gibe, just stared down at the man. He'd been around forty, a white man with thick, dark hair that was just beginning to turn gray at the sides.

What startled me was his peaceful expression. It seemed as though such a terrible murder should have left a trace on his face—shock, fury, some emotion. In the Middle Ages, people believed a dead person's eyes would hold the image of his killer, and maybe I'd been expecting something like that. This man looked as though he'd lain down for a nap.

I put my hand on his neck again, wondering if I'd been mistaken before. His damp skin was already colder, stiffer than it had been when I'd found him an hour earlier.

"We know he's dead," one of the patrol officers said.

Blood loss had turned his skin a waxy yellow, so that he seemed more like a mannequin than a dead person. Even the blood that had leaked from under his windbreaker and pooled onto the floor didn't look real.

"He couldn't just have lain down there for someone to murder," I said. "But that's what it looks like. He must have been alive when the spike went into him for so much blood to have spilled, but—was he drugged? Did someone carry him here?"

"Yeah, when we need your guidance on how to run the investigation or the autopsy, we'll get back to you," Sergeant Anstey said. "Meanwhile, I think it's time you answered a few questions about what you were really doing in here. Don't tell me you knew nothing about this poor twerp."

I was silent.

"Well?" he demanded.

"I can't speak," I said. "You don't want to hear that I knew nothing about this poor twerp, but that's all I can tell you about him."

The sergeant told his team to secure the crime scene for the evidence techs. He took me back to the station for a heart-to-heart. While I huddled, shivering and sneezing—and eyeing my mud-stained evening dress in dismay—someone phoned with the victim's identity. Miles Wuchnik, he'd been when he was alive. And, like me, an investigator. Anstey couldn't believe I didn't know him.

"Sergeant, there are hundreds, maybe thousands, of investigators in Illinois. Most are not detectives—they just do research for law firms or work in security."

Anstey ignored that answer and started to imagine a scenario where Wuchnik had been muscling in on one of my clients and I'd murdered him to get him out of the way.

I rolled my eyes. "First you wanted us to be drug dealers who'd fallen out, or lovers having a quarrel. Now, at least, you're respecting my professional status, but your theory is still a million miles from reality."

I sneezed again. "You've got your air-conditioning turned on too high. Save the city a dime, save the planet, turn it down. I'm freezing. If that's the best you can do, I'm out of here."

He didn't try to stop me; he probably didn't even really suspect me. He just was hoping the murder would solve itself for him, and I was handy.

No one offered me a ride back to my car, but they didn't tail me, either, so I walked straight to the Dudek apartment.

3. BEDTIME STORIES

When I rang the bell at the Dudek place, Petra came down to let me in. I'd called her right after I'd sent the girls over the cemetery wall, warning her of the imminent arrival of the gang of seven, and telling her not to let them leave unless she inspected their escort.

"Vic! Thank God you're here. Tyler is the only one who showed up, besides Kira, I mean. What happened to the others? Kira said she didn't care if the rest all ended up in jail, but where did they go?"

"I don't know." My eyes widened in dismay. "Have you texted them?"

"They're not answering. Anyway, I'm not sure who all was there—Arielle Zitter, I know, and if she was there, Nia was with her, but I don't know the names of the other three. Tyler, all she does is cry and say how her dad will beat her up, and then Kira says, well, at least you've got a dad, and they start in on each other."

I shut my eyes for a moment, hoping that when I opened them I'd be home in bed, waking up from a dream. Unfortunately, when I looked around, I was still in the ill-lit foyer, my eyeballs aching and scratchy. My seven dwarfs: Achy, Scratchy, Cranky, Crabby, Grim, Truculent, and Bellicose.

"I was trying to spare them being picked up on a curfew violation, not to mention giving them a chance to talk to their folks about this escapade first," I explained as I followed my cousin up the stairs. "Are those girls good enough friends that they would all stay together? That would keep them safe on the street, even if the police nail them."

The door to an apartment at the top of the stairs opened. A man stuck his head out and hissed at us to keep it down, people were trying to sleep. I felt jealous of anyone with the luxury of trying to sleep right now, but I smiled contritely and tiptoed behind Petra to the end of the hall, where she pushed open the door to the Dudek apartment.

A little girl in a yellow-flowered nightgown was standing next to a narrow couch, crying. I supposed that was Lucy, whose call to Petra had set my night in motion. Next to Lucy, not looking at her sister—or, indeed, at anyone—was Kira Dudek, the girl with the long, fair hair I'd seen at the cemetery.

The new initiate, Tyler, sat across the room at a small table that seemed to double as a desk—it held books and a computer as well as the remains of dinner. Both girls had changed from their wet clothes into dry shorts and T-shirts. Tyler looked at the open door with some alarm, but Kira didn't even move her head when Petra and I came in.

The couch, the table, and four laminate chairs pretty well filled the room, although the couch faced a wall unit holding a modest television and four or five shelves of books. An icon to the Virgin above the couch and a crucifix on the wall behind the table made up the Dudek family's art collection.

It was a small room, too small for the tension between the girls. Petra ignored the older two and made a beeline for Lucy, who grabbed my cousin's leg. With that anchor, she felt safe enough to stop crying and stare at me to see what new drama I was bringing to the night.

I pulled a chair away from the table and placed it halfway between

Tyler and Kira. "Okay, my sisters: it's time you started talking. What was going on tonight?"

"Nothing," Kira muttered.

"Only it was 'nothing' in the middle of a graveyard during a thunderstorm. This was an initiation into the cult of Carmilla—"

"The cult of Carmilla?" Petra exclaimed. "What were you guys doing? That is not part of our book club."

"It's something we do on our own. Or at least something the creeps at Vina Fields do on their own," Kira said.

"We're not creeps," Tyler said. "It's not my fault if my folks send me to school there."

Vina Fields was one of those private academies where diplomats' and entertainers' children mingled with the heirs to Chicago's great fortunes. Parents shelled out the equivalent of the price of a new home to give their children an early leg up in the race of life.

"You're not even part of our book club, but you came barging in like you owned it!" Kira said.

"That's not fair. I'd come if my dad would let me, but he won't, it's only 'cause he's out of town this weekend that I even got permission to spend the night at Arielle's," Tyler said hotly.

"Only, really, you came to Kira's," I said.

Tyler started picking at the skin around her cuticles. For the first time, I noticed how raw her fingertips were.

"Yes, she came here with all the big girls and then Kira left, even though she's supposed to *mind* me, and I was all alone and I was scared. And I'm going to tell Mama!" Lucy's indignant treble startled all of us, she'd been standing so quietly.

"Whoa, there, missy. Two in the morning and you're in the living room? That's what I'm going to tell your mama, unless you hop like a bunny back into that bed of yours!" Petra said firmly.

Lucy eyed my cousin, trying to gauge whether she meant it. Petra scooped her up and carried her from the room. I guess those five younger sisters had given her plenty of experience. We heard water running in the bathroom, Petra's bright chatter, a giggle from Lucy. After another moment, my cousin rejoined us.

"She was asleep before I left the room. Too much for a little one in one night."

"Too much for all of us in one night," I agreed. "But it's high time I started hearing some truth. Fast, before Kira's mother gets home. Let's start with the simple stuff—names and phone numbers of the girls who were there tonight."

Kira and Tyler exchanged glances and shrugged. I looked at my cousin. "We know Arielle and Nia. We have Tyler and Kira. Who were the other three?"

"Lucy told me Beata Mizwa was here. She's one of our Malina girls, like Kira here," Petra said.

"So Tyler and the others aren't part of Malina?" I asked.

"They're from Vina Fields. I told you last winter, Vic: my boss started this experimental program, pairing girls from Malina with Vina Fields. The VF girls get community-service points for participating, and the theory is they'll be kind of like big sisters to the Malina girls."

"What, patronize them, make them go to cemeteries? Sounds very sisterly!"

Petra made an impatient gesture, but Kira was startled into a spurt of laughter.

"Even though school's not in session, your book group is still going strong?" I asked.

"The book clubs meet year-round so that kids who aren't reading at grade level can use the summer to play catch-up," Petra explained.

"Is it working?"

"It is for my groups, because we're reading *Carmilla*," my cousin said. "Kids just gulp these books down! I can't believe you never heard of them."

"I spend too much time reading about the vampires in our financial institutions," I said. "That's all the excitement I can handle. Let's get this business here sorted out. You girls need to tell me what was going on in the cemetery tonight. Tyler, what happened when you were in the middle of that circle with Arielle?"

Tyler stared at me blankly. "Nothing."

"You said you hated them and their stupid club and you didn't care what they said about you. What—they'll put it out on Facebook that you're a coward? Is that what worries you?"

"Maybe." Tyler began picking at her cuticles again.

"You said this initiation into Carmilla isn't part of your book group," I said to my cousin. "Do you know what it could be, or what reprisals the girls wield against people who squeal?"

Petra's mobile face displayed a pantomime of ignorance. "There are clubs, I know that much, you write in and get a charter or something. When my friends and I got hooked on the books, only the first two or three had been published. The clubs and things came later."

"So is Carmilla a vampire?" I was thinking of the cry—Tyler's cry?—that she'd seen a vampire.

"Good grief, no. She's a shape-shifter—the Raven! Vic, I'm embarrassed that my own cousin is so illiterate!"

"They were initiating Tyler," I persisted. "Everyone warned her it would hurt, but she wanted to go through with it anyway. Were they imitating a raven? Did Arielle peck your eyeballs?"

Tyler giggled nervously, but Kira said, "No. Arielle and Nia, they stick—"

"You can't say, we swore an oath not to tell!" Tyler exclaimed.

"That was just Arielle and Nia, and they didn't even come back here tonight. You Vina Fields girls, you make me sick, acting like you want to be friends with Beata and me, but really, you only come here because you know my mom works nights, so you can sneak out and not have any grown-ups listen in. *You're* not even in our book group. I never even saw you before tonight, so don't go telling me what to say or not say in my own home!"

"Don't blame me!" Tyler replied. "They told me you liked to hold the meetings here on account of you have to babysit your little sister."

"No one's going to be meeting here again, so it doesn't matter," I said, "but, just out of curiosity, Kira, why did you take part in this group?"

"In case it's true," Kira whispered. "We thought, at least Arielle had this idea, maybe we could become shape-shifters, you know, like Giralda in the book. She learns to be a raven, and, well, I know it's a sin, calling up magic spirits, but I thought if I could turn into a raven, I could fly to Tarnow, that's where my *tata*—my dad, he left us, I thought—"

She turned a muddy pink and stopped talking.

"I think it would be good if you told me about how Arielle and Nia stick you," I said. "I won't be angry, but I need to understand."

"Arielle and Nia, they stuck each other in the palm with these big sewing needles," she whispered, speaking so fast I could barely understand her. "Then they licked each other's blood, and then they stuck me and the others and we all kissed each other's hands."

"Oh, gross! Why didn't you guys talk to me?" Petra's mouth twisted in disgust. "I could have told you there's nothing like that in any of the books. Vic, you have to believe I never talked about trying to turn into a vampire or a shape-shifter. I mean, everyone knows about Dracula and vampires, but we never talked about licking each other's blood."

I smiled faintly. "The power of the imagination. You should be proud you could unleash it." I turned back to Kira. "Is that what happened the time Lucy saw you? Is that why you went out to the cemetery this time?"

Kira nodded. "Arielle and Nia, they couldn't come last month, but the full moon before that, back in May, Lucy heard us. Jessie kind of screamed when she got stuck, so Lucy came out just when they were sticking me, and she screeched her head off. Arielle and Jessie and them took off. And then Lucy told my mom next morning at breakfast. I said some of my friends came over for a study group and we were practicing first aid and Lucy didn't understand what she was seeing. But tonight, for Tyler, Arielle and Nia decided we'd better go outside, in case Lucy saw us again."

"Everyone met up here?" I asked. "Arielle and Nia and the others?"

Kira nodded. "I told them to be quiet, but I guess Lucy woke up and saw us leave. She knew Petra's number because I wrote it on the refrigerator for Mom, so she called Petra."

"Why do their mothers let them come here?" I wondered.

Kira hunched a shoulder. "I suppose they say they're going off to do good deeds on some poor stupid immigrant family."

"It's not like that!" Tyler burst out. "Arielle said we all should say we were going to her place for a sleepover, except her, she told her mother she was going to Nia's. Then we met over on North Avenue, at the bus stop next to our school, and rode over here."

I rubbed my eyes. I could picture it all. In fact, when I thought of my own childhood, the exploits I'd committed with my cousin Boom-Boom when my mother thought I was asleep in my attic bed, I could picture it all too well.

"You headed over to the cemetery, all seven of you together, and then Tyler saw the vampire."

"I didn't really," Tyler said.

"No, really you saw a person," I agreed. "Man or woman?"

"I don't know. It was just out of the corner of my eye, it was just like a shadow, I can't talk to the cops, if I do they'll tell my dad." Her voice rose in her anguish.

I wondered uneasily about Tyler's home situation, whether her father was a garden-variety domestic tyrant, or if he was actively violent. I decided to sic Petra on that and keep my focus on what had happened in the cemetery.

"And the dead man—who was he?"

"I don't know! Don't keep acting like I killed him or something, I never saw him before."

I glanced at the clock on the television. It was almost three. If Tyler or Kira knew anything about Miles Wuchnik, the dead detective, my brain wasn't working well enough to come up with a clever question to pry it out of them. In any event, Arielle and Nia were the driving forces of the group; they had chosen the site. But did they have enough power over the other Carmilla club members to get them to engage in murder?

"What did Arielle and the others say when they left you?" I asked the girls.

"This one girl, Jessie Morgenstern, her dad gives a lot of money to, like, politicians. She said her dad would get someone who works for the mayor to take care of things with the police," Kira said. "But me and Beata, we can't talk to the police, our moms could get deported, so Beata, she went back to her place, she just lives two blocks from here. Her mom and mine work at the same hotel."

"Enough for tonight." I got up. "Tyler, are your parents really out of town? Where were you going to spend the night?"

"I thought maybe Arielle—or even Nia—but I asked them before they ran off, and they—they were mean, they said I was a coward and a crybaby and they wouldn't ever talk to me again and they'd see no one at Vina Fields ever did, either—" Tears rolled down the sides of her face.

"She can't stay here," Kira said stonily. "Me and Lucy, we share a room, and my mom has a bed, and that's it."

"I'll take her," Petra said. "Your folks coming back tomorrow, Tyler? I'll take you home in the afternoon and tell them you were meeting with my book group."

I blew my cousin a grateful kiss. Before she left, I went over to inspect the place on Tyler's palm where Arielle had stuck her. There was a small puncture hole, covered with a thin crust of dried blood. I told Petra to clean it with peroxide when they got to her place.

"If it starts swelling, or you find any red blotches on you, you get to a doctor on the instant," I warned her. "You can make up any story you like for your dad, but you ladies are playing with plague, poking each other with needles like that."

Petra put her arms around Tyler and led her gently into the night. I stayed behind to tuck Kira into bed, in the room she shared with her little sister. A map of Poland hung between the two beds, with Tarnow circled in red on the southeast side.

The wall above Lucy's bed was covered with pictures of horses. She had fallen asleep in a nest of toy horses of all sizes and colors. Kira had a poster of the jacket art for *Carmilla, Queen of the Night*, by Boadicea Jones, on her side of the room. On it, a raven grew out of the body of a young girl; behind her, just visible in a syrupy palette of browns and greens, were the tusks and gleaming red eyes of a boar.

I waited outside the bedroom door while Kira undressed. I was dozing against the wall when I heard her give a howl of anguish.

"Now what?" I was too tired for a new crisis.

"My phone," she wailed. "I must've dropped it in the cemetery. My mom will be so mad, we can't afford—"

"I'll go back tomorrow and look for it," I promised hastily. "Try not to worry about it now, just get some sleep. You're sure you don't need me to stay here until your mother gets back?"

"We always stay by ourselves," she snuffled, climbing into the narrow bed. "Promise you'll go look for my phone? Can you make sure the door is locked when you go? The key is on a hook next to the door, so can you just lock it from the outside and push the key under the door?"

I pulled a sheet over her, but left the coverlet folded at the bottom of the bed—a window fan did feeble duty, but it was hot in the room. Lucy, worn out by her own histrionics, slept through her sister's new crisis.

On my way out, I left the key on its hook, using my picks to turn the deadbolt into place. The rain had cleared, but the moon was setting and the streets were dark. I walked slowly back to my car, wondering again what had brought the girls to the very spot where a man was being murdered. Not just murdered, but pierced through the heart, as if the killer thought he was a vampire. A vampire murder on the spot where the girls were hoping to become shape-shifters. It seemed like a mighty big leap to think that had happened by chance.

4. CHARMS—
OR SOMETHING

As I walked along Chicago Avenue, a couple coming out of a bar tried to offer me a dollar for a cup of coffee. Their gift made me realize just what a bizarre vision I must present—in my running shoes and bedraggled evening gown I was an avatar for homelessness.

I'd started the evening looking like I belonged in a limo, or at least in the grand ballroom at the Valhalla Hotel, which is where I'd been headed. I've never been fond of big glitzy events, and you go to the Valhalla only if glitz is your middle name. I especially wasn't fond of them when they celebrate the life and work of people I despise: in this case, Wade Lawlor.

If you don't know Lawlor, it's because you get all your news from microform copies of the Chicago *Daily News*. Local boy made, well, "good" would be putting a values spin on it. Local boy made national superstar was more like it.

Although I tried never to watch the show, you can't live in Chicago and not know Lawlor's face—it's on the sides of buses, on billboards, on the back of the *Herald-Star*. GEN, the Global Entertainment Network, whose lead cable news show Lawlor hosts, often features him on its billboard along the Kennedy Expressway.

Lawlor's signature is a blue-checked work shirt, open at the throat to show he's a working man who scorns the suit and tie of an effete liberal journalist. His thick black hair is artfully tousled on-air: *America's in danger, I don't have time to comb my hair!*

For his anniversary carnival, Lawlor incongruously wore his checked shirt with a dinner jacket, a modern one with square pockets sewn to the jacket front. An American flag picked out in jewels was on the lapel. It had a fancy little ear of corn on top of it, as if to point out that he could afford diamonds and rubies, but he was basically a Midwest hick at heart.

Lawlor was working the room with one of those top-grossing stars whose name and face you keep seeing in *Us* and *People*. My red evening dress is a backless ankle-length number, but the star, whose smile seemed epoxied in place, made me feel overdressed. When Lawlor came over to where I was standing with Murray Ryerson, I tried, discreetly, to see how his date kept her breasts from tumbling out of the front of her dress, since it opened all the way to her waist. More epoxy, I decided, keeping a glass in my right hand and food in my left so that I wouldn't have to touch Lawlor.

"Hey, Ryerson, thanks for showing up." Lawlor's eyes scanned the room behind us, looking for people more worth his attention.

"Wouldn't miss it," Murray said with unnecessary heartiness.

Lawlor smirked. "And who's the talent?"

"V. I. Warshawski," I said.

"I haven't seen you before. Out of town?"

"Totally local," I assured him. "Steel City. And you?"

"What's 'Steal City'? The Chicago motto?"

"Very clever, Mr. Lawlor. I'll have to put that in my blog, how clever you are, and what a thrill to meet you, and so on."

I kept my voice languid, trying, for Murray's sake, to keep the venom

I felt out of it. Even so, Lawlor's lips tightened and his eyes narrowed. He put his hand on the star's elbow and started to guide her away, but she stayed put. Perhaps she didn't like him any better than I did; perhaps it was her publicist's idea that she be seen with him on the entertainment sites.

"Are you with GEN?" she asked.

"I'm a private investigator," I said. "Murray Ryerson and I have worked together on a number of stories."

Lawlor eyed me in a way that made me long to take his ribs apart. "She your legwoman, Ryerson? Why'd the network give you the one with the body and me the ugliest guy in Chicago?"

"I guess our looks match our results," I said.

Lawlor frowned; the veneer of charm vanished to expose a startling rage. "What's that supposed to mean?"

Murray knocked my arm hard enough that the wine sloshed over the rim of the glass. We all exclaimed at the mishap, and the star allowed Lawlor lead her away.

"Why the fuck did you have to say that?" Murray demanded.

"It was just banter, Murray. I didn't know he was sacred and that you're not allowed to answer back to his gibes. Is it critical for your career for me to find him and apologize?"

"No, no, don't!" Murray said. "Your apology might involve black eyes and stuff that would really end my career."

"And that flag pin—does he have that glued to every garment he owns?" I fumed. "What's with the ear of corn? Is he showing that he's the corniest man in America?"

"Where have you been since campaign season started, Vic? That's Helen Kendrick's signature—U.S. flag with corn from the heartland. Ethanol is a big chunk of her husband's family fortune, you know that. And Lawlor is her number-one booster."

Kendrick was running for Senate. She thought the last time America had been a great country was the day before Lincoln signed the Emancipation Proclamation, so it was no surprise that Lawlor backed her campaign.

Various other media and entertainment celebrities drifted by. If I did keep a blog, I'd have written up the number of national figures who felt their careers required them to get freshly Botoxed and painted, and show up in little numbers by Chloé or Vera Wang. I didn't care about spotting stars of GEN's reality show *All-American Hero*. What staggered me were the senators and even Supreme Court justices who'd flown in from Washington to see and be seen. That told a sobering tale of how influential Lawlor's voice was on America's political scene.

A few minutes later, Harold Weekes, head of GEN's news division, ambled by. Even though I thought he was the slime on the pond, I smiled, said little or nothing, and even let him leer at my cleavage.

"Keep up the good work, Ryerson! *Chicago Beat* matters to us at Global One, you know."

I couldn't help rolling my eyes at that—what a name for the ugliest chunk of glass and steel to go up in Chicago since Trump Tower broke ground.

"I'm happy to hear that, Harold," Murray said, with an effusiveness that made me wince. "I wanted you to meet Vic here. V. I. Warshawski. She's one of Chicago's most skilled criminal investigators."

Weekes's brows went up. "Expecting to find murder here?"

"Nope," I said. "Just the usual graft and corruption, nothing special."

"Vic has done background work on a lot of my stories," Murray said hastily. "Last winter's exposé on war profiteering, for instance."

Weekes frowned. "I know you thought you had a big scoop there, Ryerson, but it's always been true that war creates opportunities for the alert."

I grinned insanely, the little woman ecstatic to be in the presence of power. "For the alert opportunist, I suppose. Other people just have the chance to get their heads blown off."

There was an uncomfortable silence for a beat, and then Weekes laughed. A smiling woman in a silky red dress, she could be given the benefit of the doubt.

Murray plowed ahead doggedly. "You know the series I'm working on, *Madness in the Midwest,* on the mentally ill, from the streets to state hospitals' forensic wings—Vic could add a lot of depth to the series."

Weekes patted Murray's arm. "We'll certainly keep that in mind, Ryerson. If your friend has investigative experience we can probably find a role for her."

Like Lawlor's a few minutes earlier, Weekes's eyes were glazed over. Talking to Murray and his friend was his idea of purgatory. I couldn't really blame him—the feeling was completely mutual.

The governor of Wisconsin came along and tapped Weekes's arm. The news king moved on.

"Murray, is that why you invited me to this horror show? To help you with some story about mentally ill criminals?" I demanded. "Why didn't you tell me you had an agenda?"

"You put up such a song and dance about coming at all, I didn't feel I could go into it with you," he blazed back.

That much was true. When Murray called last week, asking me to be his date to tonight's celebration of Lawlor's tenth anniversary as GEN's star, I'd said no without thinking.

"I hate Wade Lawlor," I protested. "I hate his politics, I hate his molassied voice, and I hate his pretense of being a working-class boy. That fake work shirt makes me throw up every time I drive up the Kennedy. I bet the closest he ever got to a day's hard labor was paying a neighbor to mow his mother's lawn when he was a kid."

"You'd lose," Murray said. "He comes from some kind of broken home. I've seen him weep on camera, over how his dad ran off and left him and his sister to fend for themselves. Success hasn't just gone to Wade's head—it's made him vindictive. My job ain't so secure that I can dis the network's golden goose. And I don't want to go alone."

"What about all those blond twentysomethings you flaunt anytime I see you in public?" I snapped.

"Are you jealous?"

"More disgusted. Why can't you act your age?"

"That's what I'm trying to do here, and you're not helping. You can rehabilitate me, turn me into a boomer who's not afraid to show his age," he wheedled.

"If I could rehabilitate you, Murray, it would be to turn you back into the journalist who won a Pulitzer for *White Crime/Black Convict.*"

As soon as the words were out of my mouth, I'd wished them back. Murray had done a spectacular series for the *Herald-Star* on the white youths who bought their coke and meth on the black South and West Sides but who were seldom accused of drug crimes. He'd followed four kids—two black, two white—from the drug scene for a year. At the end of the year, the two white guys were setting off for the east coast to college at Haverford and Princeton; one of the black kids had been sentenced to fifteen years for possession, while the other was dead.

The year after Murray won his Pulitzer, the Global Entertainment Network bought the *Star,* along with several hundred other papers. Harold Weekes acquired a minor Hollywood studio for its cable potential, moved the company from the outer reaches of LA to Wacker Drive, gutted the reporting staff at Global's papers, and hired Wade Lawlor to disseminate rumors, innuendo, and outright lies, under the catchy title *Wade's World.*

Wade's World trumpeted the claim that Obama had ordered police to collect Bibles from kids on their way to school. Wade signed on with a group disputing the president's citizenship.

It wasn't Murray's fault that his new owners preferred video to print. It wasn't his fault that he had to scramble to keep a job, so I didn't hold it against him that he anchored a weekly TV show on GEN. In *Chicago Beat,* he reported on everything from politics to the arts, but most of his shows were devoted to sensational crimes, since that's what draws a crowd.

Despite Harold Weekes's hearty assurance that everyone in GEN's headquarters loved *Chicago Beat*, Murray's show aired once a week in Illinois and Indiana, although Wisconsin and Michigan affiliates sometimes picked it up. *Wade's World* was shown four times daily in every city, village, and farm in America.

I didn't believe Murray's career hung by the thread he kept claiming, but he was working in a poisonous environment. Lawlor was reported to pull in twenty million a year just from GEN, while his endorsement contracts probably tripled that figure. Other GEN cable stars made seven-figure salaries; in a milieu where the chief operating officer dismissed print journalism as "turning back the clock to the era of illuminated manuscripts," no matter what Murray earned, he was bound to feel insecure.

I felt ashamed of rubbing Murray's face in his troubles; I said I'd go to Lawlor's event at the Valhalla with him. And I'd regretted it the minute I walked in the door. After the encounter with Weekes in the Valhalla ballroom I was furious.

"You could have warned me before I met your boss that you wanted my help with a story. I could have jumped in with some intelligent backup, instead of which he dismissed me as your girlfriend."

Murray looked sheepish. "I just couldn't find a way to propose it to you, and then Weekes popped up, and I wanted to get the idea back in front of him. You saw the first piece, looking at the returning Iraq/Afghan vets who've become homeless."

"Yes, yes, I did. You did a great job with that. I didn't know it was the start of a series, though."

"It wasn't," he fumed. "I had the whole series started—I was going out to one of the state mental hospitals to look at murderers found not guilty by mental defect, I had one on the advanced practice nurses who do most of the hands-on medical care of the mentally ill homeless—I had nine shows lined up, and I had my own producer's blessing, and then, right after the one on the vets ran, Wade Lawlor stuck in an oar at the huddle, said it was banal and a resource-eater, and Weekes axed the whole series."

"I can't possibly persuade Harold Weekes to listen to you instead of Lawlor," I protested.

"No, but I was hoping you could come on board as the resident expert on evaluating criminal evidence for the segment on people found not guilty by reason of mental defect. I've tried pitching that again as a single episode; I put together a list of five people who've been held at Ruhetal or Elgin for more than twenty years, but Lawlor keeps shooting down the idea, and I never get time alone with Weekes. I was hoping if he saw you, I don't know—"

"Even though I'm not a blond twentysomething, that my sparkling gray eyes and flawless skin would captivate him."

Murray grimaced. "You have a way of putting things in the worst possible light, but, yeah, something like that."

It was then, as the noise level in the ballroom had passed the dangerous decibel mark, that Petra's call came, begging me for help. I told Murray I had a client in trouble, refused to give him details, and fled. It took a good fifteen minutes for the Valhalla valet to fetch my car. By the time I got to Mount Moriah, the girls had a substantial head start on me.

5. STIMULATING NEWS— OR IS IT MALICE?

WHEN I GOT HOME, I CAME UP THE BACK STAIRS, WHERE I could see if lights were on in Jake Thibaut's place. He's a bass player who moved in across the landing from me two years ago, and we've been spending a fair amount of our free time with each other. Friends of his had been playing at a small venue on the northwest side, and I'd kind of hoped he might still be up—musicians keep even more erratic hours than detectives. However, his place was dark. The whole building was, except for the second floor, where the Soong family had a new baby that kept them up nights.

I slid thankfully into bed. Although I dreamed of vampires and ravens, I slept soundly until the phone woke me a little after eleven. I choked out as bright a hello as I could manage, hoping it was Jake on the other end.

"Warshawski, what the hell was going on last night?"

"Murray Ryerson." I tried to wake up. "Now, there's an excellent question. I still don't understand why you brought me blind to the Wade-in last night. Thank goodness I didn't actually touch Lawlor, but just breathing some of his CO_2 nearly did me in."

"You know damned well what I'm talking about. Why did you leave to go to a crime scene and not tell me? I looked like a total moron in front of the head of the news division when the reports came in this morning."

"Murray—when I left you, I didn't know I was going to a crime scene."

"And when you got to Mount Moriah cemetery, you didn't think you could call me? You'd just left me, you know how much I could use a scoop. I told you how hard it is for me to get face time with my boss. Instead, I find out at our morning huddle that the vampire corpse not only has a connection to Vina Fields, but to Crawford, Mead."

I sat up. Murray had dropped that squib deliberately. The Vina Fields part was easy enough to understand: Kira had said that the parents of one of the girls in her group, Jessie Something, were connected to the mayor. They must have started their Sunday by calling their clout and getting him (or her) to intervene with the police for them. And once that happened, word would start floating around the city.

But Crawford, Mead? There are a handful of outsize law firms in Chicago that work for the state's heaviest hitters in politics and business. Since I specialize in financial crime—when I'm not crawling through cemeteries in the mud—I've met members of most of the big firms in court, but it's only a managing partner at Crawford, Mead whose taste in socks and sex I know. Or had known, back in the days when we were married.

Richard Yarborough wasn't a bad guy, just one who wanted power and money badly enough to sacrifice anything that got between him and his goal—such as my career, my feelings, little kittens. Not that I was still bitter or anything, twenty years later.

"What's the connection?" I asked weakly.

"If you won't share, I don't have to, either."

"Murray, I'm too tired for games—I was up past three with recalcitrant schoolgirls. How did you find out I was involved, by the way?"

"These things leak out, Warshawski, you know how that goes. I have a friend at the 13th District who thought a body with a stake through its heart was freaky enough to merit coverage. Of course, she mentioned you, because she knows you and I are pals, although a pal would have called me from the cemetery.

"This morning, I had to listen to Lawlor's broadly smeared innuendoes about what a great *leg*woman you were, and how great it was that you went out and created news for me. Of course, I pretended I knew all about it, and at least I'd had the heads-up from the 13th, but you listen to me and listen good, V. I. Warshawski: if you ever leave me looking that stupid again you will never ever get another line of print from me, even if you've uncovered proof that the president was born on the planet Krypton."

"Believe me, Murray, when you're slogging through mud with a bunch of screaming tweens, the last thing on your mind is texting your friends. Although, of course, if I'd known you wanted to take over my babysitting gig I would have called you in a heartbeat."

Murray was too angry to be placated. "It wouldn't have been so bad if you hadn't just been with me. Lawlor's an asshole, but Weekes is no dummy, and he put the twos together very fast."

"I'm sorry," I said, inadequately.

The truth was, I hadn't wanted to give Murray a heads-up. I was worried about my cousin, and about the immigrant girls in her group. Given how much Lawlor and Weekes railed against illegals in the country, I wanted to protect Kira and her mother from GEN scrutiny. Time was when you could cover Murray with syrup and send him into a nest of fire ants and he wouldn't talk. Now, given how desperate he was to make an impression on his boss, I wasn't so sure.

"Of course, you could start making it up to me," Murray said.

"Oh?"

"Get me in to see Yarborough."

"Murray, Dick and I have been divorced for a good twenty years, and the parting wasn't harmonious. It's unlikely that I could get him to talk to *me,* let alone a reporter." I sat on the edge of the bed and did a few leg lifts, flexing my toes to increase the stretch. "What on earth was Wuchnik doing for Crawford, Mead?"

"He died without confiding in me. All I know is that he was on Yarborough's payroll."

"Along with thirteen hundred other people. Dick probably didn't know his name." I put the phone on speaker and started loosening my shoulders. "I'm going back to the cemetery this afternoon. I'll be glad to show you the tomb where Wuchnik died."

"We had a photographer out there first thing this morning. And a camera crew. By the way, Helen Kendrick had a really passionate segment on her *Sunday Values* show on how a woman who wants to deny Americans the right to read their Bibles raised a daughter to worship Satan in a graveyard."

I stopped my exercises. "Murray, I don't know if it's you or me, but this makes no sense. Are you trying to say that Helen Kendrick was attacking me? Does she think Petra is my daughter? An assumption that depresses me on every conceivable parameter, by the way."

"You really don't know?"

"Don't know what?"

"Nia Durango was one of the girls at the cemetery last night." He sounded like a magician who's surprised himself along with his audience by pulling a rabbit from his hat.

"Nia Durango." I repeated blankly. "The name is supposed to mean some—oh! She's Sophy Durango's kid?"

"Give the lady the kewpie doll for firing the winning shot. Do you swear on Boom-Boom's jersey that you really didn't know Durango's kid was with you last night?"

"Murray, ten minutes ago I was blissfully asleep. I can't handle all this—Wuchnik and Dick Yarborough, Sophy Durango's daughter, Helen

Kendrick's shrieking, Satan, eliminating Bibles—too much without even a cup of coffee, let alone a trip to the bathroom. I'll call you back."

I hung up. At least I was wide awake now, but I still found Murray's call a lot to digest. What on earth was Sophy Durango thinking, to let her kid take part in an escapade like this? I guess that wasn't a fair question—Nia Durango had sneaked out pretending that she was spending the night with her pal Arielle.

Durango was president of the University of Illinois. She was also a candidate for the United States Senate. And she was running against Helen Kendrick, she of the ear of corn on the American flag. Three years ago, no one had heard Kendrick's name, except in connection with her husband's family's fortune. Then Kendrick had sued Durango and the U of I over the school's science admissions criteria—Durango refused to allow incoming freshmen to substitute Creation "science" for evolutionary biology.

"We're training young people for the twenty-first century, not the twelfth," Durango had said, and Kendrick, who believed Creationism should be taught in the public schools, had sued. The trial had brought Kendrick national attention and support, along with a slot on GEN's national cable news show (*GENuine News, No Substitutes Allowed!* scrolls across the top of the screen while you're watching Lawlor, Kendrick, and other commentators hyperventilate.)

Kendrick's followers had filled the courtroom during the trial, and had held up gorilla masks when Durango passed them in the hallway. Since Durango was African-American, their chant "to send the monkey back to the zoo" had struck some of us as a wee bit racially charged.

How had Helen Kendrick gotten hold of the news that Durango's daughter was at Mount Moriah in time for her Sunday-morning show? If parents of one of Petra's girls had gone to their tame Rottweiler in the mayor's office, their kid might have given him all the names of the girls in their Carmilla club, but that still made it a mighty fast data transfer to Helen Kendricks and Wade Lawlor. The officers at the 13th District wouldn't have known, because I hadn't known last night.

Of course, Global Entertainment probably had a dozen sources in police departments and mayoral offices all over America. It was GEN's mission to spread embarrassing news about centrist or left-leaning public figures; sometimes the reports they put out were even true. When I'd showered and had some breakfast, I'd watch the Internet replay of Helen Kendrick's show.

6. LEAKS EVERYWHERE

As it turned out, I didn't have time to look at Kendrick, let alone call Murray back. In fact, I barely had time to shower and make an espresso before Sergeant Anstey arrived, with Elizabeth Milkova. I'd met Milkova on a murder inquiry last winter, when she'd been part of the Area Six detective squad attached to Lieutenant Terry Finchley.

"Officer Milkova! Is Terry working this case? Or have you moved on to bigger and better things?"

"Lieutenant Finchley asked me to accompany Sergeant Anstey, since he's tied up this afternoon." Milkova had short, dark hair, which she played with nervously, pushing it behind her ears every few minutes. When I asked heartily after Finchley's health, her hands automatically went to the sides of her head.

Anstey glared at me, hands on hips. "Finchley warned me that you think of yourself as some kind of one-woman show, but I'm not a customer. You lied to me last night."

I didn't have a witty one-woman comeback to that, so I merely sipped my espresso.

"I knew that story about you hearing some screams inside Mount Moriah was bull-hockey. I should have locked you up last night until you told the truth. Instead, I get to hear it from my watch commander, who brings me in on my day off."

I wondered if I should put him in touch with Murray: two guys who felt I'd blindsided them with their bosses. They could get drunk together and think of horrible names to call me.

"Tough," I commiserated instead. "I don't like working Sundays myself, but here we both are."

Anstey narrowed his eyes into an expression that was frightening enough to make me glad we weren't alone in an interrogation room. He glowered for a second, waiting to make sure I wasn't going to add fuel to the fire, before continuing his tirade.

"I was taking my boy to Burr Oak Woods to play softball, and thanks to you, one of my few days with my kid is completely fucked."

Never explain, never apologize, at least not when facing an angry cop. I spread my hands in a placatory gesture but didn't say anything, which didn't really matter, because Anstey was speaking for two. Maybe for three, since Officer Milkova was standing mute by the windows.

It wasn't clear where the police had gotten their version of what the girls were doing in the cemetery last night, but the story had been garbled out of recognition as it flowed down the chain of command: after getting most of his grievance off his chest, Anstey demanded to know why I'd led a group of twelve- and thirteen-year-olds into an abandoned cemetery to perform Satanic rituals.

"That's a serious charge, Sergeant. I'll call my lawyer and you can talk to him, because I am asserting my right to remain silent."

"You're not under arrest. Yet."

"I always have the right to remain silent."

We were in my living room. I turned on the radio and went down on my hands and knees to do some core strengthening moves.

Anstey hit the off button hard enough to shake my stereo. "This isn't helping, Warshawski."

I didn't say anything. The Supreme Court's recent ruling on the right to silence had alarming implications for anyone who said anything during an interrogation. I rolled over on my back and began a sequence of abdominal presses. I could see that my toenail polish was chipped. Time to give myself a pedicure.

Anstey squatted down so that his face was directly over mine. "Why did you take the girls to that cemetery?"

I shut my eyes and lifted my butt off the floor. I could feel his breath on my face, and it took a major act of will to hold the pose for a count of thirty. I slid away from his breath, sat up, and reached for my cell phone.

I was just typing in my lawyer's phone number when my downstairs neighbor arrived, along with the two dogs we share. Mitch and Peppy were ecstatic to see me, and barked energetically at Sergeant Anstey. Mitch tried to jump up on Officer Milkova.

I got to my feet and forced Mitch to sit. "These aren't friends, and even if they were, you're not to jump on people."

Mitch grinned at me but sat, slowly, to show it was because he wanted to, not because I said so.

Mr. Contreras looked at the cops. "I didn't know you had company, doll, but what's this about you being at some cemetery last night with a bunch of vampires? I just got off the phone with Ruthie, and she says it's all over the TV and the Internet and everything! She says you've become a devil worshipper, which of course is a bunch of crap, pardon my French, but what's with you finding a corpse in a cemetery and I hear it from Ruthie first?"

Ruthie was Mr. Contreras's daughter. She had inherited his gene for nonstop talking, but not his gruff charm, which might explain why her husband had decamped when their two sons were in elementary school.

"You are the third person who's attacked me in the last half hour for learning about my business from their bosses instead of me," I complained. "Murray woke me up all hot and bothered, then these cops burst in on me, and now you. Cut me some slack! Sergeant Anstey here"—I sketched a wave in his direction—"even thinks I took the girls to the cemetery. He and Officer Milkova would prefer not to have any facts thrown their way, but to you, my beloved friend and neighbor, I will confess all. Around eleven last night, I got an SOS that some kids were out after curfew. I tracked them down to an abandoned cemetery in Ukrainian Village.

"The kids were acting like you and I did when we were their age, meaning they have more enthusiasm than sense. They got it into their heads that they were going to dance under the full moon, and nothing, not even a thunderstorm, was going to deter them. Unfortunately, they picked the same spot that a murderer had chosen. I was protecting the girls from the police until they had a chance to talk to their parents, and I didn't get home until past three, so I didn't have a chance to tell you sooner. Also, I haven't had breakfast. I don't suppose you have any leftover French toast or anything?"

"Why couldn't you tell me that?" Anstey demanded.

"Because you started with the wrong question," I said coldly. "If any of the girls, or their parents, are claiming I took the group to the cemetery, they are lying."

"Who was in the cemetery with you?" Anstey said.

I shook my head. "Wrong phrasing. You might ask whom I found in the cemetery."

"Don't push me, Warshawski." His voice dropped to a growl.

"Sergeant, you know as well as I that semantics is everything in a courtroom. I have every right to push you into not framing your questions in ways that make it sound as though I abetted the delinquency of a group of minors."

"The Morgensterns said that a Petra Warshawski was with the girls." Milkova spoke for the first time.

"Again, Officer, your language is misleading."

"We need to get in touch with her."

"Not if you're going to harass her, you ain't. You heard Vic here, you can't go around accusing people of stuff with no evidence and no reason. You got a dead body in a cemetery and you want to take the easy way out and pin it on someone, well, you ain't pinning it on either of my gals. Some man gets stabbed through the chest, you go look for someone who uses knives. You got databases, you got brains, go use them and don't come harassing—"

"We're not harassing," Anstey said, patches of color showing in his cheeks. "But your 'gal' here lied to me last night. I have a right to the truth."

"You do, Sergeant, and I gave it to you. Is there anything else?"

"I have the names of most of the girls who got together 'to dance under the full moon.'" He gave the phrase a sarcastic emphasis.

He flipped open a notebook and read the list of names. He had all the girls, but he didn't have last names for Tyler, or for the two Polish girls, Kira and Beata.

"And we know Arielle Zitter and Nia Durango were there but made it home somehow on their own. You involved in that?"

"Sergeant, who told Helen Kendrick that Dr. Durango's daughter was at the murder site last night? I haven't seen Kendrick's show myself, but a reporter just called to tell me about it. Her show goes on live at ten a.m. At that time, *I* didn't know the names of the kids I found in the cemetery last night. How did Kendrick get them?"

"I don't know where journalists get their information. I only know that trying to keep an investigation secret is like trying to hide an elephant inside a convertible."

"She didn't get Nia Durango's name from you, did she?"

The red patches reappeared on his face, but he kept his temper in check. "I'm going to pretend I didn't hear that. I need you to give me some names, though—surnames for Beata, Kira, and Tyler."

"If I could help you, I would," I assured him. "But, as I keep saying, I don't know these girls."

Anstey smacked the top of my piano. "Goddamn it, Warshawski, stop lying—"

Mitch got to his feet, growling. I grabbed his collar but couldn't stop Mr. Contreras, who said, "You got no call to start swearing, young man. You got two ladies in here with you, case you hadn't noticed, and just because one of them's a public cop and one's private, it don't mean you can't watch your language."

Anstey's expression—compounded fury and astonishment—made me start to laugh. I doubled over in a coughing fit before he could see my face.

Anstey was off balance but he wasn't stupid. He told me we weren't finished, that he'd be back after he spoke to Petra, and I'd better not have plans to leave town. He took Milkova and left, with a heavy stomping of shoes on the stairs.

As soon as they were gone, Mr. Contreras started to fret about "what trouble you got Peewee into now.".

I put my arms around him. "Don't start on me, darlin', it was a late night with a lot of worry involved. Shoe's on the other foot, anyway." I gave him the unedited version of last night's events.

At the end, although he wouldn't admit he'd misjudged me, he did say Petra was lucky she had me to turn to in a crisis. And he offered to make me breakfast.

While Mr. Contreras happily puttered around his hot kitchen, frying up French toast, I called Petra to warn her that the police wanted to talk to her.

"Call your boss at Malina today . . . Yes, I know it's Sunday, but call her as soon as we hang up: the one crime that bosses don't forgive is being the last to hear bad news from their staff. So far, no one has ID'd the two Malina girls. If anyone asks you, don't volunteer Beata and Kira's last names—if their moms have immigration issues, you could get them in hot water. Maybe your boss can get the foundation's lawyer to help you with your police interview, because you shouldn't go into it naked."

"Gosh, Vic, this is really scary." Petra's voice was subdued.

"We'll figure it out together, babe. Do you know if your other kids made it home? I just got up and I've had the police here, so I haven't made any calls."

Petra had gotten texts from the girls but hadn't spoken to any of their parents. "See, I only have the girls' cell phones on my cell. The moms' numbers are at the office, but maybe I should have my boss call them?"

By tomorrow, the parents would likely all be calling the foundation, screeching about their kids' safety. I didn't want to add to Petra's fears by saying that, so I merely reiterated my advice that she call her boss as soon as possible. "Today, kiddo. Where's Tyler, by the way?"

"I just dropped her off about ten minutes ago. Gosh, her dad is a creep. I told them I was driving Tyler home because I was chauffeuring some of the girls from the book club, and I hoped Tyler would join. She and her mom squeaked and said, oh, only if Daddy thought it was a good idea. He made my skin crawl, the way he was looking at them and me. A total reptile."

When I'd finished with Petra and eaten my breakfast, I set out for the cemetery. Mr. Contreras and the dogs came along to help look for Kira Dudek's phone. There was police tape across the gate, and a patrol car nearby, but we walked on up Leavitt until we were out of surveillance range and found a gap in the fence big enough that Mr. Contreras didn't have to crawl to get through it.

The slab where Wuchnik had died was covered with a tarp to protect any evidence in case the techs decided to revisit the scene, but there weren't any officers around. We searched the square where the girls had been dancing and didn't see the phone. Of course, if Kira had dropped it there, the evidence techs would have picked it up, but in that case, Sergeant Anstey would have been able to get her last name from the phone company.

I'd try to retrace the path the girls and I had followed to the wall. I took off one of my sandals and held it under Mitch's nose. "Find the scent, boy, find the scent."

Mitch roared off happily into the overgrown bushes after a rabbit or a snake—certainly not after my scent—with Peppy in pursuit. However, I didn't need a bloodhound to discover last night's route. I followed the trail of lost scrunchies, dropped water bottles, even a rain jacket—the evidence techs hadn't gone very far from the crime scene. I got all the way to the wall without finding a phone, so I hoisted myself up the crumbling brickwork and jumped off on the other side. Mr. Contreras protested mightily, mostly because he couldn't follow me.

I walked all the way down Hamilton Avenue to the end of the street, but didn't see a phone.

7. FRIENDS I'D RATHER NOT HAVE

I DECIDED TO SWING BY THE DUDEKS ON MY WAY HOME. Mr. Contreras waited in the car with the dogs, listening to the Sox on the radio, while I spent a fraught half hour with Lucy and Kira's mother. Since I don't speak Polish, I had to rely on the girls' translating skills to discuss what had happened last night. The only reason I had any confidence that the truth was transmitted was the quarreling that went on between Lucy and Kira: Kira was trying to put a spin on the story that Lucy wouldn't accept.

I also had to tell Kira I hadn't found her cell phone. This caused some fierce words between mother and daughter that ended with Kira stomping out of the room. I left soon after, without learning how serious an issue Ms. Dudek's immigration status was. As a matter of form, I gave Ms. Dudek my card, although the language barrier meant I didn't really expect her to use it.

"How could she be here eight years and not speak a lick of English?" Mr. Contreras demanded when I reported on the meeting.

"I don't know. The kids translate for her, she's mostly around other

Polish speakers. I suppose she keeps hoping she'll save enough money to go home. My mother never was truly fluent in English; she always spoke Italian to me. I think in some corner of her mind she kept a dream that she'd return to Italy and sing."

Maybe dreaming of a triumphal return to Pitigliano was the only way Gabriella could get through those days in South Chicago, with the dust from the mills covering everything, and no one around who cared as passionately as she did about art or music.

"My folks spoke English at home." Mr. Contreras sounded as though he was ready to start a full-scale rant, but he paused, then added in a surprised voice, "Come to think of it, they had to. My ma came from Messina and my dad was from Naples, and they neither of 'em could understand the other's dialect. It was like the fighting at Anzio to hear them going at it, which one of them spoke real Italian."

When we reached home, my answering machine was blinking. So few people call my landline anymore that it was strange to see it lit up so excitedly.

The first message was from a Julia Salanter. "It's important that we talk *today*, so please call as soon as you get this message."

My answering service had texted me that she'd called my office with the same message—I just hadn't taken time to scroll through my texts this afternoon.

I didn't know Julia, but I sure knew the name: the Salanter family were power players in Chicago. They had one of those fortunes where you don't have enough fingers and toes to count all the zeroes in their holdings. I knew a little bit about Chaim Salanter from Lotty, because he'd started the Malina Foundation. I hadn't paid close attention, but I think she said Salanter came from one of the Baltic states in his teens, made a fortune in scrap metal or commodities or something, and set up the foundation to ease the path for other immigrants.

I did a quick look at the family online. Julia was Chaim's daughter;

she chaired the Malina Foundation. A son, Michael, helped run the trading company. So Julia probably wanted to talk about the foundation's exposure to liability or publicity from last night's episode.

The next five messages, in rising levels of intensity, all came from one voice, high, bright, imperious. "Victoria! Are you there? Pick up the phone! We need to talk!"

"Victoria, this is hot, you're all I've got, I need you a lot! My situation's fraught. If *you* called *me* I'd be off like a shot."

"Victoria, you're making me crazy. You know who this is, I can't say my name, but it's not a game. Answer me, come on, I wouldn't be begging if they weren't coming after me."

I felt a sinking beneath my diaphragm. I did indeed know who that was. There had been a time when I answered Leydon Ashford's calls on the first ring. Returned the messages as soon as I got them.

Leydon Ashford was the first person I ever encountered who had two last names. We'd both grown up along the shores of Lake Michigan. The difference was, her family owned an eighteen-room mansion backing onto three hundred yards of private beach, whereas the Warshawskis' five-room bungalow was separated from the lake by a century of cyanide-laced landfill.

In our law school days, just hearing Leydon's voice on the phone conjured the glamour and excitement she seemed to embody. It was only later that she came to embody trouble—urgent summonses to places where she didn't appear, tempestuous monologues that started with a point but ended in a bewildering morass, and trips to the emergency room that became more frequent with time.

When I first met Leydon, in our Civil Procedures study group, I'd been prepared to despise her, along with her family, and the Austin-Healy Sprite her father gave her when she graduated from Wellesley. Leydon looked like a fairy-tale princess—she had hair like spun gold, and she seemed to float when she walked, like a feathery ballerina. I

wasn't a ballerina, I was a street fighter, a product of the mills and ethnic wars of Chicago's Steel City.

Even so, we became friends, sharing the same political meetings, law
school study groups, even the occasional family holiday. Leydon held
me in her arms the afternoon I'd come from taking my dad to the ER
when he'd been drowning in his own lungs. She called me "Victoria,"
not "Vic," because she said it matched my regal bearing.

Leydon had tried to talk me out of marrying Dick Yarborough: "I
know that type, Victoria, I grew up with guys like him. He only wants
to marry a strong woman so he can wrestle her to the ground and grind
the life out of her." She brought me a case of champagne and a dozen
roses the day I called to tell her we were divorcing.

It was I who'd helped her celebrate her appointment to clerk for
Justice Brennan—her family thought she was a traitor, that Brennan
was a dangerous subversive.

And it was I, not her parents, who got her to the hospital the first
time. The week before we took the bar exam, she became convinced that
her father was sending a hit man to stop her from becoming a lawyer.
Her father had opposed her law school education. He didn't like women
who were aggressive, who tried to do men's jobs, and more than once,
he and I had clashed at the Ashford dinner table.

When Leydon started talking about hit men, I thought she was joking. Then I thought she was short on sleep. It was only after I found
her huddled in a corner of the stacks at the law library that I realized
she needed help.

She recovered quickly that time, quickly enough to pass the bar in
the next exam cycle, which she did brilliantly. Her next episode didn't
occur until she was back in Chicago, on the fast track at one of the big
firms, when she started delivering all her reports by hand because the
Department of Justice was monitoring her outbound mail. After that,
the periods of hospitalization became longer, and the time in between
them grew shorter.

I had lost the stamina for Leydon's universe. I felt like a rat, but I'd stopped returning her calls. It had been over a year since I'd last talked to her, and listening to her frantic messages this afternoon, I knew I wasn't ready to deal with her again.

I called Julia Salanter instead.

"Ms. Warshawski, I want to talk to you today."

"Great. I have a few minutes right now."

"It will be better if you come to my home."

"If you're concerned about the Malina Foundation, I can't advise you. And it can surely wait until tomorrow: I have an opening in my schedule at—"

"I understand you're related to Petra Warshawski, who's working with some Malina book groups. I need to discuss what the girls were doing last night." She gave me an address on Schiller Street and hung up on my abortive protest that I was busy.

I looked at my watch. Ten to four. Jake and I were due at Lotty's at six-thirty, and I wanted to make sure I was home in time to ride over with him. I hate the assumption of the rich and powerful that when they say "jump," the rest of us salute and say, "Ma'am, yes, ma'am!" But Julia Salanter's reference to Petra worried me—if she was going to hold my cousin responsible for the girls' extracurricular behavior, I'd have to hire every law firm in town to protect her, and even then I probably wouldn't succeed. Which meant that I saluted and said, "Yes, ma'am," and walked over to Belmont and Sheffield to pick up the L.

8. MOTHERLY ADVICE

SCHILLER STREET, WHERE JULIA SALANTER LIVED, WAS BOUNDED on the east by Chicago's most popular beach and on the west by the city's hottest bar scene. At four-thirty on a sticky July Sunday, every inch of sidewalk was filled with sunburnt young people heading from beach to bar, or vice versa. If I'd driven I'd never have found parking: the traffic was bumper to bumper along both Clark and Division Streets.

I muscled my way through people texting, people carrying coolers, kids drumming on overturned buckets, mango vendors, ice cream carts. Car stereos cranked to the max shook the sidewalks, and the honking, drumming, screeching horde made me feel that my own street near Wrigley Field was a rural oasis.

Salanter's house, which was shielded from the street by a forest of arbor vitae, was reached through a wrought-iron fence whose graceful curlicues concealed security eyes. I called on a phone embedded in the front gate. As I waited to be buzzed through, I saw a nice collection of empty bottles and food bags cached in the shrubbery.

Once I was inside the grounds, a houseman greeted me with an easy courtesy, but kept me waiting outside the front door until Julia Salanter arrived.

She was a small woman, with curly dark hair cut close to her head. She was probably attractive in a gamine kind of way, but this afternoon, tension was pulling her skin tight across her face. She looked at my PI license, and then at me, and invited me inside, but it wasn't until I told her I knew Lotty Herschel that she actually smiled.

"I wanted to see you in person rather than talk on the phone because I'm hoping to persuade you to be as discreet as possible about last night. And also because I—because Sophy Durango and I—want to get a better idea of what happened than what the girls are saying."

All the way down to the Gold Coast, I'd been imagining my conversation with Salanter, scenarios that started with her arrogance, my anger. Her statement took me so by surprise that I could only murmur something disjoint. She took that as a sign that she'd offended me, but I interrupted her apology.

"You can count on my discretion as long as you're not asking me to conceal a crime, Ms. Salanter, or go against the interest of a client, but I really can tell you very little."

"Come into the back with me, where we can talk in comfort. Physical comfort, at any rate." Her mouth twisted in a wry smile. "And I'm one of those tiresome women who cares about her floors more than her guests; we ask people to take off their shoes."

She gestured at a kind of bench made out of welded bits of scrap metal. "From my dad's first scrap yard. He has a sentimental attachment to the car parts that started him on his road to success in America."

I unbuckled my sandals while the houseman shut the front door. The street noise disappeared instantly. I stood, and the marble of the foyer felt cool and caressing against my toes. If I'd known I'd be barefoot in paradise, I would have washed my feet, which were as dirty as my shoes after traipsing through the cemetery. Maybe I'd even have removed the chipped nail polish.

The houseman, a tall bald man of about forty, asked Salanter if she needed his help with our meeting. I was interested to note that he called her by her first name.

"No, thanks, Gabe: Sophy and I have our script prepared."

My hostess led me down a hall along a wood floor so polished it could have served as a skating rink. My sweaty feet squeaked as I trotted after her. We passed paintings, a couple of sculptures that seemed to be more twisted pieces of scrap metal, and a dress made out of metal mesh, but Julia was moving at such a clip that I caught only glimpses of the art, as if seen from a fast-moving train.

We landed in a small side room. Unlike the gleaming hallway, this was occupied space. Newspapers were spread across a low rattan table, a plate with half-eaten sandwiches was on another stand, and the floor was strewn with cushions so that people could lie on the thick carpet and read or dream or whatever seemed right at the moment.

It was chaotic, but reassuring, a nest where you could curl up and feel safe. And curled up in the middle of a white wicker couch was an urchin with a mop of curly hair. In the daylit lounge, she bore a striking resemblance to Julia Salanter.

I stopped to stare at her. "Arielle Zitter. What are you doing here?"

"I live here. Who are you, and what are you doing here?"

The tall girl who'd led the chanting last night was sitting on a stool near Arielle. She was drumming her middle fingers against her knees.

"And Nia Durango. Where did you girls go when you left the cemetery last night?"

"So your friend Jessie was telling her parents the truth. When her dad called me this morning, I didn't believe him." A woman I hadn't seen at first spoke from the windows behind the couch. "Nia, Arielle, you have a lot of explaining to do."

The Senate candidate was a tall, slender woman, whose hair, pulled into a knot at the nape of her neck, accentuated the severe lines around her mouth.

Nia and Arielle spoke almost in the same breath. "It was her idea!"

"You two blaming each other makes you sound like street criminals. I'm ashamed to hear you behaving like a couple of crooks caught with your hands in the till."

That was Sophy Durango; Julia Salanter added, "I'm not interested in apportioning blame between the two of you and your friends. I want to know what you thought you could gain by lying to us. Aunt Sophy and I trust you girls, because we've always believed you were mature enough to understand the fishbowl we all swim in. We trust you to behave responsibly in public. To find out you both lied to us last night is a source of grief. And you have also created opportunities for Aunt Sophy's opponents to attack her."

"But, Mom, we weren't trying to hurt your campaign," Nia said. "It's just—Carmilla, she's so cool! We thought—we hoped—we wanted it to be true. And the chanting, the full moon, it made us feel like we were part of her!"

"You girls thought you could turn into ravens?" Sophy Durango was so dumbfounded she couldn't figure out anything else to say.

"I know what they're saying about Grandpapa on the news," Arielle said. "I want to peck their eyeballs out!"

Julia sat on the couch next to her daughter. "Darling, we all know the horrible hate that they're spewing out about your grandfather, and about Aunt Sophy, and we agreed we had to ignore it, to pretend it isn't happening. But last night's escapade is going to make things worse, you know. I don't know how Helen Kendrick got Nia's name, unless Jessie Morgenstern or one of the other girls talked, or put it on Facebook, but Kendrick already attacked Aunt Sophy on her show this morning. We need the truth before Wade Lawlor starts in on your grandfather."

"Can you back up a minute?" I said. "I don't know who you're talking about. Jessie Morgenstern—she was one of the girls who was with you at the cemetery last night?"

The two girls nodded cautiously, wondering if my questions would lead to further trouble for them.

"Her father is the one who gives money to politicians?" I said. It had been Tyler, or maybe Kira, who had said that in our early-morning conversation.

"Yes, yes," Julia Salanter interrupted me impatiently. "He's a hedge-fund manager who dabbles in politics. Jessie goes to Vina Fields with Arielle and Nia. Her parents hired a PR specialist to help their lawyer coach Jessie through her police interview, but they promised me they didn't tell the specialist or the lawyer that Ari and Nia were with Jessie. Sam Morgenstern owes a chunk of his success to tips that—well, never mind that."

Julia added wryly to Sophy Durango, "I can see Lawlor's headlines: *Nazi Supporter's Granddaughter Sucks Christian Blood. Is This Who You Want Advising Your Next Senator?*"

Durango made a face. "If I'd known they were going to attack Chaim in such an ugly way, I'd never have let him sign on to my campaign. Ms. Warshawski, you didn't leak news about last night's escapade to the Kendrick campaign, did you?"

"Dr. Durango, I had quite enough on my hands with the remnants of your daughters' group without getting involved in a political campaign as well."

"Don't get on a high horse with us, Ms. Warshawski: we don't know you, so we don't know what you might or might not do," Julia Salanter said. "We need to do some damage control before the damage gets worse. Someone fed Helen Kendrick the news that Nia was at Mount Moriah last night, but didn't make the connection to Chaim. Either they didn't know Arielle was there, or they didn't realize she was Chaim's granddaughter—Zitter is her father's last name."

"I certainly didn't know that," I said. "Chaim—Mr. Salanter—he's running Dr. Durango's campaign?"

"Heading my finance committee," Durango said. "Why don't you tell us what you saw last night."

"Ms. Salanter mentioned my cousin on the phone," I said. "She's worried that she's going to be in hot water, either with you or with the cops or both. And I, of course, am concerned that she not be held responsible for last night's events. She did what she could to look after the girls in her group, but she had no authority over them."

Salanter nodded, her face grim. "We know that. Just tell us what happened."

I went through my spiel: Lucy, Kira, the full moon, stumbling on the girls by chance, finding Wuchnik's body, trying to get the girls to wait for me at the Dudek place while I ran interference with the police. "As to what lies the girls told to leave home in the first place, and whether they were really sticking needles into each other's bodies—you'll have to get that from your daughters. By the way, where did Nia and Arielle go when they left the cemetery? Petra kept trying to text them but they went blank on her."

"They went back to my house," Durango said. "They knew I was at an event downstate last night, and hoped they could con me into believing they hadn't gone out. I didn't know anything until someone called me from Chicago for a comment on the accusations Kendrick made this morning. I was *not* happy."

Nia and Arielle looked at their feet.

"What's this about needles and sucking blood?" Salanter demanded.

"It was our ritual," Arielle whispered, after a glance at her friend. "Tyler was such a crybaby, we shouldn't have let her take part, then this wouldn't—"

"I told you, I don't want to hear you shifting your responsibilities onto someone else!" Durango's voice was a whip.

"There's another problem," I said to the mothers. "A murder took place near them. Tyler being a crybaby meant that we all came on the body, but I think the murderer was still there when the girls got to their chosen spot. Someone claimed she'd seen a vampire; I think she caught a glimpse of the murderer. Arielle and Nia are going to have to talk to the cops, and the sooner you make that happen, the easier controlling your damage will be."

"Which girl saw the murderer?" Salanter asked.

"No one," Arielle said. "Tyler thought she saw a vampire, but she couldn't have, she wasn't even initiated yet."

This new grievance made Arielle bunch up her fists and pound the cushions. She was on that tightrope between childhood and young adulthood—like young Kira, hoping to fly off to her father in Poland, Arielle and Nia still hoped magic might really happen.

"Tyler?" Julia said. "I don't remember her name from your Malina book group."

"She isn't in it. Lots of kids at Vina Fields want to join our Carmilla club. Jessie and Tyler hang out; Jessie persuaded us to let her join, but now—we told Tyler it would hurt, but I guess she didn't believe us."

"Or she wanted friends badly enough not to mind—although I don't suppose anyone is prepared for a needle in the palm," I said. "When she ran away from you, after you'd stabbed her, she said she didn't care if you didn't speak to her for five years. What was that about?"

Arielle flushed but didn't speak.

"Did you threaten her with ostracism?" her mother demanded.

"Not like that," Arielle stammered. "It's a vow. Before you can be initiated you have to swear that you won't reveal the secrets of Carmilla, and if you do, no one else in the group will talk to you for the rest of the time we're at school together."

Arielle saw her mother's shocked face. "Mom! It's the only way we can keep our club a secret!"

"How did you choose your ritual?" I asked, before the conversation devolved into a mother-daughter battle.

"We tried to bite each other, but it's really hard, you need extra-sharp vampire fangs, otherwise you're just catching up a fold of skin, and then, oh, you know, Aunt Sophy, she's always doing needlepoint, so we started experimenting with her needles."

"You stabbed each other?" Julia said.

"Of course, Aunt Julia," Nia said. "We had to do it first; we couldn't ask someone else to go through it if we hadn't seen what it was like."

The two mothers looked at each other again. Some wordless communication passed, because they nodded, and Salanter spoke.

"The Vina Fields Carmilla club will go on without you from now on. Arielle, you and Nia will not see each other or text each other for two weeks."

The two girls started shrieking in protest, promising endless good behavior; Salanter raised her voice. "There's plenty of work for you to do, either for the foundation or the campaign—that will be your community service. Grandpapa's lawyer will come tonight to prepare you for your conversation with the police, which will be happening tomorrow morning, if we can arrange it."

Dr. Durango turned to me. "We've spoken very frankly in front of you, Ms. Warshawski. I want to know whether we can rely on your discretion."

"Oh, yes, I'm discreet as all get out," I said impatiently. "But I don't think you're taking this very seriously. A man was murdered last night, stabbed through the heart in a way that looked like a movie-style vampire slaying. How did he happen to be where your daughters were prancing around? Did you know him?"

Julia flushed. "Of course we care that someone was killed. As to whether we knew him—what was his name?"

"Miles Wuchnik," I said, my voice tight. "Maybe you are the good guys in Illinois politics, but this focus on damage control when a man was killed, it doesn't sit well with me."

"I don't think *you* understand," Salanter said. "My father is under constant attack, as is Dr. Durango. What our daughters did was ill advised, but we don't have the luxury of dealing with them privately: their behavior isn't just public property, it will be taken up as part of a relentless media attack machine. So I won't apologize for focusing on damage control."

I responded mechanically to her words: my attention was caught by Arielle, whose eyes had widened at hearing Wuchnik's name.

"Did you know him?" I demanded.

"Of course not!" she cried.

"You spoke to him on the phone?" I persisted.

"My daughter says she didn't know him. It's extremely offensive of you to imply that she was lying," Julia Salanter said.

"Maybe he was a genie," Nia said.

She and Arielle giggled at each other, but stopped instantly when they saw their mothers' angry faces. "I just meant, maybe he appeared out of smoke or a bottle or something."

"Not funny," Sophy Durango said.

I looked at Arielle. "You didn't care enough about the body you stumbled on to watch the news? Miles Wuchnik has been at the center of every news outlet all day long, whether on TV or online."

"I don't watch the stupid news. I hate it; there's always some hate story about Grandpapa or Aunt Sophy. And, anyway, I was trying to protect Grandpapa."

Julia blinked in bewilderment. "Why would boycotting the news help Chaim?"

Arielle bit her lips, keeping a wary eye on me. She had some connection to Wuchnik, I was sure of it.

"It troubles me that Wuchnik was stabbed in a way that echoes the ritual the girls were involved in," I said slowly. "It's as if the murderer knew what the Carmilla club was up to and wanted to make a public statement about it. How could that have happened, Arielle?"

"Who knew you were going to the cemetery yesterday?" Sophy Durango asked.

"Me and Arielle," Nia answered her mother. "Jessie, Nolan. We didn't tell Tyler because she wasn't initiated."

"What about Kira and Beata?" I asked.

Nia and Arielle shook their heads.

"I thought they were initiated," I persisted.

"They are. But they're not our real friends."

"Right. They're immigrant kids, their moms scrub toilets for a living. Hard to be real friends."

"That's unfair," Salanter said. "Arielle knows better than most girls what immigrants go through."

"Ms. Salanter, lots of girls have parents or grandparents who came here in poverty. Most of us, including me, have parents and grandparents who never had the mix of luck and drive that gave your father the ability to swaddle his grandchildren in luxury."

"Don't attack my daughter for my father's success!" Salanter snapped. "We get it hammered into us constantly on GEN as it is."

"If anything, I envy her, and the GEN commentators probably do as well. But his success does put a wall between her and a woman who cleans hotel rooms on the night shift."

Durango changed the subject. "You're an investigator. Could you find out who leaked the news to Kendrick?"

I shook my head. "These girls text everyone. They may have sworn a vow of silence, but they were videoing each other with their phones last night; someone put it on Facebook, or sent it to her friends in a text. Anyone with an axe to grind about the election could have picked it up and sent it to Kendrick. Anything else?" I turned to leave.

Julia followed me back up the hall. "And you will keep our conversation to yourself."

"Oh, yes. I don't want to add to Dr. Durango's woes with the public, but someone does. Even though I don't think you could trace the leak, someone got the news to Kendrick fast—she had Nia's name before the police knew it, because the cops only got it after one of the parents took his daughter into Area Six this morning. And then, the way the murder was committed—it was horrible, rebar through the heart. I think grounding those girls until the murderer is caught might be a smart move."

Salanter stared at me. "You think someone would try to hurt Arielle?"

"I don't know." I sat on her father's scrap metal relic to put my sandals back on. "I hope not, but if you have a security detail, I'd keep an eye on her. On Nia, too. There's an ugly mind behind this murder."

Salanter's face, tight and white with worry, stayed with me as I rode the L back north.

9. CABLE NEWS

Over dinner at Lotty's, conversation was mostly about music, or, more accurately, musical personalities. Jake was leaving for Vermont in a few days: he'd been invited to serve as an artist-in-residence at the Marlboro Festival. I'd put aside the last week of the festival to spend with Jake, a real vacation—from Marlboro, we would drive up to Canada, where we would hike the Laurentian Mountains.

Lotty and Max were planning to go in August, when some of their old musician friends from London would be in residence, and they joined Jake in dissecting conductors and performers with a happy disregard for slander laws.

It wasn't until we were sitting on the balcony with our coffee that Lotty brought up the body in the graveyard, and that was because she worried about how it might affect the Malina Foundation.

I told them about my meeting with Durango and Salanter, at least the parts that wouldn't violate their privacy: the girls' participation in the full-moon ritual was pretty much public knowledge.

Max's lips were tight with anger. "Malina has been under attack for years; this is going to add fuel to a fire that's almost out of control."

"Why?" Jake asked.

"The anti-immigration hysteria that's gripping parts of the country," Max explained. "You know that the foundation's mission is with immigrants and refugees? It's why Lotty and I sit on the board, and maybe why we follow more closely than you the way Global Entertainment keeps attacking the foundation along with Chaim. They claim that Chaim is anti-American, or trying to destroy America, and they point to Malina as proof. Malina is an old Yiddish word for a hiding place inside a ghetto, and people like Lawlor pounce on that—they say Salanter chose the name because he's smuggling illegals into the country. They say he's laughing at America by running the foundation as a training camp for terrorists."

"Yes." Lotty shuddered. "I can hardly bear to imagine what Wade Lawlor will say if he learns that the girls in Petra's group were acting out vampire fantasies."

"Julia said Lawlor will accuse her father of being a Nazi sucking Christian blood," I said, "but I thought the Salanters were Jews."

"They are." Lotty's mouth set in a hard line. "It's despicable, what they say about Chaim. He somehow survived the 1941 Yom Kippur massacre in the Vilna ghetto. His family was annihilated that day, but he slipped out and managed to survive on the streets for the next four years. Lawlor twists that to mean that a thirteen-year-old boy bartered his mother and father for his own life."

"This is completely outrageous," Jake exclaimed. "Why doesn't Salanter sue?"

"He says it will just bring more attention to the lies that Lawlor and Global are telling," Max said. "I think it's a mistake to let them get away with it—it's letting them ape Goebbels: keep repeating outrageous lies and people believe them."

"I haven't watched much of GEN's campaign coverage," I said. "I know they support Kendrick, but she's such a wing-nut—she wants to teach Creationism in the public schools, she's proposed jail terms for women who have abortions, she wants to outlaw Social Security and

Medicaid—I just assumed no one could take her seriously. But if Global is positioning Salanter as the fulcrum of the axis of evil—"

"Yes. It's dangerous, shocking, vile. I never thought I would hear such language in America—" Lotty broke off mid-sentence.

Lotty's grandfather had sent her and her brother from Vienna to London with the Kindertransport in the summer of 1939. English immigration laws meant the adults had to stay behind, and they all—grandparents, parents, aunts, as well as her cousins whose family lacked the money or connections to send them west—had perished in the death camps.

Lotty and Max—who'd come to London from Prague, also with the Kindertransport—had grown up in central Europe listening to anti-Jewish hatred on the airwaves and in their schools. I could only imagine how painful it must be to hear the same lies bleated again in America.

Jake gave Lotty's shoulder a sympathetic squeeze and went into the apartment. We heard him at the piano, softly playing "Erbarme dich," from Bach's *St. Matthew Passion*. We sat for a long time in the dark, watching the moonlight ripple on the black lake beyond, as Jake improvised on the melody. The bass is his instrument but he can handle a piano—he says it's just a bass with two hundred thirty strings.

After a time, I went to sit next to him. He put his right arm around me; with his left, he played the chords and coached me through the aria.

Later, back at our own building on Racine, Jake came into my place with me. From some perverse impulse, we turned on the television to see if we could find Wade Lawlor's show. Since GEN broadcast it four times a day, we caught the ten-o'clock broadcast.

I fetched my mother's Italian wineglasses and a bottle of Black Label—I had a feeling that we'd need something to calm our nerves. After the appropriate drumrolls and logos and ads, the camera moved in on a stern-looking Wade Lawlor, sitting in an armchair next to a small table covered with books and papers.

He was wearing his usual blue-checked shirt, his thick hair in its carefully arranged tangle. When I met him last night, I hadn't noticed the intense blue of his eyes, but I realized now he wore the blue shirt to make his eyes stand out on camera. At the beginning of the show, he leaned back in the chair, but as the broadcast wore on, his urgency moved him to the edge of the seat and his head came up and out at the viewer like a frenzied adder's.

"My fellow Americans," he began, as if he were the president of the United States. "My comrades in arms, my brothers and sisters who share my passion for liberty and my fear that we are letting Fascists, Communists, even terrorists who are hiding under protection of our Constitution"—here he broke off to wave a piece of yellowed parchment in front of the camera—"we are letting terrorists flush our precious freedoms down the toilet to Mexico."

He took a sip of water—his emotion was so powerful he had to steady himself.

I've talked to you before about one of these terrorists. He operates brazenly, boldly, right here in Chicago, and he has no use for America or Americans any more than he had use for his parents or siblings or friends in the country of his birth. That's right. I'm talking about Chaim Salanter.

"Chaim" should be pronounced to rhyme with "time," or even "rhyme," but Lawlor deliberately mispronounced it to make it sound like "shame."

When he was thirteen, *Chame* Salanter came of age, under Jewish law. Now, I've gotten ugly e-mail from terrorist sympathizers, telling me I'm not saying that name right, but I'm an American and I only know how to talk one language, American.

So back in Foreignland, the first thing this new young man *Chame* did was get rid of his parents. Yep, *Chame* sold his parents to the Nazi invaders, and they let him out, maybe the one life they should have taken, but they spared him so he could operate ruthlessly on the streets of Vilnius. *Chame* bought and sold the trinkets of desperate people and began to amass his fortune.

Lawlor opened a book and the camera panned on photos of gaunt Jews with stars on their coats, standing in a barren city square. There was no way of knowing where or when the picture had been taken.

Using the chaos of post-war Europe as a convenient cover, *Chame* Salanter came to the United States, pretending to be a refugee. A ruthless Communist like him learned how to milk the capitalist system. He'd dealt in poor people's last hopes in Lithuania; here in America he turned to the same trade, scrap metal, but he soon saw that the real money was in the fake markets, the stocks and bonds and options and other things too sophisticated for people like you and me to understand.

Chame took our savings and turned them into one ginormous fortune. And now he's using that fortune as a Trojan horse. He has a foundation, the Malina Foundation [*background footage of the Malina Building with a big wooden horse rolling through the front doors onto Van Buren Street*].

Malina looks out for the "rights" [*Lawlor made air quotes with his fingers*] of refugees and immigrants. What is that but a big cover for sneaking terrorists into America, just as he snuck here himself? What about your rights?

And last night, an American citizen, a hardworking American trying to make an honest dollar, was brutally murdered in an abandoned *Jewish* cemetery.

We saw the familiar footage of Mount Moriah cemetery, with the temple where Wuchnik's body had been found. Lawlor's cameraman added a close-up of several Jewish gravestones, with the six-pointed stars on them.

And who was right there in the middle of the cemetery, dancing around the dead man before his blood was cold? Why, *Chame* Salanter's cute-as-a-button granddaughter. And who was with her? The daughter of Sophy *Duran-goo*, the offspring of the monkey in the zoo, who thinks she needs to go to Washington to represent the good and honest people of Illinois.

And dancing right along with them? Children of illegal aliens that *Chame* and his Malina Foundation have brazenly smuggled into the United States to take jobs away from good and decent Americans like you! It's time we told *Chame* to go home, to take his terrorist pals with him, and to send *Duran-goo* back to the zoo!

And before you liberals start in with your smears and blood libels against me, remember, *Duran-goo*'s the one who brought monkeys into the debate. She thinks she's descended from a monkey, not created in the image of God like you and me. If that's racism, I totally give up on the United States of America as a place where free speech is allowed. It's *Heil Duran-goo, Heil Obama, Heil Salanter,* as we march the United States over a cliff.

By the end of the rampage, I was biting my lip so hard I drew blood. Jake was furious. "That's disgusting and obscene! How does he get away with it?"

"We let him get away with it!" I poured us both out a good dose of whisky; my hand was none too steady. "I think you're right, that Salanter should sue Lawlor. Otherwise those lies will just fill up more and more of people's heads."

"You don't think there could be some truth?" Jake suggested.

"No smoke without fire? You really think a child locked in the Vilna ghetto did some deal with the Nazis to murder his parents in exchange for his own freedom?" My face flooded with color.

"Don't give me the eye of death, V.I.! Of course I don't. But if he isn't sitting on something ugly, why won't he confront Lawlor?"

"Maybe he puts too much faith in reason, or believes Americans are too decent to be taken in. I don't know." I moved fretfully around the room. "The girls I saw last night—Salanter's own granddaughter— they're the age he was when he was living alone in a war zone. They're halfway between children and women; they're old enough to look after themselves but they don't have good judgment. If Salanter—if any child that age—did something questionable to survive—"

I broke off, as I began to imagine horrific things that Salanter could have done—or his granddaughter, come to that. If she and her friends had stumbled on Miles Wuchnik and killed him, I wouldn't believe their youth made murder acceptable. If Salanter had done something dreadful in the middle of occupied Lithuania, did the occupation excuse his acts?

"But how did Lawlor get the news that Salanter's granddaughter was in the cemetery—not to mention the two immigrant girls?" I said. "When I saw Durango and Julia Salanter this afternoon—"

My phone rang mid-sentence. It didn't surprise me to hear Julia Salanter on the other end of the line.

"Dr. Durango and I trusted you to keep—"

"Never begin a sentence with an accusation," I cut her off. "I didn't betray your confidence. I just watched Lawlor's show—it's sickening, and I don't blame you for being upset, but I am not the person who leaked the news to him."

"Then who did?" Salanter demanded.

"I don't know, and, as I said this afternoon, I think it would be close to impossible to find out. Lawlor has people trolling blogs and Facebook and police blotters, looking for little grains of scandal to use to back up his big lies. I still think your dad should sue him for slander, and libel, but I can't solve the leak problem for you."

"Chaim won't sue," Julia said. "We don't want more fingers poking through our history than happens already!"

"Then you have an insoluble problem," I said dryly. "There are no brakes on what anyone can say online these days. I suppose you could start your own PR offensive, if you wanted to change the dialogue."

"We don't have anything to hide or prove. But we talked to our lawyer and to our publicist, and we've all agreed that the best thing we can do is to be open about what happened. Our publicist arranged for the girls to appear on television tomorrow—the Rachel Lyle show. We hate doing it, Chaim most of all: we've always tried to keep our lives emphatically private, but Rachel will run a sympathetic interview, and we owe it to Sophy to try to limit damage to her campaign."

"Oh, this obsession with damage control!" When Julia started to bristle, I cut her off. "Yes, I understand why you're doing it, but I'm more interested in what the girls know about Miles Wuchnik."

"Why?" she demanded sharply. "You're not trying to suggest they were involved in his death, I trust."

"No. But they knew something, about Wuchnik, or the way the murder was committed. If one of the girls didn't tell him they were going to Mount Moriah, how did he and his killer know they'd be there?"

"It's what you just said," Julia snapped. "You can't chase down leaks. The girls texted, or one of them blabbed to someone who blabbed to someone. But don't imply that my daughter went behind my back and talked to a third-rate private eye. Or you'll find that there are some legal actions the Salanter family is willing to undertake."

"Squashing a small person, leaving a big one to go on his merry way, you mean?" I couldn't keep the words back, but it wasn't surprising that she hung up on me.

10. POLITICS AS USUAL?

JAKE HAD GONE INTO THE KITCHEN WITH A BACK COPY OF
The Atlantic while I was talking to Julia. He put the magazine down
when he saw my unhappy face, but didn't speak, just got up and led
me to my bedroom.

Our lovemaking was hard, almost furious, as if we could use our
bodies to suppress the demons invading our minds. Neither of us slept
well. I finally got up at five-thirty, trying to slip quietly out of bed, but
Jake was already awake. He joined me in the kitchen for an espresso,
but went back to his own apartment when I left for the beach with
the dogs.

Yesterday's bright, clear day had been a one-shot wonder. It wasn't
seven o'clock when the dogs and I left the beach to come back home,
but the sun on the water already had a glare that made the eyes ache,
and the air was as thick and sticky as a bowl of oatmeal.

The phone was ringing when I reached my apartment, but it had
stopped by the time I got the door open. Caller ID again showed the
incoming number as blocked. I carried the handset into the kitchen
while I fed the dogs and cut up a mango for myself. Just as I was stirring

the mango into a dish of yogurt, the phone began to ring again. I'd been expecting someone from the press, or the Salanter-Durango operation; I'd forgotten Leydon.

"Victoria! Thank goodness. I was starting to think you'd left the country, or that you hated me, which I couldn't bear, nothing would drive me to the top of the tower formerly known as Sears faster than thinking you didn't love me anymore. I need you, my little huntress, they've sent someone after me, I knew it, I knew it when I saw his weaselly face and now they'll come after me and kill me or worse."

"Ley—"

"Not my name, not on a phone, you know how it is when they don't leave you alone! They're tracking me. I need your help, you're such a clever huntress, you'll be able to think like them and tell me what I need to do."

"Take a breath, tell me what's going on."

"Not on the phone, Iphigenia, darling, it's much too Gordian for the phone. These days, it's not just who's in the room with you, it's who's on the scanner or the GPS chip with you. Just go to our old favorite meeting place. I can be there in forty minutes, or thirty if I can retrieve my car. I took it to the garage yesterday, only they said they couldn't get to it until this morning, but it's just a leaky gasket, that's an easy fix. They have loaners, although then you have to sign the paperwork, and you know how it is, as soon as you put your name on something, you've got telemarketers, not to mention Uncle Sam and your own brother tracking—"

"Leydon, I have meetings today that I can't miss—"

She cut me off again, hysterical that I'd said her name. I apologized and offered to meet her at the end of the day.

"I need you now, you need me, this could be a great story for you, this is hot, red hot, hotter than the midday sun on a July day in Chicago. A red-hot photo op, one for the photo shop, but you'd better hop!"

"Leydon, please, I can't—"

"When did I ever turn my back on you when you needed me?" she cried. "When you left Dick Yarborough, didn't I put you up for the night? When you started your detective business, didn't I get my firm to send work your way? Why can't you do this for me? I know it's not a little thing, saving someone's life, but I would do it for you if you asked, I'd be there in a heartbeat, in a half beat, in a half second, I wouldn't put you second, the way you're doing to me."

I could feel my head splintering under her pile-driving chatter. "I have to run. Give me a hint about the problem now."

"Can't on the phone, I told you, darling, it's too Gordian, it's a Gordian knot, too overwrought for the phone."

Gordian. That was Leydon's code when we were young to let me know someone was in the room while she was on the phone. The subject was too personal, too knotty, for her father or roommates to overhear.

"Then I'll meet you at five-thirty; just tell me where."

Leydon repeated that she'd be at our favorite spot, but she wouldn't reveal the address—she was too worried about eavesdroppers. "You remember it, my little huntress, our old haunts, far from the prying eyes of men; be there at five-thirty."

"Far from the prying eyes of men? You mean the women's toilet at the law school?"

"Don't joke about it, Victoria, be there, don't be square, you know where, I'll see you—"

I hung up. I'd forgotten Leydon's riddling, rhyming talk. Her clever language, filled with double or even triple entendres had added to her allure when we first met. In my family, with my slow-talking father, and a mother whose English didn't come easily, I'd never experienced such linguistic fireworks. Later, though, the brilliance had faded from Leydon's speech, leaving only difficult riddles at the core.

That was why she called me "her little huntress." It was Leydon who knew that my middle name, Iphigenia, was an avatar of the Greek goddess Artemis, the huntress. When I became a private eye, she thought it a clever joke that I was now a hunter, and she kept me up until three one morning, debating why my mother had chosen to call me that. Leydon was sure the choice had an unconscious effect on my career decision, and her chat had veered off into topics I couldn't follow, such as the Lacanian unconscious. ("Victoria Iphigenia, this *proves* that you absorbed the Greek avatar in your preconscious Italian mind, where it's hovered all these years!")

Our favorite spot, far from the prying eyes of men: that was a good example of an irritating riddle. Leydon might be thinking of almost any place, and I was supposed to unravel the code, or end up feeling responsible for the meltdown that would lie on the other side of a missed meeting.

I smacked my espresso pot down hard enough to splash coffee across the countertop and across my torso. Fortunately I was still in my T-shirt and cutoffs.

I wiped a sponge across the counter and went off to dress for work, choosing something sleeveless because of the heat. Not a sundress, since I was seeing clients today, but a severely tailored dress in gold cotton with big black buttons, cut for me by Joseph Parecki. He was an old friend of my parents' who'd made my mother's concert gowns.

Parecki was eighty-three now and didn't sew much anymore, but he'd had a crush on Gabriella, and he liked to cut for me because I looked like her—"Only you are much bigger, Victoria, not that I mean to insult you. Your mother was a small woman, but her voice—that was the size of Mount Everest. You, you are tall like the mountain but with a smaller voice—Mother Nature has a sense of humor."

While I dressed, I turned to channel 12 so I could watch Rachel Lyle's interview with Chaim Salanter's granddaughter.

"Here with me in the studio today are a couple of America's most significant women: Dr. Sophy Durango, president of the University of Illinois and a candidate for Illinois Senator. Also with us is Julia Salanter, director of the Malina Foundation. The women have brought their daughters with them to the studio today, and if Helen Kendrick, Durango's opponent, sells a moisturizer that produces those complexions, I want it, no matter what it costs!"

Her last sentence was a light reference to the skin-care products and drugstore chain that made up a big part of the Kendrick fortune.

The camera moved in close on Nia Durango and Arielle Zitter, who were sitting side by side on a couch. Lyle had placed herself at the end of the couch, sitting with her profile to the camera so she could look at the girls, who were dressed in pink sundresses that made them appear young, innocent, guileless.

The two mothers watched their daughters from armchairs at either end of the couch. The whole tableau looked like a set for a Victorian charade: anxious, doting mothers dressed in prim summer suits, hair carefully coiffed. "We drink tea and do good works," the stage set proclaimed. "We support old-fashioned family values. We may run gigantic enterprises, but at heart we are just women who long to stay at home with our daughters, baking chocolate-chip cookies."

Lyle talked with the girls about their fondness for the *Carmilla* books, and whether they'd ever expected to have adventures like the ones the girls in the series faced.

"Every kid wants adventure, as long as it isn't scary," Nia said gravely. "We thought going into the cemetery would be an adventure. It was sort of like the *Carmilla* books, but it seemed more like Huck Finn, when he goes to the cemetery with Tom Sawyer."

The comparison felt like a PR clunker—it was meant to make the girls seem all-American, but it was hard to believe kids that age would make the leap on their own. If I'd been Rachel Lyle, I would have pushed Nia to see when she'd read *Tom Sawyer.*

"Only then it got really scary," Arielle chimed in. "A man was killed where we were having our Carmilla club meeting. We were lucky that our book group leader, Petra, sent her cousin to find us. Her cousin is a detective, see, and she helped us get home and be safe again."

A nice smooth skate there over abandoning their friends and followers and running home—and trying to pretend to their mothers that
they hadn't left the Durango home all night even long enough to let the
dog out.

The mothers said that they were grateful, too, to Petra and to me,
but they wanted Nia and Arielle to understand that actions have consequences. "Like girls all over America, our daughters are swept up in
Carmilla mania. Still, they know that it was wrong to sneak out of the
house to meet with their school's Carmilla club, and they're grounded
for two weeks."

"Our moms have blocked each other's numbers on our phones," Nia
pouted. "So no texting, either."

I watched the performance through to the end. No mention of vampires, no mention of lying to their mothers, of sticking needles into one
another's hands. As the cameras rolled away from the tableau, I started
flipping through the other channels.

The story was the number-one feature everywhere I looked. A number of channels already were rolling footage of the interview I'd just
watched. No one seemed very interested in Miles Wuchnik, alive or dead,
although they all made use of the Gothic murder backdrop, showing
the crumbling pillars of the tomb where he'd been killed.

Most commentators focused on whether Nia Durango's presence at
Wuchnik's murder site would kill her mother's bid for senator.

"It's July," one pontificator pontificated. "People in Chicago have
short memories and a deep tolerance for their politicians' misbehavior.
By November it'll be forgotten."

"Typical of Chicago corruption" was Global Entertainment's response. Their color-balanced morning news team—a bleached-blond
woman with a dark African-American man—said that Durango letting
her daughter run wild in a graveyard was unsurprising, given the loose
morals you could expect from a single mom, and did Illinois need more
of that?

"Sophy's on record as being against the Bible," the female half of the sketch said. "As a result, her daughter belongs to a dangerous cult that worships vampires, or birds, or something, in a graveyard. Sophy can't recover from this kind of revelation before election day."

The *Global Morning Show* (motto: *We Spin the Globe in Your Kitchen*) also brought in Helen Kendrick to give her a chance to comment. All I knew about Kendrick's personal life was that she had married wisely, into a family whose holdings included ethanol plants along with their international drugstore chain. Helen had taken charge of Kendrick's online skin-care division and turned it into an international gold mine. Ken-Care for the skin, Ken-Hair for the head, Ken-Scare for the politics.

Her on-screen presence was a credit to the family business. Her skin glowed with health, and her hair had a gold-blond sheen that looked natural, although it was probably not as genuine as the jewel-studded crucifix at her throat. If the stones were genuine, the pendant probably represented a year's rent for someone in my childhood neighborhood— where Kendrick's support ran high in the Eastern European part of the ward.

As soon as Kendrick started speaking, it was clear that she'd avoided elitist vocal coaches who might have tried to tone down the grating nasal of the true Chicagoan. "I guess if you think your grandfather was a monkey, you don't care if your girls are worshipping animals in a cemetery. I can't believe Sophy Durango can be so casual about her daughter's behavior, calling it an innocent prank. Nia Durango was out after curfew, she was in a cemetery, she was practicing a cult, and all the time a man was being murdered nearby.

"I raised five children and saw them safely into adulthood before I turned to public life, but, like the apes she thinks are her ancestors, Sophy *Duran-goo* believes in letting her one teenage daughter loose in the urban jungle on her own."

Kendrick paused dramatically. "Who was Miles Wuchnik, and why doesn't Sophy Durango want to talk about him? Was he her lover? Was her daughter in the cemetery because Sophy brought her child there with her while she met her lover? The voters of Illinois have a right to answers to these questions."

The harsh voice went on and on with one hate-filled phrase after another. I couldn't seem to move, not even to summon the energy to turn off the television. The leap from Nia, to Wuchnik's death, to the assertion that he'd been Sophy Durango's lover, was made seamlessly, but without any regard to facts or logic. What could Durango possibly say to counter such extreme language?

The station finally turned to a commercial. The sight of women jumping up and down in a field of daisies, extolling the freedom that came from a drug to control leaky bladders, seemed like a garish counterpoint to Kendrick's onslaught. The drug might well be part of Kendrick Pharm's profit centers, but the dancing women broke the spell of Kendrick's voice enough that I could turn off the set and resume dressing.

11. HERE A MOB, THERE A MOB

As I put on lipstick and eyeliner, my landline rang a few times. In case Leydon was trying to call me again, I let the calls roll over to the answering machine. It turned out I was getting my own fifteen minutes of fame: NPR and the local CBS affiliate both wanted to talk to me about what I'd seen in the cemetery.

The third call, as I was finally walking out the door, came from Max Loewenthal. "Victoria, I will try your office number. Chaim Salanter would like to talk to you and I promised to act as a go-between."

That was so startling I turned back to pick up the phone, but Max had hung up. Anyway, I was late. I raced to my office, where I dumped my car and picked up the L into the Loop.

In between meetings and teleconferences with the clients who form the backbone of my business, I called Max. He didn't know why Salanter wanted to talk to me, although we both took for granted it had to do with his granddaughter's outing and Wuchnik's death.

"He called me because he knows me from Malina's board. We're not at all close; he's not a person one becomes close to, although of course

I've cultivated him as a potential donor to Beth Israel. He hoped you could meet him for lunch today."

"Not possible today. I've got commitments until—" I'd been about to say until five, and then I remembered my tangled conversation with Leydon. Assuming I could figure out our old favorite spot, I'd be heading there at five-thirty. "Tell him I'm free this evening after seven or so. And give him my cell-phone number; no need for you to act as his gofer."

At every meeting I went to that day, people were frankly curious about the girls and the dead Miles Wuchnik. Their voyeurism didn't trouble me particularly—we're all human, after all, we most of us take part in a gaper's gawk when there's blood and gore all over the floor. What bothered me was to find out the number of my clients who took Helen Kendrick seriously.

Kendrick's tirade this morning had been on everyone's smartphone within thirty seconds—all these lawyers and managers subscribe to news feeds, of course. And a number thought Kendrick raised legitimate questions.

"Why was Sophy Durango in the cemetery?" one corporate security VP demanded.

"She wasn't," I protested. "She was downstate Saturday night, campaigning in Jacksonville and Roodhouse for the U.S. Senate. I read about it in yesterday's *Herald-Star*. She didn't get home until Sunday."

"That's what she wants you to think," the vice president said, pitying me for my gullibility. He scrolled through his phone. "Jacksonville—that's near St. Louis. She could hop into Chaim Salanter's private jet, fly here to kill the guy in the cemetery, and get back to Jacksonville before anyone noticed she was missing."

"Salanter's private jet? Durango in the cemetery? All this is made up out of nothing!" I said. "If I gave you a report on one of your employees that had this much imagination in it, you'd be right to fire me."

"It's not just Kendrick saying it," the vice president responded. "Wade Lawlor had it on his noon podcast. I'll e-mail you the link; you can listen to it after we're done."

"Yeah, do that." If I said anything else, I'd lose a client whose chief merit was paying his bills on time. "Let's get down to the business we actually know nuts and bolts about."

My day was sprinkled with encounters like that one. To be fair, many other clients were as worried by the GEN commentators as I was.

Along the way, Salanter's personal assistant phoned. She tried to push me into agreeing to an early meeting: *Mr. Salanter is very busy and is leaving for São Paolo in the morning*, but I said he had to take his place in the queue like everyone else. She gave in grudgingly and told me Mr. Salanter would meet me at the Parterre Club on Elm Street at seven.

I managed to finish my meetings before four o'clock. I was on the northbound L, congratulating myself on having time to type up my notes before I needed to find Leydon, when a text came in from my cousin.

Help, under attck, come @1s, corner DesP &vanB.

Des Plaines and Van Buren Streets. That was the Malina Building. If the building was under attack, I hoped the police already knew about it. *On my way, 10 min,* I wrote back. *Call cops!*

I'd already ridden past the Loop stops. I got off at Division, looked at the congestion on the roads below, decided a taxi would be useless, and jumped on the next inbound train.

It seemed as though we were going three miles an hour, waiting at each stop long enough for someone to deliver a baby, crawling into town while the driver did her nails or texted her lover. I hovered by the exit, as if that would make the trains ahead of us speed up and clear the tracks. I scrolled through the news feeds on my phone but couldn't pick up anything about violence in the Loop.

We finally reached the University of Illinois exit. I sprinted along the platform in my dress sandals, up the stairs, pushing my way past slower commuters with a breathless "Excuse me," taking curses from people I knocked into.

As soon as I got to the street, I could see the cop cars starting to appear. Gapers had backed up the traffic; drivers were honking madly. Someone had stalled on the bridge over the expressway with a boiled-out radiator, and cops were leaning on their own duck-call horns, trying to find a way through the backup.

Over all the traffic noise I could hear shouts from a crowd near the Malina Building. I moved as fast as I could through the stacked-up cars, ignoring a whistle and a shout from one of the cops who'd managed to get close to the building.

Some forty or fifty people were marching around the foundation's entrance. Their posters contained such appetizing slogans as *"Nazis out of Illinois!" "Wetbacks, swim home!" "Salanter Belongs in a Death Camp."*

I tried to push past them to look for my cousin. A woman with tightly permed hair blocked my path. "Do you work for the Nazis?"

"Do you work at all?" I snapped.

I ducked under her poster, but a group of protesters had linked arms near the building's doors; I could see a cluster of people inside the lobby doors but couldn't get close enough to tell if my cousin was among them.

More cops arrived. Whistles competed with chants, and a couple of patrol officers forced the phalanx blocking the door to start moving. The officers wouldn't let me into the building, but I was close enough to see that the mob had thrown eggs, tomatoes, and even balls of paint at the façade.

I pulled out my phone to text Petra and was told by a cop I had to keep moving.

"I'm not part of this bunch of cretins; I'm looking for someone they were attacking."

The officer was uninterested in anything I had to say and told me either to keep moving or face arrest. When the cops are in crowd-control mode, it's impossible to talk to them.

WGN and GEN already had camera crews on the scene. As I moved back to the street, Fox and NBC both pulled up. I saw a GEN camera-woman I know and thought about worming my way through the crowd in her wake but decided I was better off trying to find Petra by phone.

The only new message from Petra had come in while I was still on the L: *Vic, where r u? girls terfied, me 2.*

Me, too, little cousin. I texted Petra, hoping she hadn't been so mobbed that she'd lost access to her phone. I circled the building, looking in the parking lot, and then started on the side streets. Before I went completely demented, my phone chirped at me. Petra, at a coffee bar two blocks from me.

By the time I got there, my nylons were as tattered as my nerves. Petra was at a table outside with Kira Dudek and Arielle Zitter. The two girls had huddled as close to Petra as the plastic chairs allowed. They had eggshells in their hair and on their T-shirts, and a blotch of red paint covered the left side of Arielle's face.

"Vic!" My cousin sprang to her feet, tension washing out of her face. "Thank God. This was a horrible afternoon. We were coming back from a trip to a bookstore and this mob attacked us, they chased us all the way to the expressway and threw paint and crap. I thought they were going to push Kira off the bridge, but we finally got away."

I sat down and took Kira and Arielle each by the hand. "What a dreadful afternoon for all of you. And nothing to drink?"

"They wouldn't let us inside." Arielle's face was pinched with fear. "I wanted to wash off this horrible paint and they acted like we were street people or something, but we were afraid to go back to Malina for Petra's car. I tried calling and texting my mom but I can't get through; I'm scared she's stuck in the building and they'll hurt her."

"The police are there now," I said. "I don't think anyone's getting

into the building, but why don't you call your grandfather, or his assistant? They probably have a way to get a message to your mom."

Arielle pulled out her phone and called the assistant I'd been talking
to earlier. The woman apparently put her through to Chaim. "Grandpapa? Where are you? Do you know where Mom is? Do you know
what's happening at the foundation? . . . No, me and Kira, we were the
only two from our book group to show up, the rest of the group, their
parents were like we had AIDS or something, and Aunt Sophy took
Nia downstate to campaign . . . Yes . . . I don't know, I'll find out . . .
Okay."

Still holding the phone to her face, she told me, "My mom's okay,
just she's meeting with our lawyers and not answering phone calls. He
says we should go to Schiller Street, if you want to come, Kira, if it's
okay with your mom."

"Schiller Street?" Kira said.

"Where I live, I mean. You can come home with me and clean up,
and when things calm down, Gabe, he's our houseman, he can give you
a lift home."

Kira shook her head. "I gotta get back to my place. My mom will be
leaving for work and I have to stay with Lucy."

"We'll go up to my office," I announced. "It's just ten minutes from
here. There's a shower and cold drinks and everything, and then Petra
can take Kira home, while I drop off Arielle."

We were far enough from the confusion on Van Buren to find a cab
quickly. I bundled my three into it over the driver's protests—he didn't
want blood in his cab, he wanted to see money upfront.

"Don't whine," I said. "It's unattractive and takes away from your tip."

Out of revenge, he drove as recklessly as possible, accelerating and
braking so abruptly that I began to feel seasick. When we got to my office, I counted out the exact amount on the meter.

"Besides whining, it's a mistake to drive like an idiot. It won't help
you make a living."

He took off with a great squealing of rubber. The two girls giggled at the exchange and the atmosphere lightened for a brief time.

My leasemate, the famed sculptor Tessa Reynolds, was at her drafting table. As soon as she understood what happened to the girls, she helped me scrub the worst of the paint and egg from them. Between us, we dug up enough old T-shirts and shorts to get everyone into clean clothes.

I looked at Tessa's wall clock and clucked my tongue with worry—I was going to be late for meeting Leydon, and I didn't know how well she'd handle it, especially since I still wasn't sure where I was supposed to find her. I thought about just putting Arielle into a cab by herself, but I didn't think she should be on her own after this afternoon's trauma. And besides, I wanted a private word with her.

I took my trio outside and flagged a cab for Petra and Kira. "Peetie, when you've seen Kira safe into her apartment, why don't you go up to your uncle Sal? He'll be happy to give you a drink or whatever you need. I have to drop off Arielle, then hustle down to the University of Chicago—the woman I'm meeting won't hold up too well on her own much longer."

Petra hugged me. "Vic, I know you get tired of flying to my rescue, but I'm so grateful to you."

"You got yourself out of trouble today, little cousin. And that was terrifying, attacked by a mob like that. Good heads-up thinking."

She made a face. "I wasn't thinking, just hopping like a bunny. Anyway, thanks for being our guardian angel."

I kissed her cheek, patted her shoulder, and gently pulled myself away. Guardian angel—not a role I fancied. The Divinity School Library on the Chicago campus. Angels carved into the beams soared above the readers there, and it was in that room that Leydon Ashford and I used to meet for study sessions that ran until the librarian shooed us into the hallway so he could lock the doors.

The Divinity School Library was far from the prying eyes of men.

Well, not of men, but certainly of our competitive, angst-ridden fellow law students.

I pushed Arielle into my car and maneuvered across town to Schiller Street as fast as I could, but my efforts to question her didn't go well. I was tired, she was scared, and half my mind was on Leydon, anyway.

"You had met Miles Wuchnik, hadn't you?" I said, glancing at her.

"Is that why you're driving me home? So you can worm information against my grandfather out of me?"

"I'm on your family's side, Arielle, but Sunday afternoon, you couldn't hide your dismay at hearing his name. Nia tried to cover for you: she said she'd never met him. But one of you talked to him, didn't you?"

She crossed her arms in front of her chest and stared stonily ahead.

"Why was it a joke when Nia said he was a genie?" I asked.

"Let me out!" she yelled. "I'm taking a cab."

"I let you leave on your own on Saturday night, but that won't happen again. You're too young and too vulnerable to be running around town on your own right now. You stay with me until Gabe opens the door to your house for you."

That was the end of the conversation. I tried every approach I could think of, and finally had to admit defeat. I double-parked in front of her house, walked through the gate with her, and watched while Gabe let her inside before I put on the afterburners on Lake Shore Drive. The only blessing about being late was that I easily found a parking place on University Avenue, close to the Divinity School.

12. MURDER IN THE CATHEDRAL

"Leydon? Leydon, if you're here, come out! It's me, Vic. Come out and let's talk."

I was standing in the doorway to the old library at the Divinity School. The narrow mullioned windows were so clogged with ivy that even on a bright summer evening, the room was too dark for me to see anything. I ran my hand along the walls, fumbling for a light switch, but finally had to dig a small flashlight from my briefcase.

I shone it around the room, looking for the switches, or for some sign of Leydon. I kept calling her name, but when I finally managed to turn on the lights I didn't see any sign of her.

The old library had vanished as well. The angels still soared overhead, which meant I was in the right room, but the library tables had disappeared, along with the old biblical-studies journals. I'd thought—hoped—I might find Leydon hiding in the stacks, but those were gone as well. The walls had been replastered and painted a bright white.

It was like one of those movies where the villains drug the heroine and try to pretend that the strange house in the country where she wakes up is really her home. I imagined Leydon arriving here in her hyper, anxious condition. She was so worried she was being followed that she wouldn't even announce herself by name on the phone and I hadn't been able to call her because the same fears had made her block her own number. If she'd come up to this sterile, empty room, she probably thought I'd abandoned her.

In a corner of my mind, one I didn't like to visit, I could see her as I'd found her twenty-five years ago: under her kitchen table, hugging herself, as she rocked back on her heels, weeping soundlessly. She'd been up for three days and I'd been looking for her—we were presenting a case together in moot court and I had tried to condense the hundreds of pages she'd spewed out into a document acceptable to the judges. I'd finally let myself into her apartment and found her.

I tried to think where she might have gone today when she didn't see me in the reading room. If she'd been calm enough to think, perhaps she would have gone to the coffee shop in the basement—our study sessions often started there. She might feel safe in the basement.

On my way down, I looked in all the rooms on each floor. Study rooms, classrooms, junk storage rooms. I looked behind doors and under desks but saw nothing more alarming than empty coffee cups and chip bags.

One fourth-floor room was hung with framed ivory miniatures that depicted lives of the early saints. They looked ancient, as if some early divinity professor had found them in a cave and then abandoned them here to be forgotten for another millennium or two. I wondered idly what they'd fetch on eBay, but I was a good responsible citizen these days, not the hooligan I'd been when Boom-Boom and I were Arielle and Kira's age. I left the miniatures alone and headed for the stairs.

My high-heeled sandals clattered loudly on the stone steps and set up a crashing echo in the open stairwell. I was exhausted and my feet hurt from running around after Petra and her girls. I was meanly hoping Leydon had given up and gone home: I could imagine a long cold drink, something with mint and lime and fizz, and the chance to soak my feet in a bucket of cold water.

I stopped at the third-floor landing to call Leydon's name. I ducked down to look underneath the stairs but didn't check the seminar rooms. At the second floor, I shouted her name again. I was startled when a woman opened a door at the end of the hall and stuck her head out.

"You looking for someone?"

It couldn't be Leydon, my flickering first thought, unless she'd been transformed from a slender red-gold sylph to a heavy-set gray-haired earth goddess.

I apologized for disturbing the woman. "I thought the building was empty. I used to be a student here and I'm trying to hook up with an old friend."

The woman looked me up and down, deciding whether to trust me. "Is your friend on the nervous side?"

"The far side of nervous. Have you seen her? Slim, fair, a bit shorter than me. I'm V. I. Warshawski, by the way, if she asked for me by name."

"She was sitting on the stairs, sobbing. I thought maybe someone had died, but when I asked her it turned out she was crying over the reading room in the old library—she was horribly upset because we'd turned it into a conference room. That happened years ago, but she was so distraught she could hardly take in the information. As soon as I told her I was the associate dean she started shouting that I was worse than the Taliban who destroyed the giant Buddhas, that only a heathen and a Philistine would turn a beautiful library into a conference center. You're not her caseworker, are you?"

"Just an old friend," I repeated, depressed. "I'm going to see if she went to the coffee shop."

"It closes at four in the summer. You might check the chapels, Bond, or Rockefeller. She wanted to know where else on campus angels soared and I suggested those two places to her." She hesitated. "I did wonder if I should call campus security. I can still do it if you think—well, do you think she might be a danger to herself?"

I scrunched up my mouth—I didn't know what Leydon might do. "I haven't seen her for a while, so I don't know how shaky she is these days. If I don't find her at either of the chapels, I'll call the cops myself."

I ran down the rest of the steps and jogged through the portico connecting the divinity school to its chapel. Bond Chapel was dark, too, with narrow stained-glass windows that flashed jagged prisms onto the walls. I went up the single aisle to the altar, shining my flash underneath the communion table and into the corners. The only person I found was a homeless man, asleep in one of the pews. My light woke him; he backed away from me in alarm, muttering curses.

I left Bond and moved as fast as I could on my sore feet to Fifty-Ninth Street, past the president's house, to Rockefeller Chapel, whose carillon tower dominates the neighborhood. The tower is almost twenty stories high, and I wasn't sure they locked the stairwell.

I pulled open one of the heavy doors and entered into silence and twilight. I stood at the entrance to the nave, involuntarily hugging my arms across my chest: the stones seemed so cold, so ominous, that I felt chilled, despite the heat outside.

The building is the size of a cathedral. The arched stained-glass windows didn't let in much of the late-day sun, and the lamps hanging from the vaulted ceiling were so remote they might as well not have been switched on.

I strained my ears for any sound, a sob, a laugh, but heard nothing. "Leydon! Leydon?"

My voice bounced around the walls and gave me back a mocking echo. I started up the central aisle toward the chancel, my shoes setting up what sounded like a drumroll. Too big, too loud. If Leydon were in here she'd surely hear me, but if she were feeling abandoned, depressed, she might not be able to respond. Leydon crouched under the kitchen table—the image kept popping into my mind. I pulled the pencil flash from my bag again, shining it under the pews as I searched.

I found her lying facedown near the chancel steps. Her red-gold hair glinted under my flashlight. I knelt next to her, smoothing it back from her forehead.

"Leydon, I'm sorry I was late. Was that too much for you to bear? Did you decide a nip or two of Jim Beam would carry you while you waited for me?"

I kept my voice soft, a loving croon, despite the words. I'd learned long ago how cruel it was to add my criticism to the demons already attacking her.

I put an arm under her to turn her over. That was when I realized something worse than drunkenness was going on. Her left arm flopped against me at an inhuman angle. She must have tripped on the chancel steps, then hit her head as she fell, knocked herself out. I put my fingers on her neck, praying for a pulse. I hoped I was feeling one, but my hands were cold, they were shaking, I couldn't feel anything.

"Fessa! Idiota!" I snapped under my breath. "Stop feeling sorry for yourself. Get an ambulance here, now, on the double."

I removed my arm from beneath her as gently as I could and called 911. "Inside the chapel," I said, fighting for calm.

The dispatcher took the details, told me not to move her, but to keep her warm if I could. I ran across the chancel, looking for something to wrap around her, an altar cloth, an abandoned sweater, anything. In a box behind the organ console I found a stack of yoga mats and blankets, and grabbed one of those.

The ambulance crew arrived an hour, or maybe only a minute, later—in a crisis all time spent waiting for help feels like eternity. When I heard the front doors opening, I stood and called out, waving my flashlight as a beacon.

The two techs, a man and a woman, trotted up the central aisle. They were carrying a portable gurney and neck-stabilizing gear. They had industrial flashlights that they placed close to Leydon so they could see what they were doing.

As they knelt and started bracing her neck, the man asked how it had happened.

"I don't know," I said. "I found her like this. I thought she tripped on the chancel steps."

He shook his head. "The cops will tell us for sure, but I'm feeling breaks in her arms that didn't come from tripping and falling." He gently probed her sides. "She has broken ribs, too."

He and his partner slid her onto the gurney and stood in a quick, fluid motion.

"We can't wait for the police," the woman said. "You'll have to talk to them. There's an outside chance—"

Her words disappeared under the rumble of the gurney wheels on the stone floor. I followed them to the ambulance and kissed Leydon as they loaded her into it. An outside chance, that was better than no chance at all.

Back inside the chapel, I lay on the front pew to wait for the police. I'd been running for hours, ever since I got Petra's alarm. I couldn't move, I couldn't take in another thought. If the police didn't arrive soon, I'd fall asleep with any homeless people who sought shelter here.

Above me I saw the railing around a small gallery where overflow visitors could sit during Convocation. If Leydon had gotten her injuries in falling from a height, that was probably where she'd been.

I forced myself to get up. On cement-laden legs, I walked behind the organ console to the gallery stairs. The gallery railing was only about thigh-high on me. If Leydon had stood there, working herself into a frenzy, she could easily have fallen over.

I looked around, wondering where she'd dropped her handbag. Leydon always used to carry an Hermès bag—it was one of those odd vestiges of her conservative upbringing, always carrying a handbag, almost always from Hermès, although every now and then she ventured into Chanel territory. Perhaps she'd had it over her arm when she fell. I tried to imagine the physics of the fall, the arc, where the bag would have landed.

My toes were cramping from all the pressure I'd put on them this afternoon. As I bent to massage them, I saw a piece of paper under the pew, written over in heavy black ink.

When I pulled it out, I recognized Leydon's round, urgent scrawl, the way she wrote when she was cycling high. *I saw him on the catafalque,* she'd written over and over.

I was tucking the paper into my own bag when the door underneath the gallery opened. Thinking it might be the police, I hurried back down the stairs, but it was a trio of tourists, two women and a man.

They looked at me in consternation, which wasn't surprising—I was barefoot and disheveled.

"You are rehearsing for a play?" one of the women asked.

"This is real life, I'm afraid."

"We thought we heard you shouting," the other woman said. "When we were coming earlier to look at the organ."

"You were in the chapel? What did you see?" I stepped closer in my urgency, and they backed away in alarm.

"We saw nothing," the man said. "We heard you and decided we must come back later."

"It wasn't me you heard. A friend of mine—did you see her—she fell— the police are on their way—if you saw anything, heard anything—"

"The police?" the man said. "No, we can tell the police nothing."

He said something in German to the women, and they nodded. "We cannot stay for the police, we can miss our flight, or who knows what. They can put us in prison, perhaps."

"But if you saw what happened—"

"But we did *not* see," the second woman said. "We wanted to inspect the organ, which is famous: my husband is also an organist. And now there is no time. I am sorry about your friend, but we must leave."

I was close to screaming with frustration.

"Please—"

The two women seized the man's arms and hurried back to the western door. I followed and thrust one of my cards into the man's shirt pocket. "If you remember anything that my friend said, please call me."

13. A LONG PITCH

WHEN THE POLICE SHOWED, I TOLD THEM THE LITTLE I knew—how I arrived late for my meeting with Leydon and found her spread-eagled across the chancel steps. Evidence technicians showed up and took photos in a desultory way, looking at the gallery, making little notes of angles and tangents.

"Were you a close friend?" one of the cops asked.

Close at one time, not any longer. "We hadn't seen each other for a year or so," I said.

"Do you know her frame of mind? Was she suicidal?"

"When she spoke to me this morning, she sounded very alert, very alive," I said.

There was a commotion in the back of the chapel. We all turned to squint at the narthex and in a second or two a man in a well-cut summer suit burst up the aisle.

"Sewall!" I was astonished to see Leydon's older brother.

"Victoria Warshawski? I might have guessed!"

"Guessed what?" The officer and I spoke almost in unison.

"My sister stole my car, and I got some report that she had ended up here at Rockefeller. You're the police? You came in response to my report?"

"No, Sewall," I said firmly. "They came because your sister is badly injured, nearly dead. Your car seems mighty unimportant."

"What? Did she run it into a tree? She's been out of the hospital for ten days, and if she's taken her risperidone once since they released her—against my most urgent warnings that they keep her—I'd be astounded. She talked to Faith yesterday, and Faith couldn't make head or tail of anything she was saying. It was all a jumble about spies, and then a string of obscenities directed at me! Poor Faith was so embarrassed she finally hung up!"

Faith was Sewall's long-suffering wife.

"She stole your car, sir?" The officer tried to pull a followable strand out of the tangled yarn Sewall had flung at us.

"Probably egged on by Warshawski here. The two of them have lived to make my family's life a misery ever since they met in law school. Did you actually tell Leydon to steal my car, or just suggest it would be a good way to piss me off?"

"Steal your car? What do you drive, anyway, that someone could hot-wire it?" I was rattled, and seized on the one point I could understand—perhaps I'd told Leydon how Boom-Boom and I once hot-wired my uncle's old Buick. Leydon could quote poetry by the ream; maybe she'd memorized the details of solenoids and ignition wires when I recounted them all those years ago.

"Hot-wire my Beemer? What are you talking about? She waltzed into our company garage and helped herself to my BMW and then had the gall to tell the garage man I'd given her permission to drive it. The idiot didn't check with me first."

"So your—sister, is it?—borrowed your car, sir," the officer said. "The word we're getting from the hospital is that if Ms. Ashford recovers, it's going to be a long time before she drives again, so I think we'll just let that dog lay down and sleep."

I restrained an impulse to slap him on the back and cry, "Good show." Sewall was less impressed.

"She has the keys. Did she leave them with you, Warshawski?"

"I got here too late to talk to her," I said. "I was wondering where her handbag was. I found a piece of paper she'd been writing on, something about seeing someone on a catafalque."

"Oh, that catafalque crap!" Sewall snapped. "That was part of what she laid on Faith yesterday, she kept saying she'd seen him on the catafalque and then asking, well, I won't repeat it, it's too embarrassing."

"Seen whom?" I asked.

"Oh, you know Leydon when she's jumped the rails, who knows? It was all some jumble, some garbage she likes to taunt Faith with, about 'the faith once delivered to the sinners,' whatever the fuck that's supposed to mean! She says that all the time to my wife, and then yesterday she added on all this catafalque crap."

"You weren't here earlier, were you, Sewall?" I asked. "A witness heard Leydon shouting up on the balcony. They couldn't tell who was with her." If anyone, I added to myself; it was always depressingly possible that Leydon had simply been shouting.

The officer who'd made the remark about letting the dog lay down and sleep stopped what he was doing to look more closely at Sewall. "Were you here earlier, sir?"

"I was at my office in the Loop until thirty minutes ago. And I have a dozen witnesses, including a senior officer of the Fort Dearborn Trust, and one of my attorneys. We're underwriting a bond issue and I did not need my damned sister derailing herself and my work right now."

"Your sister may not live through the night," the officer said. "You need to show some respect."

One of the evidence techs strolled over. "We found some pill bottles. Risperidone and some vitamins. We'll bag and tag just in case. Which one of you would be the responsible party, so we can get a signed receipt?"

"Do you have her power of attorney?" I asked Sewall.

"Faith—my wife—does. Did you find my car keys?"

"No, sir, but they may show up. This is a big space and it's not easy to find things."

Sewall turned to me. "What hospital did they take her to?"

I shrugged. "I don't know—I suppose the one right here, but it doesn't have a trauma center. You'd better call around."

The cops took care of that for us: Leydon was at Mitchell Hospital here on the university campus, going into surgery to deal with damage to the brain. The hospital would be glad if Sewall stopped by to give them financial information.

"Her wallet isn't here?" Sewall said. "It has her Link card in it."

"Your sister is on public aid?" My jaw dropped down to my chest. "I thought she had a trust fund—"

"She does," Sewall cut me off. "But she needs health insurance and she's disabled."

I clasped my hands tightly behind me. "You know, Sewall, it would be a really good idea for you to get over to the hospital and deal with them. Because I feel this horrible urge to break your nose and your ulna and all these other body parts you'll need if you want to locate your Beemer and drive back to the North Shore tonight."

Sewall protested, and tried to get the officer to take note of my threats, but the police were as disgusted as I was, maybe more so. They live on fifty or sixty thousand a year, but the cops I know, the ones I grew up with, scramble and scrape to care for their families. The idea that a wealthy man would cut his sister loose didn't sit well with the men I was talking to. They sent Sewall packing. A few minutes later, they took off themselves, with the advice to go home and have a good stiff drink with "hubby."

The evidence techs lingered a few minutes longer. When they finished with their photographs and measurements, I got up to go, but my legs didn't want to carry me forward.

I sank onto the chancel stairs, head in hand. I'd been galloping from point A to point B all day, not having time to reflect on anything I was doing, from my meetings with clients, to chasing after Petra, to sprinting across campus in Leydon's wake. If I'd stopped to think for one second, I could have done it all differently. Leydon would be maddening me with her chatter, but she'd be upright, alive.

I had been in the chapel choir in my student days. Leydon never came to the service. She despised church, but she enjoyed sitting in on choir rehearsals. ("Too many Sundays with Jesus after breakfast and 'by Jesus, young lady, do as I say' after lunch. The outside of the plate polished so you could see your reflection, the inside full of filth and mire, you know how that goes.")

I found myself singing the alto line to a setting of Psalm 39 that Leydon had particularly liked.

"That's Stravinsky, isn't it?" A man had joined me on the steps without my noticing. "*Let me know my end and the number of my days.* I've always found that a troubling verse. Would you want that knowledge?"

If I'd known twenty-five years ago what the end of Leydon's days might look like—that launch from the parapet—what would I have done? Tried harder, probably, to change the ending, but the day would still have come when I would have walked away because Leydon's problems were too difficult for me to handle.

I'm not prone to unburdening myself to anyone, let alone a stranger in a darkening church, but I was so tired my usual filters weren't in place. I spoke my thoughts aloud.

"It's like reading the *Iliad*," my companion said. "You want to reach into the text and tell Achilles' mother to stick his whole foot in the river. You see the danger and want to avert it, but there's nothing you can do. Sometimes events have a tragic momentum that you're powerless to halt.

"I'm Henry Knaub, by the way, the chapel dean. The police called to tell me about your friend, but I was at a meeting on the North Side and couldn't get back sooner."

"I'm a detective," I said. "It's not my nature to be so—so passive in the face of events. I've been like one of those tether balls that we used to play with in school, getting batted round and round a pole, so much so that I can't think!"

"I heard the end of your quarrel with—Leydon, did you say her name was?—with her brother," Knaub said. "Crisis makes people behave oddly, but if that's how her family typically responds to her, she was lucky to have you as a friend."

I shook my head in the gloomy chamber; I hadn't been much of a friend lately. "She has a phenomenal memory; when we were law students she could remember almost the page where she'd seen a citation or a case reference. If she started to argue with you, or most especially, with her brother, she'd start pulling poetry or legal precedents, or who knows what, out of her hat.

"I was on her side, always, but I didn't blame her brother for getting wound up. For instance, her brother's wife is called Faith, and Leydon always refers to her as 'the Faith once delivered to the sinners,' meaning Sewall and their parents—they live with Sewall's mother."

Knaub chuckled softly. "Oh, yes, that was a favorite line of the reformers in the sixteenth and seventeenth centuries; they were trying to recapture 'the faith once delivered to the saints.' Yes, I can see your friend could be trying. Brilliant, but trying."

"The last few days, according to Sewall, Leydon was going on about a catafalque. She suffers from hypergraphia when she's cycling high, and she'd written it over and over on a piece of paper I found in your gallery." I pulled the crumpled paper from my pocket: *I saw him on the catafalque.*

Knaub squinted at it. "*Portrait of the Artist;* the child Stephen Dedalus is overhearing adults talk about the death of Parnell." He was apologetic, as if he thought I'd be embarrassed at having my ignorance exposed.

"One of the differences between Leydon and me." I smiled with difficulty. "We both read Joyce as undergraduates but his words stuck in her head and not in mine."

"Could she have seen someone laid out on the communion table here?" the dean asked. "Is she delusional?"

I shook my head. "I can't tell you; I got here when she was already on the floor. It's all extremely—Gordian—in her favorite phrase."

My cell phone buzzed in my briefcase. I pulled it out—incoming from Chaim Salanter's personal assistant. Mr. Salanter was waiting, and no, he didn't want to reschedule to a more convenient time: this was his only convenient time. He was leaving for Brazil in the morning.

"Oh, my God!" I got to my feet. "I'm supposed to be meeting the world's twenty-first richest person for dinner. Another thing that didn't stick in my head."

The dean stood with me. "The twenty-first richest person? How odd that they can be counted that way, from top down. I wonder if they know the twenty-first poorest person in the world?"

"I looked up the *Forbes* list this afternoon between meetings," I said. "Five of the top fifty are women. I don't know if *Forbes* could figure out where the fifty poorest live, but a dollar says they're all female."

"I'll be praying for your friend," the dean said. "In return, if number twenty-one is feeling charitable, the chapel can always use a billion or two."

He held out a bronze leather handbag with a distinctive "H" picked out in the leather. "I found this behind the pulpit, with Ms. Ashford's name on a nearby pill bottle. I put in the papers and a car key that might belong to her, but if she's missing something let me know; our cleaning crew is very good about turning in the oddments people drop in church."

I took the bag but pointed behind him at a little tower on the right side of the chancel. "Is that what you mean—behind that?"

"That's the pulpit, yes. Is that a problem?"

"Leydon had to have been up in the west gallery to fall as she did. If she was carrying the bag, it traveled up the steps and thirty feet away from her."

"If she's bipolar and cycling high, maybe she threw it from the gallery." His voice was diffident.

I went back to the gallery staircase. "Can you turn on a light?" I called as I climbed.

I waited a moment at the top until the dean had found the right switch, then went to the balustrade.

"Okay. Here I am, filled with irrational exuberance. I fling my bag."

I did a windup and released the bag, throwing it as far as I could. It landed in the middle of the chancel, a good fifteen or twenty feet from where Knaub said he'd found it. The force of my throw propelled me forward; I had to clutch the low railing to keep from following Leydon over the edge.

"I can see how throwing the bag might have made her fall," I conceded. "But she doesn't have nearly as strong an arm as I do. You'd have to be Johnny Unitas to get that handbag from here to the back of the pulpit. Someone else dumped it there, but who?"

14. ONE ARMAGNAC TOO MANY

IT WAS CLOSE TO EIGHT WHEN I REACHED CHAIM SALANTER'S appointed meeting place. The sun was low in the horizon and the air had that quiet warmth, a lover's embrace, that it offers at twilight in summer. I left my car in the club's loading zone and stood for a moment, eyes shut, listening to the birds cheeping their end-of-day messages, breathing the heavy scent from the flowers planted around the club's stairs.

The Parterre Club was housed in one of those discreet old greystones on Elm Street, just off Lake Shore Drive—and a short walk from the Salanter mansion on Schiller Street. When I finally summoned the energy to climb the stairs to the front door, I saw a framed placard next to the bell: the club had been founded in 1895 for "Ladies and Gentlemen with an Interest in Ornamental Horticulture." That was reassuring—all during my drive north, I'd been thinking of the parterres under cathedral balconies.

An attendant came to the door and took my car keys, while a stooped woman who looked old enough to be my grandmother escorted me to the ladies' lounge so that I could "freshen up"—a euphemism for doing something about the blood that had dried in stiff brown Rorschachs down the right side of my dress. When I saw myself in the full-length mirror, I winced: my hair looked like Tom's fur after Jerry had run an electric current through him. My olive skin had a gray sheen, fatigue mixed with sweat.

There was nothing to be done about the blood tonight, unless I stripped to the altogether and gave the dress to the attendant. I sponged off my feet. I'd sprouted blisters on the soles and around my little toes from running in high heels, but the lounge's toiletry counter included Band-Aids along with combs, deodorant, and mouthwash. When I'd taped my feet and made myself presentable from the cleavage up, I let the elderly woman escort me to the second floor, where Chaim Salanter was waiting for me in the members' dining room.

The ornamental horticulturalists had lined the club stairwell with bonsais and decorative shrubs. There had even been an array of sweet-smelling flowering plants in the ladies' lounge.

My guide turned me over to a waiter, who led me to Chaim Salanter. The billionaire half-rose to his feet when I reached him, but told the waiter to take me to the bar while he finished a phone call.

I ordered an Armagnac and wandered around the room with it, admiring the paintings. Most were of plants, but there were several startling Expressionists by Lasar Segall. When I finished my tour, Salanter was still on the phone.

I moved to an empty table and took Leydon's Hermès bag out of my briefcase. Her wallet was in it, with her driver's license and her Link card and about forty dollars in cash. No credit cards, perhaps a wise precaution, although hurricane-like shopping sprees had never been part of her bipolar illness. Dr. Knaub had stuffed in the handful of papers he'd found floating behind the pulpit, the news stories that Leydon followed obsessively—one on an *E. coli* outbreak in Germany, one on a woman who'd been killed in a hit-and-run accident, three on the nuclear reactors in Fukushima, and two on diets that help improve brain function.

Leydon had written heavily on all of them, mostly about the huntress and the catafalque.

Dr. Knaub had found some pills the evidence techs had overlooked. He'd also discovered the key to Sewall's BMW under the altar, but he hadn't found Leydon's personal keys. Perhaps she lived in a group home, where some manager buzzed you in. I checked the address on Leydon's driver's license. It was on Sheridan Road, near the Loyola University campus. I pulled out my iPad and found the building, a high-rise that seemed to be a mix of condos and rentals.

I was clicking on a link to the building's Realtor when my cell phone rang. A blocked number, which made me think of Leydon, but it was a man's voice on the phone, speaking so softly I could barely hear him.

"There was a person in the church with your friend this afternoon."

"Who is this?" I demanded.

"I'm sorry, I cannot be involved in American police matters. And I saw nothing, only I heard the shouting. A man and a woman, with the woman saying most of the words. The emotion was too intense for an outsider to follow; also, the English was too fast for us, so we left the church. That is all I can tell you."

Behind him I heard a woman's voice, sharply telling him the plane was closed, all cell phones had to be shut down. The connection went dead. I stared at the bottles on the bar, so fixedly that the bartender thought I wanted another drink. I shook my head.

Leydon had been arguing with a man. Maybe she'd just been shouting at a man. Perhaps a lover, perhaps even her brother, although I didn't think so. I could imagine Sewall being angry enough to fling Leydon over the balcony, but he wanted his car keys, and if he'd found her earlier and fought with her, he'd have extracted his Beemer keys then.

Chaim Salanter appeared next to me, apologizing for keeping me waiting. A billionaire's apologies! Exciting, worth waiting for!

"I understand from my assistant that you were involved in a tragic event this afternoon," he said. "I wouldn't have insisted on our meeting

going ahead, but I have to leave for Brazil in the morning and I needed
to talk to you before I left."

He took my elbow and ushered me to his table. Salanter was a small
man: the top of his bald head just came to my ears. His voice was soft,
but both voice and movements were authoritative. As soon as we sat, a
waiter had menus in front of us. Salanter didn't look at it, just nodded
at the waiter, who nodded back. Bring me my usual? Put rat poison in
my guest's food?

Although the day had been hot and sticky, I found myself craving
heavy food. A steak, mashed potatoes, broccoli with cheese sauce.

"I like to see women eat heartily," Salanter surprised me by saying.
"Too many women starve themselves these days. Even my daughter
thinks she needs to diet. If age didn't force me to take the low choles-
terol special, I would join you with pleasure."

His face was brown and lined, like a leather book that had cracked
with time. What remained of his hair was white, but his eyebrows had
stayed black; they formed a startling smear across his forehead, as if
someone had drawn across the book jacket with a fat Magic Marker.
The heavy brows made it hard to pay attention to how he was saying
what he said. Maybe he dyed them to keep people off balance.

"I was at the Malina Foundation this afternoon," I said. "My cousin
runs one of your book groups, the one your granddaughter is part of.
Arielle was showing the flag, coming to the group even though most of
the parents had pulled their kids, and she, my cousin, and another girl
were attacked by the mob."

"Yes, that was disturbing. I spoke to my daughter, and to the police.
Perhaps that discussion can wait until we're on our own."

Until the waiter had finished delivering the food, Salanter talked
idly, about the history of the Parterre Club, his own interest in growing
ornamental plants—"a good hobby for a desk-bound man. You can
groom them while you're waiting for the markets to open in Tokyo or

London"—and about the Segall paintings I'd admired. His English was impeccable, but the remains of an Eastern European accent floated underneath it.

"My grandfather knew the Segall family because he lived around the corner from them in the Vilna ghetto. My grandfather acquired several of the paintings in the nineteen-twenties, out of sentiment—he thought Expressionism was trash. As did Hitler, actually. Lasar Segall himself was long gone from Lithuania by the twenties, and the Orthodox thought it was good riddance.

"Of course all my grandfather's art was stolen once the war started. The advantage of a billion dollars: I was able to trace all but one of his Segalls. Those I keep at home, but the two here are very fine and I like to see them while I eat."

It was disconcerting to hear a hyper-wealthy man speak so frankly and casually about his wealth. The waiter appeared with our food— cold salmon for Salanter, steak for me. My appetite disappeared as soon as I saw the food. The blood oozing onto the plate was uncomfortably like Leydon's blood oozing onto the chapel floor.

Salanter didn't comment on my unheartiness—he was ready for the meat of the meeting. "My daughter explained how you came to be involved in Wuchnik's death, but she couldn't say what you planned to do about it."

"No, we didn't discuss that," I agreed.

The heavy black line contracted, but he asked, with exaggerated patience, "What do you plan to do about it?"

"There's not much I can do, Mr. Salanter. He's going to stay dead, no matter what I plan."

"This is a serious matter, young woman. Flipness like that is out of place."

"Mr. Salanter, you called this meeting. I have no idea what you want out of it, but I have had an extremely long day, what with dealing with the attack on your granddaughter this afternoon, and finding a good friend close to death. I am still covered with her blood and I would love to go home and take a bath. Tell me what you want as directly as possible and I'll keep my flippancy to myself."

"Are you investigating Wuchnik's murder?"

I had a flash of glittering fantasies, on retainer to the twenty-first richest man in the world. "Would you like me to?"

"I would like you to leave the matter alone."

"Leave it alone?" My voice rose half an octave. "When your foundation was attacked today as a result of Wuchnik's death?"

He shook his head. "The foundation was attacked because of anti-immigration hysteria in this country, not because a man was killed."

"But at least two commentators, Wade Lawlor and Helen Kendrick, tied your granddaughter's presence at the murder site to their rabid commentaries. They accused Sophy Durango of being Wuchnik's lover and there's a ton of filth circulating the Net saying she killed him."

"All the more reason to leave it alone," he said sharply. "The more you dig, the more avid the flies who feed on filth become. Ignore the story and it dies on its own."

"With respect, Mr. Salanter, is there anything in the history of the Jews in Europe that makes you believe that?"

"Americans use Hitler and Stalin as political insults far too freely, without any understanding of the context. The people spewing garbage, at me, at Sophy, at my foundation, are a tiny handful on the fringe. Most people in this country are decent and don't act on hate."

I thought of lynchings, and the murders of abortion providers, and the assaults on Muslims and gays, but I was too tired to argue. I needed what was left of my wits to try to understand what he really didn't want to come to the surface about Wuchnik's death.

"Did Miles Wuchnik work for you?" I asked.

"No, Ms. Warshawski. When I need information, I use a staff of more sophisticated investigators than this Wuchnik seems to have been. I'm asking you to leave the matter alone to keep from getting more hands on the spoon that's stirring up pond scum."

"Are you making the same request of the police?" I signaled to the waiter: I needed coffee. Armagnac on an empty stomach after a major trauma hadn't been the best way to approach a meeting with a man like Salanter.

"The police understand that their duty is to find Wuchnik's killer."

I tried to parse this. Leydon would have done so standing on her head. No one had been more skilled at taking apart arguments.

I thought through the problem out loud. "To find the killer, period. You have asked the police to limit their investigation in some way. Perhaps the coincidence of your granddaughter playing at vampire and Wuchnik having a stake through his heart?"

He nodded courteously. The affable gesture told me my guess was wrong.

"I wouldn't go out of my way to hurt your granddaughter," I said. "You don't think Arielle killed Wuchnik, do you?"

His upper lip curled in disgust. "Of course not. Is this how you spend your time? Making obscene suggestions?"

I smiled. Once the opponent was angry you had the upper hand. "A better detective than I'll ever be said you have to start an investigation by eliminating the impossible. It may be obscene to imagine how two girls as enterprising as Arielle and Nia got a grown man to lie passively on his back, but it isn't impossible. Do you think your daughter killed him to protect Arielle?"

"Also not impossible." He had recovered his equilibrium. Years of practice at high-stakes poker.

"And it's possible you killed him yourself."

He nodded. "More possible than my daughter or granddaughter, certainly. Why do *you* think this man Wuchnik was murdered?"

"I have no idea. Because of something he was working on? Because his wife was furious that he was sleeping with someone else? Because he was spying on your granddaughter and a mugger came on him randomly?"

"Was he sleeping with another woman?" Salanter asked the question a shade too eagerly.

"I don't know if he was gay or straight, married, divorced, or had a steady partner. I'm just tossing out possibilities. Why do *you* think he was murdered? Because of your family?"

"Like you, I have no idea. How many of your possibilities are the police likely to follow?"

"All of them," I said. "The detective in charge is one of the most competent investigators on the force."

"So you will leave the matter in his hands, then."

"What is it you're afraid will come out, Mr. Salanter?"

"Merely I want to protect my family from further harassment."

The waiter brought my coffee, which was bitter and caramelly; it had sat on a warming coil all evening. "Did your daughter tell you I harassed her yesterday? It was she who summoned me, just as you did today. Truth to tell, I'm starting to feel a mite bit harassed by the Salanter family."

The thick black brows went up in a skeptical line. "I promise you we won't bother you anymore if you leave the investigation to this most competent of police detectives."

I tried again to think like Leydon. What could I do that the police—with their evidence technicians, their thirteen-thousand-strong force, their forensics lab, and the power of the law—could not?

Detective Finchley was not just an inspired investigator, he was beyond corruption. But he was also part of a military-style organization with an inviolable chain of command. Salanter, and some of the other parents in Petra's book group, had connections in the mayor's office. If the word came from the mayor through the superintendent to leave the Salanters alone, or to put the Wuchnik murder on a back burner, then Finchley would have to obey it.

But if I wanted to ask questions, I would do so. I have been known to ignore threats, orders, and attempts on my life, and someone may have told Salanter that.

I saw him on the catafalque, Leydon had scribbled. Was it Miles Wuchnik she'd been referring to? She surely hadn't been in Mount Moriah cemetery Saturday night—in her manic state she wouldn't have been able to keep her presence a secret. She'd seen his picture in the newspaper or on TV, then. But why did she care? She had something that was "hot," she'd said. What could she know about Wuchnik?

And then, the German organist had heard Leydon arguing with a man this afternoon. Maybe she'd had evidence that led her to Wuchnik's murderer, and the man, whoever he was, had tossed her over the balustrade onto the chapel floor.

I was staring at the congealed blood on my plate, not seeing it. I had a duty to Leydon, and I had a duty to my cousin and her book group. I didn't agree with the billionaire: I tied this afternoon's mob at his foundation to the exploitation of Wuchnik's murder.

"I'm sorry, Mr. Salanter, but I agreed earlier today to look into Miles Wuchnik's activities. I don't think they have anything to do with—"

"Who hired you?"

I shook my head. "If I don't respect the confidentiality of my clients, in a short while I won't have any clients."

"Whoever your client is, if you only agreed to do the work this afternoon, you can't have had time to start. I'll pay double whatever you're charging this other person to leave the investigation alone."

I couldn't help smiling, since twice zero is still zero, but I was annoyed all the same. "I don't work that way. I drop investigations very rarely, and then only if they are futile, or if the client has been lying to me. I don't send my investigations out to bid."

Salanter pressed his hands together with the forefingers steepled against his lips. The gesture apparently helped him think, or at least kept him from blurting out the first thing that came to mind.

"I'd like to hire you to report your findings to me before you make them public," he said at length.

"Your biography says you started out as a poor boy on the streets of Vilna. You can't always have believed you had an absolute right to whatever you want."

"If you've read my biography, then you know that I have had to be ruthless in order to survive." His voice was still soft, but the implied threat was credible.

"You didn't hire Wuchnik but you think he was investigating you," I said slowly. "You think he found something to your discredit, or perhaps to your daughter's or Dr. Durango's. Is that why you won't sue Wade Lawlor over the sickening statements he makes about you on his show?"

"Wade Lawlor is an annoying mosquito. People on the left take him far too seriously. I don't sue him because I'm past eighty; I want to spend my remaining energy on more attractive pursuits than the courts."

"If that was what you cared about, you wouldn't have summoned me to dinner, nor waited an hour and a half for me. I don't know who you wait for, but a PI like me, you'd be up and out of here if I were thirty seconds past due unless you wanted to quash this investigation more than you want to pack for Rio. No, you've got something weighing on you. It could be your granddaughter, of course. I'm pretty sure she had met Wuchnik, or at least talked to him, but she refuses to tell me."

"You can do as you please about who you work for, but I will not allow you to talk to my granddaughter."

The words were sharp, but something in his movements, a restless moving of his knife and fork, meant he was worried—about what Arielle had done? Or about what might happen to her?

When I didn't say anything, he added, "I'll be checking up on you from time to time to make sure you leave her alone."

"With your highly competent team of investigators." I got to my feet. "I hope whatever skeleton you're draping with velvet and sable to keep out of the public gaze isn't about Sophy Durango. I like her. I'd like to see her in the U.S. Senate and it won't happen if anything discreditable emerges. Thanks for the Armagnac."

15. A HARD DAY'S DAY

Despite my fatigue and my bloody dress, I stopped at Lotty's on my way home. Max was with her. I joined them on the balcony and felt better as soon as I drank some of Lotty's rich Viennese coffee.

"Why can't a private club that caters to the wealthy and horticultural make good coffee? Don't they understand that coffee is a shrub, that the berry requires careful tending?" I complained.

Max laughed, but Lotty swept aside my comment, demanding a report on my meeting with Salanter.

"I hope our conversation doesn't cost Beth Israel the funding for the Chaim Salanter wing, or whatever he's pledged to you. He wanted to hire me *not* to investigate Miles Wuchnik's death." I summarized our Byzantine conversation. "The trouble is, I'm committed to looking into, not Wuchnik's death exactly, but the cases he was working on leading up to his death. Do you know anything about Salanter that I should know before I jump onto a land mine?"

"No," Max said slowly. "I know next to nothing about his history, and I'm not sure anyone knows those details. He arrived in Chicago around 1950, but I only met him after I became executive director at Beth Israel and started cultivating potential donors. His response was tepid, so I was surprised when he asked me to be a director of the Malina Foundation."

"His past, that's his business," Lotty said crisply.

She'd sat on her own wartime secrets for decades. She would have preferred that they never come to light, but her past had overtaken her and forced her into some partial revelations, and reconciliations. I wondered if the same thing might be happening to Salanter.

"His past is his business," I agreed, "unless it's responsible for Miles Wuchnik's death. Wuchnik was investigating Salanter, or Salanter is afraid he was. What is Salanter afraid that people will find out?"

Neither Max nor Lotty had any ideas, although both agreed he would go to great lengths to protect Arielle, his only grandchild. The Malina Foundation was important to him, too.

"Not important enough to take on the creeps who drove a mob into an attack on the foundation. Not to mention his own granddaughter, besides my cousin and another of her charges."

Max and Lotty had seen the coverage of the protest but hadn't realized Petra or Arielle had been assaulted. I explained what had happened, and Salanter's insistence that I not pursue the matter. "I don't think the mob knew Arielle was there, or the attack would have been even more savage. As it was, she and one of the other kids were pelted with eggs and paint bombs. So was Petra. I'm worried that these girls will find it hard to recover from such an assault."

"We should get a private security firm to look after the children in the book groups," Max said. "At least until this episode blows over."

"According to Petra, there are seven groups. It would be a big financial burden to look after—what—a hundred or so kids?" I said. "Better to cut the head off the snake."

We talked that idea back and forth without reaching a conclusion.

"Salanter's from Vilna," I said. "But the name sounds Polish or Russian to me."

"Like Warshawski?" Max laughed softly in the dark. "You can't tell country of origin that easily with Eastern European surnames, especially not Jewish ones. 'Wuchnik' doesn't sound Jewish, however. The word means 'archer,' or 'bowman.' Which is ironic, when you think how he was killed, almost as if he'd taken an arrow in his chest. Are you thinking Wuchnik and Salanter knew each other in Europe?"

"His father or grandfather," I admitted. "Wuchnik was only forty or so."

"It's possible," Max grunted. "Anything is possible in that neck of the woods, but Salanter is a guy who faces forward, not backward. You don't amass all that wealth by dwelling on past grievances. Look at how he brushes off Wade Lawlor's attacks. I would be astounded if he had anything but a 'publish and be damned' attitude toward any bilge a private eye could turn up."

"Not that you think *I* sink my net into bilge," I said.

Max, whose courtesy is legendary, was embarrassed. He apologized but added, "I suppose I am worried about you digging up something Salanter would find painful. I don't want him harmed—not because he's rich and deserves more respect than the average person, but because, like Lotty and me, he lost his childhood and came here, like us, as a refugee."

Lotty nodded, her expression bleak. Like Salanter, though, or Max himself, she faces forward, in this case to an early surgery call in the morning. She said she was shooing me out.

I got up but asked if she could check on Leydon before I left. Max and I carried coffee cups to the kitchen while Lotty went to her study to work her network at the University of Chicago hospitals.

She came into the kitchen, shaking her head. "Your friend is out of surgery, but it's hard to say what the prognosis will be. Right now she's in a medically induced coma. The good news is that she doesn't need to be on a respirator; the bad news is that she bruised the brain badly—she hit her head on stone, I gather. The family have left a DNR order, claiming that the jump was proof that she wished to end her life. You don't know if she left any written directives, do you?"

"She wasn't thinking in such a linear way the last decade or so, but I don't think she was trying to kill herself this afternoon. I think if she fell it was by accident, and it's even possible she was pushed."

"Pushed?" Max said. "What makes you say that?"

"Some German tourists went into the chapel. They heard her shouting with a man, and fled, not wanting to be part of someone else's quarrel. And then there's this business with her handbag." I explained where the chapel dean had found Leydon's bag, and how impossible I'd found it to throw it that far.

"She might have dropped it herself before climbing to the gallery," Lotty objected.

"Yes, that's always possible. Anything is possible, especially where Leydon is concerned," I agreed.

Lotty caught sight of my dress for the first time and her eyes widened in dismay. "Victoria—I didn't realize you'd come straight to us from the accident—you're covered in blood. No wonder Chaim Salanter reacted to you so negatively. Go home, change, take a hot bath. But no more alcohol, do you hear?"

She held me tightly for a moment, then propelled me gently out her door. Max rode down with me in the elevator and escorted me to my car.

He held the door open for me with old-fashioned grace, and apologized again for his "bilge" comment. "You've had too stressful a day; I shouldn't have added to it by insulting your profession. I know you work hard for those who are poor and needy. But don't assume the rich don't also sometimes need care."

I was too tired to argue, and too grateful, anyway, for his concern.

As I drove off, though, I argued with him in my head, the way one does. *Salanter implied he could order the police to limit their investigation. He didn't exactly threaten me, but he didn't exactly not.*

Petra was still with Mr. Contreras when I got home. I put my beautiful gold dress in a bag for the cleaners, although whether all the dry-cleaning fluids of Chicago could ever sweeten that little frock I didn't know. Between that and my scarlet party gown, my involvement with the Salanters had already taken a terrible toll on my wardrobe.

When I'd showered and washed my hair, it took every ounce of will I could muster to avoid bed and go back down to check in with my cousin.

Mr. Contreras and she had long since moved out of the worry-and-fear phase of her experience to revenge fantasies, which they'd spelled out over burgers on the grill. They were sitting on the back porch, my neighbor with some of his abominable homemade grappa, my cousin with a beer.

Petra said her boss had called, to tell her that enough parents had canceled their daughters' participation in the Malina book groups that they were consolidating the groups from seven to four.

"But they're keeping me half time," Petra said. "They like what I'm doing, and maybe something else will open up with kids that doesn't require an advanced degree. You don't have to worry that I'll want to be on your payroll or anything."

I grinned. "You are right about that, my sister. I'll buy *StreetWise* from you before I put you on my payroll again."

Mr. Contreras began a protest, but Petra just laughed. I kissed them both good night and was on my way out the door when Petra called to me.

"I forgot to tell you, but Murray phoned me to talk to me about the protest at the foundation today."

"Murray?" I echoed. "How did he know you were there?"

"I guess me and Kira showed up on TV when we were trying to get back to the Malina Building. So he had some questions about what it felt like, the attack and all."

"Did he ask you about the cemetery?"

"I can't remember. I'm pretty sure he did, but of course, I wasn't there, so I couldn't tell him anything."

I was too tired to figure out why that made me uneasy. I just told Petra to make sure her boss knew she'd been talking to the press. "The one thing bosses hate is surprises, especially surprises involving their underlings and publicity."

As I climbed the stairs, my legs so itchy with fatigue that I could hardly lift them, I thought enviously of Lotty's high-rise. Glossy floors, elevators, doormen. I should have become a surgeon instead of a private eye.

I fell instantly and heavily asleep, but my night was filled with unquiet dreams. Over and over, Leydon jumped or flew or fled from terror while I stood frozen to the spot, watching but not acting. She taunted me, reminding me that she could quote James Joyce, poets, Puritans, while I was only a bailer of bilge.

In another dream, Chaim Salanter knelt on Miles Wuchnik's chest, sticking darning needles into his neck and sucking his blood. Arielle and Nia Durango danced around him, shrieking, "Do it again, Grandpapa, do it again!"

I got out of bed the next day leaden of brain and foot. I drove the dogs to the lake, too groggy to run that far. The air was already hot and heavy, but the water was icy, and the flies were biting hard. The dogs could keep swimming to get away from the swarms of insects, but the water was too cold for me. I threw balls for the dogs as long as I could stand it, running up and down the beach, swatting at the flies that were stinging me, but I finally had to drag my pair back to the car. At least my frenzied movements had taken my mind off my troubles and brought some life to my dull brain.

16. ANGEL MOTHER—NOT

I LEFT THE DOGS TO THE COOL OF MR. CONTRERAS'S FRONT-room air conditioner and drove myself to the eighteen-room mansion in Lake Bluff where Leydon Ashford had spent her childhood. The journey took me along congested expressways, where grinding trucks belched gray smoke into the heavy air.

The route north led past the city's sleeper suburbs, past Ravinia, where the Chicago Symphony had its summer home, and decanted me into paradise. As soon as I left the expressway, the air was bright and clear, the lawns a miracle of tightly clipped emerald. No empty chip bags or McDonald's wrappers spoiled the gutters. Children biked or skateboarded along the streets, terriers barking happily at their heels. It was as if the drawings in my first-grade reader had been pasted onto cardboard and set in motion.

There must be an app for this somewhere in the Apple or Droid worlds. You clicked on it and suddenly the temperature dropped eight degrees, pollution and congestion evaporated, and everyone around you turned miraculously wealthy. And white.

It had been a good twenty years since I'd last been to the Ashford home, but I found my way there without stopping to check apps or maps. I'd spent a lot of weekends there with Leydon, swimming off the private beach between bouts of studying, and then going inside to argue about civil rights or economics with Sewall and Mr. Ashford. There'd been an especially hideous Thanksgiving when my dad was in the hospital and I'd let Leydon persuade me to come north with her. I'd almost come to blows with Mr. Ashford over the laziness of immigrant workers.

Before turning in to the Ashfords' private drive, I called Lotty's clinic nurse for any fresh news about Leydon. Jewel Kim put me on hold and returned to say that Leydon was still unresponsive but still able to breathe on her own. It was impossible to know how she was doing.

Ashford money, like Salanter money, had come originally from steel, although the Ashfords had been in the production, not the scrap, end of the business. At one time, Ashford mills stretched from Gary, Indiana, to the Canadian border, with a bunch of iron-ore mines tucked in here and there along the way.

I don't know what they did for money now that the mills were closed, but they didn't seem to be suffering. Trees, grass, flowers, shrubs were all well enough tended that the Parterre Club would have admitted the Ashfords on sight. I saw a dark-skinned man in an orange vest cleaning out the ornamental pond, while another was riding a mower around the three acres of lawn.

When I reached the house, a Lincoln Navigator was in the drive, but I didn't see a BMW. That was a relief—Sewall was presumably downtown, doing whatever he did all day long; it was his wife I'd come to visit.

I didn't know her well: we'd met at a handful of big events—her wedding to Sewall, and fund-raisers for that small circle of causes where our ideas of the worthwhile intersected. Lyric Opera was the only one I could think of.

A maid answered the front door. That was a change from the last time I'd been here—the elder Mrs. Ashford liked butlers. Perhaps women's lib had reached the North Shore. The maid took my card and went to find Faith.

The house was built in two wings around a wide hall that led directly from the front door to a garden room and the grounds beyond. I watched the maid walk down the hall and out through the garden room. After a few minutes, Faith came hurrying toward me. She was wearing cutoffs and a dirty T-shirt, but she'd dropped a tool-filled apron and kicked off her clogs in the garden room.

"V. I. Warshawski. You were with Leydon in the church yesterday, Sewall told me. What a terrible ordeal. Sewall was very upset." She looked at her dirty hands. "I've been staking up my dahlias and the weather is unforgiving. I know you and Leydon were—are—good friends. I hope you haven't come here in person because there's bad news?"

The dahlias and Leydon seemed to be vying for the front of her mind. "Leydon's condition hasn't changed, but she isn't worse, which I guess is a good thing," I said. "I came to find out what she was doing the last few months. Leydon hired me to make some inquiries for her, but she fell before she could give me any background and we hadn't talked for a time."

"Oh, my." Faith pushed some sweaty wisps of hair out of her eyes with the back of her hand, leaving a dirty smear across her forehead. "I don't know—we don't see her that often. Sewall and she—and then, I suppose if you've known her a long time you know that sometimes she can be, well, a little unpredictable."

"That's a charitable way of putting it," I said. "Leydon is the most brilliant person I've ever known, but I know how maddening she can be."

Faith smiled gratefully. "Can you come out back with me? Mother Ashford will be as unforgiving as the weather if I stand here dropping dirt on the floor; this marble was imported from Carrara when they built the house in 1903 and she just about killed Terence—my eleven-year-old—when she caught him skateboarding on it."

I followed her to the back of the house, to a large stone patio on the bluff overlooking Lake Michigan. Stairs led down to the beach, which was littered with water toys, including a small sailboat. A trio of boys was windsurfing twenty or thirty yards from shore; farther out we could see a phalanx of sailboats.

Dahlias of all colors and sizes filled the borders around the patio, and Faith looked at them wistfully before gesturing me to a wooden deck chair. She used a cell phone to ask the maid, or a maid, to bring us iced tea.

"Sewall mentioned that Leydon had left the hospital a week or so ago," I said.

Faith nodded. "She has an apartment in Edgewater, but she was getting very wound up. One weekend she drew pictures on all the walls, not just in her own apartment but all over the halls. She wouldn't stop, she wouldn't take her medication. In the end the building manager called Sewall and he got the police to take her to Ruhetal."

Ruhetal was a state mental hospital in Downers Grove, one of the suburbs west of Chicago. It annoyed me that Sewall wouldn't use Leydon's own money to get her private care, but I tried to put the feelings aside.

"I don't suppose you know what the pictures were about?"

Faith looked again at her flowers, and a wagon filled with stakes and twine. "No, I never went down there and if the manager described them to Sewall, he never said. You don't think they were valuable, I mean, you don't think they were real art, do you? We had to pay to have them painted over!"

"I never knew Leydon could draw at all," I admitted. "I'm just trying to find out what was going on in her life. Sewall said Leydon called you two days ago and talked to you in an obnoxious way."

Faith's sunburnt face turned redder. "I got upset at the time, but if I'd known—if I'd had any idea she meant to—do what she did—I would give anything to be able to go back two days and be more patient with her!"

I smiled sadly. "I've been beating myself up, too, for not taking her more seriously. It would be a help if you'd tell me what she said."

"She called because she thought Sewall was spying on her. She wanted me to tell him to stop, especially if he was using her own trust fund to pay for spies, that was how she put it. She called him *See-all,* which always makes him furious. He got on the line and told her he was fed up with her not taking her drugs, and then she said, did he want her to take a drug test, and she asked—she said—did he want to hold out his hands so she could—pee—in them."

Faith ducked her chin like a guilty seven-year-old. "She could be so dirty in how she talked," she whispered. "She talked about how it would be incest, brothers and sisters exchanging bodily fluids, and how distressed Mother Ashford would be, but she'd do it if he wanted to know her drug profile."

I couldn't keep back a crack of laughter.

Faith looked at me with startled, wounded eyes. "It wasn't funny at all, Victoria."

"Leydon has always had the knack of driving Sewall around the bend," I said. "Sorry I didn't see his face when she said that. But is he spying on her?"

Faith grimaced. "You know, he and Leydon don't agree on one single thing. He doesn't think about her unless he has to."

"So he wouldn't have hired a private detective to follow her when she got out of the hospital?"

"I can ask him." Her voice was doubtful, as if asking him would be a painful exercise. "Or Mother Ashford."

"Ask me what?"

Mrs. Ashford had appeared on the patio. She was about eighty now but still moved easily, holding herself erect. She was dressed for day in a silk print shirtwaist, her makeup complete, despite the heat. On her collar she sported the pin of an American flag topped by a corncob: Helen Kendrick's campaign button for high-end donors.

I got to my feet. "Hello, Ms. Ashford. I'm sorry about Leydon; I was with her—"

"You were with her when she jumped. Sewall told me that you had encouraged her to steal his car."

I felt the pulses in my temples begin to throb but made a halfhearted effort to control my anger. "She didn't jump. I was with her when Sewall came in, yapping about his car keys. The cops were as disgusted as I was that he didn't even pretend to care about Leydon." Okay, very half-hearted.

"Leydon always did her utmost to upset her family," her mother said. "I'm sure that's why she used to invite you out here, for the pleasure it gave her to see you enrage my husband. If you came out here today to see how angry you can make me, you might as well leave now, because I'm already angry."

Faith shifted uncomfortably in her deck chair. She picked up a pair of binoculars from an occasional table and looked at the windsurfers. "I think Terence has gone out too far; I'll just go down and wave him in."

She scurried down the stairs to the beach. Ms. Ashford didn't look at her, or at her grandson out on the water.

"You could be right," I said. "I think Leydon enjoyed having a blue-collar friend to flaunt at her dad. But with all her flaws, and despite her illness, I continue to love her, and I've agreed to do some work for her. I wondered—"

"If you think Sewall or I will pay you, you can stop wondering."

"Leydon has her own money, no?"

"She has a trust fund from her father, but Sewall is her trustee and he certainly won't authorize payments to a private detective." She bit the words off as if she were spitting out cigar ends.

"Would he pay a different detective?" I asked. "I mean, would he, or you, hire someone to follow Leydon to make sure she didn't commit any major new embarrassment? Although it would be hard for someone to stay in her apartment with her, making sure she didn't paint all over the walls again."

"Are you trying to suggest that we employ you?" Ms. Ashford's nostrils dilated in her outrage.

"Not at all. Leydon has hired me and it would be a conflict of interest for me to work for both of you. Merely, I wondered—"

"Hired you to do what?" Ms. Ashford interrupted.

I smiled. "To conduct a confidential inquiry. Did Sewall spy on Leydon when she left the hospital? That's what she told Faith."

Down on the beach I could see Faith waving small colored flags, trying to signal the windsurfers, who seemed to be paying no attention to her. Her fate in the Ashford family, apparently.

"What we do about Leydon is our business. All I can do is ask you to leave us alone. Leydon has caused us many decades of heartbreak and embarrassment, and if she dies from yesterday's injuries, we will all be—" She stopped, unable to think of a graceful way to finish the sentence.

"Ecstatic?" I suggested. "Jubilant?"

The lines around her thin mouth deepened. "We would be within our rights to feel some relief from the misery she's caused us all these years."

"Your daughter has been a hard burden," I said, squeezing her hand in mock sympathy. "And yet you bear up nobly. I'll make sure her doctors know that you're too distraught to be interrupted with bulletins about her health."

17. CLEANING OUT THE DEAD

I TOOK THE LONG, SLOW ROUTE DOWN SHERIDAN ROAD BACK to the city, forty miles of meandering roads, with the lake on my left hand keeping the worst of the summer heat at bay. Leydon's mother had depressed me, as she doubtless meant to, with her dig about why Leydon used to bring me up here. Mr. Ashford had been an overwhelming presence in the family and Leydon had never felt able to stand up to him directly. I might not have been as clever at remembering Joyce or quoting Puritan preachers, but I wasn't afraid to tackle Sewall Senior, over everything from his disdain for women in public life to his virulent racism.

"Leydon loved me," I said aloud, as if Leydon's mother could hear me. "She might have used me to give herself a stronger voice, but none of you Ashfords are worth as much as one strand of her red-gold hair. So there!"

I finally meandered to my office. Heat rose from the sidewalks in translucent sheets. The tree that my leasemate and I had planted in a hole she'd drilled through the concrete outside our front door was gray from smog and humidity. And no one seemed to care that we'd put a large trash can along the curb—the usual dreary detritus of the heedless lined the street—empty bottles, cups, plastic bags.

Inside my office I resisted the urge to collapse onto the cot I keep in my supply room. I returned e-mails and phone calls, did some desultory work for my paying clients, and then asked LifeStory, my favorite search engine, to fetch me details on Miles Wuchnik.

While the computer searched, I called Nick Vishnikov, the deputy chief medical examiner. Even though I'm not with the police, we serve on a human rights committee together, and he's willing to give me autopsy results.

"He died where you found him, which you probably already guessed from the amount of blood. But he'd been whacked on the back of the head first, which explains why he was lying so peacefully on his tomb."

I saw him on the catafalque. Leydon's line, or Joyce's, ran through my head. Still, it sounded as though I could end my inchoate fears about Nia Durango and Arielle Zitter having lured him to the vault. They were two very enterprising young ladies, though—maybe they'd whacked him before they met the rest of their friends at the Dudek apartment. Perhaps they figured out a way to drag him up the steps onto the vault. Or agreed to meet him in the tomb and then hit him.

I put the possibility cautiously to Vishnikov.

"I doubt it. I can't see two young girls being strong enough to heft an unconscious body onto a slab as high off the ground as that one was. Anyway, he didn't have the kind of scrapes and abrasions you'd find if he'd been hoisted up the side of the slab. Whoever put him there lifted him. Unless your girls are junior weightlifting champs, I'd strike them from my 'possibles' list."

By the time I finished talking to Vishnikov, LifeStory had finished its study of Miles Wuchnik. He, and his two brothers and one sister, had been born and raised in Danville, Illinois, home of Dick Van Dyke,

Bobby Short, and the Danville Correctional Center. He'd played high school football, and studied criminal justice at Eastern Illinois University, taken a job with the Illinois State Police, and then moved to the Chicago area nine years ago, where he set up as an investigator in private practice, specializing in finding lost and missing people but willing to do pretty much anything.

His sister still lived in Danville; both parents were dead and his brothers had moved farther afield. Like me, Wuchnik had been married once and divorced; his ex-wife, Sandra, had remarried five years ago and was living in the southwest suburbs. Miles lived alone in Berwyn, a modest town on the border of Oak Park where Frank Lloyd Wright was king. As far as I could tell, Wuchnik's office had been in his home and his car.

LifeStory couldn't tell me whether Wuchnik's family had come from Vilna, and whether Chaim Salanter had been pals with Wuchnik's father, or perhaps grandfather, when they were little boys before war spattered and scattered Lithuania. Neither could my other favorite violator of privacy, The Monitor Project, although the Monitor told me Wuchnik had left an estate of thirty-two thousand, less whatever his outstanding debts were.

That depressed me further. If I died tomorrow, I wouldn't leave a whole lot more to my heirs. My car, almost paid for, my condo, ditto. A modest 401K. Why hadn't I followed my ex into private practice?

I went back out into the heat, stopping at La Llorona for a cold vegetable sandwich. I couldn't resist Ms. Aguilar's hot sauce, which meant that by the time I got back to my car, I had a line of red juice across my white knit top. Good thing I'd started the day in Lake Bluff—I never would have survived Mother Ashford's withering scrutiny.

Even though I didn't expect ever to bill Leydon for my work, I scrupulously entered my mileage, as I had on my way to Lake Bluff. In yesterday's excitement I'd forgotten to include the mileage down to the university and back. That would be my donation to Leydon's trust fund.

Berwyn, Little Bohemia, it used to be called, when Chicago's Czech population filled its streets. There was a time when they called Cermak Road—the town's main commercial strip—the Bohemian Wall Street, but the area had long since changed identities. A handful of the famous Czech bakeries remained, but they were outnumbered these days by taquerias. No matter what the ethnicity, Berwynites were house-proud: when I left the expressway and headed south, I saw that the bungalows were carefully painted and tended. Even without a phalanx of gardeners to clip the shrubs and fertilize the grass, the small front yards were tidy and well groomed.

Wuchnik's home, mostly owned by the Fort Dearborn Trust, turned out to be the top floor of a two-flat on Grove Avenue. At three on a hot afternoon, there wasn't any foot traffic. I'd passed some parks where a few kids were playing ball, but anyone looking at the Wuchnik place would be doing so behind the closed blinds in their air-conditioned front rooms.

I rang the bell for the ground-floor apartment, but no one answered. Just to be safe—after all, the guy hadn't been married, but many people didn't bother these days—I rang Wuchnik's bell as well. When there was no answer, I pulled out my picks. It took me only a minute to undo the front door, which said more about Wuchnik's carelessness than my skill. The stairs to the second floor weren't carpeted; I found myself tiptoeing my way up, as if someone might hear me.

At the top, it took me no time at all to get into his apartment. That was because someone had been here before me and not bothered to lock up when they left. The six rooms had been searched thoroughly. Not violently, but the searcher hadn't bothered to be careful: drawers stood open, the dead man's few books were splayed. If he'd owned a landline, that had been removed. In fact, no electronics remained, unless you counted the microwave and the television. Certainly no computers, discs, flash drives, or cell phones that might give me some kind of clue about who Wuchnik had been working for when he died.

The searcher had apparently been angry at not finding what he— she?—was hunting, because he'd slashed a book to ribbons. In the kitchen wastebasket, I found a chunk of paper as if someone had scooped out a book like a pumpkin. Little puffs of gray print clung to my fingers after I'd sifted through the trash.

The first intruder had dumped the contents of Wuchnik's files onto the living room floor, and I looked through those, without much hope of finding anything useful. Wuchnik had kept clippings about old murder cases, mostly unsolved murders, and he'd made a few notes in the margins: *no next of kin; mother wouldn't speak to me; wife remarried & left for ca 5 yrs ago.* On a piece of scrap paper that clung to the back of one of the clippings, he'd written, "'In death they were not divided'? Told me to look it up."

Just because nothing else in Wuchnik's place seemed to mean anything, I tucked that scrap into my briefcase and went back into the July heat, where I called Terry Finchley, the Area Six detective in charge of investigating Wuchnik's murder.

"V. I. Warshawski," Finchley said. "That would be 'Vexatious Investigator' Warshawski?"

"Try 'Veracity In Person.' I'm outside Miles Wuchnik's place. It's been thoroughly tossed."

"And it's in Berwyn."

"I know you always got A's in geography; you don't have to show off for me." I was sitting with the windows down, hoping for a breeze, but sweat was trickling down my neck.

"Don't ride me when it's ninety-three outside. You know it's a jurisdiction issue. You call the locals?"

"I thought you'd be interested. And I also thought the locals might inspect the scene more thoroughly if a highly decorated Chicago PD lieutenant alerted them, instead of a vexatious investigator."

Finchley laughed. "So your skin is thin in places. Wuchnik's homicide isn't at the top of our pile here—no physical evidence at the scene, nothing in his private life to indicate someone with a grievance. His ex married a guy in pharmaceuticals and is living way better than Wuchnik ever hoped to. He hadn't dated anyone for about fifteen months and we couldn't find anyone with a grudge."

"I had dinner last night with Chaim Salanter." I decided I had to sacrifice a polar bear: I turned on my engine so I could run the air-conditioning.

"I ate with my wife and little girl at Navy Pier. Which one of us do you think was happier?"

"I'm sure you were, Terry. Salanter wanted to hire me *not* to investigate Wuchnik's death. It didn't occur to me to ask if he was making the same offer to all the other PI's in the Chicago area, but I suppose a guy that rich can pay everyone off and not notice it."

"If you are implying that I can be—"

"Scout's honor, I am not trying to ride you. I told Salanter last night you were an inspired investigator, and an incorruptible one, and both those things are true. But guys like Salanter don't deal at the Area detective level—they go to the mayor's office."

Terry was silent for a beat or two. "That explains—the directive we got on the murder. Not to stand down, just to acknowledge, well, what I told you at the outset. No physical evidence, et cetera. Do you have any idea why Salanter cares?"

"None at all, although it stands out a mile that he thought Wuchnik was investigating him. Do you have a list of what the guy was working on? You weren't the people who made off with his computer, were you?"

"No. We dropped the ball there." Terry was bitter, with himself for not getting out to Berwyn. "Thanks, anyway, for the call, Vexatious—can I call you Vexie for short?"

"Only if I'm not there in person to tie your tongue into a bow."

"I'll call Berwyn. You might not want to be sitting in front of Wuchnik's place when they arrive. You can't keep being spotted around the guy when the police show up. Sooner or later some dumb cop is going to get suspicious."

He hung up before I could thank him.

18. THE WRITING ON THE WALL

I HAD THOUGHT ABOUT CANVASSING THE NEIGHBORS, TO SEE if anyone had spotted someone carting off computers and flash drives from Wuchnik's home in the last two days, but Terry's warning was very much to the point. I joined the long, slow crawl back to the city, getting off the Ike at Ashland Avenue to avoid congestion on the Kennedy, only to get stuck in a backup of similar-minded people.

At Chicago Avenue, I abruptly turned west again. Wuchnik hadn't walked from Berwyn to Mount Moriah cemetery. If his killer hadn't driven him, his car might still be somewhere in the neighborhood.

I pulled out my Monitor Project report on him. Wuchnik had driven a Hyundai Tucson and he probably hadn't parked far from the cemetery, as heavy as Saturday night's rain had been. I made a slow circuit of Mount Moriah, but it wasn't until I widened my search that I found the car. It was parked nearer to the Dudek apartment than to the cemetery.

The streets here were crowded with people returning from work, mothers laden with children and groceries, kids skateboarding, kids throwing balls in the street, and everyone texting like mad no matter what they were doing.

It had been a long time since I'd broken into a car, but I was relying on people's focus on their handhelds to keep them from noticing anything I might do. However, when I got to the car, I saw I didn't need a cover: someone once more had been ahead of me. The rear window was smashed and the locks were popped.

I looked at the mess, depressed. Except for the broken glass, and the empty pizza boxes that showed how much Wuchnik lived behind the wheel, the car was empty. No files, no car fax, not even a GPS tracker.

"This your car, miss?"

A couple of boys on skateboards had stopped near me.

"Friend of mine. He sent me down here to collect his papers, but someone got into his car ahead of me. I don't suppose you saw anything, did you?"

"No, miss. It must've happened in the night, 'cause it was okay last night, but it was all busted up this morning."

So if I'd just come here yesterday—although yesterday, I'd been pretty tied up, come to think of it. The boys were rocking back and forth on their skateboards, ready to take flight. I thanked them for stopping.

The second boy said, "Whoever broke in, they dropped one of his papers. It was half under the car when we come down this morning. You want it, miss?"

"Absolutely!"

They skated off toward one of the three-flats up the street. I poked around in the detritus while I waited and found several credit-card slips, which I tucked into my briefcase. The boys returned quickly, holding a grimy spiral notebook, one wider than it was long.

"What's your friend's name, miss?" the first one asked as I stuck out a hand.

"Miles Wuchnik."

They studied the notebook and whispered to each other. "It's just got an address."

"On Grove Avenue in Berwyn?" I asked.

That did the trick. They handed over the notebook and I gave each of them a five, which made their faces light up. I also handed each of them a card.

"I'm a detective, private, and so was Miles. You know the dead man who was found over in the cemetery?" I jerked my head toward Mount Moriah. "That was Miles. I agreed to take on his old cases and try to solve them for him, but I think the murderers broke into his car to keep me from finding out what he was working on. So if you see anything, or hear anything, give me a call. And for pity's sake, don't tackle them on your own. You are two very brave and resourceful young men, but the killers are ruthless."

Their eyes grew big with excitement. "What's that, miss, ruthless, that where they were born?"

"It's a word meaning they are utterly cold-blooded with no regard for human life."

"So was your friend killed by a vampire, like they're saying?"

"Nope. Not a vampire. A very human sort of being, just not a nice one."

They raced down the street on their boards, so excited they almost collided with a woman pushing a baby carriage. By five p.m., everyone on the street would know they were helping to track down the vampire.

I took the notebook back to my car. When I opened it, I couldn't believe my luck. It was Wuchnik's mileage log. I started to read it but realized how much I'd exposed myself, identifying myself to the boys, asking questions, and now sitting near Wuchnik's own car. Since I had no idea what the vampire killer looked like, it could be any of the people looking at my Mustang as they walked up the street. Not enough of them were buried in their texts for my comfort.

I turned back to Ashland Avenue. Traffic had become marginally lighter; I made it home in half an hour. Jake was leaving for Marlboro in the morning. We were going out for dinner and dancing, and I was not bringing my cell phone with me: no one was going to break up my evening, not even if the Malina Building was on fire and Petra was stuck on the top floor with fifteen screaming twelve-year-olds.

Back home, I showered and put on a pair of black silk pants and a shimmery silver top. I wished I'd kept my scarlet dress for tonight, instead of letting it get wet and dirty Saturday night. My cleaners had said they'd do their best with it, but they hadn't been optimistic. Maybe Joseph Parecki could make me a new one, if I made some money this month. I taped up my blistered feet with enough padding that I could put my dancing shoes on without feeling the pain, or at least, without feeling much pain.

While I waited for Jake to finish his packing, I started working through Miles Wuchnik's mileage log. Some of the entries were in pencil, which had smeared and blurred with time, others in ballpoint. He seemed to have entered every place he went, with dates, times, and miles. The last column on each page identified the client, or at least the case he was working on, but he'd used a code here, probably the case number he assigned to the investigation, and I didn't have a way to crack the code. Somehow it made him become a real person to me, touching the numbers he'd written moments before his death.

Wuchnik had been a busy detective, so busy that the notebook covered only the last four months and was already almost full. He'd trekked from the county buildings dotting Greater Chicago's six counties to the Metropolitan Water Reclamation District's headquarters, to hospitals, restaurants, and to Ruhetal in Downers Grove.

I put the spiral notebook down, carefully, as if it were made of glass and might shatter. Ruhetal, the state mental hospital where Leydon had spent the month of June. This was Gordian indeed.

I picked up the notebook again. Wuchnik had made six trips to Ruhetal, starting on the Wednesday before Memorial Day, with the last one ten days before he died. I'd have to get the exact dates Leydon had been out there.

Wuchnik had also carefully noted the eight-point-nine-mile trip from his home to the parking space on Augusta. The code in the margin was the same as for the trips to Ruhetal. I tried to analyze Wuchnik's numbers. All of them ended in eleven, so that probably referred to the year. Brilliant, V.I. Keep this up and you'll have a job at Langley in no time.

But the first two numbers couldn't possibly be a date. It had to have something to do with how he labeled his cases.

"Victoria Iphigenia. You are the most beautiful thing I've seen—I don't know—in my whole life, maybe."

I'd left my front door open for Jake but hadn't heard him come in. I sprang to my feet—a skintight top that wows your lover—the best cure for the puzzled and weary detective's sore feet and baffled brain.

I went to my bedroom safe for my mother's diamond earrings, and tucked Wuchnik's notebook into it. Not that I expected the vampires to come after it, but it was the only thing I'd been able to salvage from his belongings, that and the little scrap of paper that said, "In death they were not divided." And a few credit-card slips, but those I left in my briefcase.

Jake and I closed down the Peacock Walk at two Wednesday morning. I resolutely kept my mind on dancing, food, and sex, using a small corner for sadness at saying good-bye to Jake for a month or so. Anytime Wuchnik or his notebook popped up, I counted backward from eleven. But at ten-thirty Wednesday morning, as soon as Jake had driven away with his two basses, I was on North Kenmore Avenue, at Leydon Ashford's apartment.

Any lingering ideas I'd had that Leydon might have been in a group home, or even Section 8 housing, disappeared when I saw the glossy high-rise, with a uniformed doorman. When I explained who I was and what I wanted, the doorman phoned through to the manager, who directed me to his office on the second floor.

The manager was a man in his fifties or sixties, wearing a short-sleeved shirt and a tie but no jacket. When I arrived, he was handling a complaint about a water leak in 4J while listening to an elderly lady whose cat had run into the stairwell on twelve and not yet returned. The nameplate on his small desk announced that he was Saul Feldtman.

"What can I do for you, ma'am?"

Feldtman froze when I mentioned Leydon's name, but when I explained that she was seriously injured and wouldn't be home for some time, he was perfectly willing to look up the date he'd called the cops to come get her.

"She's on the ninth floor. We didn't know at first that she was doing all this painting, but she covered the stairwell, and then started on the halls. When I tried to get her to stop she became very agitated. And then it turned out she'd been painting the common room—and not like she was Michelangelo, mind, more like—well, I took photos, in case, you know."

In case it came to court. America, land of the fee, home of the litigant. Feldtman pulled up his photo album on a computer and let me look while he calmed down the woman whose cat was missing and called a plumber to deal with the leaky showerhead.

Leydon's painting was dramatic, but she definitely belonged more to the R. Crumb school than Michelangelo's. She had used black and red house paint. Much of what she'd done was hard to make out in the photos because she'd gone over and over the same space with a thick brush, but there were places were I could make out male figures. They had large penises and tiny heads where only a large mouth was drawn, and they said things like, "Don't move or I'll fuck," or, "I am thinking with my big head, dude." I hated to sympathize with Sewall Ashford and his mother, but I could barely bring myself to look at the photos.

Leydon hadn't gone to Ruhetal until four days after Wuchnik made his first visit. When the manager finished with the plumber and the cat lady, I asked if he could find when he'd first noticed Leydon's behavior.

Feldtman was methodical, organized: he had a log of all his calls and tenant complaints. Someone first saw one of the cartoons in the stair-well about ten days before she was hospitalized, but in the beginning, she was just making a few drawings and it took a few days to trace them to Leydon.

"Then we called the brother, because he pays the bills and it's his number in our files, and him and the mother, they came and tried to talk to her. So then she locked herself in her own place for a few days and we didn't see her, but then suddenly there she was in the middle of the night, painting up and down the stairwell; we couldn't get her to stop.

"And then, my God, when I and the super forced her back into her own apartment—it was such a mess—she'd painted on the tables and couches, it was unbelievable. So the brother told me he'd call the cops, and they took her out to Ruhetal. There's a real good private place just a mile from here, and I told the cops to take her there, but the brother, he wouldn't pay for private, so they took her out to Ruhetal."

19. THE AUGEAN STABLES

I FOUND AN INDIE COFFEE BAR AND SAT AT THE COUNTER, trying to decide if I should drive out to Downers Grove to look at Ruhetal. Even if the Ashford family had sent Miles Wuchnik out to the hospital to spy on Leydon, I couldn't see how it connected to his death.

But why would the Ashfords have hired a private eye at all? He wouldn't be allowed into the wards, and since Sewall's wife had Leydon's medical power of attorney, they could get all the information they wanted from the hospital. Maybe Sewall was denuding Leydon's trust account and he wanted a private eye to see if she'd figured it out. I tried to imagine how a client would frame such a query: *Wuchnik, my friend, disguise yourself as an orderly and get my sister into conversation about her trust fund. Shouldn't be hard—her mind jumps from topic to topic like a kangaroo.*

I shook my head. I couldn't come up with a scenario to validate Leydon's fears. But the fact remained that Wuchnik had made numerous trips to Ruhetal last month. Perhaps he had a different agenda than spying on Leydon Ashford.

I looked again at Wuchnik's mileage log to see if I could make any sense of his case numbering system. The scrap of paper I'd found in his apartment had somehow ended up in the log: "'In death they were not divided'? Told me to look it up."

If someone had given the detective a quotation and a riddle, that someone was likely Leydon. The dean at Rockefeller seemed to have the same portmanteau memory as Leydon. I called down to the chapel and was lucky enough to find Dr. Knaub in his office.

"Sorry to treat you like a walking dictionary," I said, after updating him on Leydon's condition. "But I found, well, call it a clue that I'm guessing she left behind."

"Second Samuel," Knaub said, when I read what was on the scrap of paper. "It's a famous passage, David lamenting the deaths of Saul and Saul's son Jonathan. Is that a help?"

"Not that I can see. Not unless Leydon had a lead on a father-son death that she discussed with Miles Wuchnik."

"It could be something else," the dean said. "David adds that his love for Jonathan surpassed the love of women. Is there a homosexual component to your case?"

"If there is, Leydon was way ahead of me on that, as on so many things before. Thanks, Dr. Knaub."

"Not at all," he said courteously. "I like puzzles. And please call me Henry."

I wrote Knaub's suggestions in my notebook. You never know. Although there was so much here I didn't know that adding "Homosexual love? Father-son double slaying?" to my notes just confused me further.

If it was indeed Leydon who'd given Wuchnik that cryptic message, then she'd known what he was working on. And she'd known that because she'd met him at Ruhetal. Or someplace else? Had they connected earlier and he'd followed her to the hospital?

I went back around the corner to her apartment building. The manager was between complaining tenants. Once he'd satisfied himself that I had a legitimate interest in finding out what had led up to Leydon's fall from the chapel balcony, he took me up to the ninth floor and let me into her apartment.

"I'll just watch you, miss, while you look around." Feldtman unlocked the door and then hesitated. "You may not want to go in there."

I peered over his shoulder. The door opened into a large living space with a glass wall that faced Lake Michigan. If you kept your chin up and your eyes on the lake, you could ignore the chaos that billowed underneath. Papers filled the floor and the chairs—newspaper clippings, computer printouts, brown paper bags, all covered in Leydon's large, reckless script. A few plates with uneaten food were scattered in the wreckage, along with some of the wispy lingerie Leydon favored. Feldtman was right—I didn't really want to go in.

"At least she hasn't started writing on the walls," I said, trying to put a hopeful spin on it.

I sat cross-legged on the floor and started to pick up clippings, which covered topics ranging from reports on the supercollider in Geneva to health claims for the goji berry. Leydon clipped stories on election reform, on Chicago's electoral politics, on personnel changes at my ex-husband's law firm. She'd printed out reams of stories from Internet sources, on hit-and-run accidents, on climate change, on mammograms. Some were covered in her own handwriting, with incomprehensible phrases: *The Fire Last Time, No Smoking Gun Without Fire.* I wished her hypomanic phase had led her to collect something large and disposable, like sleeping bags, instead of news.

I found two articles from the *Herald-Star* and the *Sun-Times* that covered Wuchnik's death. The *Times* had mentioned me as finding the body. Perhaps that's what prompted Leydon to call me—she'd circled my name with such a heavy hand that she'd almost obliterated it. Both papers showed the Byzantine vault where Wuchnik's body had been found. Under the photograph in the *Times,* Leydon had scrawled, *He is dead. We saw him lying upon the catafalque but no wail of sorrow went up, instead a gleeful cry, He is dead, he is dead!*

She'd gone on at greater length in the *Herald-Star*, crisscrossing the page and the margins. *Home is the hunter, home from the hill, from the dale from Happy Dale, the hunter of the haunted, tormentor of the damned, who else hated your haunting hunting?*

"Are you going to look at all of these?" Feldtman asked.

"I don't have the stamina or the time. If you want to help give them a quick once-over, you might look for Miles Wuchnik's name."

His eyes widened. "Was Ms. Ashford was involved in the vampire murder?"

"I don't think so, but there's some connection that I don't understand. Ms. Ashford thought he was spying on her. Did you ever see him hanging around the building?"

The *Herald-Star* had found a good headshot of Wuchnik, but when I showed the picture to the manager, he said he'd never seen him.

"I'll check with Rafe—the doorman—but realistically, if someone comes around snooping on one of our tenants, Rafe tells me right away. It happens, you know, stalkers, or even"—he lowered his voice, as if about to say something too vile for normal speech—"repo men. These hard times affect our tenants along with everyone else."

Feldtman made a stab at the papers, while I took the dishes to the kitchen and threw out the food. I emptied perishables from Leydon's refrigerator, washed the dishes, then went back to the front room and picked up the lacy bits of Natori and La Perla. When I took them into the bedroom, I found Leydon had been writing on Post-its and sticking them to the wall around her bed. A whole box of them sat on the table by her bed, on top of a stack of books and magazines.

In death they were not divided, she'd written more than once, along with her messages about the catafalque and Happy Dale. And her crude comments to her brother. *Sea-wall See-well Pee-well.*

What I didn't see was her computer. The printer was in the front room, buried under back copies of *The New Yorker,* but the computer itself was gone.

I pointed this out to Feldtman. He turned huffy, thinking I was accusing him, or Rafe the doorman, of theft, until I made it clear that I wanted to know only whether he or Rafe had seen Leydon leave with it.

"Maybe her brother took it when he picked her up in June," Feldtman suggested.

"I don't think so—she's got printouts with dates from after she got out of the hospital. Maybe she took it in for repairs. Maybe it's in her car; she said that was in the shop when we spoke Monday morning."

Feldtman didn't know where Leydon took her car for service but referred me again to the doorman, Rafe. Feldtman was getting beeped on his cell phone and was anxious to return to his battle station. I didn't see what else I could do in Leydon's apartment. In fact, the shambles was so disturbing, not just in itself but as a reminder of various past episodes I'd experienced with her, that I was eager to leave with him.

On my way out of the lobby, I stopped to talk to Rafe. He liked Leydon—a classy lady, not like some of the women in the building who were full of attitude because they were professors or something. He was sorry to hear of her troubles, but he didn't remember whether she had her computer with her or not.

"Everyone has one these days, miss, so it's not something you notice special."

He did know where Leydon took her car for service, or at least he knew the garage he'd recommended to her. It was a place on Devon, about a mile from the apartment. I copied the name into my notebook and gave him a couple of bucks.

The garage manager didn't share Rafe's enthusiasm for Leydon. He'd done $2,700 worth of work on her car, and she wouldn't pay for it. Her credit cards were maxed out, and her brother wouldn't release any money from her trust fund to cover the bill. Leydon apparently had had a molten phone argument with Sewall in the garage manager's office, and when that didn't get her anywhere, she'd jumped into her car and tried to drive out of the garage, almost hitting one of the mechanics.

The manager was still angry. It didn't calm him any to learn that Leydon was in a coma: "I've still got this car that no one's paying for taking up room on my lot."

"I'll talk to her sister-in-law," I promised. "She has Ms. Ashford's durable power of attorney and can authorize getting the car paid for, even if the brother won't release any money from Ms. Ashford's trust fund. In the meantime, all I want is to find out if she left her computer in the car."

The manager refused to cooperate, but on my way out, I casually waved a twenty at one of the mechanics. He waited until the manager was busy at another end of the garage, then led me behind the building to Leydon's car. The car wasn't empty: she'd filled the backseat with newspapers, magazines, recipes, and a few odd pieces of junk. But there was no computer, nor, as far as I could tell, anything that related to Miles Wuchnik and his trips to the hospital in Downers Grove.

20. CHATTER IN THE PEACEFUL VALLEY

"RUHETAL? THAT MEANS 'A PEACEFUL VALLEY,'" LOTTY SAID. "What an idyllic spot for the mentally ill—or any ill person, for that matter."

Today was one of her days in her storefront clinic off Irving Park Road. I had stopped by on my way from Leydon's apartment to see if Lotty could give me any advice on how to get information about Leydon from the staff. Faith Ashford had Leydon's medical power-of-attorney, but I hadn't wanted to drive the forty miles to Lake Bluff to try to wheedle a signed permission to talk to Leydon's doctors about her condition.

"You know I am not going to violate the law, especially not the law that protects confidential records, for any reason, even if you are convinced it's in your friend's best interest," Lotty told me severely, when I explained what I wanted. "And I don't know Philip Poynter, or any of the other physicians attached to the hospital."

Poynter was the prescribing physician's name on a bottle of Risperdal the police had picked up at Rockefeller.

I held up my hands in surrender. "Okay, okay. I'll just show Wuchnik's photo around and see if anyone remembers him."

"A word of advice," Lotty relented marginally. "Don't ask for Poynter. The doctors often don't see the patients, they just write prescriptions. Find out who the advanced practice nurse and the therapists are and see if any of them will talk to you. Now, you'd better get going—I'm keeping patients waiting."

"Would it violate your code of ethics to find out how Leydon's doing? The hospital won't tell me anything because I'm not a family member."

"Talk to Mrs. Coltrain on your way out. Tell her I asked her to call down to the U of C for you." She was out of her office and on her way to an examining room before I had a chance to thank her.

Leydon's condition was unchanged, Mrs. Coltrain said, but the neurological team wasn't optimistic.

"People do recover from head injuries, Ms. Warshawski," Mrs. Coltrain comforted me. "Look at that congresswoman in Arizona, shot in the brain, and up and walking six weeks later."

"You're right," I agreed, but I drove down to my office in a somber mood.

I used my search engines to turn up a staff directory for Ruhetal. I was starting to feel like an automaton, going through the motions of the same job over and over. Search the Web, spy on people's private data, drive around town like a madwoman, get shot, do it all over again.

LifeStory gave me the names of the psychiatric advanced practice nurses and the social workers. It also told me a bit of the history of the place. Ruhetal had been started in 1911 by German Evangelical missionaries who had advanced notions of how to treat the mentally ill. The photographs of limestone buildings set in the prairie made it seem like an idyllic setting, and, indeed, it had been a fashionable sanitarium for writers and movie stars in the twenties.

In the thirties, it proved impossible to keep the place going. The

Nazis, with their brutal ideas about murdering the mentally ill, cut off the aid coming from Germany, and the U.S. froze Ruhetal's assets once the war started. The place might have disintegrated completely, but in the fifties, the state of Illinois bought it and turned one of the buildings into a state mental hospital with a wing for "the criminally insane."

I looked at an aerial photo: the place was huge, with acres of grounds surrounding five buildings. In 1911, the founders had included tennis courts and a baseball field, but Google's photo didn't show whether they still existed.

It was late morning before I finally got on the road. I packed lunch and picked up a cortado from the coffee bar across the street. There may be good coffee in the western suburbs, but I didn't have time to hunt for it.

By the time I reached Downers Grove, it was one o'clock. I found a park where I could eat my lunch. The park had public toilets, where I washed and fixed my makeup—even with air-conditioning, a long drive in the July heat had made me grimy.

I'd been up and down Ogden Avenue a thousand times over the years, but I'd never noticed the turnoff to the Ruhetal State Mental Hospital. I finally saw a little sign on the curb by a Ford dealership. Ruhetal sat on Therbusch Road, a small side street that ran between the dealership and a Buy-Smart superstore.

The hospital complex loomed into view as soon as I passed the parking strip. The lawns and sports facilities that I'd read about online were just a memory now. The state's budget today could barely pay the hospital staff; no one was maintaining the grounds. Such grass as had been hardy enough to outlast the weeds formed islands in the large stretches of bare soil. The leaves on the surviving trees and shrubs were a sickly gray-green.

Ruhetal's forensic wing was separated from the general population by three sets of fences, but the whole complex looked like a penitentiary. The state had kept the original limestone building, but they'd augmented it with the gray concrete blocks beloved of builders like Stalin. Gray façades, narrow barred windows. If you weren't already depressed when you got here, it wouldn't take long to bring you down in a place like this.

Poor Leydon! A spasm of anger against her brother rose in me. How could he put his sister in such a place? Maybe Sewall really was stealing from her trust fund. Maybe I'd have to find a way to inspect his finances—although the probability was that he stuck Leydon here out of a punitive rage.

Acres of asphalt, easier to maintain than grass, surrounded the buildings. Cars that looked as tired and dirty as the hospital filled the parking lot. It was a busy place. The lot was full; I had to drive around for ten minutes until I found a space a quarter mile from the administrative wing.

I wasn't the only one arriving, either. Cars kept pulling into the lot, some even left, and I noticed a Pace bus drop off a clump of people outside the main gate. I had to wait in line for several minutes just to get into the front door. When I explained that I wanted to talk to Alvina Northlake, the head of the social work department, the woman guarding the entrance told me to step aside.

"You need to talk to Mr. Waxman."

"And I can find him where?"

"You can't. He'll find you. Step aside and let me deal with the rest of this line."

She was in her fifties, an experienced bureaucrat who enjoyed the opportunity to control people's lives. And where better to control them than in a state psychiatric hospital, where people were depressed or confused and very likely poor. If I showed any resentment or sarcasm, she'd take it out on me by not calling Mr. Waxman, so I wandered over to look at portraits of the founders that hung in the entryway.

They had been a serious bunch, those Brenners and Altmans and

Metzgers. They looked at us without smiling, men and women both, yet with a certain ardor in their faces. They had been successful in setting up compassionately run mental health hospitals in Hesse and Niedersachsen, the plaque said, and they were sure they could succeed in Illinois.

I looked at the scuffed linoleum on the floor and the painted cinder-block walls and wondered what Dr. and Frau Brenner would have made of Ruhetal's current incarnation.

"Miss!" my bureaucrat shouted at me. "Do you want to see Mr. Waxman or not?"

"I do, I do," I said hastily. "And does he want to see me?"

"Want? That I can't tell you, but he will see you." She scanned my driver's license and printed out a pass for me. "Down corridor A on your left, and then turn right when you get to corridor D, follow that up the stairs to two, and you'll find corridor K. Mr. Waxman's is the second door on your right."

When I'd followed the yellow brick road to Waxman's office, I decided the hospital tucked the senior administrators out of sight so that patients and their families couldn't see how much more money was spent on their maintenance than on the patients themselves. Corridor K was carpeted, the lights in the hall were in sconces, not overhead fluorescent banks, and the walls were painted a soft yellow.

Eric Waxman's door card identified him as deputy chief of operations. A deputy chief gets a secretary, a bottle blonde about my own age, who sat at a faux-wood desk so crammed with paper there was barely room for her computer and phone.

She looked up and demanded my business with Mr. Waxman.

"I'm a lawyer, Ms."—I squinted at her nameplate—"Ms. Lilyham-merfield. A lawyer and a licensed investigator. I want to talk to Alvina Northlake about a client of mine who was recently a patient here."

"And your client's name?"

"This is a confidential inquiry, Ms. Lilyhammerfield—"

"My name is Lily Hammerfield. They put it all together as one word when they made the nameplate."

"Sorry. Ms. Hammerfield. This is a confidential inquiry. I can rely on your discretion?"

"I see confidential papers day in and day out. I wouldn't have lasted my first year here if I had a big mouth, and I'm coming up on twenty."

Twenty years fielding inquiries about patients or budgets, or whatever it was that Eric Waxman did all day long. I hoped Ruhetal employees got a discount on Prozac.

"Well, this has nothing to do with litigation, Ms. Hammerfield. It concerns some of my client's visitors. As soon as I can talk to Ms. Northlake, I'll be gone. If you'll direct me to her office?"

Eric Waxman stepped out of the inner office. He was a young man, in his early thirties, with a tan mustache that was groomed to curl at the ends, making him look like an advertisement for the wax he was named for.

"What's going on out here, Lily?"

Maybe it was my calling her by her last name, maybe it was his officious tone—the little woman can't handle a simple query without management direction—but Lily Hammerfield smiled and said, "This woman is looking for Alvina Northlake's office, Mr. Waxman. I was just giving her directions."

He looked me up and down, nodded condescendingly, and went back to his own office. Ms. Hammerfield told me where to find Alvina Northlake—back down the stairs to corridor B. "I'll tell her you're coming."

When I reached Northlake's office, it was to discover she was in a meeting that would run another hour. Her office was a step down from Waxman's in every way. It was on the ground floor, with beat-up furniture, and an antechamber that held not just the group secretary but four other desks. A woman sat at one of them, going over a file with someone on the phone; the other three desks were also covered with papers, but the owners were away.

The group secretary said that Lily Hammerfield had called to warn them I was on my way; why did I want to talk to Alvina Northlake?

"I really want to talk to the person who worked with Leydon Ashford," I said. "I don't need to disturb Ms. Northlake."

"And why is that?"

"Ms. Ashford thought she was being stalked while she was out here. I need to find out if there's any truth to that."

The other woman hung up the phone and said, in unison with the secretary, "We can't give out any confidential information."

"I know. This is a difficult situation. Ms. Ashford was badly injured in a fall two days ago; it's not clear whether she'll live."

There was a shocked intake of breath. "Did she—is there any evidence—"

"I think she was pushed," I said. "But I can't prove it. And I can't prove it's connected to the man she thought was stalking her. But I thought if I showed her social worker, or maybe the advanced practice nurse on the ward, his picture, someone could tell me if he'd been out here, and if his business had been with Ms. Ashford."

The second woman got to her feet. "I'm Tania Metzger, one of the social workers here, and by coincidence, I was Leydon's caseworker during her stay."

"V. I. Warshawski," I said. "Are you related to the Metzgers hanging in the front hallway?"

Tania Metzger laughed. "That's such an odd-sounding way of putting it, but yes, they were my great-grandparents. They died long before I was born, of course, but I knew from my dad how passionate they felt about this place, and I suppose that guided my decision to go into social work. Now, let's see what you want to know, why you want to know it, and what I can tell you without violating confidentiality laws. Chantal here might be able to help, so let's just go into the conference room."

I followed her into a small side room where a table and six chairs had been fitted, leaving just enough space for a not-very-wide person to get in. I slid into a chair. Chantal, who was on the substantial side, grimaced and lifted a chair over her head in order to get close enough to the table to sit.

"It's terrible space," Tania apologized, "but we won't get any privacy if we stay in the hub."

The huddle, the hub, oh, the portentous names organizations give their workplaces. I would have to start calling my own office the command module.

Something in Metzger's manner made me decide to be frank with her. "I am an investigator and a lawyer, but I'm also a friend of Leydon's, going back to when we were in law school together. She—she was a challenging friend and I'm afraid I wasn't up to the challenge the last few years; I let the relationship slide."

I went on to describe Leydon's phone call, our date, and where I found her. "It was because of Miles Wuchnik that she wanted to talk to me. At least, I'm ninety percent sure it was—she wouldn't spell it out in so many words on the phone."

Metzger nodded. "Yes, she's brilliant, as you said, and maddening as well. My last name means 'butcher' in German, and she knew that; our sessions together often devolved into wordplays on whom or what I might be slaughtering." She put a hand over her mouth in dismay. "Even that much information is off-limits. I'd better just listen to you."

Metzger and Chantal both had followed the news about Wuchnik's death. It was so melodramatic that almost everyone in the six counties knew most of the details.

"Leydon thought her brother had hired Wuchnik to spy on her out here," I said. "I found Wuchnik's mileage records. He did come out six times while Leydon was a patient here. The question is, was he really spying on her?"

I spread out a sheaf of photos that I'd printed from my LifeStory report on Wuchnik, and the two women looked at them.

"He was here," Chantal said. "He came in one afternoon to ask questions about a patient, but it wasn't about Leydon."

"What did you tell him?" Tania asked.

"I told him he had to speak to Alvina. She wouldn't give him the time of day, of course. But I saw him later talking to one of the orderlies from the forensic wing."

The place for people found not guilty by reason of insanity or mental incompetence. If medication couldn't make arrestees fit to plead, they might end up serving a de facto life sentence.

"The patient he was asking about is in the forensic unit?"

Tania and Chantal exchanged glances and then gave the barest of nods. They wouldn't reveal the person's name, nor would they give me the name of the orderly. I wheedled in vain: they couldn't see any connection to Leydon, and they didn't believe one lapse in discretion, assuming someone had blabbed to Wuchnik, was any excuse for a second one.

"Would Leydon have gone to the forensic wing?" I asked.

Again the women exchanged looks. "It's completely secure," Tania said, "and you can't get there from the other buildings, I mean, not through any interior hallways. But Leydon is a lawyer, and she did sweet-talk her way over there one afternoon. She apparently persuaded one of the men that she could help him with his case."

"Who?"

Tania shook her head. "That isn't confidential, but I just don't know. The warden was furious with me for letting her get over there, as if I was supposed to run twenty-four-hour surveillance on her, but if he knew who she was talking to, he didn't say. Just that the whole wing was in an uproar for days after her visit."

21. SOMETHING WAS HAPPENING HERE, BUT YOU DON'T KNOW WHAT IT IS

THE TWO WOMEN COULDN'T TELL ME ANYTHING ELSE ABOUT Wuchnik. I pulled my photographs together but said idly, "Wasn't it strange that Leydon was admitted out here, instead of in the city? She has private money, even if she doesn't have private insurance."

"We didn't ask about that," Chantal said. "It was an involuntary admission, as you know, and we were focused more on her well-being than her financial health."

"Is that true for most of your patients?"

Tania grimaced. "More and more in these times, when Medicaid budgets are being slashed. The state is so hard up for funds they make us jump through fifteen hoops before they'll let us admit anyone. A lot of our patients get pretty unraveled, even the ones who seek a voluntary admission, before we're allowed to find a bed for them."

"But you must be pretty full—the website says you have forty-three social workers on staff."

Tania's cell phone beeped. She looked at the screen. "I have a patient in five minutes. She's an outpatient and that's true of about half our

load. We run group therapies as well as one-on-ones with a lot of people in DuPage County."

Tania got to her feet. "If you visit Leydon, tell her everyone here is
rooting for her. Remember, people in comas or with brain damage can
still hear what we say to them! It does them good."

I pulled my photos together. By the time I'd helped Chantal extri-
cate herself from the table, Tania had disappeared into some counsel-
ing room.

Instead of heading for the main entrance, I wandered on down
corridor B until I came to a side door. This led to a recreation area, where
a few people were sitting on the patchy grass, or walking aimlessly
about. A group of children was kicking a soccer ball in the distance. I
wondered if they were inmates, or just waiting while their parents went
to one of Tania's group-therapy sessions.

The forensic wing, a few hundred yards to my right, was surrounded
by the triple fences of all prisons. When I walked over to look at it, a
guard surged forward to demand my business.

"I'm a colleague of Miles Wuchnik. I'm trying to find the orderly he
was talking to last month. Before he was killed, you know." I pulled out
one of my pictures of Wuchnik and held it up to the gate, with a twenty
beneath my thumb.

The guard looked at the photo, and then looked beyond me. "We don't
give out any confidential information here, young lady. Anyone you
need to talk to, you go through Mr. Waxman in the main building."

I looked behind me. Eric Waxman was standing near the door I'd
just come out of with a woman and another man, who looked a bit like
David Niven, if Niven had just had an attack of reflux. The guard saw
them; they apparently had enough authority that the guard didn't think
he should be seen talking to me. Even so, he'd learned some nimble
tricks over the years—the twenty was missing when I tucked the photo
back in my briefcase. I handed him a business card.

"Call me if you think of something nonconfidential you can tell me," I said, before ambling back to the door where the trio was standing.

"What were you doing there?" the Niven look-alike demanded.

"And you are asking because?"

"Because I'm in charge of security for the hospital," he said.

He had that aura, the suit, the tie, but I asked for identification. "This is a mental hospital," I said. "Anyone could impersonate the head of security and fool a stranger like me."

The security chief glared, but the woman laughed. "She's right, Vernon. Show her your ID."

He turned out to be Vernon Mulliner, not David Niven at all. The woman shrugged but held out an ID identifying her as Lisa Cunningham, director of patient services.

Vernon was seriously annoyed by now. His demand that I tell him what I'd been doing at the forensic wing had a real bite to it this time. I gave him a card and repeated what I'd told the guard.

Vernon didn't bother looking at Wuchnik's photo. "Why do you care?"

"I'm tying up loose ends on Mr. Wuchnik's cases," I said. "This is one of them."

"No employee gives out information here," Lisa Cunningham said. "Everyone signs a strict confidentiality agreement, and if they violate it in the slightest, they are terminated instantly."

"Have you fired anyone recently?" I asked her.

"I can't tell you that, Ms."—she looked at my card—"Warshawski. But we all want to know why you're interested in what goes on here at Ruhetal."

"Miles Wuchnik was murdered last Saturday night," I said. "Maybe it didn't make the news out here, but he was found stabbed to death in a cemetery in Chicago."

"Oh, yes, the vampire murder," Cunningham murmured.

"And he was out here when a client of mine was hospitalized. She wanted to know if he was stalking her. I'm talking to the people he talked to."

Cunningham took the photo I'd tried showing Vernon. "I never saw him around the building. Did he check in with you, Vernon?"

Mulliner glanced at it this time but shook his head.

"It's time you left," Eric Waxman said to me, his mustache handle-bars puffing out. "We're running a state hospital on a small budget; our staff can't spend time with private eyes who are trying to drum up business."

I didn't argue; if I wanted to return, I didn't want to make my persona completely non grata. Waxman went back inside, but Vernon and the director of patient services walked me to the main entrance.

It was time for the shift change; there was a lot of traffic in and out, and I quickly disappeared from my escort's sight. The queue to the exit was slow; I waited a good ten minutes before I eased back onto Ther-busch Road. Before heading back to Chicago, I made a circuit of the hospital, looking for any breaches in the fences around the forensic wing. However little they spent on the grass, the state did a good job of keeping their razor wire in good shape. I didn't see any place where I might slip through.

The shift change meant it was also the start of the evening rush hour. Since the city-bound expressways were glue, I turned south toward Palos, where Wuchnik's ex-wife, Sandra, now lived.

She had just gotten home herself when I pulled into the cul-de-sac where she lived with her second husband. She came to the door still holding her handbag, a little girl of about four clinging to her pant legs. She was a heavy-set woman whose cheerful smile disappeared when I explained that I was investigating her ex-husband's death.

"Oh, Miles! I was sorry to read about his murder, of course I was, but he was a dreary, depressing man who dragged me down with him. He didn't want children, I don't think he even wanted me. The only person he seemed to care about was his sister, Iva, and she was just as dreary as he was. When I learned he'd made her the beneficiary of his 401K instead of me, that was when I found a good divorce lawyer and took a hike. And met my new husband, and got my little precious here, right, sugar?"

She bent over to hug the little girl, who was trying to fill her in on the day's activities. These involved going with Gram to the park, making a bear out of Play-Doh, and getting an ice cream.

"So you hadn't heard from him lately?" I tried to get part of her mind back to her ex. "He wouldn't have talked to you about his current investigations?"

She shook her head: she hadn't heard from him since the divorce. "And frankly, miss, if I was you I wouldn't bother. Miles had these big vague schemes that never went anywhere. In fact, he did really creepy things, like listen in on people's phone conversations. As far as I'm concerned, that's just dead wrong. Which I told him more than once. It wouldn't surprise me if someone caught him eavesdropping and let him have it."

There was definitely food for thought in that commentary. As I crept along the Eisenhower, I wondered who had been furious enough over Miles's eavesdropping to murder the detective, and then ransack his home and his car to make sure all traces of his investigations were obliterated. Was it anyone connected to Wuchnik's tour of the locked wing?

Leydon had managed to get into the forensic unit, and Wuchnik had been talking to one of the orderlies. What did the two of them know that I didn't? What magical skills had Leydon possessed to breach the security there?

I had reached the grim row of Cook County detention buildings, block after block encased in the same triple fencing that had surrounded Ruhetal's forensic wing. Guard towers on top. It looked like the German prison camp in *Stalag 17*.

When I'd been a Cook County public defender, you could trade money or drugs or sex with many of the guards for access or power, and the same was probably true at Ruhetal. The guard had taken my money, and he might even have given me access if the bosses hadn't appeared. I didn't want to think of Leydon having sex with him, but even if she had, what was on the other side of that gate that she wanted that badly?

"You always were smarter than me, babe," I murmured. "Smarter and nimbler."

Saying the words out loud reminded me of the social worker's advice, that Leydon needed to hear her friends speak to her. I turned onto Roosevelt Road and made my way east and south to the University of Chicago hospitals. Leydon was still in intensive care. I said I was her sister, which was true enough in the broadest sense of the word.

The ward head clucked her tongue. "We wondered when her family would show up. ICU is hard on people; they need love, they need to know they're not forgotten."

She helped me encase myself in a protective shield—Leydon's skull was open; they couldn't risk my transferring any germs. When I got into the unit, I found it hard to look at her, with her head shrouded and the shunt sticking out the side, but I took her hand in my own latex-gloved one and gently massaged her fingers.

"I don't think Wuchnik was following you, Leydon," I said when we were alone. "You just kept running into him. Did you see him in the forensic wing? Was that what made you nervy? You'd seen him in the general population wing and then over in the forensic building. Or did you follow him there and try to confront him?"

That was possible. If Wuchnik had bribed a guard to let him into the forensic wing, Leydon could have—and would have—run after him to demand his business.

I wanted to believe that her expression was changing, that she was following what I was saying and was trying to offer a comment of her own. I pressed my fingers against her palm.

"You worked out something that he wanted to know, and you told him the clue lay in that Bible verse, 'In death they were not divided.' Was someone in the prison wing because he murdered his father, or his own son, or a queer lover?

"Babe, I wish you weren't so brilliant. I wish you just said what was going on, beginning, middle, end. I could follow you then, but it's like all those classes we took together—you always saw where the case was going and danced to the conclusion. I had to put my head down and work it out one step at a time. You were a greyhound, I was a Newfoundland."

At the end of fifteen minutes, the nurse took me away. "Try to come back. I know it's painful to see her like this, and it's difficult to put on all the gear, but you being here will do her good, believe me."

When I got back onto Lake Shore Drive, heading north toward home, I knew I wasn't in the mood for solitude, but I wasn't up to an evening with Mr. Contreras. I drove to the Golden Glow, the bar near the Board of Trade owned by my friend Sal Barthele. The traders had finished their postpartum gulping. Only a handful of dedicated drinkers, with a sprinkling of local residents, sat at her mahogany horseshoe bar.

I persuaded Sal to turn the Glow over to Erica, her senior bartender, and come out with me for a meal. We went to a quiet restaurant in the west Loop, and ate a civilized dinner. Sal knew Leydon, and she shared my sadness over the trajectory of Leydon's life.

Even while I was relaxing with Sal, in the back of my mind I continued to fret about what I'd learned at Ruhetal today, enough that I looked up some of the players when I got home. Although Tania Metzger, Leydon's social worker, had seemed like a level person, I wondered what swings in fortune had moved her family from running Ruhetal to working there.

I did a search on Metzger through LifeStory. What if she had taken a job at the hospital to get back at the people who she imagined had wrested control of the hospital from her family?

Just because Eric Waxman and his waxed mustache had rubbed me the wrong way, I requested information on him, as well as on the woman who was head of patient services, and on the director of security.

The Metzger family's control of the hospital had ended when German funds dried up in the mid-thirties. LifeStory couldn't tell me what her grandparents had done next, but her parents had served as missionaries in Korea for an Evangelical church. I lifted my brows: Metzger had grown up in Korea and apparently was fluent in the language. That was quite an accomplishment but not one that made you think of revenge fantasies, although it did explain her hobby—Korean drumming and dancing.

Social workers don't earn extravagant salaries. Metzger had bought a small ranch house in Forest Park, one of the suburbs close to Chicago's western border. That seemed to be the limit of her assets, along with a CD for twenty-five thousand left to her by her grandparents.

The administrators all made better money, of course, and spent it in flashier ways as well. The woman who directed patient services liked to take spa vacations in Mexico, Eric Waxman belonged to two very pricey golf clubs, and Vernon Mulliner, the head of security, had just moved into a five-million-dollar home in Naperville. Six bedrooms and seven baths—the extra one was attached to the pool—might offer just enough space for Mulliner, his wife, and their two teenage children.

I watched a slideshow of twenty photographs of the house. It was huge, and ugly in a way that was embarrassing—the dining room appeared to be a Disney version of a European wine cellar, and the bedrooms had vaulted ceilings covered in paintings that looked, at least in the slideshow, like bad Fragonards.

I imagined a blackmailer who threatened to divulge Mulliner's lack of taste to the Ruhetal management. More likely, someone who spent that much money on something that garish bragged about it. What really interested me was where he'd gotten the money to buy such a monstrosity. LifeStory didn't show him inheriting a windfall, and he wasn't over his head in debt.

Jake called while I was looking at the financial reports on the other administrators, just to say that he'd arrived safely, the place was beautiful, and he couldn't wait for me to see it. It felt good to be missed, and I got a solid night's sleep for a change.

22. WADE'S WORLD

MY COUSIN PHONED THE NEXT MORNING AS I WAS DRIVING back from the lake with the dogs.

"Vic, I think I'm in trouble at work."

I pulled over to the curb and put on my flashers. "I thought they gave you a big vote of confidence after that riot or whatever it was two days ago."

"Vic, didn't you see the paper yesterday? You know how I said Murray called me about the attack on me and Kira and Arielle? I think, I mean, I know I shouldn't have talked to a reporter without clearing it with my boss, but he's a friend of yours, so I didn't think he'd use what I said—but now I just had a message from Julia Salanter. *She* wants to see me. What should I say to her?"

"I didn't read yesterday's paper, so I don't know how bad the damage is, but tell her what you just told me. Tell her she can call me if she wants to talk about Murray further. If he abused his personal relationship with me, well, I'm going home; I'll read the paper. I can't do anything until I see what he said. Call me after you've seen Julia."

I hotfooted it home with the dogs and left them in the backyard while I ran up to my place and found yesterday's paper. I'd tucked it into my briefcase but hadn't remembered to read it.

The protest at the Malina Foundation was inside, in the *MetroBeat* segment. Time was when the local news had its own ten-page section, but that was before Harold Weekes and Global's top brass decided to turn the *Star* into a version of *My Weekly Reader*. All the national and international bureaus had been closed; any major news came from Reuters or the AP and was trimmed down to a bite-sized paragraph that wouldn't tax the brain of the texting generation. The front page looked as though it was the inside of a celebrity magazine.

Only my waning loyalty to Murray kept me as a subscriber—a loyalty that waned down near zero when I read his story on the mêlée at the Malina Foundation. After a brief paragraph about the violence, which was described as a "demonstration," Murray turned to Petra.

> *Petra Warshawski is a cousin of Chicago's well-known private eye, V. I. Warshawski. Petra, who's been leading book groups for the Malina Foundation that focus on the popular vampire series* Carmilla: Queen of the Night, *seems to have been a special target of the protesters. It was girls in Petra's group who were with another private eye, Miles Wuchnik, when he was murdered vampire-style in Mount Moriah cemetery on Saturday night. Nia Durango, daughter of U.S. Senate candidate Sophy Durango, was part of the graveyard group, as was Arielle Zitter, granddaughter of billionaire trader Chaim Salanter, who is advising Durango's campaign.*
>
> *Petra Warshawski refused to comment on the connection between Nia or Sophy Durango and the vampire murder. She also denies any connection between her book group and Wuchnik's death, or the* Carmilla *series and the demonstration outside Malina's Van Buren Street headquarters. Petra agreed that if the foundation was harboring illegal immigrants they were in violation of the law.*

*She added that even if they were breaking the law, that was no
reason to throw rocks or eggs at her and her girls.*

When people say they see red, it's because a mist of blood covers the
eyes and coats everything they look at. I returned the paper to my
briefcase. I took just enough time to wash the sand out of my hair, then
flung on the first clothes I picked up from the chair in my bedroom. I
was so angry on the drive downtown, it was a miracle I didn't smash
into anyone else.

I found a meter around the corner from the *Star*'s building on Kinzie
and Canal. One of Global's economizing measures had been to close
down the *Star*'s beaux arts building in the Loop and to move the reporting and editorial staff out to the press building along the Chicago
River. Given the four-hundred-million-dollar price tag for Global's corporate headquarters on Wacker, I suppose every penny saved on investigative journalism was essential; through my haze of anger I felt a brief
twinge of sympathy for Murray, moved into this dingy building in the
shadow of the rail yards and expressways.

The twinge was fleeting, but it helped keep the fury out of my voice
when I demanded a meeting with him. When the security guard asked
for my name and business, I said I was one of Murray's street sources,
and that I preferred not to give my name.

The guard told me to wait; "Mr. Ryerson" would be right out. He
waved a vague arm toward a long bench near the front door, but it was
covered with dust. I paced up and down the sidewalk outside the front
door until Murray showed.

He was startled to see me, but he tried for a light touch. "The mighty
goddess is coming down from Mount Olympus to meet and greet the
mortals?"

"If I were a goddess, you would be watching your family jewels fry
on the sidewalk in front of your eyes." I pulled the paper out of my

briefcase. "Your report of your conversation with Petra didn't cross a line, it drove right over a median strip into oncoming traffic."

Murray flushed. "I thought you didn't do bodyguard or babysitting work. You Petra's publicist? She have to clear everything she says in public with you first?"

"What happens in that damned 'huddle' in the morning?" I said. "Did Harold Weekes call you and say, 'Global's official line is to make it sound as if Sophy Durango and Julia Salanter's daughters brought Miles Wuchnik to the cemetery, therefore, if you write anything connected with the Malina Foundation, ignore all other issues and twist the story to be about Malina girls in the cemetery?'"

"The story isn't about the book group. It's about girls who want to be vampires—that brings people to TV and even to the printed word."

"And that's a reason to lie?"

"You *are* on Mount Olympus." Murray was now as angry as I was. "What 'lies' are you talking about?"

"Those girls were not with Miles Wuchnik when he died."

"What? They were in the south of France? I thought they were prancing right in front of him."

"But they didn't know he was there," I shouted.

"Sez you! And since when do I take your word, oh, Queen of Crime, instead of checking it out?"

A trio of *Star* employees came outside to smoke. They moved a few feet up the sidewalk from us but stayed in earshot, making no secret of their interest. Murray and I were both too angry to care.

"Oh. You've checked it out, and Wuchnik's ghost came back and said, 'Yes, I brought Nia and Arielle and their girlfriends to Mount Moriah with me?' Were they also the ones who tossed his apartment?"

"Tossed his apartment?" Murray echoed. "When did that happen?"

The anger had gone out of his face, but I was still furious. "Don't ask me—check it out for yourself."

I turned to leave, but Murray grabbed my arm. "Warshawski, you can't go marching out of here in the middle of this conversation. When did it happen?"

"Why would you believe my answer if I gave it? You've accused me of lying, you've put my cousin's job at risk by implying that she knows Malina is harboring illegal immigrants—"

Murray put both hands on my shoulders. "Vic. Come inside and talk to me before we need a federal mediator."

Still smoldering, I followed him into the old press building and up a flight of metal stairs to the newsroom. The trio of smokers seemed to sigh with disappointment as we left.

Back when the old presses ran here, they took up the equivalent of two stories. Global had gutted the building, saving one of the presses as a sort of museum piece. They'd installed two floors of offices and cubicles, but they'd left an opening at the north end, with a catwalk where you could look down at the heirloom press.

To do the company justice, despite the building's seedy exterior, they hadn't stinted on the interior. Not that they'd spent the bucks they'd given to furnishing Global One, where all the TV operations were housed, but the computers and the networking system were modern, sleek, and fast.

Flat-screen monitors on the walls showed competing networks as well as GEN's own local and national output. GEN's national monitor was on commercial break; the local station was showing a fire at a South Chicago factory. On the CNN screen, rioters in Ivory Coast were throwing things at soldiers. On yet another monitor, I could see the pulsing green of worldwide stock indices. As I watched, the Dow went down and the fire turned to a commercial for an anti-anxiety drug.

I was turning to follow Murray to his cubicle when Wade Lawlor appeared on the screen that was airing GEN's national programs. And in a pop-up window to his left, I saw my own face.

I was so stunned that I stopped where I was. "How do I turn up the sound on this thing?" I called out.

Murray was out of earshot, but the smokers had come up the stairs behind me. One of them handed me a set of earphones and asked which channel I wanted to listen to.

"Lawlor," I said grimly.

He looked from the screen to me and did a double take. "That's you, isn't it?"

"I believe it is, and I'd like to know what the King of Slime is saying."

The smoker pushed a button on the earphone control, and Wade Lawlor's voice filled my head.

"I met Warshawski at my tenth-anniversary party last Saturday. I thought she was just a friend and collaborator of one of my colleagues on the print side, Murray Ryerson, but I see now her mission is to bring illegal aliens into this country and take jobs away from hardworking Americans like you and me. She's teamed up with our own favorite Communist, *Chame* Salanter, to protect illegals at the Malign Foundation."

A cartoon picture of the Malina Foundation building covered in oozing sores appeared on the screen. The camera zoomed in on the pustules. Each had a little message: *Communists*; *Nazis*; *illegals*; *drugs*; *disease*; *crime*.

"The billionaire invited her to dinner at his Gold Coast club, which must be where they hatched their plot. Of course, Warshawski's own mother was an illegal, just like Salanter, so I guess she knows what she's talking about."

Salanter and I had been Photoshopped to appear arm in arm on the steps of the Parterre Club. How had Lawlor known we were there? I didn't have time to worry about that little question; he was moving on to his main attack, his voice like syrup mixed with acid.

"Warshawski has a reputation as a private eye, just like the guy she found dead in a cemetery last Saturday night. I was celebrating my tenth anniversary of being able to bring the truth to you, my good friends and loyal listeners, and she was in a cemetery doing—what?

"I've looked into her record. She supports the 'underdog,' so-called. Well, I am sick and tired of bleeding hearts shoring up underdogs."

He leaned forward into the camera, spit flecking his lips. "My own sister was murdered by one of those 'underdogs' when we were teenagers. Magda was seventeen, the most beautiful girl I've ever seen."

The camera gave us a close-up of the tears spilling out of the corners of Lawlor's eyes, and then a photo insert of Magda Lawlor. Like Wade, she had thick black hair, cut in the style that Madonna made popular in the eighties.

"I was three years younger and I adored her. My wife knows however much I love her, I'll never feel as close to any other woman as I did to Magda. They found my sister's body in Tampier Lake. One of these underdogs, these mental incompetents that Warshawski bleeds all over, had murdered her, strangled her, and dumped her in the water, as if she were a used condom. I would have killed him myself if I'd known they wouldn't give him the death penalty. I'll never get over Magda's death, but Warshawski is one of the people who protected her murderer."

I felt as though my legs had turned to cement. Lawlor went on and on, and I stood there taking it.

When a smooth female voice finally said that "*Wade's World* will return after these messages," I couldn't even lift my arms to remove the earphones.

Murray appeared behind me and took the headset away. His face was ashen. "Jesus Christ, V. I.—I had no idea that was on tap."

23. A REPORTER'S LOT IS NOT A HAPPY ONE

The trio of smokers had stayed with us in the hall, and another fifteen or twenty people had drifted out of the newsroom to watch. Someone had turned on the sound so that everyone could hear it. At the commercial break, they turned to look at me with the same expression people have for plague victims: pity mixed with fear that it might be catching.

"He attacked Gabriella," I said to Murray. "He is such a low and loathsome piece of bottom-feeding, scum-sucking garbage that he slandered my mother."

Murray put an arm around me. "He attacked you way worse. Or doesn't that count?"

I tried to smile. "I think it's so shocking I can't quite look at it head-on. This is what Sophy Durango deals with every day. And Chaim Salanter. There must be some way to stop him."

"Second Amendment remedies," someone in the news crowd said. Everyone laughed, that kind of raucous laugh you give as an antidote to shock.

I turned to face the group. "How many of you go to the huddle? Besides Murray, I mean."

After looking around to see if anyone else would speak up, a woman in a miniskirt and leggings said, "There are several huddles. The big one is at Global One. Murray goes to that, and so do the assignment editors—me, Klaus Hellman, and Gavin Aikers. Then the assignment editors have our own huddles with the newsroom teams."

"So what was the official line at Global One when they brought up Malina and Warshawski and so on?" I asked.

"There wasn't a line about you," Murray said. "Of course, Harold Weekes is obsessed by illegal immigrants, and he hates Chaim Salanter, or at any rate is targeting him. But no one said, 'Go after the Warshawski family, including V.I.'s dead mother.'"

The woman in the miniskirt nodded. "They told us to do some digging on Malina, see if we could come up with the foundation's policy on illegals, or find out who the girl with your—is that your daughter in the photo?"

"No. Petra is my cousin." Lawlor's assault had left me exhausted; the words came out slowly.

"They wanted us to find the girl who's with your cousin in the photo," the young woman said.

"And has anyone?" I asked.

The group in the hall exchanged glances, but there were head shakes all around.

"Do you know who she is?" someone else asked.

"Not a clue. But I'll call Petra." I speed-dialed my cousin. "Have you seen Julia? How did it go?"

"I don't know. She didn't fire me, but she chewed me out in a really scary way. I mean, she never raised her voice, or called me names, but she made me feel like I might have jeopardized the whole foundation. I did like you said, told her Murray was your friend and I didn't know he would take what I said and turn it into a story. She called my boss and the two of them talked it over and decided I was just naive, which is better than being unemployed, but gosh, they made me feel like I was a puppy who'd messed on the Persian rug."

"I can call Julia if you don't think that would make things worse." I described the drubbing I'd just taken.

"Just don't say anything that'll get me fired," Petra fretted.

"I have talked to Murray," I said. "We agreed that we all need to be more professional. But I can tell Julia that Harold Weekes, the head of GEN's so-called news division, apparently put out a hit on the foundation in his infamous huddle."

"Huddle?" Petra repeated doubtfully.

"Darling, they used to call them news conferences, but that was when journalists were journalists and looked for news, instead of going on air and in print to destroy people's lives."

Murray looked like another puppy caught on the Persian rug, and I smiled grimly but said to my cousin, "GEN seems to think you know who that kid was next to you in their picture, but I don't think you'd ever seen her before, had you?"

"Vic! You remember Kira Du—"

"That's right, babe. She was a complete stranger, whom you saw being attacked by the mob and pulled to safety. Isn't that right?"

My cousin was silent for a second. "You mean if anyone calls to ask—"

"Is that what happened? You pulled her to safety, and then she ran off in the direction of the Green Line? You didn't get her name?"

"Okay, okay, I get it," Petra said. "You'll tell Julia about, well, what happened at the news thingy? How they decided to target me?"

"Yep," I said. "And if anyone, either Julia or the press, tries to move you to the center of the story, we'll be taking legal action."

When I put my phone away, a man around forty, in a necktie and short-sleeved shirt, said, "That sounds as though you just coached your cousin to lie to the press."

"And you would be?"

"Gavin Aikers," Murray supplied. "He's the city desk assignment editor."

"Mr. Aikers, I don't think anyone at GEN can get more hysterical and lie-filled than they already are, but by all means, call Harold Weekes and tell him to bring it up at the next cuddle."

"Huddle," Aikers corrected.

"I thought it was the meeting where you cuddled each other and said what a swell job of creating an alternate reality you were doing. Maybe it's the muddle."

Murray put a hand on my shoulder. "Vic, let's go somewhere private before you actually slug someone. I don't think you have enough liability insurance to cover the damages."

I let him guide me out of the viewing area. Behind us I could hear Gavin Aikers telling his staff they had work to do, they couldn't watch TV all day. Reporters began to trickle in behind us.

Murray took me to his cubicle, which wasn't exactly private space, but no one was at any of the closest desks. "Vic, I'm sorry. The text in my story about Petra and the Malina Foundation got edited in rewrite. If you'd like to see the original as I posted it, I'll show you."

His face was still pale, making his freckles and blue eyes stand out as vivid splashes of color in his face. I noticed that his red hair was streaked with gray. So much time had passed since he and I worked on our first story together, corruption in the Knifegrinders union. We not only hadn't cleaned up the city, we hadn't even made a dent. Instead, fraud had spread along every corridor of American life and had infected the newsroom.

"I'll take your word for it. But if you call Petra again, I want her to hang up on you. As soon as she says anything, it'll go into Weekes's distortion machine and come out as a claim that she caused the tsunami that hit Japan."

"I won't call her." Murray held up three fingers, the scout salute.

The young woman in leggings came over to his cubicle with mugs. "Hot tea. It's better than our machine coffee and maybe it'll help calm you down."

I accepted the mug meekly.

"I'm Luana Giorgini—in charge of froth. You know, books, music, comics, the stuff that the paper wants to edge out. Every now and then they turn movies or videos over to me."

"Luana is my only spiritual ally on the editorial side," Murray added.

"That's why I'm in charge of froth." Her small round face didn't change expression, but Murray laughed.

"You can say anything to Luana that you say to me."

"Which isn't much right now," I said, lips tight.

"Tell me about Wuchnik's place being tossed," Murray said.

"Someone had been through it with a sieve." I described the condition of Wuchnik's apartment. "They'd broken into his car, too. The one thing I found was his mileage log—whoever cleaned out his car must have dropped it in the dark. I got the log from a couple of kids."

Murray recovered his color. "Let's see it, Warshawski."

"There's nothing to see," I said. "He tells where he's going but not who he's going to see, or who hired him."

In the interest of restoring harmony, though, I pulled the photocopied log out of my briefcase and showed it to Luana and Murray. I didn't point out my special interest in Ruhetal—Murray had a very deep hole to climb out of before I trusted him with much again.

Murray and Luana bent over the photocopies. I leaned back, sipping my tea and reading the cartoons and notices Murray had pinned to the corkboard on his cubicle walls. He had all the predictable *Dilbert* strips, along with *Doonesbury*'s Roland Hedley's spurious reporting.

One wall was devoted to his scrapped series on mental illness, *Madness in the Midwest*. I leaned forward to read the proposal, which began with nineteenth-century farm women going mad from the isolation of their lives and burning down their farmhouses with themselves and their families locked inside.

He'd also posted the e-mail chain that ended with Weekes telling him that the series was "too narrow, too downbeat for our demographic."

Murray looked up and saw what I was reading. "Oh, yes. My dead series. I can't quite let it go."

He ripped the e-mail from the corkboard and handed it to me. It looked like a good story to me, starting and ending with the veterans on the streets: in 2001, they included 150,000 survivors of Vietnam. In 2010, those numbers had been swelled by 9,000 vets from Iraq and Afghanistan.

In between, Murray had proposed a look at mental health institutions like Ruhetal. Who got treated, who got turned away, who paid the bills. And his segment on "not guilty by reason of mental impairment": he'd suggested five names to Weekes, three at Ruhetal, two at Elgin. "All these people have been on locked wards for more than twenty years," he'd written the head of GEN's news division. "We're looking at incarceration with no end date and no judicial oversight. Why isn't this worth a story?"

And Weekes had written back, "Because everyone is glad to see these scum stay locked up. Too bad we can't do that with the rest of our murderers."

Murray had written, "Sounds like China. Or Iran."

Not too surprising that Weekes had canceled the series.

"Did you figure out why he canceled?" I asked. "Was it because of your Iran comment?"

"Nah. He'd already made up his mind by then. He was never very interested, but it was either the segment on homeless Iraq vets—GEN is still pounding their war drums—or the forensic-wing stuff. He doesn't think mentally ill criminals deserve a sympathetic hearing—he made that clear in the huddle." Murray scowled in remembered resentment.

"Lawlor added some choice sarcasm. It was like being back in eighth-grade gym, with the coach egging the rest of the guys on to bully kids like me who didn't play football."

I couldn't believe I was feeling sorry for Murray, working in that poisonous environment, only half an hour after I'd been ready to kill him.

"By the way," I said, "you told me on Sunday that Wuchnik did a lot of work for my ex's firm. How did you know that?"

"Who's your ex?" Luana demanded.

"Richard Yarborough, at Crawford, Mead."

"Just think—if you'd stayed with him, you'd have the capital to start a newspaper, or an international security firm. You wouldn't have to deal with people like us," Murray said.

I smiled sourly. "I never thought there was an upside to my marriage, but you're making it sound attractive. Anyway, how did you know about Wuchnik and Crawford, Mead?"

"It came up in Sunday's extra-alarm huddle, I think," Murray frowned in an effort to remember. "Weekes must have told us, because it's not something I knew on my own. Luana?"

She shook her head. "I was out sailing with my brother and his partner on Sunday. I didn't get the news until later and then all I was supposed to do was a feature on the *Carmilla* books and why tweens all over the world love them so much."

"If it's true, I can't figure out why Crawford, Mead use him," Murray said. "I've called around, and he was a two-bit kind of guy. Solo shop, but not the kind of sophisticated work you do, Warshawski. If you wanted private information on someone, he got it for you, sometimes by pretty—well, unorthodox methods is the charitable spin."

"So if you were trying to undermine someone in court and you wanted the goods on their fetish for sleeping with goats, he'd find that out? That kind of thing?"

Murray nodded.

"That also seems beneath Crawford, Mead's dignity," I said, "but I'll check in with Dick. Maybe that will cheer me up, watching his face, although the tea helped. Thanks, Luana."

Back in my car, away from the need to keep up a public face, I felt so pummeled that I dozed off behind the wheel. A passing ticket writer rapping on my windshield woke me. She pointed at my parking receipt, which had expired three minutes ago. I was grateful that she hadn't issued the ticket—the city is so cash-hungry that many of the enforcers wouldn't have cut me the slack.

I wanted to go to my ex-husband's law firm, but not in this condition. I drove to my office, where I fell instantly asleep on the daybed in my back room.

24. TALKING TO THE EX. SIGH.

WHEN I GOT UP AGAIN, IT WAS A SHOCK TO OPEN THE PHONE log on my computer: I had more than fifty messages from clients and friends who had seen Lawlor's tirade. Some commiserated, but others worried that being on *Wade's World*'s hit list would make me unreliable as a detective. *Give us a call; we want to know your mind is on the job* was the gist of about fifteen messages. At the same time, to my astonishment, simply being mentioned by Wade Lawlor made me interesting to other people. I had queries from various non-GEN media outlets, wanting interviews, along with a good half dozen potential new clients. Maybe I'd have to share their retainers with Lawlor.

I buckled down and sent e-mails, made calls, and organized interviews with a couple of local television stations. All the time that I was reassuring clients of my undying commitment to their needs, the back of my mind was thinking about Lawlor's harangue. Who had he talked to about my mother? He'd said Gabriella came here as an illegal alien, but how had he known to ask about her? How had he known her memory was so sacred to me?

Gabriella had come to America as a refugee during the Second World

War. The drama of her escape was what I always thought about, not whether she'd had the right papers on her when she arrived. She had been hiding with her father in the hills northeast of Siena when one of her music teachers arranged passage for her on a ship bound for Cuba. My mother had never seen her father again, nor her only brother, who'd been fighting with a group of partisans in the north.

My grandmother's sister Rosa had grudgingly given my mother a place to stay in Chicago, but I'd never asked Gabriella how she made the journey from Cuba to the States. Wade Lawlor apparently had made discovering that his business. It was frightening to think what a deep and wide network of spies Lawlor could call on, to get information that was almost seventy years old.

In the middle of my fretting, I dimly realized that Lawlor could have made it up, that he'd learned my mother was an immigrant and decided to say she was illegal. He fabricated so much of what he screeched on the airwaves that when he hit home, he might only have made a lucky guess.

I had to remind myself that his real goal had been to attack me, not my mother. Why, though? I'd been a little rude at his anniversary bash on Saturday. Was his ego so inflated that he went after anyone who was sarcastic to him?

When I'd cleared my inbox, I called my lawyer, Freeman Carter, to tell him about Lawlor's attack. He'd heard about it already.

"All week, Lotty and Max and I have been fuming over why Chaim Salanter doesn't sue him for slander," I said. "Now that he's assaulting me, I'd like to explore the possibility of suing him myself."

There was a long silence at the other end of the line. "I was just reading the online transcript of Lawlor's remarks about you," Freeman explained. "I'm no expert on L and S law, but I don't think his broadcast meets the requirement for slander. He was offensive, but he doesn't accuse you of anything worse than being a liberal, which you are."

"But he attacked Gabriella," I protested.

"Vic, no one should make a decision about a lawsuit when they're in the heat of strong emotion. You know that as well as I do. I can talk to someone I know who does libel and slander law, but if you sue, your legal fees and court costs could go to half a million. Since Lawlor has some of the deepest pockets in America, he could keep a suit going until you were in so deep you'd have to scrub toilets in Soldier Field to pay your bills."

My face contorted into a horrible scowl, as if looking like a gargoyle could somehow menace Wade Lawlor. Freeman was right. Which made it all the more infuriating that the Salanters, with pockets as deep as the Grand Canyon, wouldn't take on Lawlor and GEN.

"Out of curiosity, what did you do to get on Lawlor's radar at all?" Freeman asked.

"I tweaked him a little at his anniversary party, but I didn't threaten him."

"If you show him you care, he'll sink his teeth deeper into your calf. He's like any other bully. If he sees you're not paying attention, he'll go away fast enough."

"That's exactly what Chaim Salanter and his daughter say, but Lawlor, and Helen Kendrick, for that matter, keep gunning for both Salanter and for the Malina Foundation."

"Don't do anything rash before next Tuesday," Freeman said dryly. "I'm going to Martha's Vineyard for a long weekend and I don't want to have to find someone to post emergency bail for you."

I promised I wouldn't do anything either reckless or criminal in the next four days, but I hung up with a little resentment. It wasn't Freeman's fault that people like me gave him a seven-figure income that allowed him to lease a plane for weekend jetaways, but I still wished I could get ahead of the game for once. I was tired of racing around in Chicago's hot sticky heat. Big security firms bill their clients the same way lawyers like Freeman do—at four hundred an hour and up, but solo ops like me or Miles Wuchnik don't command those kinds of fees.

One of my clients—mercifully, not one who'd been on my case about being a feature in *Wade's World*—had once offered me the use of her Michigan weekend retreat. When I called, she told me her place was free this weekend. Not only that, I was welcome to bring the dogs. When I got home, I invited my neighbor to join us. Mr. Contreras was delighted; he packed a hamper with enough provisions to keep us through Labor Day and we set off early enough the next morning to avoid the backups on the roads.

We spent three days swimming, hiking, and rebuilding our relationship while sitting around my client's gas-fueled barbecue grill. Mitch had a glorious time rolling in the rotting buffalo fish on the beach, but we just poured shampoo on him and sent him into the lake. I kept in touch with clients by text but resolutely stayed away from the television. We came home late Sunday, tired but refreshed. No emergency calls from my cousin, no horses' heads in my bed. All good.

Monday morning I went early to the cleaners to pick up my good clothes. My lovely scarlet frock would never be the same. They'd done their best, but they couldn't get out the grass stains without tearing the delicate silk.

"It's just a dress," I scolded myself for wanting to cry. It may be, as the Romans said, that clothes make the man, but for women, or at least for this woman, clothes are a projection of the self: I felt personally damaged.

At least the gold cotton dress had come out okay: you couldn't see the blood unless you stuck your nose into the fabric. I couldn't imagine Dick doing that, so I slipped it on for my trip to his office.

While I did my makeup, I gave in to temptation and looked up the new *Wade's World* segments on YouTube. He'd attacked Sophy Durango and Chaim Salanter, along with his usual venom about filthy immigrants and vile health-care reform. Nothing new about me. Maybe I'd been a one-day filler on his show.

I drove to my office and rode the L into the Loop, getting off at Wells and Lake, near the Chicago River. My ex-husband's firm occupied seventeen floors of the Grommet Building, one of those glass towers that make you think of Darth Vader—the glass façade was black and all you could see was the reflection of the skyline and the clouds, not any signs of life within.

Crawford, Mead had changed offices since the end of my marriage; this was my first trip to their new headquarters. When I got off at the elevator at the fifty-second floor, I was glad I'd taken the trouble to pick up my dress, do makeup, and so on. I felt cool and professional, as if I belonged in a space that proclaimed, *We bill at a thousand dollars an hour and we're proud of it.*

The reception area, decorated in soft greens and golds, had several tasteful pieces of sculpture strewn about, while the two women behind the marble counter were as glossy as the glass on the building.

I handed my card to one of the receptionists. No, I agreed, or perhaps stipulated, I didn't have an appointment, but Mr. Yarborough and I were old friends; I had a quick question for him.

Dick was in a meeting, naturally enough, but I had to wait only twenty minutes before he strolled into the reception area. His greeting was unenthusiastic. "I have five minutes, Vic. Try not to blow me up in that length of time."

I put my fingers on his jacket sleeve and batted my eyelashes. "Why, Richard Yarborough, what a thing to say after all we've meant to each other."

The receptionists looked at each other, eyes widening: my arrival was adding a little excitement to the workday.

Dick's mouth twisted in a reluctant smile. "It's because of what we've meant to each other. What do you want?"

"Information about Miles Wuchnik."

"Miles Wuchnik? Who is—oh, the vampire killer's victim. I don't know anything about the guy, sorry."

He slid his shirt cuff up to check the time. His watch was impressive, covered with gold dials and a revolving star map. Maybe the millennium gen have given up watches because they tell time on their cell phones, but nothing says "I'm important" quite like a handmade timepiece.

"He worked for you, Dick. He was one of your firm's investigators. Surely that was on your 'important news affecting Crawford clients' report when you logged on last Monday morning."

Dick turned to the receptionists. "Celeste, look up Wuchnik—spell it for me, Vic."

He could have said please, but it was too late to teach him now.

Celeste shook her head. "Mr. Yarborough, I checked when I heard he was dead. He was freelance, mostly working on projects for Eloise Napier, but sometimes for Mr. Ormond."

Dick turned back to me. "If I say we don't know anything, you'll just hack into my firm's computers, or disguise yourself as an electrician and break into our vault, so let's settle this now. Celeste, get Ms. Napier and Mr. Ormond to meet us in conference room J for ten minutes."

Dick had Celeste escort me to conference room J, another tribute to the firm's billable hours. Webcams were mounted at several stations around the table for ease of teleconferencing, a flat-screen TV took the place of old-fashioned dry-erase boards, and a large oil painting of a woodland scene dominated the facing wall.

The room overlooked the Chicago River. Dick followed me in as I was watching the drawbridges go up for a sailboat. He offered me a drink from a collection on a wood trolley in a corner. In fact, he was more solicitous than I ever remembered him being during our marriage, a fact that made me eye him thoughtfully.

"You remember Leydon Ashford?" I asked, sipping a glass of grapefruit juice.

"That's right: you two were tight in law school. Sewall and I have worked on civic committees together; she hasn't aged well."

"Sewall didn't look too good when I saw him last week," I said. "His sister had just been carted off to the hospital with her head bashed in, and all he cared about was his car keys."

Dick hadn't heard about Leydon's accident. He was appropriately shocked but added, "The two of you brought out the worst in me when you were together. It wouldn't surprise me if you threw Sewall off balance."

"Who brings out the best in you?" I asked.

The question startled him, but he was saved from answering by the arrival of his colleagues. Eloise Napier, very blond, with a good coating of cosmetics covering any signs of age, held out a hand heavily weighted by gold bracelets. More gold at her ears and throat, and the wheat-colored suit in slubbed rayon, made her look like a giant daffodil. Only her eyes, a cold, shrewd hazel, belied the appearance of a Gold Coast lady who lunched. I noticed she sported one of those jeweled American flags topped by an ear of corn worn by Helen Kendrick supporters.

Louis Ormond looked like a quiet middle-aged rodent next to Napier, his thinning gray hair combed back behind his ears, making his long beak of a nose appear even longer.

The meeting was short, to the point, or really, to no point. Of course all client affairs were confidential, Eloise Napier explained, so she could neither confirm nor deny that Miles Wuchnik had worked on any cases for her clients. If I was a cop with a court order it might be a different story, but even then, privilege, liability, confidentiality, couldn't promise there'd ever be a time when Wuchnik's workload could be disclosed.

I smiled, to help me keep my temper: the last thing I needed was for Dick to see me get angry. "Was he working for one of your clients—of course, unspecified—when he went to the cemetery on Saturday night?"

Napier and Ormond exchanged glances with Dick. "We have no idea why he was there," Eloise spoke for the trio. "We understand that Sophy Durango's daughter was there, and we've heard talk that Durango might have had an assignation with the dead man."

"Yes, I've heard that talk, too, but only in one place: on Helen Kendrick's program on GEN. Dick, I don't know your colleagues, but I know you're too smart to repeat actionable lies in public."

Spots of real color burned beneath the rouge on Napier's cheeks. "Helen is a good friend. I've known her for years, and I can assure you that she doesn't make up stories like that unless she has reason to believe they're true."

"From messages she gets in her fillings?" I asked.

Ormond sucked in an audible breath, while Dick performed one of those eye-rolling routines spouses do when their exes are unusually obnoxious. Napier's glare could have peeled off my own makeup.

"Is Crawford the official law firm of the Kendrick campaign?" I asked Dick.

He shook his head. "We don't take political positions as a firm. Individual attorneys, of course, may work for specific politicians, or hold fund-raisers for them."

"So Eloise advises Kendrick." I waved a hand toward Napier's American flag pin. "Wuchnik might have gone to the cemetery to do something for Kendrick."

"I can assure you that did not happen. But if you don't believe me, you can listen to the messages in your own fillings," Eloise said.

I laughed, hoping it would calm the waves if she saw I could take heat as well as dish it out. "You're right—I shouldn't have said what I did. Let's see if we can agree on one or two things, even if we disagree on Helen Kendrick's political views.

"The medical examiner says Wuchnik was hit on the head and then laid on the tomb, where someone pounded the rebar through his chest—that was what killed him, but he was unconscious, or barely conscious, when he died. No defensive wounds on the hands, no signs of a struggle."

"We agree on that?" Eloise Napier said spitefully. Okay, the waves weren't calm yet.

"Please talk to Dr. Vishnikov over at County yourself; you don't need to take my word that those were his findings."

I paused for a moment, to give her a chance either to call Vishnikov or to challenge me further, but she seemed willing to go forward.

"Wuchnik's mileage log tells us that he went to Ruhetal five times between Memorial Day and July Fourth." I handed out photocopies of the log—the original I'd moved from my apartment to my big office safe.

Dick didn't bother to look at his copy, but Napier grabbed hers with an eagerness that told its own story. When she'd studied it, she demanded to see the rest of the log.

"That's the only part of it I have. And it's the only remaining piece of his documents—someone cleaned out his condo within a day of his murder. Computer, files, the works." I watched Eloise as I spoke; maybe I imagined it, but she seemed to breathe a little sigh of relief on hearing that all Wuchnik's papers were gone.

"I was hoping you might know about his trips to Ruhetal," I said. "The dates—do they correspond to anything he was working on for you?"

"Did he leave a code for who the clients were?" Ormond asked.

I shook my head.

"Then why are you bothering us?" Napier asked.

"Oh, that—apparently the Global Entertainment honchos announced it in the puddle, or whatever they call their news briefing. They said Wuchnik worked for Crawford, Mead."

The room was quiet for a beat, while Ormond and Napier both looked at Dick. He pushed himself back from the table.

"Right, Vic, it's where you came in. He wasn't on our payroll. Lou and Eloise hired him sometimes, but only as an independent contractor. They don't know anything about his trips to Ruhetal. We were not his only clients, right, Eloise?"

"No, indeed." She took her cue a little breathlessly. "Louis and I often had to wait several days before he could fit us in."

Dick again looked ostentatiously at his wrist: he was a busy man with a lot of demands on his time. I was close enough that I could see a glass panel that showed the works moving in little circles. A separate circle showed the time. "F.P.Journe, Invenit et Fecit" was engraved across the bottom.

The meeting was over. I exchanged a few joking comments with Dick, just to make his colleagues think we were closer than we were, but I left more puzzled than when I came. I didn't know about Louis Ormond, but smart money said that Eloise Napier had a pretty good idea why Miles Wuchnik had visited Ruhetal.

25. IN THE HUDDLE

THE GROMMET BUILDING WAS JUST TWO BLOCKS FROM GLOBAL Entertainment's monster headquarters on the Chicago River. Global One was a chunky building whose architect hadn't been able to decide if he was putting up an amusement park or a Gothic cathedral—the steel frame was encased in concrete after about the fourth story, but the high lobby held an entertainment corner with a merry-go-round, a small putting green, and some giant video screens.

Global One had become such a popular tourist destination that the city had blocked off an entire lane of traffic in front of it for buses and cars to drop off their loads. People signed up for tickets to live tapings of *Wade's World* and other popular shows, for tours of the studios, and for the round-the-clock screenings of Global's archive of movies and TV series. If you had insomnia, you could wander over to the lobby and watch old TV shows at three in the morning.

When I strolled over from Dick's office to take a look, the tourist line was already around the block. To keep the populace from feeling bored or fractious, vendors plied them with food and drink, and the big screens in the lobby showed reruns of *Nerve Center,* a spy drama set at the National Security Agency. Local actors worked the line dressed up as animals from Global's kid show *Gator Under Cover.*

I walked down the stairs to Lower Wacker Drive, where you usually find the service entrances to buildings that front the river. Global's service bay had all kinds of trucks coming and going. I hadn't really thought through what I would do if I went inside. To be honest, I hadn't thought about it at all—I just followed one of the truckers as he went into the loading dock in search of a signature, nodded at the guy checking off items in a load, and got into an elevator. As the doors shut, I heard someone calling to me angrily to get out, I couldn't go inside without a pass.

One thing about makeup and a beautifully cut dress: you look as though you belong in corporate headquarters. I got off the service elevator at the fourth floor, where a knot of employees were waiting at the elevator banks, carrying bags of chips, coffee cups, and other accoutrements of having been on break.

I followed them into a car and interrupted a spirited replay of this morning's project meeting by saying, "I have an appointment with Harold Weekes, but I forgot what floor they said he's on."

The group stared at me in silence—the sheep herd realizing there's an ibex in the mix—and then one woman muttered, "Forty-eight." The group shut down for the remainder of the journey: no one wanted to risk revealing themselves in front of a stranger bound for the head guy's office.

On the forty-eighth floor, a locked glass wall separated me from the executive offices. A woman at a high desk on the far side of it spoke through an intercom, demanding my business.

"V. I. Warshawski to see Harold Weekes," I said.

She worked her phone. "You're not on the calendar. Are you sure you're in the right place?"

"I don't want to bellow private information around the hall," I said, "but everyone at Crawford, Mead is wondering how he knew that Miles Wuchnik worked for them."

"I didn't get those names."

I pulled a business card out of my bag and wrote my message on the back. I felt like an inmate in the lockup, pasting messages to a window, but I held my card against the glass panel for her to read. After hesitating for a moment, she must have decided she felt as stupid as I did; she released the door lock and let me present the card to her in person.

The woman muttered into her headset, listened, pronounced Wuch-nik's and my names with passable accuracy, and finally told me I could be seated, someone would be with me in a minute.

The minute stretched on to twenty-eight, but I couldn't complain: I was unexpected, uninvited. I got out my laptop and logged on to one of my private databases so that I could start some research for an actual paying client; I answered a few e-mails. The Monitor Project blinked to let me know it had something for me.

My furious emotions this morning had made me forget that I'd asked for reports on the people I'd met yesterday at Ruhetal. Eric Waxman, the guy with the handlebar mustache, was badly in debt. He seemed to gamble on sporting events, along with belonging to those expensive golf clubs: he had a bill with a Las Vegas firm that was close to half his annual pay.

Lisa Cunningham, the director of patient services, wasn't paid as well as Waxman, but her husband was a pharmaceutical company exec; they apparently stayed on top of their hefty credit-card and mort-gage bills.

Vernon Mulliner, the security director who'd just moved into his garish mansion, was the only one with a real investment portfolio. Be-sides his house, he had a tidy nest egg, several million dollars. He was a shrewd investor, or his wife was. Or her suburban school district paid its first-grade teachers a handsome bonus. I was annotating the report when an emissary from Harold Weekes arrived.

"Ms. Warshawski? Todd Blakely, Mr. Weekes's personal assistant. He's got a two-minute gap between conference calls coming up soon, when he can talk to you, but he wanted me to find out what you're doing here—he didn't recognize any of the names Amber read from your card." Blakely was a youngish man, in a crisp white shirt and tie, as if he were with the FBI in mid-February instead of an entertainment conglomerate in mid-summer.

I got to my feet. "Crawford, Mead—they're one of Chicago's biggest law firms. Miles Wuchnik—he's the PI who was killed in the cemetery ten days ago. In the news cuddle the morning after Wuchnik's body was found, Mr. Weekes mentioned that Mr. Wuchnik worked for Crawford. All up to speed now?"

Amber, the receptionist, was listening, but Blakely didn't care, or maybe didn't notice, what mere clerical workers did. He led me down one of those lushly carpeted halls to the executive offices at the east end of the floor. I was left in an antechamber with another secretary, who offered me a chair in a group that faced the window. People waiting for Weekes weren't given a TV screen, but the great show of Chicago's river winding through the skyscrapers toward Lake Michigan was entertainment enough.

A pair of binoculars on a glass table in front of me proved irresistible. I watched the sailboats out beyond the breakwater, the gulls swooping down behind the aquarium, and, on the river, the tour boats, where people's sunburned heads appeared startlingly close to me.

When Blakely reappeared, I put the binoculars down reluctantly. Whatever else you could say about Global, they knew what entertained the public.

Blakely had his suit jacket on this time; as he held the door to

Weekes's office open for me, I noticed he had one of Helen Kendrick's corn-flag pins in the lapel.

On the other side of the door, Weekes was bent over a computer screen with Wade Lawlor. Both of them were too busy to look up when we entered, which was just as well: I had time to school my face to keep the fury I felt at seeing Lawlor out of my expression.

Like his PA, Weekes was wearing a business suit; the jacket was for more than show—the air-conditioning was cranked up so high that my bare arms were sprouting goose bumps. Lawlor had on his trademark checked blue shirt, but both of them wore Helen Kendrick's jeweled corn flags.

"V. I. Warshawski is here, boss," Blakely said.

"Right. So, Wade, we'll focus more on books in that sector"—he tapped the screen—"but this one clearly responds most to our foundation's work. Ms. Warshawski—we met at Wade's anniversary party, but I don't believe I handed you an invitation, did I?"

"No. You left that to Mr. Lawlor, who apparently is fascinated by my family's history. I wish you'd called me first before you ran your segment. I could have given better stuff—Boom-Boom Warshawski's mom's involvement in block clubs would have really spoken to your anti-Durango sector." My aunt had been a spit-spattering racist who'd joined one of the sixties block clubs that sprang up in an effort to keep South Side parishes all-white.

If I'd hoped to rattle Lawlor, I'd underestimated him. "Glad to know you catch my show, Warshawski. From what I've heard of you, I wouldn't expect you to agree with my viewpoint, but it's nice to know that a liberal can keep an open mind."

"Gosh, Mr. Lawlor, I didn't realize you were so interested—you know my politics, you know where my mother came from. I almost feel like we had a date where you were the only one who showed up. I'm going to have to blog about this." I made my voice seductive. "Every middle-aged woman's dream came true for me this week: Wade Lawlor was stalking me."

"A stalking charge is a serious one," Lawlor said. "I'd be careful what I posted, if I were you."

"She doesn't have a blog, Wade," Weekes said. "She's just yanking your chain."

"All of which proves my point," I said. "You guys have an unhealthy interest in me. And you apparently kept an equal interest in Miles Wuchnik. They wondered over at Crawford, Mead how you knew that Wuchnik sometimes worked for some of their lawyers."

"How do you—" Lawlor began, but Weekes cut him off.

"We have a lot of tipsters," he said. "People hear something, see something, they know that we give away fifty dollars for every tip that makes it on air."

"So someone thought it was newsworthy that Miles Wuchnik worked for a law firm?" I lifted my brows.

"You'd be surprised at what people send in, and sometimes the oddest tidbits turn out to be useful," Weekes said. "And then we have a whole team of in-house investigators who can do background checks, verify leads, that kind of thing."

I thought of Dick's clerical staff. Would any of those receptionists slip information to Harold Weekes in exchange for fifty dollars? If you made thirty or forty thousand a year in a firm where the managing partner pulled in seven figures, you might feel you were entitled to a bonus by letting out nonessential information. You might not reveal a witness list, but if the firm worked with a PI, that could seem like a harmless thing to reveal to Harold Weekes.

Come to think of it, maybe that was how Lawlor knew I'd been at the Parterre Club with Salanter last week; the old woman in the restroom, the bartender, any of them might privately feel that Salanter's guests were Wade Lawlor's business.

"I can't imagine Eloise Napier blurting out team secrets for a measly fifty dollars," I heard myself say.

"Eloise?" Lawlor smirked, the way kids on the playground do when they know a secret they're not going to let you in on. "Fifty dollars doesn't pay for a pair of Eloise's stockings, from what I hear."

"Eloise is a good team player," Weekes rebuked him. "We sit together on several committees and she would never reveal a client or a firm's secret, to me or to anyone."

"You feel equally confident in Louis Ormond?" I asked.

"I don't know Ormond," Weekes said, "but even if I did, I don't reveal our tipsters' names without their permission. It could put them in danger. Speaking of people we know, you're close to Ryerson over at the *Herald-Star,* aren't you?"

"Close?" I said. "I know him, and a few other reporters around town. Beth Blacksin on your news crew, for instance. I used to know a lot more reporters, but what with axing news bureaus until they look like a rainforest after an agribusiness bulldozer's been through, there aren't that many reporters left to know these days."

"So Ryerson didn't blab secrets out of the huddle?" Weekes played with his pencil as if the question weren't terribly important.

"The huddle!" I snapped my fingers. "I kept trying to remember what you called it—I thought it was the news muddle, where you imagine how to dirty up the news until the viewer can't tell truth from fiction. No, like Eloise Napier, Murray Ryerson is a good team player. But, like you, I have a lot of sources around town."

26. CAR TALK

WHEN I GOT BACK TO MY OFFICE, I SAT FOR A TIME, TRYING to figure out what I'd learned from seeing Lawlor and Weekes up close. Or what I'd revealed. I hoped my defense of Murray had been believable: until now, I hadn't taken seriously the notion that his career might hang by a thread. I started to send him a warning e-mail, then wondered if Weekes might be monitoring his mail, and decided it would be more prudent to leave it alone.

Hearing Napier and Ormond's names had made Lawlor smirk. Had the two lawyers said something, say, at a Helen Kendrick strategy meeting, that had led Lawlor to find out about Wuchnik? Or was Wuchnik one of Lawlor's own tipsters?

I hadn't brought up Salanter's name in the meeting, because it seemed to me that Lawlor was hammering on him chiefly as part of Global's effort to discredit the Durango campaign; I hadn't thought I'd get anything useful from mentioning him. In fact, what useful fact had I gotten from either of my meetings with the city's rich and powerful? Back to work, Warshawski, I admonished myself.

I couldn't resist looking up Dick's Journe watch first. I'd never heard of the make, but it apparently was the ultimate watch if you needed every platinum screw carved by hand. The price, when I found it, staggered me. What was Dick trying to prove, buying a watch that cost as much as a house—assuming you didn't need six bedrooms and a swimming pool? Even if I could afford a watch like his, I wouldn't spend the money on it. I had a moment's happy fantasy of Dick leaving his Journe on a bathroom sink. Good-bye, five hundred thousand dollars.

All the arguments we used to have came back to me: Dick's insecurities, needing the most expensive car, the best wine, an impressive address, even when we couldn't afford them. My belligerence, the chip on my shoulder that made me combative with his firm's managing partners. I worked for the public defender—I was a loser, wasting my time on losers, Dick said, demanding that I quit my job so that I'd be at home, preparing delightful meals and making enchanting small talk with those partners.

I said he already had scoliosis from bending double in front of his bosses all day long, and he retorted, and I snapped back, and then we were divorced. I wouldn't take alimony. In those days, I'd imagined myself as too idealistic to want a lot of money. And now, it just depressed me, how hard I worked, and how little I had to show for it.

"Money doesn't matter," I announced grandly. "Just what you can do with it."

I opened the call log on my computer. I have an answering service, even in these days of voice mail and text messaging, because people with urgent problems need to talk to a live person, not a machine. The service posts calls to my computer as soon as they answer them. They also text me if an emergency comes in.

I ran down the list, picking out the urgent calls, which the service marked with a red asterisk. Halfway down was a message marked with a tiny blue crankshaft, the signal that alerted me to possible crank calls.

Anonymous caller, left message specifically for you, as follows: Xavier

Jurgens has a new Camaro. Double-checked all spellings. Phone number blocked.

Despite the last sentence, I called the answering service, but they couldn't tell me more than what was on my screen, not even whether the voice had belonged to a woman or a man: gruff, deep, whether a woman pretending to be a man or a man roughening his voice; either way, the operator who'd taken the call figured the caller was disguising their voice.

I looked up Xavier Jurgens. There were two, one in central Pennsylvania, and one in Burbank, Illinois. The one who lived in Burbank was thirty-nine years old; he shared his address with a Jana Shatka. Life-Story said he drove a nine-year-old Hyundai. There was nothing about a new Camaro, but if it was really new the information might not be showing up on the DMV database yet.

Shatka was on long-term disability, for reasons not specified. Nor could I find where she'd worked, but Xavier Jurgens was employed. He was an orderly at Ruhetal State Mental Hospital, making just over twenty-four thousand a year.

I sat back in my chair and stared for a long time at nothing in particular. The secretary in Ruhetal's social work unit—I looked in my notebook—Chantal was her name. Chantal had seen Miles Wuchnik talking to one of the orderlies from the forensic wing. Perhaps it had been Chantal who had left the anonymous message with my answering service.

If I called out to the hospital, I doubted very much that anyone would give me Xavier Jurgen's work hours. But if I drove out to Burbank, I could see for myself if the guy owned a red Camaro.

I drove home and changed out of my gold dress into khaki cargo pants, an outfit more suited for stakeout work. A loose white knit top. My iPad, so I could do a little paying work if I had a long wait. A Thermos of coffee, some fruit.

Mr. Contreras was ostensibly tending his small vegetable patch behind our building, but after a weekend in the country, he and the dogs were all snoozing. I didn't wake him, just left a note next to his chaise longue asking him to take care of the dogs this evening, since I didn't know how late I'd be.

I managed to get on the expressway before noon, and, despite the construction on the Ike, I had a fast run, relatively speaking, to the western suburbs. I stopped in Downers Grove and toured the employee parking lot at Ruhetal. I saw a couple of Camaros, but none that looked especially new.

Jurgens lived a pretty good hike from the hospital, but on twenty-four thousand a year, there weren't a lot of places he could afford out here. I drove the twenty miles to Laramie Avenue in Burbank. Jurgens's address was a duplex across the street from a small park, just big enough for a single baseball diamond, a set of swings, and a sandbox.

I parked near the swings and walked up the street to the duplex. Midway Airport was nearby; a jet on its final approach seemed so close that I instinctively ducked my head, but none of the kids in the park paid any attention.

The north half of the duplex was painted a pale green, with the windows trimmed in rosy brick. The Jurgen-Shatka ménage, which occupied the southern piece, needed some attention. However, you didn't notice the peeling siding, or the cracked paint around the windows, when you saw the car. A shiny fire-engine-red Camaro, it stood under a carport next to the duplex.

I walked up the short drive. The car still had its orange temporary license plate, but the plateholder announced the dealership: Bevilacqua Chevy in Cicero. I bent down to look at the wheels. The hubcaps must have been a special order, with their intricate wiring and the Camaro logo on the cap. The wheels were by Sportmax, picked out in red trim.

"What are you doing here?"

I'd heard a door slam, and had hoped it might be Xavier Jurgens, but this was a sturdily built woman in her forties, whose thin sundress didn't quite cover her impressive bosom. She had thinning bleached hair that hadn't been tended for several weeks—the dark roots were showing. Her freckled face was red, from the midday sun or maybe chronic anger.

I got to my feet. "Admiring the car."

"You're on private property. Admire it from across the street."

"Is Mr. Jurgens at home, Ms. Shatka?" I asked.

"How did you know my name?"

I gave a thin smile. "It's in our files, Ms. Shatka. You're on long-term disability, but that doesn't seem to prevent you from getting around."

"What files? Are you with Social Security? Show me your identification." She had an accent that was hard for me to place.

"I'm not with the government, Ms. Shatka. I'm private. And I want to talk privately with Mr. Jurgens."

"He's at work, and he has nothing to say to anyone, either privately or to the government."

"I think he'll want to talk to me, Ms. Shatka. I'm following up on Miles Wuchnik's old cases."

A couple of women with a number of small children in tow had stopped at the foot of the drive to stare. Although she whirled to glare at them, I didn't think it was their arrival that made Shatka become suddenly quiet.

"Yes, Miles Wuchnik entrusted his work to me when he died," I added. "And I'd like to think he got his money's worth from Mr. Jurgens."

A triumphant smile played at the corners of Shatka's mouth. "I don't think you ever met Miles Wuchnik."

I had made a misstep there. I'd been convinced that Wuchnik gave Xavier Jurgens the money for the Camaro, but that apparently wasn't right.

"Oh, I met him," I assured her. "Miles was disappointed that after all the trouble he went to, Jurgens did a deal for the Camaro behind his back. As I tidy up the loose ends of Miles's old cases, that's one I want to clear up. The things he had to say about your disability claims, well, we can let those die with him."

The smile disappeared. "Whoever you are, you leave my property now."

"Technically, of course, it's not your property. You rent it from the Makkara family, but I understand what you mean. I'll wait for Mr. Jurgens in my car."

I strolled back to the street, where I stopped to talk to the women. Two children were in strollers; three were old enough to whisper and punch at one another while their mothers chatted. Jana Shatka scowled at us from the top of the drive.

"That's quite a car your neighbor has," I said.

One of the women snorted. "Have you come to repossess it? Jurgens can't afford to make the payments, and that *puta,* when did she ever do a day's work to pay the bills, let alone buy a car?"

"I heard he paid cash for it," I objected.

"If he did, where did he get the money?" the second woman said.

Jana Shatka stomped down to the sidewalk. "I know you two are standing there telling lies about me. What about your own lives, huh? Who pays for those spic children you're breeding like flies in a warm dung heap?"

"And you, you dried-up Russian *puta,* you are like a rotted squash, no seeds to bear fruit."

Russian. That explained her accent. The fight was getting interesting, but I needed the conversation back on track. "If Xavier isn't earning enough money at the hospital to pay for the car, how could he afford it?"

"That's our business!" Shatka's massive front heaved with fury.

"Probably he stole drugs and sold them," the second woman said, and both mothers laughed boisterously.

Jana drew her hand back to slap the speaker. I grabbed her wrist and pulled her hand behind her back.

"Ladies, let's not get physical here. It's too hot a day, and the police overreact in the heat, okay?"

An ice cream vendor pushed a hand cart up the street; the three older children tugged at their mothers. *"Helado, Mamá, helado."*

The cry for ice cream gave everyone a face-saving way to leave the fray. The women turned to the vendor. I walked back to my car and Jana Shatka returned to her home.

I was betting she'd be calling Xavier, but if he was working days, the shift didn't change for another two hours. I had time to drive over to the Bevilacqua dealership. The glare of the summer sun on the cars hurt my eyes even through my sunglasses.

No one was out on the lot, but as soon as I parked, a man in shirt-sleeves and tie surged over to greet me. His smile could have lit most of the South Side. He looked at my nicked and dusty car as if it were a precious piece of art.

"You're a lady with a discerning eye for a quality sports car. Let me tell you, if you liked this Mustang, you'll love one of our new Camaros."

I smiled regretfully. "I've come about a Camaro, but not to buy. To check the legitimacy of a sale."

Like a turtle retreating into a shell, he switched off his heartiness and appeared more like a funeral director greeting the bereaved. "If this is a legal matter, you need Mr. Bevilacqua." He spoke into a mike that hovered a few inches from his mouth, announcing to someone inside the building that trouble was arriving.

I walked through the sliding glass doors into air-conditioning so in-tense that I hugged my arms to try to get some warmth back into them. The cold air carried an unpleasant odor, maybe the glue they used in the carpeting.

A receptionist waved me toward a corner office. I wasn't a customer, I didn't deserve a personal greeting, let alone a smile. As I threaded my way around the cars and trucks that filled the showroom, I couldn't resist stopping to stroke a Corvette. My dream car, the 1938 Jaguar SS 100, was reselling for about half a million these days—the price of Dick's watch, come to think of it—but a Corvette wouldn't be a shabby second choice.

The receptionist coughed loudly and pointed toward the owner's office. Carm Bevilacqua was waiting in the doorway. A heavy man who would have had trouble squeezing into a Camaro, with eyes as cold as the air-conditioning, he demanded to know what authority I had to question any sale on his premises.

"Easy does it, Mr. Bevilacqua. This isn't about you but about one of your customers. He has a long list of creditors and they're licking their chops over the Camaro he just bought. If he wrote you a check, it's probably bouncing around like a kangaroo right now, but before I let any of my clients seize the car, I'm doing you the courtesy of seeing how he financed it."

My glib patter was essentially meaningless, but Bevilacqua didn't pounce on the faulty logic. He didn't even demand my ID, so relieved was he to find out I wasn't raising a legal issue about his dealership. Instead, he wanted the name of the customer.

I looked around to see who was in earshot, and prudently closed the door. "Xavier Jurgens," I murmured.

He asked for the spelling, sat at his desk, and busied himself on the computer. I perched on the visitor's chair. The smell in the showroom seemed to come from the upholstery.

"Yes, here it is," Bevilacqua said. "Jurgens bought a new model Camaro eighteen days ago, with premium wheels and the extended warranty. He paid fifteen in cash and financed the remaining ten, but we ran a credit check, Ms., uh—"

"Cash? You mean actual dollar bills?"

"Actual hundred-dollar bills, to be precise." Bevilacqua permitted himself a chuckle; we were teammates now. "He has the title, and our financing company looked at his employment."

"I know: he's at the Ruhetal hospital," I said absently. "Works in the forensic unit, so he's probably got good job security. Which he needs, since the woman in his life doesn't seem able to work."

"I wouldn't know about that. She certainly was the one who asked the tough questions during the financing session—he was all about the car. Between you and me, he would have paid an extra half point in interest if he hadn't had her along. If your clients are dealing with her, well, they'll have a hard time getting that car away."

"I'll make sure they know." I was out the door and back to my Mustang before Bevilacqua remembered he didn't know my name.

Word must have traveled fast that I hadn't come to challenge the dealership's financing policies. My hearty friend personally opened the Mustang's door for me and handed me his card. "When you're ready to trade in your baby, you come talk to me!"

27. JUST A FLESH WOUND

I drove back to Xavier and Jana's with the windows open. Muggy air, even stained with exhaust fumes and grease from the fast-food chains, still sat easier in the lungs than the frozen gluey smell inside the car dealership.

When I got back to Burbank, the Camaro was still in the carport, but no one answered the Shatka-Jurgens bell. A couple of women were sitting on a bench in the little park across the street. I asked if they'd noticed anyone coming or going, but they just shrugged. They were texting, even while sitting next to each other, and hadn't been paying attention to the neighbors. A boy bouncing a ball nearby spoke up: he'd seen Jana Shatka get into a taxi about half an hour ago. Another jet was closing in overhead; I wondered idly if Jana was heading back to Russia.

I got back into my car and started returning e-mails, but I couldn't focus on my clients' needs. I kept wondering where Jurgens had gotten fifteen thousand in cash. Not from his twenty-four-thousand-a-year job, not unless he'd skipped lunch for twenty of his thirty-nine years.

At the same time, Wuchnik's own finances weren't that brilliant. If he'd bribed Jurgens, where had he gotten the money? Anyway, Jana had smirked when I'd suggested that Wuchnik had paid for the car. Someone else had paid off Jurgens, or maybe it was what one of the women had suggested this afternoon: Jurgens was stealing drugs from the hospital and selling them.

But Jana knew Wuchnik's name. Her smirk suggested that she'd met him, done business with him. Bevilacqua said it was Jana who drove the bargaining over the Camaro, not Jurgens. So maybe Jurgens had called in his lady friend to deal with Wuchnik. Maybe Wuchnik had welched on a deal and Jana Shatka had impaled him with a spike at Mount Moriah. She had enough fury to do it, and she might have the strength, as well.

Speculation, speculation. I needed facts. I turned resolutely back to my iPad and focused on e-mails for forty minutes. In fact, I got so focused that I almost missed Xavier Jurgens's return home in his beater. Another jet was screaming overhead, so I didn't hear him slam the door to his Hyundai; it was just the motion out of the corner of my eye that made me look up in time to see him go into the duplex.

I turned off the iPad and followed him. The women who'd been on the park bench when I arrived had left, replaced by a couple of older men. One of them shouted after me, "You can do better than him, baby. Try me."

Xavier Jurgens was still in his hospital whites when he answered my knock, but he'd taken time to open a can of Pabst. "Yeah?"

I opened the screen door. "Mr. Jurgens? I'm a coworker of Miles Wuchnik's. We need to talk."

Jurgens filled the doorway. He wasn't a big man, but he had impressive neck muscles, which his shaved head made appear more pronounced. In his uniform he looked like the guy on the Mr. Clean bottles.

"What do you mean, coworker?" he said.

"I mean someone like me, who works with someone else, in this case, Miles Wuchnik. I'm clearing up loose ends on his outstanding cases."

"I know what a fucking coworker is. But he told me he worked alone."

"You can't trust anyone these days, can you?" I mocked him. "Bevilacqua Chevy isn't sure they can trust you for the remaining payments on that Camaro, for instance."

"What are you talking about? Are you from the car dealer? I signed the papers, they know I'm good for the money."

"But what nobody understands is where you came up with all those lovely portraits of Benjamin Franklin."

Jurgens shook his head, not in denial—he just wasn't following me.

"Mr. Jurgens, you paid cash. You counted out a big stack of hundred-dollar bills. You were proud of them, everyone in the dealership came around to look. But if you stole that money, or got it from drug sales, the government will come and take your shiny red Camaro away from you."

"I didn't steal the money, and Miles knows—knew that. So go away."

"Like Jana," I said. "Jana explained to me that it wasn't Miles who gave you the fifteen grand, but she was jittery that I was even asking questions about him and you and the car, so she took off about an hour ago."

"So what? It's a free country, she can come and go when she wants."

"Yes, indeed. She hopped in a taxi. Now, I will confess that I didn't hear her give the destination to the driver, but my guess is that she went off to talk to the person who gave you all that lovely money. What do you think?"

"I think you'd better leave."

I was able to slip inside when he backed up to shut the inner door. He was used to dealing with obstreperous patients. He grabbed me and wrenched my arms behind my back. I went limp and fell toward him. My dead weight took him off balance. While he struggled to hold me up, I hooked my right leg around his and upended him. The beer can hit the floor and sprayed the room.

He rolled over and sprang to his feet. "Goddamn bitch."

"No." I moved behind a chair. "A fight isn't a good idea. We'll both end up hurt, and we still have to have this conversation. Tell me who gave you the money for the Camaro."

He lunged at me over the chair. I shoved it into his abdomen and he doubled over with a horrible grunt.

"Who did Jana go see so fast? She called you after I left, and told you what she thought you needed to do."

He started to dance around me. I kept turning, chair in hand. It was exhausting.

"Who did Miles Wuchnik want to see in the forensic wing?" I panted.

"You think you're smart, but you're not," he said.

"You could be right," I agreed. "Was it a guard or a patient?"

Jurgens grabbed a butcher knife from the kitchen table and started slashing at me. I flung the chair at his head and fled through the back door.

A cab pulled up just as I reached the street. Jana Shatka got out. She had changed for her appointment from the thin sundress and flip-flops to a tight-fitting navy skirt with hose, heels, and a white jacket.

"You! You have been breaking into my home while I was out? I'm calling the police!" It wasn't an idle threat—she pulled her cell phone from the outsize blue handbag she was carrying.

"Xavier let me in." I was gulping in air. "He ran into some chair legs, so he's in a bit of pain. But he agreed you must have been off talking to the money pot who funded the Camaro."

"What? You went into my house and attacked my man? You are a crazy person! You belong in that hospital with the other lunatics Xavier works with all day long. Get away from here!"

We had drawn a crowd, homebound commuters along with the people hanging out in the park.

"You told your donor I'd come around asking questions, didn't you? What advice did you get back?"

"To put you in a straitjacket and take you to the locked ward at the hospital," she snapped.

"Hey, she's bleeding," one of the spectators called. "What did Xavier do? Bite her?"

"No, man, he cut her—look, he's there with the knife!"

I turned with the rest of the crowd to stare at Xavier, who was standing next to the Camaro, brandishing the butcher knife. It was pathetic, in a way: the car was perhaps the dearest thing he'd ever owned. I'd threatened it, and he was standing guard.

I hadn't noticed until now, but blood was seeping through the front of my knit top. Xavier had managed to strike me, and I hadn't even noticed. My shirt was sliced open at the shoulder. I craned my neck to squint at the wound. It didn't seem very deep, but in the aftermath of the fight, the sight of my own blood suddenly made me weak in the knees.

"Better call the cops," someone said. "He's turned violent, cut this lady, who knows what he'll do next."

"She started it," Jana growled.

"How do you know? You weren't here—you were off on a date with your fancy-pants guy, weren't you?" one of the women cawed.

"She admitted it out loud," Jana said. "She hit him with a chair."

"Maybe she hit some sense into him. A smart man would get rid of a lazy bitch like you, pretending to be on disability."

"I am on disability," Jana said. "It's my lungs, the doctor agreed!"

I went over to the woman who'd said Jana was off on a date. "Have you seen Mr. Fancy Pants?" I asked. "I'm anxious to find him."

She shook her head. "It's just talk around the street. You know, she goes off like this, makeup, pantyhose, the whole bit, when most of the time she is wearing some old housedress."

Another woman chimed in. "Of course she has a rich boyfriend. Why else would a whore like that who spends her day listening to Wade Lawlor make up lies about Mexicans—"

"What, that Mexicans are lazy vermin?" Jana interrupted.

The other woman lunged at Jana, calling her a *cerdo ruso perezoso,* a lazy Russian pig, but a man stepped between them. I decided I'd had enough excitement for one day and slipped off to my car while the crowd's attention was on the new contestant.

A woman at the fringe of the group nodded at me as I was crossing the street. "Those two women, they're always at each other's throats. You should get to a doctor. Out of curiosity, why did you come to fight Xavier?"

"I didn't come to fight him." I leaned wearily against the Mustang. "But there are questions about where he got the money for the car. You wouldn't know, I suppose."

She shook her head regretfully: she longed to know. Everyone on the street longed to know. "Xavier works hard, you know. He's not a lazy man, but he's an unlucky man—especially to get tied up with a *neryacha* like that Jana. I'm from Eastern Europe, same as her, but I work for a living! But we all know what they pay over at the hospital and it's not enough to buy a car like that."

"You think that's where money for the car came from—from Jana's lover?"

"Who would pay a creature like her that much money? I'm thinking he maybe stole drugs from the hospital."

Oh, the word on the street—it was like revisiting my childhood, all the local feuds, with each set of immigrants trying to push the other off the bottom rung of the ladder they were all trying to climb. What is it we fear in those who aren't part of our tribe? Is it the old sibling rivalry—who gets the most love, or the last piece of chocolate cake?

As I eased into traffic, I watched the crowd in my rearview mirror. People were drifting away, home to dinner, or in search of better entertainment elsewhere.

I stuck to the side streets heading back into the city. My wound, or maybe the fight, had caught up with me; I wasn't alert enough to be safe on the expressways. I called Lotty while stalled in a backup on a bridge over the Sanitary Canal. She told me she would wait in her clinic for me.

As I drove slowly north, I wondered how I could have made so many mistakes. "You think you're smart, but you're not," Xavier Jurgens had said, and I had to agree with him.

When I reached the clinic, on the western fringe of Uptown, Lotty's clinic manager gasped in shock, as did the handful of patients still waiting for attention. "Ms. Warshawski! Dr. Herschel told me you'd been injured, but this is terrible. I'll let Doctor know you're here."

Despite having known me for twenty years, Mrs. Coltrain still addresses me formally. Before she could pick up the phone, Lotty swept into the waiting room, looked at my bloodstained shirt, and ushered me back to the examining room attached to her office. I could hear one of the waiting patients grumble to Mrs. Coltrain.

While she cleaned the wound, Lotty demanded a report on how I'd come by the injury. "We don't need stitches or staples; it's not deep, the knife just glanced your shoulder." She used surgical tape and carefully pulled the edges together. "You're up to date on your tetanus, yes?"

"Yeah, when I got cut up two years ago. I'm just not up to date on my detecting skills. Maybe I can get a booster shot for those."

Lotty wrapped a sheet around my shoulders. "A course of antibiotics. And even though it is contrary to your nature, *Liebchen,* some rest as well. What mistakes do you think you made this afternoon?"

"I didn't do any homework. I'm grabbing at straws, so when I got the anonymous call about the guy's Camaro, I raced off to confront him, instead of coming up with some other strategy."

"What other strategy?"

"That's part of my problem—I don't know. Xavier Jurgens certainly has a car that he likely can't afford, but maybe he has rich parents—I didn't even bother to check that. Or maybe his girlfriend got some big insurance settlement. She's on disability, for her lungs, she says."

I leaned back in Lotty's reclining exam chair. "The neighbors are divided. Most think Xavier got the money from stealing hospital drugs, but some think his girlfriend, or business partner, or whatever she is, has a sugar daddy. My own thought was that Wuchnik bribed Xavier to get into the forensic ward, but Jana, the girlfriend, made it clear that wasn't the story. I started off with Xavier by asking him about the money, and that was where the conversation ended, too—he tried to fight me, and when that didn't work, he grabbed a knife."

"I don't understand, Victoria. Wuchnik—he's the detective who was found stabbed in the cemetery? Why do you think he bribed this orderly?"

"The social worker at the hospital said that Wuchnik had been seen talking to an orderly in the forensic unit. Leydon thought Wuchnik was stalking her, that her brother had sent him out to Ruhetal to check up on her, but I'm convinced he was on a different mission."

Lotty opened a closet and handed me a white blouse. "Unless the top you wore in here is a sentimental favorite, I'd advise throwing it out. You can borrow this, if you promise not to fight anyone while you're wearing it."

I smiled weakly. Joke, recognized.

"And I'm driving you home to spend the night with me. Your car will be safe in the lot until morning, and I want to make sure you get soup into you."

"Yes, ma'am." I sketched a salute, but the tension eased out of my shoulders. Even though a high-speed chase in a motor boat on the north Atlantic was safer than riding with Lotty, it still felt good to relinquish my responsibilities to her.

I was her last patient of the day; Jewel Kim was taking care of the people who'd been in the waiting room. I snoozed in the recliner while Lotty finished dictating her day's notes.

Jewel came in to tell Lotty she'd finished, but she needed Lotty to double-check a lump in a woman's armpit. While Lotty went off to the other examination room, Jewel looked at the job Lotty had done on my shoulder with a grudging approval: ordinarily this was the kind of injury she'd handle herself.

"You did a good job," she said when Lotty came back. "You could be a nurse if you get tired of surgery."

Lotty laughed but took Jewel aside to confer. My cell phone rang while Lotty and Jewel went off to talk to the woman with the lump.

It was Henry Knaub, the dean of Rockefeller, who asked politely if this was a convenient time.

I bit back a bark of sardonic laughter. "Fire away."

"You called me last week with a quotation."

"Yes, 'In death they were not divided.' I'm afraid Second Samuel didn't give me much guidance."

"I was having dinner with a colleague in the English department last night; I hope you don't mind, but I mentioned the matter. She is on the Rockefeller Chapel board, and of course the entire university community is worried about the unfortunate accident to your friend."

His voice was apologetic, as it always seemed to be when he was speaking to me. I wondered idly if he sounded as hesitant when he spoke to his English colleague. I felt a twinge of annoyance that he'd discussed my question with his colleague, but I murmured something noncommittal. I was too beat for a discussion.

"She reminded me that George Eliot used the verse as an epigraph in *The Mill on the Floss*."

Another book I'd read as an undergraduate. I searched my tired brain. "It's about a brother and sister, right? Maggie somebody?"

"Maggie Tulliver. The novel is based loosely on Eliot's own life, particularly her relationship with her older brother, whom she idolized as a child. In the novel the brother and sister drown together when the River Floss floods. My English colleague asked if there were a brother and sister involved in your case."

Lotty returned to her office and announced that we were leaving. I thanked the dean and climbed out of the chair. I was moving stiffly; after sitting so long, the muscles I'd used in my fight had tightened up.

Lotty eyed me without pity; she knew exactly why I was limping and she has made her position on my fighting skills clear plenty of times. Today she merely shook her head. At least she didn't tell me I was getting too old to fight.

As Lotty ran red lights and zipped around UPS trucks, I kept my eyes shut and thought about brothers and sisters. The most obvious were Leydon and Sewall Ashford, but it was hard to see how Eliot's epigraph applied to them.

Had there ever been a time when Leydon idolized Sewall, or vice versa? Not that she'd ever talked about. Perhaps they'd been born fighting. "Look it up," she'd told Wuchnik. "In death they were not divided." Was she thinking about brothers and sisters, or fathers and sons, or something even more obscure?

As Lotty pulled into the garage underneath her building, I remembered my conversation with Miles Wuchnik's ex-wife. She'd said the only person he seemed to care about was his sister, Iva. He'd even made her the beneficiary of his 401K. Maybe he'd bequeathed her some information, along with his thirty-two thousand dollars.

28. BOOK CARVINGS

HEAT ROSE IN SHIMMERING WAVES FROM THE CARS AND TRUCKS around me as we inched our way south. It was after one and traffic on the Ryan was at its miserable worst. The Interstate signs told me I'd be heading to Memphis in another quarter mile, which sounded like excitement, a road trip, but the reality, when I finally made the turn, was more of the same congestion.

I'd hoped to be under way earlier, but yesterday's fight, or maybe the tablet Lotty ordered me to swallow at bedtime, had knocked me out for a solid ten hours. When I finally got up, it was after eight and Lotty was long gone. She'd left instructions for how to protect my wound while bathing. *If the surgical strips come loose, see Jewel before you do anything strenuous, such as arm-wrestle a boa constrictor.*

Out hunting for a boa with arms, I scrawled under the note. Lotty also left a Thermos of her rich Viennese coffee, along with a basket of the fresh rolls someone on her staff at the hospital bakes. I scratched out my snarky comment—it felt too wonderful to be pampered.

When I'd stretched the worst kinks out of my muscles, I returned to Lotty's clinic for my car, but I couldn't set out on my journey immediately. Aside from a pressing need for clean clothes, I needed to reassure Mr. Contreras, never a speedy activity. I'd called him last night, of course, but he had to see me for himself, cluck his tongue over my wound, remind me that there were better ways to solve problems than fighting.

"Darling, that comes strangely from the man who swings a pipe wrench first and asks questions second!" I kissed his cheek.

"Yeah, but you need your looks, doll. Jake Thibaut may be a good guy, but there are a lot of beautiful girls half your age playing the violin around him day and night out there in Vermont."

That thought had also occurred to me, but I said, "That'll help me stand out in a crowd—middle-aged, scarred, no violin. He won't be able to miss me."

Mr. Contreras shook his head in disapproval. "I seen you go through a lot of guys in the years I've known you, cookie. This Jake is better than most of them, but you can't keep beating them up or beating them off. One of these days you'll be as old as me, always assuming you don't let some punk stab you to death first, and who's going to look out for you then?"

That was unanswerable, so I deflected him by telling him my day's travel plan. I further deflected his desire to accompany me by reminding him that if I got stabbed to death he'd have to be in Chicago to take care of Mitch and Peppy. He did drive over to the lake with me to give the dogs a long swim, since the heat was building too much to let them run. And he made lunch for me while I changed into my last clean pair of summer slacks. I packed an overnight bag just in case, and finally made it to the Kennedy Expressway a little after noon.

Before setting out, I'd run a couple of searches on Miles Wuchnik's sister, Iva. I was still annoyed with myself for doing so little preparation before calling on Xavier Jurgens yesterday. I let my iPad read the search reports to me while I drove.

There had been four children in the Wuchnik family—Iva, Miles, and two other brothers. All three boys had moved from Danville when they were in their twenties, but Iva had stayed behind, looking after their aging parents in the time-honored tradition. In another time-honored tradition, the parents hadn't rewarded her sacrifice. Their father had died back in the nineties; when their mother died three years ago, the family home and her modest savings had been divided equally among the four children, with no special recognition of Iva's work. The house had been sold, right after the market fell out of real estate, and Iva had moved into an apartment near the claims office where she worked as a clerk.

It was a depressing story. I shut off the iPad and put in a CD Petra had created for me of her favorite indie bands. I was pleasantly surprised by my cousin's taste, especially Neko Case, who took me down to 138th Street, where the road finally opened up. After that, I had a smooth drive south to Danville.

I found Iva Wuchnik's apartment easily enough, but I'd gotten into town before the end of the business day. I didn't think it would help either of us if I showed up at her office, so I found a park, where I ate the chicken sandwich Mr. Contreras had packed, then wandered along the Vermilion River for a bit.

At four-thirty, I went back to Iva's apartment. The five-story building wasn't run-down, exactly, but it had an air of shabbiness, as if the management company had gotten too depressed to care about the dirt in the corners of the lobby. Poor Iva, first caring for her elderly parents, then having to move into this.

I rang her bell, but there wasn't an answer. I went back to my car, where I could watch the front entrance while pretending to work my cell phone. Just one of 286 million U.S. texters, as unnoticed as the setting sun. I didn't pay close attention to the cars going into the building's underground garage, and would have missed Wuchnik if she hadn't had to fumble around with her card key.

Something about the depressed set of the lines around her mouth, or the square forehead, similar to her brother's, made me stare over the top of my phone. I gave her twenty minutes to settle in before ringing her doorbell.

"My name is Warshawski," I called through the intercom. "I'm the person who found your brother's body last week."

There was a pause, as if she were wondering whether to believe me, and then she buzzed me in. When I got to the third floor, she opened her door the length of a short chain.

"Who did you say you are?"

"V. I. Warshawski. I'm sorry for your loss; I'm the person who found Miles's body at Mount Moriah cemetery last week."

"Let me see some ID," she demanded.

A sensible precaution. Although it really was no proof of anything, I showed her the laminate of my PI license. This satisfied her enough that she undid the chain.

She ushered me into a living room so stuffed with old furniture it looked like a showroom to a down-market antiques store. Iva had apparently grabbed every piece of furniture from her parents' home when she and her brothers sold it. A sectional couch in aqua Naugahyde took up the most space, but there was also a card table and chairs with the spindly legs so popular in the fifties and sixties, an overstuffed armchair and a scarred teak cabinet with a stack of old books on top.

Next to the books stood an eight-by-ten of Miles in a decorated frame. It dated from some earlier epoch, before his hair had started turning gray, before the jowls had begun to grow heavy, before someone stuck a piece of rebar through his heart.

Iva saw me looking at the picture and said, in her flat, heavy voice, "So you're a private investigator, like Miles. He never mentioned you to me."

"No. We never met."

"Then how come you were in that cemetery where he died?"

"A missing-persons search," I said, not exactly lying. "I had a tip that my target would be there, but I found your brother. The medical examiner told me he had been hit on the head hard enough to knock him out. His body was then carried to the tomb, where he was stabbed to death."

"I see." She kneaded her hands together. Despite her thick shoulders and short, square body, she had long, slender fingers. Another woman might have painted the nails to draw attention to a fine feature, but Iva Wuchnik's hands were rough, untended, like the skin on her face, or her hair, dyed a shoe-polish brown.

She roused herself. "I was making some iced tea; you want a glass?"

She led me past the furniture storeroom to a kitchen that was also cluttered, this time with racks of pots hanging from the ceiling. I sat on a bar stool next to the counter while she poured cold tap water into two glasses of powdered tea.

"It looks as though you're quite a cook." I gestured toward the pots.

"Oh—those were my mother's, and my grandmother's. I don't have time for that kind of thing. Most of what I eat is take-out, although I suppose if I had company . . ." Her voice trailed off; she couldn't imagine herself with company.

I couldn't, either. I hastily changed the subject.

"I'm trying to follow up on some of your brother's cases. He seems to have been a very generous man."

She dropped the glass she'd been about to put on the counter next to me. "Oh! I always was the clumsy one in the family, Mother said that a thousand times if she said it once."

"Let me." I slid off the stool and squatted to pick the pieces of glass out of the mass of brownish ice.

"These glasses, Mother got them as a wedding present. I shouldn't have been using them for everyday."

"I know," I said sympathetically. "I've destroyed two of the wine-glasses my mother carried with her from Italy, and I think a piece of my heart breaks off every time I lose one of them. No matter how often you tell yourself that accidents happen. Like just now, I shouldn't have sprung that information about your brother on you."

"What information?" She tried to laugh but she wasn't good at it.

"How generous Miles was. I know he gave a Camaro to a complete stranger, for instance. How many people would do that?" I didn't actually believe Miles had given Xavier the money for the Camaro, but I had to find some wedge to pry information out of Iva Wuchnik.

"Miles gave—a Camaro is a sports car, right?"

"A kind of baby Corvette. Worth about twenty-five thousand. I'm wondering where Miles got that kind of money." I stood, my hands full of shards.

"He was a brilliant investigator, brilliant!" Her voice thickened with emotion.

"Yes, I'm sure he was," I said sycophantically. "He had dozens of clients; I've seen his log just for the last three months. Where is the garbage can, by the way?"

"Oh! Oh, thank you, sorry, I wasn't focusing." She opened the door under the sink and pulled out a garbage can filled with the empty microwave pans for frozen dinners.

I dumped in the glass shards and pulled a length of paper towel from a roll above the sink to blot up the mess. It was so much easier a way to consume instant tea than drinking it.

"He talked to you about his cases, didn't he?" I suggested. "None of your other brothers paid as much attention to you as Miles, did they?"

"You did know him, didn't you? He must have told you that, because no one outside the family would have known that."

"I didn't know him personally, but he talked about you a lot to a friend of mine." When I was a child, you were supposed to cross your fingers if you were telling a lie: that meant, sorry, this doesn't count as a sin. My fingers were full of wet paper towel and the remaining slivers of glass I'd found; I couldn't cross them.

"Did he ever mention my friend to you?" I continued. "Leydon? Leydon Ashford? He met her at a case that took him to a big mental hospital outside Chicago."

She frowned over the name. "You mean Ruhetal? He told me he was going out there, but he never mentioned that person's name. Miles said it was the biggest case of his career and if it turned out the way he thought, I'd never have to work again. Not that I'd know what else to do with my time; I sometimes wonder what I'll do if I have to retire, but Miles said he'd take me to Europe, take me to the town in Poland where our grandparents came from, go to London, all those places you see on TV." She started pleating her fingers again, pushing her thumbs against the palms.

"Did he give you any hint that the case was dangerous?" I dropped my load into the garbage can and rinsed my hands under the tap. I'd managed to slice a finger open. Shedding blood two days in a row on this investigation. Not a trend I wanted to continue.

Iva's eyes grew round in her square face. "You mean one of the inmates killed him?"

"I don't think so. He died fifty miles from the hospital and there's no suggestion that any of the patients was involved. But he wanted to go into the wing where the criminals are housed, and that's a risky place to be. Did he tell you why?"

I eyed her surreptitiously as I wrapped a strip of paper towel around my bleeding finger, but her worried frown and head shake seemed genuine. I returned to one of her earlier comments.

"When Miles said you could retire, was he imagining that the two of you would live together?"

"We didn't talk about that, because he has—had—his work in Chicago and I have a job here. Anyway, I moved in here when Mother passed."

"Your mother's house was too big for one person?" I asked, even though I sort of knew the answer.

"Sam and Pierce—my two other brothers—they made us sell the house after the funeral. Sam, he moved to Indianapolis, and Pierce went down to Louisville. They never even helped out when Mother needed nurses round the clock, even though they both have good jobs. You wouldn't believe the medical bills, almost a hundred thousand and Medicare wouldn't cover any of it. Anyway, Sam and Pierce, they said we had to sell the house, the place our parents bought back in 1958, they didn't care for one second about sentimental value, let alone where was *I* going to live?

"Miles said I ought to get to keep the house, seeing as how I looked after Mother and Daddy and everything, but the other two wouldn't give one nickel to help with the bills. Their wives, they're just as bad."

Iva Wuchnik paused, her jaws working, all the grievances of the last few years welling up as if they had happened yesterday.

I murmured something sympathetic, to keep the spigot flowing, while I tried hard to think what had scared her into dropping the tea glass. It was when I'd said her brother was generous, but before I mentioned the Camaro. Maybe she resented his bestowing that much money on a stranger, but it was the comment about Miles's generosity that upset her. She was afraid I knew something particular about her brother's money. The question was how to ferret it out.

"I'm trying to follow up on Miles's open cases," I said. "Did the police tell you someone had broken into his home and stolen all his papers, his computers, everything?"

She clutched involuntarily at her throat. "No." She mouthed the word, cleared her throat, said it again in a harsh croak. "Everything? Who—was it—that means they know—they want—"

"Who will know what, Ms. Wuchnik?" I said gently when she stopped mid-dither. "You think the people who killed Miles may come after you?"

She gave another of her unconvincing laughs. "That's ridiculous, when I don't know who killed him myself."

"He was sending you money, though." I spoke with the kind of certainty we learned in the Public Defender's Office: *I know you were holding the gun for your homey. Better tell me now before we're in front of the judge.*

"How did—who did he tell? Your friend with the weird name?"

I smiled enigmatically. "He sent you cash. But did he tell you where he got it?"

"He—he thought it was better for me if I didn't know. Is that why he was killed?"

"I don't know why he was killed, but I'm trying to find out. How did he send you the money?"

Her eyes darted toward the front room and then quickly fell to her hands. "Your tea, I never made you a fresh glass of tea, and you did all that work cleaning up after me."

Twenty questions. Miles sent his sister cash. And he sent it to her via something in the living room, and—the image of the dismembered book in Miles Wuchnik's kitchen garbage popped into my head. I'd thought the intruder in his home had slashed a book to shreds, but it was Wuchnik himself, carving books like a pumpkin.

29. TALKING TO A SPECIAL SISTER

I SLID OFF THE BAR STOOL AND RETURNED TO THE FRONT room. The old books that Iva had stacked on the teak storage cabinet made up one of those motley collections you see at garage sales. *A Girl of the Limberlost*, *How to Win Friends and Influence People*, *Ramona*.

While Iva twittered nervously behind me, I started flipping through them. The *Better Homes and Gardens Junior Cookbook* held more than two hundred dollars in twenties and fifties. An old twenty was stuck inside *Daddy-Long-Legs* but *Sanders of the River* was as dry as a dead riverbed.

I closed the books and put them back on the sideboard. "I don't care about the money, Ms. Wuchnik. I mean, I don't care if you give it to the Humane Society or use it for a trip to Poland. But I'd like to know where your brother got it."

"He didn't steal it!" Her square cheeks turned a blotchy mahogany.

"I'm not suggesting he did. But you must have wondered; you surely asked him when he started sending you hollowed-out books full of money."

"I don't know where he got it, but he told me he was working hard, harder than he'd ever worked in the past. He wanted to quit, and there wasn't enough in his 401K for him to retire, so he was taking extra jobs. If people wanted to pay him in cash, was that a crime?"

Only if he didn't report it, but I kept that to myself—I didn't want to get onto a side track about income taxes. "So you put it in a bank account to keep for him?"

"What I do with it is none of your business."

"You're right, you're right." I held up my hands, surrender mode. "My business is to try to figure out who killed Miles, who pounded on his chest hard enough to split the ribs and reach his heart. I found him, as I told you, and his blood was still warm."

Her lips quivered. "That's not right, that's not fair, to come into my home and describe my own brother's body to me like that."

"It was even harder to be there with him," I said. "What I'm trying to find out is who he'd made so angry that they ambushed and killed him."

"They said on TV it was the black woman, the one who wants to be Senator. They said on TV she was having an affair with him."

So Iva was one of Wade Lawlor's legion of fans. I sat on the sectional couch. The aqua cushion gave a small poof, air escaping, and with it, a cloud of dust that made me sneeze.

"Do you believe that?" I asked, trying to keep contempt out of my voice. "Did Miles ever give any sign to you that he was having an affair with anyone?"

"If he thought it would hurt my feelings to hear it, he might not say." She spoke to the floor, her voice thick with shame, as if there were something wrong with her for being hurt by her brother's sex life.

"He cared more about you than anyone. Everyone I've talked to who knew him says that." Okay, 'everyone' was just Wuchnik's ex-wife, but she still counted. "Aren't you the one he sent his money to? Aren't you the one he promised to help make famous? Not Dr. Durango, or Helen Kendrick. But his sister."

I was afraid I was laying it on with too heavy a trowel, but Iva Wuchnik brightened. She even sat down, across from the couch on one of the old armchairs, unleashing another cloud of dust.

"I'm thinking that one of these cases your brother was working on so hard got him killed. And I'm especially interested in his trips to the Ruhetal Mental Hospital. He somehow made it into the locked wing there, which is just one sign of how skilled he was as an investigator— I'd love to know how he managed it."

Iva agreed that Miles was way smarter than anyone gave him credit for, but she couldn't shed any light, either on how he got into the locked ward or on who he was trying to see there.

She added, darting a glance at his photograph, "He said he couldn't tell me anything because it wasn't safe, if someone was listening in on his phone calls."

"He knew a lot about that, didn't he?" Sandra, the ex-wife, had talked about his eavesdropping. "Detectives have to employ a lot of methods that ordinary citizens can't, and your brother was an expert on electronic eavesdropping, so he'd know he had to be careful."

She nodded cautiously, not sure where I was going.

"Did he ever talk to you about his techniques? Some of that equipment isn't just expensive, it's hard to get access to it."

She frowned. "Were you talking to Sandra? She totally did not support Miles's work, or understand it, and he finally had to leave her because of it. But if you're on her side—"

"The only side I'm on is finding Miles's killer," I interrupted before she worked herself up into enough anger to throw me out. "It's just— devices to intercept cell-phone calls, if they're really effective, they cost thousands of dollars, and I wondered if they were something your brother ever discussed."

"Miles never talked about his methods with me, but he got results."

"Would he call you when he was getting ready to send you another book?"

"E-mail," she muttered to her hands.

"Could I see how he phrased the messages?" I was scraping past the bottom of the barrel into open air.

Iva communed about it with her hands, plaiting her long, slim fingers together again. She seemed torn between wanting to show me that her brother trusted her and wanting to tell me to mind my own business, but she finally took me to her bedroom, where her computer sat. This was the one room that was authentically hers, not a storeroom of her parents' furniture. Drapes with pink peonies, a matching duvet, everything else in white, including a vanity table with a frilled skirt, and a painted white desk.

"He told me to delete them, but I couldn't bear to, not after he died and they were what I had left of him," she whispered.

That and the money.

There were eight e-mails from Miles altogether. Iva wouldn't let me print them, or forward them to my own computer, so I focused on the dates and the headers. The first three were hush-hush, burn before reading, hints of a lucrative new project.

> Can't tell you more, sis, but you will definitely ride to heaven with me when I come into my kingdom. I think I've finally found the goose that will lay our golden eggs.

"It was after he sent me that one that he drove down here in person, to tell me about his idea for sending me the money in books," she said.

"And that would have been about when?"

"May seventeenth. I got in from church and he was waiting for me on the doorstep, with the first book."

So six cash deliveries in all. I got up from the stool in front of the painted white desk, but there was one more topic I wanted to bring up before I left. "Did he ever mention Chaim Salanter?"

"Who? Oh, you mean *Shame* Salanter." She mispronounced the name in the manner of Wade Lawlor. "Miles said it was terrible what rich people get away with in this country."

At last there was something we could genuinely agree on: the free ride America gives its hyper-wealthy. I started to say as much, but Iva's outrage with Chaim Salanter burst out of her.

"You see Salanter on television all the time, how he wants to fill the country up with illegal immigrants, probably just so he can get his garden looked after for nothing with Mexican workers. That isn't right."

"Did Miles have a plan for stopping Salanter?" I asked.

She didn't say anything, but a smile lurked at the corners of her mouth. She knew something, but what?

"It would take a lot of courage to go up against a powerful billionaire," I said, coaxing. "It doesn't sound as though your other brothers had the moral fiber that Miles possessed."

"You're right about that. Sam and Pierce always called Miles a loser, because he didn't own his own home or drive a fancy car, like they do. But he was going to show them. That's why he was giving me the money to keep for him; it all had to be a secret, from the FBI and everyone."

"You mean the IRS?" I couldn't figure out what the FBI had to do with a stash of cash.

"Oh, them! No, Miles said the FBI was on his trail, along with Shame Salanter, so we couldn't talk until the whole operation was finished, and then we'd be on Wade Lawlor's show, and be national heroes and everything for exposing Salanter."

"Maybe you can keep up the good work," I suggested. "Miles must have shared *some* of his strategy with you."

She stopped in the doorway between her bedroom and the living room. "Why are you really here? Are you trying to horn in on Miles's business?"

"No, ma'am! I have no interest in the kind of business that gets you a spike in the chest. But if I don't understand what he was working on, I'll never get close to finding his killer. He never told you who hired him to investigate Chaim Salanter?"

"No. Clients' business stayed confidential with Miles. Didn't you say you were a PI, same as him? You should know that."

"Of course. It's just, someone suggested that your grandparents and Chaim Salanter's family might have known each other in Europe, before they all came to America. I wondered if somebody doing genealogy research might have hired your brother to look into that."

"Who told you that? Who said we might be related to a—a liar and a cheat like Shame Salanter?"

"Oh, Ms. Wuchnik, you know how it is: like your brother, I have to protect the confidentiality of my clients." I moved past her into the furniture showroom. "If you think of anything at all that you want to tell me, please call. I'm leaving my card on your table here."

The July heat swallowed me as soon as I walked into the hall outside her apartment, but it was a relief to be away from the dusty room. It wasn't until I started down the stairs that I saw my hand was bleeding again, too freely to drive comfortably with it. I didn't really ever want to see Iva Wuchnik again, but maybe she could slip me a few Band-Aids across the length of the chain lock on the door.

Her phone rang as I was lifting my fist to knock. Some Miles-like impulse made me wait, my ear to the door. At first I couldn't hear anything except her husky voice muttering the conventional greetings, brief answers to questions, but then she gave out a sudden protesting squawk.

"I didn't tell her anything because I don't know anything. Who is this, anyway? Miles *protected* me. He didn't want me to get hurt, and—"

She was silent for a moment, then said quietly, "No. Of course not . . . I understand."

I crept down the hall again. I could wrap my hand in the T-shirt I'd packed in my overnight bag.

Someone had been tracking me. But who, and why? I thought of Jana Shatka, going off in a taxi yesterday to talk to someone. As I got into my car, I shivered, despite the heavy summer air.

30. LOST DAUGHTER

I WOKE THE NEXT MORNING TO BLOODSTAINED SHEETS. EVEN though it was just from the cut on my hand, it seemed like an ominous echo of Miles Wuchnik's death. I couldn't shake a sense of oppression from my strange conversation with his sister. Her own depression, her determined devotion to her blackmailing brother, they were like an illness that had infected me through the cut on my hand. I knew I should write up my notes before I forgot too many of the details, but the encounter felt so sordid that I found it hard to think about it head-on.

The most puzzling, and ultimately most worrying, part of the conversation was what happened at the end. Who had called her? Who knew I was there, and what was their stake in the conversation? Iva's protest, that she hadn't told me anything because she didn't know anything—had her caller been asking, as I had, about the source of the money? Or was there something else that she'd played close to her chest, so close I hadn't realized she was sitting on a second secret?

I walked slowly to the kitchen to put on water for coffee. Iva Wuchnik had gone on about Chaim Salanter: she saw him on television all the time, she'd said, wanting to fill America with illegal immigrants. I didn't think Salanter was on television—he wasn't a publicity seeker. Iva saw his face or heard his name on Helen Kendrick's or Wade Lawlor's show. Miles had been doing some dangerous investigations that would show up Salanter, Iva said. And Lawlor would heap fame and glory on her brother.

Did that mean Lawlor had hired Miles Wuchnik? The two-bit Berwyn PI and the man with the twenty-million-dollar annual contract from Global? Wade Lawlor had hundreds of investigators at his command, but maybe he was spreading his net wide, trying to snare Salanter.

On a whim, I logged on to Lawlor's website, to see if he was offering some kind of reward for nailing Salanter. I didn't see a header that said "Wanted, Dead or Alive," but he did have a tip line.

If you have information on any topic Vital to the Survival of Our Republic and Our Christian Values, e-mail me: Wade.Lawlor@Global.Net

The website showed photos of some of his stalwart tipsters, with a little blurb about the vital information each had supplied. Other tipsters had written under a cloak of anonymity: "This information is so damning that our reporter's life could be in danger for revealing it," the caption read.

As I scrolled down, my own name jumped out at me. An anonymous source had claimed that my mother was an illegal immigrant.

The fury I'd felt at the *Herald-Star* offices two days ago welled up in me again. How dare they, *how dare they,* these faceless, mindless, cowardly, jackboot-licking pond scum? I was shaking with rage, halfway to my closet to collect my gun, when a night soon after I'd learned my mother was ill, that she might not get well, came to my mind.

One of the women on South Houston whom Gabriella had scorched for her advice on how to control me—*Your daughter is a disgrace to the neighborhood,* the woman had said, and Gabriella had said, *She's growing up to inhabit a larger world than you'll ever visit.* As I walked past the woman's house she'd spat out an insult about Gabriella, *Melez,* she'd called her. I'd grown up hearing that Croatian word: my mother was a mongrel, a half caste—half Jewish, they meant. I'd jumped up the stairs in the dark and been on the point of punching her when my father materialized.

"Come on home, Tori," he'd said.

I was fifteen and almost as tall as he was, but he picked me up and carried me down the stairs. He didn't berate me and he wouldn't listen to my side of the story. He sat me down on our back stoop, where we'd listened in the darkness to Gabriella working on her breathing exercises: cancer was not going to still her voice, she was determined about that.

After a time, Tony said, "The worst cops are the ones whose gun is their first weapon, instead of their last. The best cops go into a situation head-first, not hand-first. You remember that, Tori: you get yourself into trouble you don't need with that hot temper of yours. And anger doesn't make a bad situation better. It depletes your strength and it depletes your mind."

I was letting rage at Wade Lawlor and his minions deplete my mind. I sat back down in front of my laptop. It was almost as though someone was trying to keep me so angry that I wouldn't be able to see my way clear.

Was it Wade Lawlor, with his attacks? I thought of my meeting with Harold Weekes. Lawlor was his—GEN's—money machine, but Weekes was the brains. Lawlor had smirked all through the meeting like the smart-aleck kid at school, but every time he was about to blurt out a revelation, Weekes shut him up.

I remembered my Monitor Project report on Vernon Mulliner's finances. Where had he gotten all that money? From Harold Weekes? In which case, what was Mulliner doing for him out at Ruhetal?

I rubbed my eyes. None of this made any sense.

I turned back to Wade's site and looked for the tipster entries on Chaim Salanter or the Malina Foundation. There was a lot of vitriol, a lot of speculation about Chaim Salanter's past as a Nazi collaborator, and his present as Sophy Durango's financial adviser, but nothing that sounded like a damning fact.

And yet Miles Wuchnik believed he was on the trail of such evidence. And there was another fact: Chaim Salanter had tried to bribe me to stay away from the Wuchnik investigation. That sounded as if he was hiding something shameful. And he knew that if Wuchnik hadn't found it out, he was close to doing so.

My espresso pot had boiled all over the stove. I turned off the burner and looked at the mess in disgust. Cleaning Iva Wuchnik's spilled tea last night, my own stove this morning. Mopping up messes, it's what I did for a living, but that didn't mean I wanted to do it in my kitchen as well.

Had Chaim Salanter murdered Miles Wuchnik? Salanter was small; he was old. He couldn't have dragged a man so much bigger than him onto the catafalque on his own, but his daughter might have helped him. When I'd first found Wuchnik, I'd had unsettling ideas about the girls in the Carmilla book club luring him to the catafalque and then stabbing him.

Now I wondered if Julia Salanter could have done it. Nick Vishnikov, the ME, had said Wuchnik had been bashed on the back of the head before he was stabbed. If Julia thought Wuchnik was going to reveal some nasty secret about her father, she could easily have persuaded him to meet her in the cemetery. I wondered if any of her mother's family were buried at Mount Moriah—that could explain the choice of venues. Gabe the houseman was big enough to heft any number of Wuchniks onto slabs. And his role in the household seemed very much more active than that of a garden-variety servant.

I shivered. I didn't like this line of thought at all. It wasn't just that

I'd taken a liking to Julia Salanter, but it also meant that Wade Lawlor would be vindicated for his pile-driving attacks on her father. It would be a blow to Lotty and Max, as well.

And then there was young Arielle to consider. She was sitting on some information about Wuchnik. What if it had to do with Julia, rather than with Chaim? What if Gabe's role in the household was intimate enough to include being Julia's lover?

I put the soiled rags in the sink with some bleach and refilled my little pot with water and grounds. This time I shut everything else out of my mind until I'd poured espresso into a cup.

The money that Miles Wuchnik had been sending his sister, that screamed *BLACKMAIL!* at the top of its lungs. My hand kept creeping across the kitchen table toward my phone. My hand wanted to call Julia Salanter and ask what secret Miles Wuchnik had uncovered about her father. And what would she say? *Oh, Daddy murdered his mother and all his sisters to save his sorry ass?*

If I could find out who had hired Miles, then maybe I could follow the trail from the other direction. It's true that someone had swiped his computer, his cell phone, and all his files, but I had a little more information today than I'd had yesterday. I knew Miles's e-mail address, from looking at Iva's computer, and with some luck I might get into his server and recover them.

I also knew that Miles had gone to see his sister on May 17. Maybe he'd considered that journey a deductible expense. I'd locked the original of his mileage log in my office safe, but I had the photocopies in my briefcase.

Mr. Contreras came up the back stairs with the dogs while I was spreading the pages out on my kitchen table. He turned a dark umber when he realized I was wearing only a T-shirt and underpants.

"Not to worry," I said kindly, but I went back to my bedroom and pulled on a pair of cargo pants.

When I returned to the kitchen, he was standing at the sink, washing my week's accumulation of dishes, carefully not looking at me. "How'd it go yesterday, doll?"

"Weird. Very weird. You can turn around now."

I assembled a bowl of fruit and yogurt while I described my visit to Iva Wuchnik.

"Wuchnik was sending her money in hollowed-out books," I said. "Either it's cash he found lying around and stole, or someone agreed to pay blackmail."

"Or drug sales," my neighbor said.

I nodded thoughtfully; that hadn't occurred to me. "Yes, the women out in Burbank think that Xavier Jurgens is selling drugs that he steals from the hospital. Maybe Wuchnik found out about it, and either tried to muscle in on the deal or blackmailed Xavier, until Xavier had had enough and lured him to the cemetery."

It made sense; proving it would be another story. "And in a way, it's disappointing if that's the end of the story. I was kind of hoping it had something to do with Lawlor, or Helen Kendrick, or even my ex's law firm. Just out of spite, I suppose. I don't think Xavier could make enough out of filched hospital supplies to put fifteen thousand down on a new car. That kind of money sounds more like recreational drugs, unless he had help."

I stopped, thinking about Vernon Mulliner's finances. "Mulliner's brokerage account appeared out of nowhere seven years ago, when he started at Ruhetal," I told Mr. Contreras. "I suppose he could be ordering large quantities of hallucinogens; Xavier could be selling them and getting a cut. If Miles found out, he'd have put the bite on Mulliner.

"But that's not what took Wuchnik out to Ruhetal in the first place. If there were allegations of drug fraud, the state attorney general would know about it. She has a team of investigators on her payroll; she wouldn't pick a bottom feeder like Wuchnik to investigate."

Mr. Contreras picked up the mileage log the boys had found next to Wuchnik's car. "What's this here?"

"It's Wuchnik's mileage log for his visits to his clients. You can see how many miles he logged for different trips, so that pretty well tells when he went out to Ruhetal, or down to Danville. What I don't have is a way to crack his client code system. All his electronics are missing— computer, phone, the works. I'd had high hopes for this log when the kids handed it to me, but it's just one more frustrating dead end!"

I slapped the book back on the table. "And even if Wuchnik found out about a drug deal once he got out to Ruhetal, who sent him there to begin with? If it was Ormond or Napier, at my ex's firm, who was their client? And come to that, why would attorneys from Crawford, Mead hook up with a two-bit guy like Wuchnik, when they can afford the cream of the investigative universe?"

"Meaning you, doll? Not that you'd take a job for your ex."

I kissed his cheek. "Crawford, Mead usually go for the big-name firms, Baladine, Tintrey, one of them. How did they find Miles?"

"Maybe they figured a big company would have too many ears listening in on their private business," my neighbor suggested shrewdly. "They wanted a solo op, and if you're right that he was putting the bite on them, they picked the wrong guy."

I whisked my coffee pot off the stove seconds before it exploded again. I really needed one of those fancy electric espresso makers, where you didn't have to mop off your stove every time you forgot you'd started to make coffee. Maybe for my birthday, next week, if I solved Wuchnik's murder by then. And if anyone paid me for doing so. The good machines cost more than a thousand dollars.

My cell phone rang as I was divvying the fresh coffee between Mr. Contreras's and my cups. I didn't recognize the number, but a strange male voice said, "Ms. Warshawski? This is Gabriel Eycks. Julia Salanter needs to see you. Please come to Schiller Street at once."

Gabriel Eycks—Gabe, the Salanters' houseman.

"I'm tied up right now, Mr. Eycks. If Ms. Salanter wants to make an appointment, I'll be glad to see her at my office."

"We have an emergency here, Ms. Warshawski. Arielle has disappeared, and Julia hopes you or your cousin know where she is."

31. WHERE, OH, WHERE DID THE DAUGHTER GO?

As I drove, Gabe directed me to the mansion's garage entrance. This was behind the house, via an alley that could be entered only through a locked gate. The garage was underground; Gabe was standing inside it between a Land Rover and a Mercedes sedan. He told me to leave the car where it was, not to bother parking properly, and led me up a back stairwell to the side room where I'd first met Julia Salanter last week.

Julia was walking back and forth in a short circuit, clutching her hands. Her face seemed to be all eyes and mouth, two dark pools over a skull-like rictus. She started talking as soon as she saw us, without preamble.

"Chaim is flying home, but he won't get here before five. She isn't with Petra, is she? I tried reaching Petra, but she wasn't answering her phone. Sonia Appelzeller—your cousin's supervisor at Malina—Sonia says Petra doesn't come in on Wednesdays until afternoon. I need to reach her now!"

"I stopped at my cousin's apartment on my way here. She was sleeping and hadn't heard her phone ring, but she hasn't seen or heard from your daughter since the attack on the Malina Building last week."

Petra had been cross when I leaned on the doorbell hard enough to wake her, but as soon as she heard about Arielle, she came fully awake in a hurry. "But, gosh, Vic, if she isn't with Nia I don't know what to suggest. Unless she ran off to join her father? I don't know where he is or what their story is."

I thought Petra's suggestion was a good one, so I asked Julia whether she'd talked to Arielle's father.

"He's dead," Julia said. "He died of leukemia when Arielle was four. It's how Sophy and I became friends, on the cancer ward, husbands with the same illness, daughters the same age. Are you sure Petra isn't hiding something?"

I bit back a snappy retort. Your kid goes missing, you get a free pass on the things you blurt out.

"Let's start from the beginning," I suggested. "When did you last see or talk to Arielle? When did you decide she was missing?"

Julia blinked—the recent past, the past where she didn't know something was wrong, seemed incredibly remote. "At seven-fifteen. I was getting ready to leave—I had an early meeting, and I didn't want Arielle sleeping all day. She has chores, and her community service. I think everyone needs a schedule—none of that matters!" She wrung her hands. "When I saw her bed was tidily made I thought perhaps she'd gone for a bike ride—really, I thought she'd sneaked out early to see Nia Durango, and I was starting to lose my temper, when Gabe said she left through the garage at two!"

I turned to the houseman. "Why didn't you tell Julia sooner?"

"I didn't know at the time." His voice was calm, but his brown eyes were watchful. "Julia came into the kitchen asking if I'd seen Arielle. When I realized she was gone, I looked at all the security camera footage. That's when I saw her letting herself out through the garage."

"No one was with her?"

"Not that I could see. You can look at the footage yourself, if you want."

"I guess, in a minute. It's the police you should be showing it to. When are they arriving?"

"The police?" Julia said. "What can they do? It's not as if she was snatched; she walked out of here on her own. Are you a hundred percent sure she's not with Petra?"

"Julia—Ms. Salanter—you're not thinking. You have to call the police and the FBI. You and your father must have discussed this terrifying eventuality."

"I've called Thor Janssen. He's on his way, but what can the police do? No one snatched my daughter, but why did she leave? Where did she go?"

"Thor Janssen?" I interrupted.

"The family lawyer," Gabe answered for Julia.

"If someone phoned Arielle, the police can discover that instantly," I said. "Trying to pretend that this is a normal event, it's costing you precious time."

Gabe nodded. "She's right, Julia. Thor will tell you the same thing when he gets here."

"And the one person who might know why Arielle left is Nia Durango. Maybe they're off at some shape-shifter ritual together. Have you talked to Nia, or to Dr. Durango?"

"It was Sophy's and my punishment to the girls that they couldn't text or see each other for two weeks. They haven't spoken since we did our TV show last week!"

"And you know this because?"

"Because Sophy and I ordered them not to! We blocked their respective numbers on their cell phones just to make sure!"

"Give me Nia's or Sophy's number," I said. "If you think two girls as tight as your daughters paid any attention to a command not to talk for two weeks, you must have led the life of a cloistered nun when you were a kid!"

Gabe was typing onto a cell phone while I was speaking. "Gabe Eycks here, Diane. We have a high-alert situation here; do you know where Nia and Sophy are?"

After a pause, he spoke to Sophy Durango, explained the situation, asked that she send Nia to the Schiller Street house immediately. It was another instance of how central Gabe's role in the household was. Doorman, crisis manager, what else did this houseman do? Arrange bodies on catafalques?

Julia took the phone from Gabe and began a longer conversation with Sophy, a distraught, detailed version of her crisis. I started to get agitated myself. The longer we waited to talk to Nia, the longer it would take to follow any trails she could lead us to.

"Dr. Durango's housekeeper is on her way with Nia," Gabe assured me. "It's good for Julia to talk to Sophy. While we're waiting for Janssen, let me show you the footage of Arielle."

Gabe took me to the control room. The house had security cameras at every door, as well as in the security fence and on the corners of the roof and garage. They were expertly mounted, not readily visible, and the footage streamed to a backup system that ran frequent checks to see whether the same faces were peering through the fence on successive days. If anyone tried to climb the fence, a buzzer sounded on Gabe's cell phone.

"You're the only staff member?"

"The only one who lives in. Two women come to help with the cleaning and the laundry; they're in the kitchen now. Julia already spoke to them; they don't know anything. They've been with her for over a decade, both of them, and they're completely reliable. There's Livia Barradas, who used to be Arielle's nanny—she still comes to stay when Julia and Chaim are both out of town. Chaim's PA Wren has a key, but she works out of his office on LaSalle Street."

He showed me the footage of Arielle's departure. There were no cameras in the bedrooms, but there were two in the halls. We saw Arielle in cutoffs and a T-shirt, carrying her shoes; the time stamp was 2:03.33. At 2:05.17, she ran down two flights of stairs, stopped in the kitchen, where she put on her shoes and picked up an apple, and went down to the basement. At 2:11.08, she pushed the button that opened the garage door.

"Is there a reason she didn't use the front door?"

Gabe nodded. "Once the family is at home for the night, I turn on the interior cameras and set the alarms on the doors and windows. If any of them are opened, my phone buzzes me. The garage alarm only rings if it's opened from the outside. That's a security lapse which we didn't think about, but apparently, Arielle did. And it may be that someone else did as well."

"It's why you need the police," I reiterated wearily. "They can interrogate the security company, and the lovers of the women who clean, and the children of Livia Barradas, and so on and on." I looked at him squarely. "Not to mention your own connections. You're at the heart of this household; you know all its secrets."

Gabe's lips tightened in anger, but he said levelly, "You're right: you don't know me, or my history with the family. I've been with Chaim since I was a junior in college. I don't expect a stranger to take my word that I've never given a lover access to any security codes or family secrets, but by all means—investigate my past, my friends, my family."

I nodded, not agreement, just acknowledgment that I would do all of that if it became necessary. "In the meantime, call the cops. Don't wait for Julia's okay, just do it!"

The front door rang in the middle of my plea. We both looked at the monitor. It was a tall man, dressed in a suit, despite the heat.

"That's Thor Janssen." Gabe released the front-door lock. A moment later, Nia Durango appeared on the monitor at the front gate, accompanied by a middle-aged white woman. Gabe released the lock again, but I sprinted down the hall to the front door, beating the staff from the kitchen as well as Julia.

There was a flurry of confused greetings, the lawyer suspicious, Nia scared, Sophy's housekeeper unflappable. Gabe arrived a moment later; he and Sophy's housekeeper sorted us into our component parts. Gabe took the lawyer off to see Julia in the library. Diane Ovech, the house-keeper, accompanied Nia and me to the family room.

"Nia, how were you and Arielle communicating this past week?" I said as soon as we were sitting on the wicker chairs.

Nia looked from Diane to me.

"This has gone way beyond whether you violated your mothers' or-ders to separate for two weeks," I said. "This is about Arielle's safety. Did you use Facebook?"

When Nia still didn't answer, Diane Ovech said, "You need to speak." Her voice was calm but implacable.

"Our moms look at our Facebook pages," Nia whispered. "We used old-fashioned stuff, like the landlines if our moms weren't home, but mostly e-mail."

At any other time I might have laughed to hear e-mail characterized as old-fashioned. "Did Arielle e-mail you that she would be going out last night?"

"No. If she decided at the last second, she couldn't tell me because we couldn't text. That's the trouble with e-mail, you don't know you've got it, not unless you've got, like, an iPhone or something, and we just have ordinary phones, they don't have e-mail, so we have to use our computers."

"Do you know how to get into Arielle's computer?" I asked. "Let's see if someone else was reaching out to her the old-fashioned way."

Nia admitted that she and Arielle used the same passwords. She led her minder and me up two flights of stairs and down a short hall to her friend's room. The computer was sitting on a small desk. While Nia turned it on and logged on, I had a quick look around.

It was the typical bedroom of a modern affluent teen, with the requisite sound and video systems, the laptop with its webcam, a wardrobe with a minimalist collection of clothes.

Arielle's bookshelves included books on the Holocaust—*How Dark the Heavens; From That Time and Place; How to Document Victims and Locate Survivors of the Holocaust*—sprinkled among the novels of her childhood. The seven books in Boadicea Jones's *Carmilla* series held pride of place, but she'd branched into other vampire novels, like the original *Dracula*. A collection of stuffed animals, including a large bright-eyed raven, looked down on her bed from a shelf at the foot.

"Okay, Nia. Let's see what you two girls have been talking about this week," Diane said.

I took Nia's place at the desk and scrolled through the correspondence. They e-mailed each other four or five times a day, nothing compared to the texts they would have sent, but they still managed to fill each other in on the minutiae of their lives. Arielle's included volunteer work at the Malina Foundation, a day's sailing with an aunt and uncle, a trip to Ravinia, where a famed singer who knew her mother had entertained them with a late supper. Nia had gone to campaign events in Kankakee and Edwardsville with her mother, had done data entry at the campaign office, and gone for a long bike ride with Nolan Spaulding and Jessie Morgenstern—*Loser crybabies!*

Last night at ten-thirty, Arielle had written, *Surprise message from one of our Ravens. Very mysterious, she wouldn't ID herself. Got to go out, call the landline if you get this message before one a.m.*

Nia and Diane were reading over my shoulder.

"One of your Ravens?" I asked. "Would that be Nolan or Jessie?"

Nia's oval face was scrunched into a circle of worry. "It could be them, or Tyler."

"Anyone in your Carmilla group except you and Arielle, in other words."

Nia nodded.

"Any idea what this was about?"

"No," she whispered. "It's the first time I even saw the message. Mom woke me up to tell me about Arielle, and I didn't log on or anything before Diane and I left home."

I looked back up through the messages but didn't see anything from the other girls in the Carmilla book club. "How would she have gotten the message?" I asked Nia.

"On her cell phone. It was only my number that Aunt Julia blocked, just while we did our punishment for breaking curfew and—and lying, and stuff."

"I'll call my cousin. She might have heard from another girl in the group and not connected the dots when I woke her this morning. And even if no one called Petra, she can help us reach all the girls in the Malina club to see who contacted Arielle. But we really need the police involved," I added to Diane. "They can get a log of calls to Arielle's phone fast."

"I'll go down and tell Julia," Diane said. "I don't know why she's dragging her feet on this. Nia, you come with me: you need to tell Julia everything you just said to us. At least we know Arielle wasn't coerced into leaving."

We didn't know that: we knew only that Arielle had left the house under her own steam, but the video footage already told us that. Anyone could have texted her, pretending to be part of the Malina group. I didn't say this to Nia—she was too scared already.

I phoned Petra and explained what I wanted.

"I'm all over it," Petra said. "I'll call them all until I find which one contacted Arielle. I've been feeling totally useless and scared."

"You and me both, babe," I said. "You and me both."

32. TRUNK LINE

WHILE I WAITED TO HEAR BACK FROM MY COUSIN, I TROLLED through Arielle's computer, looking for any mention of Miles Wuchnik. I went back two months but didn't see e-mails from or about him. Nor had she had gone to his website. The only messages she'd sent yesterday had been to Nia. Any other friends she could still have reached by text.

I realized I'd only gone as far back as early May, around the time Wuchnik had first visited Ruhetal. My unconscious mind was insisting on a connection between Arielle and Wuchnik, despite Mr. Contreras's suggestion that Wuchnik might have been horning in on a drug ring out at Ruhetal.

I conscientiously scrolled through Arielle's e-mails all the way back to the first of the year. I didn't see anything of interest, except Arielle's efforts to interview the author of the *Carmilla* novels. She'd done a school project on the *Queen of the Night* books, and Boadicea Jones, or an assistant, had sent back answers to Arielle's questions—gracious of a writer who was probably deluged with fan mail.

I felt agitated and immobile at the same time; going through websites was treading time, but I didn't know what else to do right now.

The sites Arielle had visited repeatedly dealt with genealogy and the Holocaust. She had spent a lot of time at the Holocaust Museum site, and had even e-mailed them, careful not to trumpet her connection to vast wealth.

> My name is Arielle Zitter. I am twelve years old and I am trying to discover my roots. My grandfather's family is called Salanter and they came from near Vilna in Lithuania, but he won't tell me anything about his history. I think my grandfather's mother's name was Judith because my mom is called Julia after her. Everyone but him died in the Holocaust, I think, but I don't know if it was at Ponar or somewhere else. I think his mom died in 1941 but maybe it was 1942. Can you help?

The museum had written back, suggesting that Arielle and her parents make an appointment with a museum archivist if they were coming to Washington. They also gave her a list of recommended resources, including some of the books I'd seen on her shelves.

I wondered if Arielle's interest in her grandfather's history came out of Lawlor's attacks on him. It made sense: Global was accusing Chaim Salanter of terrible atrocities; Arielle wanted to know the truth.

My cell phone rang. Not Petra, as I'd hoped, but Gabe Eycks, asking me to join the team in the library. "On the second floor, just below Arielle's room," he instructed.

Julia and her lawyer had been augmented by a tall woman with cool hazel eyes, who eyed me narrowly—I wasn't surprised to find she was with the FBI.

"Special Agent Christa Velpel," Gabe said. "Fortunately, Thor called the Bureau as soon as he got here."

Mercifully, unlike most cops I meet, Special Agent Velpel didn't waste time by demanding an accounting from me on why or where or what I'd been doing. She'd already heard about Arielle's early-morning e-mail to Nia from Nia and Diane, and had sent them back to the family room.

"Nia may know something she doesn't think is important; I'll talk to her again in a bit. The same thing is true of your cousin Petra, so let me have her phone number and so on."

I explained that Petra was already phoning all the girls in the book club to see who'd been in touch with Arielle.

"Have her call me. A skilled investigator will think of questions that may elicit information she doesn't think she has. And if *you* think of something, let me know. I understand from Ms. Salanter that your main interest has been the death of this private eye, not the girls?"

I tried not to let my hackles rise at Velpel's bland assumption that I wouldn't know how to elicit information, from myself or my cousin. This conversation wasn't about me, it was about saving Arielle, after all.

"It's true I'm looking into Wuchnik's death," I said, "but it's an odd coincidence that he was killed in the same time and place they were having their full-moon ritual. Maybe the Bureau has the skilled interrogators to find out if there's a connection there. His phone and computer and so on were all taken from his home within two days of his death. And his sister in Danville, who's his heir, doesn't have them."

"Oh, leave that alone!" Julia begged. "*You* may care about some dead slimy investigator, but I only care about my daughter."

"You're right, you're right," I said soothingly.

Velpel frowned. "It's an oddity, and we'll follow up on any oddities right now."

She pulled a small notebook from an inside jacket pocket and scribbled a note. The movement lifted the skirts of her jacket, revealing the bottom of her shoulder holster, and her Armani label. My eyebrows went up: the Bureau must pay its senior agents well.

"Right. Thanks, Ms. Warshawski. I don't think we need you any longer this morning."

Despite the brusqueness of the dismissal, I was relieved: the atmosphere at the Schiller Street mansion was so full of distress and secrets that it was wearing me down.

When Gabe said he'd take me down to the garage to let me out, Velpel shook her head. "I'll go with Ms. Warshawski. We don't know whether anyone's watching the house from across the street, and I'd like to see if we provoke special interest when the garage door is opened. Your cameras pick up the sidewalk outside the house but not buildings across the street."

Velpel called another agent who was outside, watching the street, and told him what she wanted him to focus on, then escorted me to my car. She walked up the ramp in front of me when the garage door opened. I didn't stop to see whether she'd spotted anyone—she didn't need my help for that kind of operation, and I wanted to get to my cousin.

It was as I was bouncing through the potholes on my way to the Kennedy that the word "genie" suddenly hit me, so much like a blow between the shoulder blades that I pulled abruptly off the road. Cars honked; a passing driver gave me the finger.

Genie. Genealogy. When I questioned Arielle about whether she had met or talked to Miles Wuchnik, Nia had said, "Maybe he was a genie," and both girls had giggled.

Had Arielle gone behind her family's back and hired Miles to investigate Chaim Salanter's history? Should I race back to the Schiller mansion and demand an answer from Nia? I was trying to imagine how to guide such a conversation when my cousin called.

"Vic, I've talked to everyone in the group except Tyler and Kira. Tyler's away at summer camp, some place down in Texas, her mom said, where the kids have to keep their phones off during the day. Kira's in town, but she lost her cell phone that night in the cemetery and I don't have her mom's phone number. Do you want me to drive over to her place?"

"No, I'm only a few blocks away. I'll make sure she's okay and get back to you."

It took me only a few minutes to reach the Dudek apartment on Augusta. My heart was beating uncomfortably as I rang their doorbell. When no one answered after the second ring, I ran to my car to get my picklocks from the glove compartment. I reached the front door again just as Kira, carrying a large bag of groceries, arrived with Lucy.

Kira eyed me warily. "Are you here because of the book club? My mom doesn't want me to go back."

"Yeah, she got painted on, she got egged on, she can't be in such a stranger-danger place," Lucy chimed in.

"I'm here to make sure you're okay." My voice was thin with relief. "Arielle got a message from one of the Ravens and disappeared from her home in the middle of the night. I wanted—never mind. Did you ever find your cell phone? Did you cancel the service?"

Kira shook her head. "It's a pay-as-you-go phone, so if someone found it, they can use up my minutes, or they can buy some more minutes. What happened to Arielle?"

"We don't know. Look, just to be on the safe side, can you stay home with Lucy today?"

"We're going to the park," Lucy said.

"I'm not one of those rich Vina Fields kids who has a nanny and a private boat and all that stuff," Kira snapped. "My mom cleans hotel rooms all night, she sleeps during the day, and it's better for her if I take Lucy out for the day."

"So you're bringing home breakfast and then taking off? Clouds are building, looks like rain. I don't think you'll be able to spend much time outside. I'll help you get these bags upstairs and then you can spend the day at my home, with a couple of friendly dogs and a wonderful old man to protect you. Petra will drive you there."

"Dogs?" Lucy said. "Do you have a horse?"

"Nope. And I don't have a boat, either. But my neighbor will let you watch horse races on television." And he would feed them spaghetti and ice cream, and basically do all the things that are supposed to be bad for you, but he would shower them with affection, which is always good for you.

I took Kira's big sack, and the smaller one Lucy was clutching, and followed them into the building. Their mother was in the front room, with breakfast bowls and glasses laid out on the eating side of the small table. She was still wearing the beige uniform of the Hotel Beaumont's housekeeping staff, with her name badge ("I'm Ivona. How can I serve you?") clipped to the breast pocket.

She looked at me in astonishment and rapped out a question in Polish. Kira and Lucy started answering her in unison. I walked over and put down the groceries. I had met Ivona Dudek two weeks ago, after I'd searched the cemetery for Kira's phone, but I wasn't sure she remembered me.

"*Pani* Dudek? *Mam* V. I. Warshawski." That was the extent of my Polish, but the fact that I knew any words in her language, or maybe the reminder of my connection to Petra, seemed to calm her down. With the girls chiming in as a chorus, I explained my wish to have them in a safe place until we knew what had become of Arielle.

The three Dudeks had an animated conversation, with the word *"miliarder"* popping up—close enough to the Italian *"miliardario"* that I knew they were discussing the billionaire grandfather. They also talked about the *"Fundacja Malina."*

"My mother is upset that we have to suffer for the problems of a billionaire," Kira explained. "But she knows you took care of me when we were attacked last week at the foundation. And she knows she can trust Petra. She'll let Petra take us up to your home."

I called my cousin again. Her energy vibrated over the line: yes, she'd be at the Dudeks' place at once, well, at least as soon as she'd shaved her legs, she'd been in the middle—I thanked her and hung up. When I called Mr. Contreras, he, too, was delighted at the prospect of a visit from the girls. Like Kira and Lucy, he doesn't get many adventures, or changes of pace in his life. Besides, as I'd expected, the chance to play protector appealed to his romantic vision of himself.

By the time Ms. Dudek had helped her daughters pack what they would need for a day, and perhaps even a night, away from home, Petra had arrived. Ms. Dudek kissed her on both cheeks, and said—through Kira—that she was happy that she could go to work tonight without worrying about her girls.

As I helped Petra pack the girls into her Pathfinder, I told her I was still worried about Tyler. "I'd better talk to her mom, get the number at that camp in Texas. If anyone actually saw the killer, it was Tyler— she's the one who screamed that she'd seen a vampire, right as I found the girls in the cemetery."

Petra pulled out her phone to text me Tyler's mother's details. Rhonda Shankman, real estate agent and part-time media escort, whatever that was.

I told Petra to take Ashland Avenue north, instead of the expressway, so I could check for tails. After a mile of cutting in and out around her, when I was pretty sure she was clean, I turned south again, to Leavitt Street and the entrance to Mount Moriah cemetery. Kira had dropped her cell phone there. I hadn't found it the day after the murder, but maybe the murderer had. He (she? I thought of Helen Kendrick or Eloise Napier) saw himself in the photographs, looked for old text messages, and found Arielle's number.

A message from Kira's phone would show up on Arielle's screen as a number she recognized. No, he must have blocked the number: I remembered Arielle's e-mail to Nia, *one of our Ravens*, she'd said. *Very mysterious.* But he'd have to have signed it in a way that made Arielle believe it was from someone she knew. I imagined the message: *Meet me in the cemetery. Raven.*

But why did the finder want to lure Arielle from home? And why had she slipped out once again in such a secretive way?

Perhaps the text read, *Meet me in the cemetery; I can tell you your grandfather's secrets. Raven.*

When I parked outside the cemetery's padlocked gates, the clouds were thickening, swirling, and the wind was picking up. We hadn't had a storm since the night I'd found the girls and Miles Wuchnik, and I'd forgotten to bring any rain gear with me.

The police tape had come undone from one of the posts and was trailing across the broken sidewalk. A cache of empties and the remains of some kind of carry-out food lay nearby—something about the crime-scene tape had attracted picnickers. I jogged up Leavitt to the gap in the fence we'd all used ten days ago and made my way to the Saloman family mausoleum as fast as I could in the failing light.

Police tape still festooned the pillars. I slipped under it. The tomb where Miles Wuchnik had lain still had his bloodstains on it, but it was empty. I picked my way through more empty Colt 45 bottles, more cigarette butts, and condoms on the mausoleum floor but couldn't find anything that looked as though Arielle or her Raven had been here.

I'd been convinced I'd find something—afraid it would be Arielle's body but sure there would be some trace of her. Now I was so disconcerted I didn't know what to do next. As if to underscore my failure, a loud clap of thunder sounded; a moment later rain poured down in thick sheets.

I stood under the tomb's small rotunda to call Special Agent Velpel, to tell her that all of the girls denied having been in touch with Arielle in the night. If Velpel had any news herself, she didn't report it, just said she would call Petra to get the girls' numbers.

I told her about Kira's missing phone, and the possibility that someone who'd picked it up had used it to lure Arielle out of her home.

Velpel agreed it would be helpful to try to trace Kira's phone—if it were still turned on—and the Bureau had the resources to do that. She even agreed that my theory was plausible, so I overlooked her reiteration that she needed to talk to Petra and the Malina girls herself. I didn't tell her that I'd sent Kira and Lucy to my own place—I wasn't comfortable with handing over a couple of girls who might be illegal to the Bureau. Even a soft interrogation could lead to their mother's deportation.

The rain started blowing into the little mausoleum, soaking my legs. I might as well continue my search, if I was getting wet anyway. I went into the downpour and made a slow circuit of the clearing where the girls had been dancing.

The rain was beating the ground, digging up little pebbles and bits of glass, and it was impossible to tell if anyone had walked through here—or dragged an unconscious girl through here—recently. Lightning kept crackling, so close that the hairs rose on my arms several times. I knew that it was dangerous to stay here among the stones and the trees, but I was too frightened about Arielle's fate to worry about my own safety.

By the time I finished exploring the area, my T-shirt was clinging to my wet torso. Not only was I having trouble thinking clearly, I was blinded by the rain dripping from my hair into my eyes. I couldn't bring myself to leave the cemetery, though, until I had retraced the path the girls and I had taken after their Raven ritual.

The thunder had died to a faint growl and the rain had lightened to a mist by the time I reached the cemetery's east wall. I found the place where I thought I'd sent the girls over and scrambled to the top, my running shoes slipping on the wet bricks.

I jumped down to Hamilton Street and continued my blind search of the grass and the gutter. And found myself looking at some Sportmax wire wheels, picked out in red trim. They were attached to a red Camaro, its paint shiny in the wet. The tinted windows were hard to see through in the rain, but I thought there was a body inside.

I had my picks with me, but it was no time for finesse. I pried two loose bricks from the wall. Used one as a hammer and the other as the nail and smashed the window. When I opened the door, I saw Xavier Jurgens in the driver's seat, his head flopped against the steering wheel.

Jurgens had thrown up violently. The vomit had already begun to rot in the thick July air. The stench was so horrible that it was all I could do to make myself feel for a pulse. I didn't find one, but the vomit was well mixed with alcohol; he might be alive at some minimal level.

The keys were still in the ignition. I'll never know what impulse made me do it, but I pulled them out and opened the trunk. Wedged against the spare wheel, her head near the backseat pass-through, was Arielle Zitter.

33. SUICIDE OR MURDER: TAKE YOUR PICK

ARIELLE WAS GOING TO MAKE IT, ALTHOUGH I DIDN'T GET THAT reassuring news from anyone on Schiller Street. When I realized the Salanter ménage, including Gabe Eycks, was on lockdown, not answering calls, I had tried the FBI's Christa Velpel.

"How is Arielle?"

"Her condition isn't something I can discuss with you."

My eyebrows and temper went up at the same time. "Ms. Velpel, you and I both know you're a truly skilled investigator because you told me that about a dozen times this morning. I'm just the bumbling private eye who found Arielle Zitter. Now I want to know if she's going to make it—she wasn't in good shape when I bumbled my way to her location this morning."

Somehow that approach didn't make the fed feel more cooperative. It was Lotty who finally got me some news; she worked her network and found someone at the hospital where the EMTs had rushed Arielle.

"She was given a strong antipsychotic, in fact, some of the Abilify that you say was at the scene. She would have suffocated if she'd been in that car much longer. What kept her alive until you found her was that she'd vomited up a lot of the drug and miraculously hadn't sucked it back into her lungs. They're flooding her, trying to wash the rest of the Abilify out of her system."

"Abilify?" I said. "Isn't that some kind of antidepressant?"

"Oh, it's one of those drugs that TV is begging doctors to prescribe," Lotty said. "It does a lot of things, but it's a powerful antipsychotic. It shouldn't be handed out as if it were candy. Arielle had much too much of it for safety; it's left her very confused. The neuropsychiatrist I spoke to says she can't remember anything of the past twenty-four hours and is hazy on other matters, but he hopes that will clear up in another few days. You are a true heroine in this story, Victoria."

"Not a heroine, Lotty, just incredibly lucky—I don't even know what made me climb over that cemetery wall to find the car."

The other piece of luck for Arielle had been that Xavier Jurgens started the night with a full tank of gas. The evidence techs who came to the Camaro told me Xavier had kept the car on, with the air-conditioning at full bore, until it ran out of gas on its own. Arielle had been lying in the stifling heat for only an hour or so before I found her.

Xavier Jurgens hadn't been as lucky. He'd drunk too much vodka with his Abilify, and had been dead himself before his car died.

Evidence techs aren't usually very chatty, especially not with private eyes like me, but one of the team had done his rookie partnership with my dad at the old Twelfth District. When Cosimo Draco connected my name to my father's, he told me he was the luckiest graduate in his academy class, getting assigned to Tony Warshawski.

"He was a real teacher, and the steadiest guy in the district. If he'd been watch commander, the Twelfth would have been a different place. It was Tony who encouraged me to get the training to work crime scenes."

In the wake of the morning thunderstorm, the sun had come out with a humidity-laden ferocity. My wet T-shirt and jeans dried to an unpleasant clamminess, and the stench from the car became unbearable.

Draco kept talking, though, sharing his team's findings, so I fought back my nausea and stayed close to the scene.

Jurgens's cell phone was on the floor at his feet, splattered with vomit but still usable. Draco held it delicately by the corners, put it into an evidence bag, then showed me the text message that he was able to bring up on the screen.

I shouldn't have done it, Jannie, any of it, Wuchnik or the kid. Sorry to screw up your life. I'll always love you, xxx Xavier.

My brows went up. "When I saw Jurgens, he was swinging a butcher knife at me. And Jana, his 'Jannie,' was screaming the street down, calling her neighbors 'whores' and spitting nails. It's hard to imagine them exchanging love notes."

Draco shrugged. "People behave differently behind closed doors. And he was probably panicking, feeling the drug and not being able to do anything. Who was Wuchnik?"

"The vampire killing, Drake," one of the other techs said.

"Oh. Guy was found here, wasn't he? I didn't work the scene, but Lurie here did, right, Lure?"

The youngest of the three-man crew nodded. "Yeah, and it turned out a bunch of girls were in here dancing in the rain while the guy was having a spike pounded through him. This sounds like a confession, don't it—'I shouldn't have done Wuchnik.' Why'd he snatch the girl, though?"

"She was one of the crew dancing in the rain," I said, "but if he was planning on killing himself, why would he bother with her?"

"Maybe he wanted to blame her for his troubles," Draco said. "Her grandpa is the rich guy, right? If he blamed the rich for his troubles, he wouldn't be the first, but that's for the detectives to sort out."

I wasn't convinced, but there was no point in arguing with the tech team. "Arielle left home because of a text message she got, we know that much. Can you see what other texts he sent?"

Draco pulled the phone back out of the evidence locker and scrolled up through the plastic. "He didn't write to the kid, at least not last night. In fact, he doesn't look like much of a texter. There's not a lot else on here for yesterday."

"Did you find another cell phone on him?"

The youngest tech said they only found Jurgens's personal phone. "We went through his pockets; we found the bottle he'd taken away from the Ruhetal pharmacy—it's labeled 'Abilify'—and his house keys, a wallet, but we didn't find a second phone. You think there should be another one?"

"One of the girls had lost her phone here at the cemetery ten days ago; I was sure the killer found it and used it to lure Arielle here."

"Theories are for the detectives," Draco repeated. "We, thank God, get to deal in facts. But bear in mind, kids lie all the time if they think they're in trouble. I'd wait to see what they say to a skilled interrogator."

Ah, these mythical interrogators with their highly honed skills. If the detectives talked to the Ravens—the loser crybabies, as Nia had called two Vina Fields girls in one of her e-mails—the police might learn what codes or language the Carmilla club members used with one another. But what could the girls tell even the most skilled interrogator about Xavier Jurgens or Miles Wuchnik?

If the two men's connection was simply a drug ring operating out of Ruhetal, the Ravens wouldn't know anything about it. Not that tween girls can't be users or dealers, but none of the Ravens had shown signs of that: the only needles they used were the ones they pricked their palms with to become shape-shifters.

But if my little brain flash about Wuchnik being a "genie" in Nia and Arielle's minds because he was connected to Arielle's genealogy search was on target, then Nia might well know more than she'd told me this morning. And if the feds or the local cops talked to Nia, the story would be all over the broadband waves in a trice. Leaks sprouted from the Wuchnik interrogation faster than holes in the sides of the *Titanic*.

I could imagine Wade Lawlor and Helen Kendrick's innuendo-laden scripts. *I don't know about you, but my kids are home after curfew. What is it about the billionaire Salanter family and "we're all apes" Durango that lets them think their kids are special and don't have to play by the same rules as ours?* Or words to that effect.

"I wish I knew what had happened to the kid's phone," I said to the techs. "It has the evidence of who sent her the text message that brought her here last night. And then—I don't know. I can't imagine Jurgens being that subtle."

"For the third time, Warshawski, we don't do theories," Draco said. "Anything could have happened to the girl's phone—kids lose them all the time. I know mine do—it's like the phone is the beating heart that keeps them alive, only they leave it at the mall or at a friend's or drop it when they get out of the car."

"You're imagining this like some kind of TV show, but criminals don't act like that most of the time." The youngest tech stopped in the middle of repacking his equipment bag to look at me. "The detectives will decide, of course, but your guy Xavier was just flailing around. He drugs the girl, gets her into his car, starts to write a ransom note, and then realizes how high the odds against him are. So he mixes the drug into his booze, knocks it back, and drifts off to Jesus."

"Or whoever," Draco said. "I've got everything photographed. Lunchtime, boys."

What do you eat after spending a couple of hours inhaling vodka-laced vomit? For me, a tall cold one. Water, not beer. I took the long way back to my car, and was lucky to find a street vendor hawking bottles of water at Augusta and Leavitt. I bought two and sat on the curb drinking, trying to make sense of the things I'd seen and heard since leaving my own home a century or so ago.

The evidence techs were willing to label this a kidnapping gone wrong. And who was I to say they weren't right? You could interpret Jurgens's farewell message to his true love as a confession that he'd killed Miles Wuchnik, and then killed himself. End of story, sort of.

It still didn't explain where Jurgens got the money to buy the Camaro, or where Wuchnik had gotten the money he was sending his sister, or who had sent Arielle Zitter whatever message had brought her onto the mean streets.

I got up and walked back to my car. I needed to change clothes. And probably, despite the dull nausea I felt in the wake of Jurgens's death, I needed to eat something—I'd gotten the SOS from Gabe Eycks in the middle of breakfast, and that had been six hours ago. Maybe if I ate, I'd be able to think of what I needed to do next.

By the time I reached home, I found that Mr. Contreras was running out of steam. He'd been on his own for an hour, since Petra had to go in to work, and little Lucy not only had the energy of an atomic pile but a certain ruthlessness that made her realize she could get pretty much what she wanted from "*Dziadzio* Sal" by opening her blue eyes as wide as possible and looking like an orphan about one second away from death.

The girls had been playing with the dogs: red ribbons festooned Peppy's neck and tail, but Mitch was wearing a pink babydoll pajama top and a baby bonnet. When I laughed at the sight, he gave me a look of burning indignation and slunk behind Mr. Contreras's couch.

"Did you find Arielle?" Kira asked.

"Yep. She'd gone back to the cemetery where you had your initiation ceremony."

"Why'd she do that?" Mr. Contreras said. "And the middle of the night, too, like she hadn't already caused her ma and her grandpa a carload of grief!"

"You know her better than we do, Kira," I said. "Why do you think she did it?"

Kira hunched a thin shoulder. "I don't know. Arielle does what she wants and the rest of us are supposed to clap."

"Everybody clap your hands," Lucy started to sing, but her sister told her to shut up.

"You know, girls, your *Dziadzio* needs a little time alone if he's going to stay up to watch a movie with you tonight. You'll be sleeping in my apartment, so I need you to come upstairs and help me put clean sheets on the bed."

Despite his humiliating wardrobe, Mitch bounded up the stairs after Lucy and Kira. I set them to changing the bed while I took a shower and found some clean clothes. When I was dressed, I logged on to my laptop as a guest, to keep the girls out of my confidential files, and downloaded a Nancy Drew puzzle for Kira to solve. Lucy was happy enough in front of the television, so I went back to my neighbor, to tell him the full story on what had happened to Arielle.

"The techs are slanting their findings toward suicide, but I'm not convinced," I said. "We don't know why or how Xavier got Arielle into that car. Teens and their phones are glued to each other; Arielle's is missing. The techs say she probably dropped it struggling with Xavier, but if that's the case, where is it? And then there's Kira's phone, which I'm pretty sure the killer used to send Arielle that bogus text."

"It's not that I'm questioning you, doll, because I seen you before, you been right when the cops say you're wrong, but why couldn't it be like they said. This guy Xavier, he even cut you with a butcher knife last week. He coulda killed Wuchnik and then figured the law was closing in on him, just like your techs say. 'Specially if Wuchnik was blackmailing him over drugs."

I thought it over. "That might be right, but someone gave Xavier money to buy that Camaro. You don't shell out fifteen thousand for doing nothing. I think whoever gave Xavier the money orchestrated last night's event, set it up to look like a kidnapping-suicide."

"Then how are these two gals involved?" Mr. Contreras jerked a thumb toward the third floor.

"The girls were all taking pictures with their phones and one of them shouted that she'd seen a vampire. She probably really saw either Wuchnik lurking in the shadows, waiting to meet the person who killed him, or the killer himself. If Kira took a picture with her phone and the killer found the phone, he may be trying to track her down. She doesn't have a service plan, so there isn't a way to ID her from the phone itself. I may be completely off base here, but just in case, I don't want anyone to get a whiff of who or where Kira and Lucy are. I know it's a lot of strain, especially the little one, but—"

"Oh, come on, doll. The day a couple of cute little girls are too much for me is the day you send me off to live in Ruthie's basement."

I hugged him and gave him a grateful kiss. Ever since he turned eighty, his daughter has been lobbying to get him out to her family room in Hoffman Estates. Since she whines and complains whenever she's around him, I don't understand why she wants him to live with her, although I know jealousy of his closeness to me plays a role.

"But why did he text the other gal, this Arielle?"

"Can't answer that one—we don't have her phone or Kira's. Maybe I'm wrong, anyway—Kira's phone could be in some drunk's pocket right now. And until Arielle gets her wits back, we can't ask her anything. Although I will talk to Nia Durango before the day is done."

But my first stop would be Burbank, to see how Jana Shatka was bearing up under her loss.

34. DRUG REQ

Word of Xavier's death had reached Laramie Avenue: when I pulled up across the street, I saw a little knot of women pause on the sidewalk in front of his duplex and point.

I crossed over to them. "Is Ms. Shatka home, do you know?"

One of the women shrugged, but another looked at me. "You were here before, weren't you? Xavier, he slashed you for asking about the car. Are you with the bank? Because he is dead, and the car is gone, I don't think you'll see it no more." She apparently thought I'd come to repo the Camaro.

"I'm a detective."

"Oh, the police, they were here already. Breaking the news. Is it true Xavier killed himself?"

"It's too early to know what happened," I said. "He died in the car, though."

"You saw him?" A current of excitement ran through the group. "What happened? He drove that car into a tree?"

"Nah," second woman said. "He realized he had to come home to her and put the hose in his mouth."

The woman who'd recognized me reminded them that I was with the police. "But how did he die, can you tell us?"

"He mixed alcohol and drugs," I said. "But he went into Chicago to do it, which seems strange."

The blinds in the front window twitched. Jana was watching us. I walked up the drive, where the battered Hyundai sat in the carport, and knocked on the kitchen door. The women watched expectantly at the bottom of the driveway, but Jana didn't answer. I could hardly pull out my picklocks in plain view, so I knocked again.

When she still didn't answer, I went to the Hyundai and tried the doors. They were locked, but the car had a lot of papers sitting in the backseat. You never know—they could hold information about Xavier's sugar daddy. Or mommy.

The window on the passenger side was loose in its tracks. I went back to my own car for a piece of wire, then wiggled the Hyundai's window enough to get my wire inside to undo the lock. When I had the rear doors open and was sifting through the papers, Jana charged out the kitchen door. She was holding the same knife that Xavier had used on me last week.

"Get away from here. This is private property."

"It's part of an investigation into a crime, Ms. Shatka." I stepped back, hoping to keep out of range of the knife.

"What are you talking about? Xavier is dead. That is a tragedy, but it is not a crime."

"I don't know about Russia," I said, "but in the United States, we consider murder a crime."

The skin beneath her freckles turned pale, making her blue eyes seem very dark. "What are you saying? The police came. They told me that Xavier killed himself. And this I already knew because he wrote to me from his car, wrote me his apology so that I would know he can be buried as a Christian. The police said not one word about murder."

"Maybe they didn't want to scare you, Ms. Shatka, but Xavier was definitely murdered."

"No!" she said fiercely, waving the knife at me.

I backed up another step. "When I was out here last week, we talked about where Xavier got the money to buy his Camaro. The neighbors think he was selling drugs, and I thought he'd been bribed by Miles Wuchnik. You knew we were both wrong, because Xavier told you who paid him off and why. You called a cab and went to see the person—was it a man? A woman?"

She sucked in a breath, astonished that I knew this much. The arm holding the knife went slack.

"This person—shall we call him your banker?—persuaded Xavier to drive into Chicago in the middle of the night. Your banker then persuaded Xavier to kidnap a young girl and put her in the trunk of that Camaro. After that, somehow this financial friend got Xavier to drink vodka laced with toxic drugs. I think it's time you told me your friend's name. Or you will be the next person he kills." Or she, I added to myself, thinking again of Eloise Napier and Helen Kendrick.

"You are crazy." The words lacked conviction. "No one will kill me, because no one killed Xavier."

"Who did you go see after I was here last week, Ms. Shatka?"

She rolled her eyes as she thought and then produced, "My hairdresser."

"I'd sue, if I were you: your roots are longer than they were a week ago. Who gave Xavier all that cash?"

"Xavier saved his money for many years. That car was his dream car; from the time I met him he talked about it, wanting a Corvette."

"Not to be picky in your time of grief, but it was a Camaro."

"He decided to cut his dream down to size. Everyone does; me, too. I came here thinking America is where everyone gets rich quick. Instead, it's like anyplace else—work, work, work."

"What work did you do in Russia, Ms. Shatka?" I got sidetracked out of curiosity.

"I don't come from Russia, from Vilnius, Lithuania."

It was my turn to be silent. Vilnius, Vilna, Chaim Salanter's hometown. "I thought you were speaking Russian last week," I finally said.

"I am ethnic Russian, my family lives in Vilnius, there are many Russians there. Why do you care?"

The hot sun, the strange conversation, my long day, I couldn't think clearly to pick and choose my questions. How had she met Xavier, I wanted to know, and how long had she been in America—quite a time, judging by the quality of her English.

Instead, I heard myself blurt out, "If Miles Wuchnik didn't approach you with questions about Chaim Salanter's past, who did?"

She ran back to her house. I sprinted after her, but she already had a chain lock in place. When I tried to push against it, she stuck the butcher knife through the crack and sliced at me.

"Ms. Shatka, you are going to need something more powerful than that knife if the same person comes after you who killed Xavier. If you tell me who you talked to, I can help you, but if you hug that information to yourself, well, I sure wouldn't sell you a life-insurance policy today."

"Go away, busybody. I can look after myself with no help from you!"

I'd dropped my bag next to the Hyundai. I went back for it and took out a card. She'd shut the door all the way, but I slipped the card through the mail slot cut into the jamb.

A jet was screaming overhead. I cupped my hands around my mouth and shouted, "If you change your mind, call me."

She didn't answer. I stood at the door for several minutes, my ear against the jamb, but heard very little, even when the screaming from the airplane had died down. I think Jana tiptoed over to the door to pick my card up from where it had fallen inside, but I wasn't even sure of that.

At length, I returned to the Hyundai and started looking through the papers Xavier, or Jana, had tossed into the backseat. Most of them were store receipts—Jana seemed to buy a lot of clothes with her disability checks. Three pairs of shoes from a discounter on Roosevelt Road just last week. The same date that I'd been out here, in fact. Maybe I was wrong. Maybe she really had been out shopping, not calling on Xavier's sugar parent. I looked more closely at the receipt: seven p.m. She'd bought shoes to cheer herself up after her hard day of neighborhood confrontations.

I found ticket stubs from the Kane County Cougars, wadded up detritus from McDonald's and the Colonel, a past-due notice for unpaid parking tickets, and a receipt from the county assessor's office. Stuck to a greasy napkin, I found a carbon of a requisition slip to the Ruhetal pharmacy for twenty ten-milligram tablets of Abilify. The pharmacy had stamped it at ten a.m. yesterday, and Xavier had countersigned it; I could just make out the blurry capital "X" at the start of the signature.

A doctor had signed the requisition, but again, the carbon was so blurry I couldn't make out more than the flourish of the "MD" at the end of the line.

"Hey, you! What are you up to?"

I'd been so intent on the papers that I'd lost track of what was going on around me. A man in a patrol officer's uniform had come up the drive; his squad car, labeled "City of Burbank, Illinois, Public Service with Honor," was parked at the curb. In the best movie tradition, he was wearing wraparound mirror shades; I couldn't see his eyes.

I introduced myself as a licensed private eye. "You know Xavier Jurgens died this morning? I'm the person who found him, in that fancy new Camaro he was so proud of. I'd hoped to ask Ms. Shatka a few questions, since Jurgens had a missing girl locked in the trunk of the car."

He grunted. "Maybe you found Jurgens, maybe you dug up a fortune in gold coins you're trying to hand over, but we got a call from the home owner that you're trespassing. Whoever you are, whatever you're here for, if the home owner doesn't want you on the premises, you get off the premises."

I thought about trying to explain myself, but even as I opened my mouth I couldn't imagine how to put my tangled nest of assumptions into one short, plausible sentence: Wuchnik's death and *Carmilla, Queen of the Night's* devotees; Xavier's death and Arielle's kidnapping; Leydon's fears and her fall from the Rockefeller balcony, and Jana Shatka's reaction to my suggesting she'd been investigating Chaim Salanter's past. Instead, I nodded meekly and went down the drive.

The Burbank cop didn't seem to notice that I was taking a piece of paper from the Hyundai. Maybe his wraparound shades were too dark for him to see me clearly, or maybe Jana Shatka had rubbed him the wrong way, because he didn't knock on her door, the way a cop usually would, to make sure the home owner knew the trespasser had been successfully rousted.

He followed me to the foot of the drive and leaned on his open squad-car door until I'd gotten into my Mustang. He followed me up Laramie until I turned west on Seventy-first Street, and then took off, his lights rotating and sparkling under the hot sun.

I drove on out to Downers Grove, followed the path to the hospital, lined up behind the other supplicants, pulled out my ID, and told the woman guarding the entrance that I had an appointment with Tania Metzger.

The gatekeeper handed me a pass and a map and moved on to the person behind me. I followed the dull brown paint on the floor to corridor B and the social work area. Tania Metzger wasn't at her desk, but two other social workers, one a man about my age, the other a young woman, were in the bullpen. The woman was on the phone; the man was doing something with his computer.

Chantal, the secretary I'd met last week, greeted me. "Tania's with a patient. Did you have some new information about Leydon?"

I shook my head, my conscience pricking me—I hadn't checked in on her for several days now. I could have asked Lotty for an update when she was filling me in on Arielle's condition.

"I went to see her, as Tania recommended, but I haven't been able to get to the hospital this week. I actually came here today because of the orderly who was murdered this morning."

"Murdered?" Chantal cried. "You mean Xavier? But they told us he killed himself."

"It's a convenient theory," I said, "but it leaves a few questions unanswered. One of them I'm hoping you can answer for me."

The woman finished her phone conversation and stood up. "I'm Alvina Northlake, director of this unit. Who are you?"

"Oh, Alvina, this is a detective"—Chantal looked at me—"I'm sorry, I forgot your name—yes, V. I. Warshawski—anyway, she's a friend of Leydon Ashford. I told you she was here last week, asking questions about Leydon, which, of course, we couldn't answer."

"And now you're asking questions about an orderly from the forensic wing?" Northlake's brows rose above her outsize glasses. "If you have questions about him, I can give you the name of the supervisor of that unit."

I pulled the greasy carbon of the Abilify requisition from my bag. "I'd welcome a chance to talk to someone in the forensic wing, but before you send me over there, can you look at this req? The signature's too blurry for me to read—I was hoping someone who knew the staff here might recognize it."

Northlake was interested despite her desire to make me follow hospital protocols. She skimmed the document, her mouth pursing in anger. "Where did you get this?"

"It was in the backseat of Xavier Jurgens's car. Not his lovely new Camaro, where he died on a side street in Chicago. This was in the back of his old Hyundai, the car he usually drove to work."

"Orderlies aren't allowed to handle medication unless they're being supervised," Northlake said. "And this is an enormous amount of the drug, enough for twenty patients for a day—why would he have it? Why did they let him sign it?"

I put on my most saintly, trustworthy face. "That's what I'm hoping you can tell me, Ms. Northlake. Do you recognize the doctor's name?"

She squinted at the signature. "I can't make it out."

Chantal and the male social worker, who'd abandoned any pretense of working, joined her, looking at the form over her shoulder. Northlake started to fold it up, out of their sight, then shrugged and held it out to them. The two frowned over the signature but agreed it could belong to anyone.

"I can take it up to Lydia in Dr. Poynter's office," Chantal offered. "She might know if someone had asked Xavier to get the drug."

Northlake grudgingly agreed that might be a good idea, then demanded to know how I'd gotten the form at all.

"I found Xavier Jurgens in his car this morning; he had a young girl locked in the trunk. When the doctors told me that both the girl and Jurgens had ingested Abilify, I went to his home to talk to his partner. This requisition was in the back of the car he usually drove to work. I'm curious about a couple of things: did he get hold of the drug because he wanted to kill himself? Why did he involve the girl? There doesn't seem to be any connection between him and her. Unless it's through the investigator who was murdered two weeks ago—in just about the same place where Jurgens died."

Chantal looked at her boss, then at me. "Alvina—she might as well know—"

Northlake bristled. "Know what? Not about any patient here, even if she's the woman's mother."

"No, no—about the dead detective." Chantal turned to me. "You were asking about him going to the locked wing—well, Xavier was the person who let him in."

The information didn't startle me. "But Miles Wuchnik, the murdered detective, isn't the person who gave Xavier the money for the Camaro; a third party did. Any hunches about that?"

"We wondered, or our security director wondered, where Jurgens got the money for it." The man spoke for the first time. "They did an audit on the controlled substances, and there weren't abnormal levels of filching. There's always some in a hospital, you can't get it down to zero, but no spikes, and nothing of the size that would have the street value of a sports car."

"What about at the other end of the chain?" I asked, thinking of Mr. Contreras's and my drug-ring theory. "Could someone be ordering massive amounts of drugs for the hospital, say, double what you'd normally use, and then reselling them on the street?"

Chantal and Northlake exchanged horrified looks with the male social worker. "I hope that isn't possible," Northlake said. "We're supposed to have strict procedures in place for signatures and so on . . ." Her voice trailed off as she looked at the requisition I'd brought in.

"The resale price for antipsychotics can't be that great," the man ventured.

"We get plenty of other drugs," Northlake said sharply. "Percocet, Xanax, all those pain meds and tranquilizers have a good street value. But if you ordered such vast quantities that someone could buy a Camaro with the proceeds, then I think it would set off alarm bells in the pharmacy; it's their cost center that would be affected. I'll call around, see what I can learn—the last thing we need is for this hospital to be turned on its ear by having the state investigate us."

"If you find out anything, please, can you let me know?" I said. "Wuchnik was blackmailing at least one person and likely more. Leydon thought he was spying on her, but she doesn't have easy access to her trust fund to pay off someone like him, and anyway, I can't imagine her letting a blackmailer get away with anything. But if you had some corrupt employees who were dealing drugs, I can easily see a blackmailer having a field day. Although how he found out, that's another question."

Tania Metzger had come into the bullpen at the tag end of the conversation. "I never heard any talk of Leydon being blackmailed."

I looked at her. "When I was out here before, you told me that Leydon went into the forensic wing one day. I know you can't repeat anything she said in therapy, but is there anything you can tell me about why she went there?"

Tania hesitated, then said, "She thought Wuchnik was spying on her and she took the opportunity to follow him."

"Tania!" Alvina Northlake spoke sharply. "You are crossing a line here on confidentiality, and if you say anything else, you could be suspended."

Tania started to apologize, then changed her mind. "That detective is dead, Leydon's in a coma, and now one of our orderlies is dead, too. I understand the issues, but I really think the time has come to bend a little bit. Garrett McIntosh is the guard who let Leydon into the forensic unit. If you can get him to talk to you, he may know what she did when she was over there."

Alvina glared at her, but her cell phone rang before she could say anything: her next patient was arriving. She and Tania were both spared an unpleasant confrontation.

35. A HARD DAY'S HUNT— WITH PEASANTS

WHEN I WENT TO THE FORENSIC UNIT'S GATE AND ASKED TO speak with Garrett McIntosh, the guard on duty made it clear that I needed permission from Ruhetal's security chief if I wanted to talk to any of the staff. This wasn't the same guy who'd pocketed my twenty last week; today's guard got pretty starchy when I casually held out a bill.

I went back to the hospital to see if Tania Metzger would help plead my case in the security office. Fortunately, Alvina Northlake was with a patient, and Tania had a few free minutes. She took me to the back of the hospital, where Vernon Mulliner, the security director, oversaw the hospital complex on a bank of monitors. Tania tried her hardest with Mulliner, telling him it was important for therapeutic reasons that we find out who Leydon had talked to when she broke into the forensic wing back in May; Tania explained that Garrett was the guard who'd assisted Leydon at the time.

Mulliner remembered me from my visit last week, and he wouldn't budge. "Even a real detective would need a court order to question anyone in the forensic wing, and you, you're an ambulance chaser who lies so she can sneak into places."

"The last PI who snuck into the forensic wing ended up dead." I pretended I hadn't heard the part about my being a liar. "That's why I'm coming to you. I expect the next people you'll hear from will be Chicago cops, because your orderly was found dead in Chicago, and he left a text message apologizing for the death of Miles Wuchnik, the murdered PI. And Wuchnik's sister may well sue you for negligence, letting one of your docs help Jurgens slip two hundred milligrams of Abilify from the pharmacy. I can help you prepare for this incoming flood, but I need to find out what Wuchnik and Xavier Jurgens were up to. Which means talking to your staff over there."

"You tried to bribe your way into the locked wing." Mulliner ignored my speech. "That may play well in Chicago, but here in Downers Grove we think the law is meant to be obeyed. By everyone."

"Someone is spreading a lot of money around this hospital," I said. "Orderlies get enough extra pay to buy new cars, senior staff get enough to buy mansions with swimming pools. Once the attorney general gets hold of that news, everyone working here at Ruhetal is going to see their bank accounts go under a microscope."

Mulliner's David Niven mustache quivered. After a long pause, he said, "You'd better leave the premises before I call some guards to carry you out. And you, Metzger, your family may have built this hospital a century ago, but your job depends on your adhering to *our* guidelines, not telling hospital secrets to outsiders."

Tania dragged me out of the administrative offices as fast as possible and hurried me to the parking lot. "You'd better go. I really don't want to get fired, not in this economy. I can't jeopardize my conscience or my professional standing to help you."

"I wouldn't expect you to," I said, hoping I meant it. "But if Leydon did tell you what she saw or who she spoke to, it matters that I hear about it now. It's not just that your orderly died this morning—he had kidnapped a twelve-year-old girl, and she'd be dead, too, if I hadn't arrived when I did. Miles Wuchnik was murdered ten days ago. Leydon Ashford may spend the rest of her life in a vegetative state. This is a scary body count. If Leydon gave you any other names or information about who she saw or what, tell me now, before the numbers get bigger."

Metzger bit her lips, debating how much she could say without jeopardizing her professional standards and standing. "She didn't tell me anything, not in direct words, which may be just as well—it makes my crisis of conscience easier to manage. She came back from the forensic wing shouting that everyone in America needed a lawyer and a video camera with them twenty-four hours a day, and then she started talking about being on fire, aflame with news. I didn't know there were so many ways to talk about being burned until I listened to her the rest of that week. Singeing, she talking about that, and smoking out dead rats, and how it would take the mightiest of huntresses to blow on a dying coal and bring the conflagration back to life."

My heart sank. "I'm the person she means when she talks about the mightiest of huntresses, and I have no more idea what all that symbolism means than, well, than you do yourself."

A car marked "Ruhetal Security" pulled up next to us. "Mr. Mulliner sent me to ask if you needed help getting rid of this woman, Ms. Metzger."

Tania flushed. "No, no, I'm fine."

"And you, lady," the guard said to me, "he asked me to remind you there's no loitering in the parking lot."

His tone was respectful, but the message was unmistakable—time for me to move on. I waved good-bye to Metzger, told her to call if anything else came to her, and left the hospital grounds.

I drove into the center of Downers Grove to find coffee and a snack.

While I ate, I looked up McIntosh's home address in Lexis. Aurora, eighteen miles to the west.

I got on the westbound tollway just after the afternoon shift changed at Ruhetal. The speed limits in the western suburbs were apparently posted as fictions to entertain drivers, who hurtled homeward as if a prize awaited the person who reached their driveway first. The sun, drifting lower in the summer sky, created a glare on my windshield that was giving me a headache, but the traffic was so wild I couldn't relax.

McIntosh's ranch house on Fifth Avenue was about fifty years old and needed work. I felt a certain kinship: I, too, was about fifty, and my techniques for getting information definitely needed work. I'd failed this morning with Nia Durango, and then with Ruhetal's security director. And, as it turned out, I didn't fare better with Garrett McIntosh.

McIntosh had been one of the winners in the commuting race. He came to the door still wearing his guard's uniform, although he'd taken off the tie and undone the shirt. Like so many people from Ruhetal, he wasn't happy to see me and he wouldn't let me into his house. At least he didn't attack me with a butcher knife, but he did tell me to mind my own business if I didn't want to get hurt.

"What, you mean like what happened to Miles Wuchnik, after you helped him get into the forensic wing and all? What do you know about the way he was murdered?"

"Nothing. It wasn't nothing to do with me."

He was a bulky man, and his bulk filled the whole doorway. We were standing close enough that I could smell the onions he had for lunch on his breath. That old line of Lily Tomlin's came to me—the trouble with the rat race is that even if you win, you're still a rat.

"And Ms. Ashford—you don't know anything about her being pushed from the balcony at Rockefeller Chapel?"

"I don't know any Ms. Ashford," he growled. "And I sure as hell don't know any Rockefellers."

"Leydon Ashford. You let her into the forensic wing the same day Miles Wuchnik was there."

"Oh, her. You got me confused there, calling her Ms. Ash-something."

"Yeah, it can be confusing to hear people called by their actual names. Speaking of which, what was the actual name of the person in the locked ward who Miles Wuchnik spoke to?"

"I don't know. I mind my business and let other people mind theirs." He leaned forward so that his Adam's apple was almost butting my forehead.

"How was Miles Wuchnik's trip to the locked wing your business?" I asked.

"I made a mistake," he said. "I thought Wuchnik was with the state, so I let him in. Then Mr. Mulliner told me he was private, same as you are, and I was deep in doo-doo. So from now on, I only talk to people when Mr. Mulliner says it's okay."

"Must be a handicap in your social life," I commented.

"Huh?"

He wasn't exactly the nimblest goat on the mountain. "If you have to okay your—never mind."

"Never mind is right. Mr. Mulliner said not to talk to you if you came around, so good-bye and good night."

"'Good night and good luck,'" I corrected, but he was shutting the door and didn't hear me.

I walked slowly back to my car, massaging the area between my shoulder blades, where the stresses of the day were lodging. I was fifty miles from home right now, and if I hadn't left Kira and Lucy with Mr. Contreras, I would have checked into the Comfort Suites I passed on my way back to the tollway.

I did pull into a strip mall to call my neighbor before getting onto the expressway. All was quiet so far on the eastern front; it was after five and Petra had come over to help grill hot dogs for the girls. She was going to teach them how to make s'mores when the coals died down.

Once I hit the eastbound Ike, the traffic turned to glue. It was almost seven when I finally pulled into the alley behind my apartment. My phone had rung a number of times as I crept home, but I resolutely refused to look at it. Too many people who'd been weaving around me had had one hand on the wheel and the other on their devices—someone had to pay attention to the road, and I was the designated driver this evening.

I looked at my call log after I turned off the ignition. Chaim Salanter's PA had phoned three times. The other calls were from other clients. I returned those first, and then phoned Salanter's PA, Wren Balfour.

"How is Arielle doing?" I asked.

"The family aren't issuing any new progress reports; they're hoping to keep her health private. Mr. Salanter wants to see you."

"I have some time free in the early afternoon tomorrow."

"Tonight. He got in from Brazil a few hours ago and would like to discuss his granddaughter with you. He's at the Schiller Street address."

"I've had a very long day, Ms. Balfour, which actually started with a summons to Schiller Street. I'm not responding to those anymore. I found Arielle locked in the trunk of a car, and rescued a couple of other girls, and in return, the Salanter family has refused even to let me know Arielle's status. I've driven a hundred miles in the heat and bad traffic, and I don't have a PA to organize my life for me. I'm taking a bath and going to bed."

"But—"

"Good night, Ms. Balfour." I hung up and climbed stiffly out of the car.

The s'mores party was hard at it in the backyard. The Soongs, the family on the second floor with a new baby, had a boy around Lucy's age; Mr. Soong had set up a badminton net for them. The kids and Petra were playing, while Mitch chased the shuttlecock, barking as he went. He'd shed the babydoll pajamas, I was thankful to see. The Soongs were talking with Mr. Contreras, the new baby asleep between them. Other neighbors were out on their porches, enjoying the party atmosphere happy children create. I felt better already.

I smiled and waved, told them I'd be down in a bit, and went up to soak the tension out of my shoulders and legs. I lay in the tub, sipping whisky, watching the water turn dark from the day's dirt.

I'd been planning on sleeping in Jake's place, letting the girls use my bed, but I decided it would be better to do it the other way around. A lot of people knew I was asking questions. Whether Jana Shatka or Vernon Mulliner—or even Chaim Salanter—was behind the murders of Xavier and Wuchnik, I didn't want any bears who might come hunting me to find the Dudek girls sleeping in my bed.

For that reason, too, when I finally climbed out of the tub, I went to the safe in my bedroom and got out my Smith & Wesson. *There are no bears on Hemlock Mountain,* I murmured. But on Racine Avenue, that was a different story.

36. ENTER A BILLIONAIRE

THE COALS FROM MR. CONTRERAS'S GRILL GLOWED SOFTLY in the dark backyard. I sat on the ground-floor porch with Mr. Contreras and some of our other neighbors, watching as Petra and Kira toasted s'mores. Even the medical resident from the first floor, who is usually vituperative about the dogs' and my noise, had put on blue jeans and brought out a six-pack.

All my play clothes were filthy, I'd realized when I got out of the bath. I had carried a load of jeans and T's down to the basement laundry, and put on my gold cotton dress for the party. Lucy Dudek then smeared marshmallow onto the skirt, but somehow that didn't bother me.

Lucy and Alan, the Soongs' seven-year-old, were asleep at our feet, their arms twined around the dogs. It had taken an hour and another whisky, drunk with a bowl of Ms. Soong's vegetable-rice salad, before I stopped feeling the porch rolling as if it were the interstate. Now I leaned against one of the stairwell posts, drowsing contentedly. Mr. Contreras's desultory comments were as soothing as a lullaby; I needed only to grunt in reply whenever he paused for air.

Mitch's short, sharp bark roused me from my torpor. He extricated himself from the sleeping children, the hairs on his neck high. When Peppy joined him, tail low like his, I brought my gun from the folds of my dress and followed them around the side of the building. I was barefoot, and the concrete dug into the blisters on my feet.

"What is it, doll?" Mr. Contreras had come after us.

"I don't know," I murmured. "Stay here with the girls, okay, and holler if someone comes in at the alley."

Before he could huff about not needing to holler for my help, I undid the side gate and followed the dogs to the front of the building. A Mercedes sedan was idling at the curb.

A tall woman stood at the front door, pressing doorbells. She spoke into her cell phone. "No one's answering. Do you want to go over to Dr. Herschel's?"

I tried to signal the dogs to stay next to me, but Mitch bounded to the front door. The woman screamed as Mitch pinned her against the building. Peppy and I jogged after him. I kept one hand on my gun but pulled Mitch away with the other.

"Who are you, and what do you want with Dr. Herschel?" I demanded.

The driver's door of the Mercedes opened. I stepped back so that I could cover both the woman and the driver. I had to let go of Mitch, who promptly returned to the woman.

"Is that you, Warshawski?" the driver shouted. "Call off your dogs!"

It was Gabe Eycks, the Salanters' houseman, doubling as a chauffeur. I lowered the Smith & Wesson and ordered the dogs to sit. Peppy quickly obeyed. After a reluctant moment, Mitch agreed, but he kept his hackles up, and the muscles in his haunches were quivering.

I looked sourly at the woman. "Wren Balfour, I presume?"

"Yes, I'm Wren. Mr. Salanter needs to talk to you."

"And since I wouldn't come to Schiller Street, you decided you had to butt in on my evening with family."

She was watching Mitch, not listening to me. "Will that dog bite?"

"All dogs bite, but as long as you don't threaten me in some way, you're probably safe."

Gabe Eycks joined us just as Mr. Contreras burst through the front door—he'd come through the building from the backyard.

"Is everything okay, doll? I got worried when I didn't hear nothing. You know these people?"

"Not very well. They're minions of a billionaire, which means they disregard anything an ordinary person says—like my telling Ms. Balfour here that I was too tired to talk to her boss tonight. She interpreted that as a signal that they should track me down at home."

"If Vic here said she was too tired to talk, that means it's time for you to leave," my neighbor said. "We got a new baby you woke up, people are trying to have a little peace and quiet after a hard day. Not everyone in this economy even has a job, that ever occur to you?"

Balfour looked bewildered, as people often do when they first meet Mr. Contreras, but Gabe said, "We're not quite as insensitive as you think, but Mr. Salanter is eighty-three, and he's worried about his granddaughter."

"Well, I'm eighty-seven, and I'm worried about Vic," Mr. Contreras snapped. "And I don't have a secretary or a chauffeur or whoever else your boss has to drive him around and paint his toenails pink."

I choked back a laugh. Out on the street, the back door to the Mercedes opened. As soon as he realized the billionaire was emerging, Gabe trotted back to the car. Wren Balfour looked nervously from her boss to Mitch. The dog grinned up at her to show it had been a game, just good fun, but the sight of all those teeth kept her glued to the front door.

In the brief quiet, I could hear the Soong baby wailing from behind the building, and then Chaim Salanter and Eycks joined us.

"I'm sorry to bother you at home, Ms. Warshawski. My staff tells me you are tired, and I am weary myself, at my age, after a long flight. But

I hope you will put your gun away and let me speak to you for a few minutes."

I made a face but told him we could talk in my apartment. When Salanter assured me he could manage the three flights without difficulty, I let him and the rest of the entourage into the building.

I pulled Mr. Contreras aside so I could give him a key to Jake's apartment, explaining that I wanted Lucy and Kira to sleep in there.

"I don't want Salanter or his acolytes to see the girls or Petra," I muttered. "It's not that I don't trust them, but—I don't trust them."

Mr. Contreras had a better plan, to put the girls up in his own place, on the beds his grandsons use when they spend the night with him. He assured me he wouldn't let Kira or Lucy into the front of the building until Salanter was out of sight, but it was high time they were in bed, not good for little ones to be up at all hours.

Mitch decided the fun part of the encounter was over and followed Mr. Contreras through the hall to the backyard, but Peppy stayed with me as I led Salanter and his pals to my home. My feet were filthy. I was also trailing little specks of blood from where the blisters had come open, I saw when I switched on my entry light.

I waved an arm toward the front room and went into the bathroom to rinse my feet. I still hadn't found time to take off my flaking nail polish—I, too, needed someone to follow me around, painting my toenails pink.

When I came back to the living room, Salanter was standing at the piano, softly picking out a few notes from my *Don Giovanni* score with a halting hand.

"You sing Mozart?" he asked.

I sat cross-legged in my armchair, smoothing my frock over my knees. Lucy had managed to rub chocolate into the fabric as well as marshmallow. "Surely you didn't drag your weary bones all this way to discover my musical tastes."

"Pleasantries are permitted even in a crisis," Salanter said.

He sat on the piano bench, his shoulders hunched, his heavy black brows low over his eyes. Wren Balfour tried to urge him to the couch but he gave a tired smile and stayed where he was. I wondered if the pantomime was meant to make me feel sorry for him.

When I didn't respond, Salanter said, "I need to know everything you can tell me about how my granddaughter ended up in the trunk of that orderly's car."

I held out my hands, palms up. "Mr. Eycks knows everything I do, and a whole lot more besides. The only thing I can suggest is that you talk to Nia Durango: Arielle shares all her secrets with Nia."

"I've talked to Nia. She can tell me nothing."

I hesitated, then said, "Did you know Arielle had written to the Holocaust Museum, looking for information about your family's history in Vilna?"

He looked up, his poker player's mask slipping briefly—I couldn't tell if he was angry or astonished, or even, perhaps, afraid. "How do you know that?"

I told him about looking at Arielle's e-mails. "I assume the FBI is doing the same thing, and that they're reporting back to you. What is it you don't want her to find out?"

"Why would she seek that information when I told her I never wanted to revisit that past?" His voice was soft but charged with bitterness.

"Children need rootedness," I suggested. "Beyond that, though, Arielle is deeply troubled by Wade Lawlor's attacks on you. She wanted to know what lies behind them."

"I've told her time and again that nothing lies behind them, that he's attacking me because it's a way of reaching his paranoid audience, and it's a way of attacking Sophy Durango. Arielle knows that!" He smacked the piano and the keys crashed discordantly.

I rubbed the middle of my forehead, trying to ease an eyestrain headache. "The last thing a bright child believes is something she knows her parents are lying about. And frankly, I don't believe you, either.

I am ninety-five percent certain that Miles Wuchnik was murdered because he was blackmailing someone. He thought he'd uncovered a big secret about you. Had he put the bite on you?"

Salanter's expression didn't give anything away this time, but the glance he exchanged with Gabe told its own story. He opened his mouth to say something, but I cut him off—I didn't want to hear another evasion.

"So he had," I said. "What had he found out? And was it something Arielle had hired him to look for?"

"How would she even know to look for a detective?"

"Oh, please, Mr. Salanter. Whatever went on in your life in Vilna all those years ago, you were no older than Arielle when it happened. She has your brains, your wits; even if PI's weren't all over TV, she'd find an investigator if she wanted one. The bigger questions are: What did Wuchnik find out about you? Who hired him to look? Why was he murdered near your granddaughter? And was it Mr. Eycks here who hoisted him up on that tomb and murdered him?"

"The implication being that I'd do anything Mr. Salanter commanded?" Gabe said. "I'm not a vassal; I get to say yes or no to anything asked of me, and I would certainly say no to murder."

"What does this have to do with the attack on Arielle?" Wren Balfour demanded. "That's what Mr. Salanter needs to know."

"Oh, that. There's a connection between the dead orderly, Xavier Jurgens, and the dead PI. There's a connection between Jurgens's partner, Jana Shatka, and Vilna. She knows something about Mr. Salanter's past. So there's a connection between Arielle's kidnapping, Mr. Salanter's past, the dead orderly, and the dead PI. You can fill in the blanks." A yawn cracked my face in two as exhaustion swept over me.

"How do you know all this?" Salanter demanded.

"Sheer dogged work. Anyone who cares enough can follow the same paths I did. If Jana Shatka knew something about your past in Vilna, anyone can find it out." I yawned again. "How is Arielle, by the way? Or is that information still classified?"

"It is not classified, merely so distressing that it's hard to discuss," Salanter said. "She will live, they are sure of that, but when she will become her bright quicksilver self again, that they cannot say. Her brain waves are returning to normal, but she still is confused and can't speak coherently, let alone remember what happened. That's why I'm here, hoping that you can tell me why she did what she did, going out in the middle of the night, presumably to that cemetery."

"That part's easy—she had a text message from a phone number in her database. What the message said we don't know, but she thought it was from a friend. She sent Nia an e-mail about it, because their mothers had shut down texting between the two girls, but Nia didn't look at her e-mail until this morning. The FBI was going to track down that text, come to think of it, find out who used the phone, what the phone message said." I sat up, my fatigue dissipating as the implication of what I'd said struck me.

"Anything I can tell you about why Arielle went back to Mount Moriah cemetery you can learn from the FBI," I said. "They might not tell me, if it was my granddaughter, but billionaires get caviar treatment from law enforcement. So you didn't come on Arielle's account: you're here because you want to find out how much of Miles Wuchnik's discoveries I've learned. That answer is easy, too: not much, but if Jana Shatka is the next person who turns up dead, I don't think even being the world's twenty-first wealthiest man will protect you from some serious police scrutiny."

37. PARANOID DELUSION?

AFTER MY VISITORS LEFT, I WAS SO EXHAUSTED I COULD BARELY stay upright. I was going to go straight to bed, then remembered the Dudek sisters. I staggered back down the stairs to Mr. Contreras's place, too tired to bother putting my clothes in the dryer. I softly undid the bolts to my neighbor's front door and tiptoed across the living room.

I could hear the old man's snores through the closed door to his bedroom. Kira and Lucy were asleep, spoonlike, in the top of the bunk beds my neighbor had put in his dining room for his grandsons. Mitch was on duty at the bottom of the ladder; he thumped his tail in greeting but wouldn't leave his post. That was reassuring.

Back upstairs in my own place, I collapsed into bed, just taking time to drop my gold dress on a chair. I fell instantly asleep, but it was into another night of tormenting dreams, where I was tracking Chaim Salanter through a maze. When I tried to peer through the hedges, the leaves and twigs turned into barbed wire. A death camp lay on the far side. I tried to run back to the entrance but found myself instead inside Ruhetal, where I wandered around the lobby, studying the photographs of the hospital's founders. In their midst, I discovered Leydon, hanging crucified next to the social worker's great-grandmother. Fire was bursting from her hands and feet.

When I woke at six-thirty, I was still tired, but it felt like a release to leave my bed. Peppy had stayed the night with me. She followed me down the stairs while I put my laundry into the dryer. We went back into Mr. Contreras's place, where everyone was still asleep, including Petra, who'd crashed on the sagging sofa bed in the front room some time after I'd looked in last night. I dragged a reluctant Mitch to the lake with us.

When we got back, everyone was still sacked out. I looked resentfully at my cousin: she turned over when Mitch raced to lick her face but didn't really wake up. I wished the gods had given me the gift of untroubled sleep but I refrained from taking out my resentment by shaking her awake. Instead, I scribbled a note, asking her to call me with updates during the day. I left the dogs on patrol and drove south to the University of Chicago, my clothes clean if unpressed, my gun in an ankle holster under my jeans.

My dream of Leydon's crucifixion had been so vivid, I'd been scared she'd died in the night, but the ICU nurse assured me her condition was unchanged. That was the less-bad news; the bad news was that Leydon would have to be moved soon to a nursing home.

"Your brother says the family won't pay for private care, so it will have to be a public-aid home," the nurse said, as she helped drape me in protective gear. "But I thought your family had a lot of money."

I'd forgotten saying that I was Leydon's sister. "The Ashfords do, but I'm not a legitimate part of the family. Sewall has never liked Leydon, and he's always been annoyed with her for staying close to me. I'll talk to him and his wife, but I'm sure he won't pay attention to anything I say."

The nurse's eyes widened. "I'm sorry—I wouldn't have said anything—I didn't mean—"

"How could you know?" I smiled and patted her shoulder with my latex-covered hand.

As I sat with Leydon, stroking her face where it showed through its protective bandaging, I told her what I'd just said. "Can't you picture Sewall exploding if he finds out I let that nurse think I'm your illegitimate sister? But I will talk to him, or at least to Faith, darling, I'll try to swallow my bile and be persuasive, because you sure don't need to be warehoused in some rat-infested hellhole. Ruhetal has a staff that cared about your welfare, even if they're underfunded, but a public-aid nursing home—not even Sewall can condemn you to that."

Leydon's blue eyes rolled sightlessly in her gaunt face. Her breath came in short, harsh pants. I blinked back my tears and brushed a strand of red-gold hair from her cheek.

"Oh, why can't you wake up? Why couldn't you just tell me on the phone why you wanted to talk to me? If you'd said two weeks ago what you saw in the locked wing, you wouldn't be here now."

I pressed my lips together: if the brain-damaged can hear what we say, Leydon would suffer from listening to my recriminations. "Sorry, girl, sorry. We do what we're strong enough to do, I know that. But what did you see? Does Chaim Salanter have an illegitimate child who's been warehoused there for unspeakable crimes? Talk to me, babe, talk to me straight, none of those riddles about huntresses and fires!"

The nurse came in to tell me my time was up. I walked slowly from the hospital across the quadrangles, to Rockefeller Chapel. A yoga class was happening in the chancel, but no one paid attention to me as I climbed to the balcony.

I sat for a long time, staring at the spot where Leydon had landed. I ignored incoming texts and calls from clients, just looking at the phone long enough to make sure they weren't distress signals from Mr. Contreras or Petra.

If I was ever going to find out what had happened, I needed to get inside the locked wing at Ruhetal. I could go in as a lawyer but not without a client. It might be easier to climb the fence in the middle of the night.

"Are you all right?"

I jumped. I'd been so lost in thought I hadn't heard the chapel dean come up the stairs. Maybe this was how Miles Wuchnik had been killed, by someone sidling up next to him. He'd been lost in thought, imagining his next blackmail target, when Gabe Eycks hit him over the head and hefted him onto the slab. Was that how Wuchnik had come to be at the site where the Carmilla club was meeting? Had Chaim, or Arielle, promised a payoff if he'd go to the cemetery, only to have the payoff be a spike through the chest?

The dean repeated his question.

"My mind is slipping; it keeps withdrawing from the present and sliding off to other places," I said. "Not good. Detectives need to be aware of what's around them."

"That sounds like a very advanced spiritual practice."

I made a face. "I think it's the opposite—a quintessential animal wariness. Do you think Chaim Salanter could be cold enough to engineer a murder that he knew his granddaughter had a good chance of witnessing?"

"Chaim Salanter? Oh, the options magnate. The human heart is incalculable in its heights and depths. Even if I knew Mr. Salanter, I wouldn't pretend to know what he could be capable of." The dean spoke with a seriousness that robbed his words of pomposity. "By the way, did any of my suggestions about that verse from Second Samuel help?"

"The George Eliot link took me to the dead man's sister down in Danville, where I learned he'd been an enterprising blackmailer, but she couldn't—or wouldn't—tell me who her brother had been targeting."

Brother and sister, in death they were not divided. Maybe it was husband and wife, maybe Jana Shatka and Xavier Jurgens—could Leydon have seen it that way? She would have met Xavier at Ruhetal; Jana might have shown up there, too.

I'd slipped away from the present again. The dean brought me back with a question about Leydon.

"The prognosis is very poor but not impossible. I need to know what she saw in the forensic wing at Ruhetal and no one will tell me."

"Didn't you used to be a criminal defense lawyer?"

"A million years ago. I couldn't mount an effective courtroom defense today—I'm far too rusty."

"I'm not suggesting that," the dean said. "Look at the patient roster. Maybe one of your former clients is in there. It would give you a reason to talk to someone on the inside."

I slapped my forehead with my palm. "You're right—I'm an idiot. I should have thought of this yesterday. It's been twenty years since I left the PD's office, but I can still go into the DOC—Department of Corrections—database and see who at Ruhetal is there on an arson charge!"

I pushed myself to my feet. "Of course, Leydon was pretty hypergraphic her last week; maybe she left a note in her apartment. I didn't really sort through the papers when I went there the first time."

As I jogged back to my car, I thought of the landfill in Leydon's condo. The idea of returning to it was so depressing that I decided to confront Leydon's sister-in-law about her care instead.

Before driving north, I remembered Tyler. I'd been on the run all day yesterday and hadn't taken the time to call her mother, but I couldn't afford to let any more time go by. I was about to make the call from my cell phone but decided I'd better be prudent, in case anyone was listening to my calls. I drove around the area until I found one of the few remaining pay phones in the city.

Rhonda Shankman proved to be a breathless, skittish woman who giggled when she was nervous—as she was throughout our conversation. I explained who I was: Petra's cousin, and a private investigator. Ms. Shankman giggled so hard at the thought of talking to a private eye that it was hard to get the conversation on track.

"How much did Tyler tell you about the night she spent away from home twelve days ago?"

"Why, why, just that she was with girls from Vina Fields who share her love of the *Carmilla* series. Is there something else? Something her father should know?"

"She didn't tell you that the girls went to the cemetery where the vampire murder took place?"

"Oooh," Rhonda shrieked, and then gave another nervous staccato of laughter. "Oh, do I have to tell Perry? He'll be so angry!"

"This isn't about whether your husband will lose his temper, Ms. Shankman, it's about your daughter's safety. It's possible that she caught a glimpse of the person who murdered Miles Wuchnik. If the killer knows that, he may try to silence Tyler—he took a good shot yesterday at Arielle Zitter, the girl who organized the escapade in the cemetery."

We went round in circles for several frustrating minutes, during which I kept feeding quarters into the phone. Finally, in exchange for my promise not to say anything to Perry Shankman, Rhonda agreed to call the Texas camp and tell them to deny Tyler's presence there if anyone called asking for her. "Lots of famous people send their kids there; it's why Perry chose it, so they're used to having kids be there under fake names and stuff."

I had to be satisfied with that arrangement, although I wished I had the time and the resources to fly to Texas myself. Not just to reassure myself about Tyler's well-being but also to try to get a description from her of the vampire she'd seen.

I'd been so troubled by my nightmares that I hadn't been able to eat this morning. For someone whose family motto is "Never skip a meal," this seemed like part of a disturbing trend, two mornings in a row without breakfast. When I reached the far northern suburbs, I found a kind of a diner, a clinically clean space painted in perky pinks and golds, where I ordered a BLT and a bitter espresso. At least, I ordered an espresso—it just turned out to be poorly made.

When I got to the Ashford mansion, the Lincoln Navigator wasn't in the drive, but as I was wondering if I should wait or hurl myself against Leydon's mother, Faith Ashford pulled up. A girl of fourteen or so flounced out of the passenger seat, ignoring Faith's call for help with the groceries.

"Let me." I stepped over to the back of the Navigator, where Faith was wrestling with four overflowing bags.

She gasped. She hadn't noticed me until then, and she was so startled she almost dropped one of the bags. "Vic—sorry—have you been here long? This is Trina's day for her flute lesson and she's upset that I kept her waiting. I guess I spent too much time at the market."

I didn't say anything, just followed her into the house. Faith's mother-in-law, trailed by the sullen Trina, came into the kitchen as Faith was unpacking the bags. The eldest Ashford woman criticized the strawberries—"You didn't inspect the ones underneath again, did you?"—and the salmon—"The tail piece, Faith? When Helen is our guest tonight?"

"Howdy, Ms. Ashford," I said. "The tail is the leaner part of the fish, of course, and your health-conscious friends will be glad to see it on your table. Why don't you finish critiquing the food while I take Faith outside for a private word."

"If this has to do with Leydon, Sewall will make those decisions. And you need to mind your own business, not intrude into my family's."

"Ma'am, with respect, Faith holds Leydon's durable power of attorney for medical decisions as well as legal ones, and if she lets Sewall make those decisions, she is liable for an action at law by the public guardian."

I didn't know that my statement had any effect on Leydon's mother, but it made an impression on Trina. Her jaw dropped, and she started putting away groceries, as if I had threatened her personally with legal action.

Faith took me into a side room and shut the door. "Vic, please don't get Mother Ashford upset, she just takes it out on me later."

"Faith, everyone in this household takes out their frustrations on you, including your bratty daughter. You can choose to let that go on or choose to stop it—I don't care which. But I do care about Leydon's welfare. I know you do, too, or Leydon wouldn't have given you her various powers of attorney, would she?"

"I suppose," Faith muttered, wringing her hands in misery.

"The hospital told me this morning she has to move into a nursing home. You have the power to choose a good private home for her. The ICU staff told me Sewall is talking about a public-aid clinic, but that's not his decision to make—"

"Father Ashford's will left Sewall in charge of her money. It's in a trust; she wasn't reliable . . ." Her voice trailed away.

"Yeah, well, if he's been robbing her so that there's nothing left in her trust fund, I can hire a forensic accountant to find evidence of fraud. If Sewall is threatening to put his sister in a substandard nursing home out of spite, it's not just a pathetic revenge, it's laying him open to a serious legal charge. If that's where Leydon lands, I will know about it and I will make sure that the public guardian also learns about it. That's really all I have to say."

I waited for her to respond. She gulped miserably. I was one more strong personality pressuring her, but she finally nodded. On my way back through the kitchen I stopped beside Leydon's mother, who was pulling bad strawberries out of the boxes Faith had brought home, laying them on a gold-rimmed serving plate.

"I don't fault you for getting worn out by Leydon's illness," I said.

"It's hard on everyone around her. But you always accused her of being ill on purpose, and you never appreciated her amazing gifts—that's what infuriates me."

Behind me, Faith gave a nervous gasp, but her mother-in-law said, "You and Leydon never had any standards of decency, so it doesn't surprise me that you would think it proper to lecture me in my own home. Faith, I'm putting these where you can clearly see their flaws, so that you know what to look for next time. We couldn't give these to the maid, let alone to Helen."

"Helen?" I did a double take as the name finally registered with me. "Would that be Helen Kendrick?"

Faith murmured, "Sewall is one of her Gleaners and is an adviser to the campaign. She—we—"

"The Warshawski woman has no need to know our private business, Faith," her mother-in-law interrupted. "I am only grateful that Leydon won't be here. The last advisory committee meeting she disrupted in a disgraceful way!"

"What? She argued with Kendrick and made her look stupid on abortion or immigration or Social Security?" I asked.

"She was funny." Trina Ashford, who'd stood silent in the background, startled all of us by speaking. "She quoted all this Shakespeare. At school they never tell us he wrote about real life, but she was going on and on—something about the country and all the offices being for sale—I didn't even know it was Shakespeare at first, because she made it sound like it was right out of the news. Then she told me and Terence how—"

"It was a vulgar display and utterly typical of how Leydon and the Warshawski woman disregarded normal social conduct," Mother Ashford said to her granddaughter. "It was the next week that we had to go to her apartment and see the disgusting drawings she'd created. You may want to lecture Sewall on his financial responsibilities, Ms. Warshawski, but paying to clean and repaint the stairwells in Leydon's

building did not come cheap, I assure you. And that was on top of trying to clean up the mess she was making at Ruhetal."

"What mess was that?" I asked. "The social workers who talked to
me never said anything about her destroying any hospital property."

"She thought she was still a lawyer. She thought she was in a position
to represent someone else, when she couldn't begin to look after herself.
We had to send—" Mother Ashford clipped her lips shut.

"Had to send what?" I thought of my meeting at Dick's law firm.
"You sent Eloise Napier out to stop her?"

Ms. Ashford smiled, a grim, sly smirk that would have looked coarse
on anyone, even a vulgar person like me. "You don't need to know. Suf-
fice it to say, we put a stop to all that nonsense, but it didn't come cheap."

"So the only thing you really care about is the money you spend on
your daughter. Interesting. Maybe that's why you live with your son, to
save yourself a few bucks." I picked up the plate and dumped the moldy
berries into the garbage disposal. "If you treated Leydon the way you
treat Faith, all she ever learned was how little respect you have for
others. And, by the way, Leydon is still a lawyer."

I set the plate in the sink. The maid materialized as I marched down
the hall. She gave me the ghost of a smile before shutting the door
behind me.

As I walked down the drive to my car, Trina surprised me, running
around from the back of the house to intercept me. "Are you friends
with my aunt Leydon?"

I answered her honestly, although I wondered what had made her
approach me. "We were close friends in law school. Not so much in the
last few years—my fault. I wasn't strong enough to cope with her
illness."

"Is she going to die?"

I looked at her seriously. "I don't know. I've been to see her several
times and she still hasn't recovered consciousness. But she can breathe
on her own, so there may be some hope."

"I know Aunt Leydon can be a pain, but no one out here is, I don't know, energetic the way she is. Maybe you think I'm rude to my mom—I saw how you were looking at me—but I wish she'd stand up to Grandma the way Aunt Leydon did!"

"Maybe your mother realizes your household would explode if everyone was standing up to each other all the time. Although if it was me, I would solve the problem by moving out."

When Trina's eyes widened in amazement, I added casually, "Who did your dad and grandmother send out to stop Leydon's nonsense at Ruhetal? And what nonsense was it?"

Trina shrugged. She hadn't paid attention to those battles. She could tell me only that her grandmother had announced at dinner one night that she'd *solved that problem,* meaning the problem of Aunt Leydon, but not what the solution had been.

I drove back to the city, mulling over the situation at Ruhetal. Leydon had gone into the locked wing. To offer legal services to someone there, because, in Mother Ashford's charming phrase, she thought she was still a lawyer.

And this had annoyed someone, maybe Vernon Mulliner, the director of security? He'd told the Ashford family and they'd dispatched—of course, they'd dispatched Miles Wuchnik to deal with the situation. I wondered if Wuchnik had threatened Leydon in some way, if that was why she'd been so frightened of revealing her name on the phone to me. He certainly had made it clear he could eavesdrop on people.

Back in my office, I called Tania Metzger at Ruhetal. She was furious when I told her about the Ashford family's sending someone—probably Wuchnik—out to the hospital to deal with Leydon.

"More than most people, even those with her illness, Leydon creates drama around her, and when she got back from the forensic wing, everyone was stirred up, the guards, the patients! It's an outrage that the family intervened in some way without consulting the therapeutic staff. How can we possibly look after our patients if we don't know what's happening to them? As Leydon became more agitated, I thought she was having paranoid delusions. Now it turns out that an outsider actually was involved. She thought she was being stalked, and maybe she was! I'm taking this up with the head of the hospital, you can be sure of that. I need to find out who allowed a third party to interfere with one of my patients." She put the receiver down with a bang.

The warehouse where I lease space is hot in summer and cold in winter—I can't afford the utility bills to cool such a large office properly. I put on a fan, weighting down my papers so they didn't fly across the room, and used a program designed by one of my old colleagues from the Public Defender's Office to hack into the Department of Corrections database. I asked it to find me anyone who'd been convicted of arson, anywhere in the prison system.

The computer told me it would take twenty minutes to do the sort. I was too wound up from my meeting with Leydon's mother to wait patiently. I needed to do something active.

It was Xavier Jurgens who had taken Wuchnik into the locked wing. If Wuchnik had been sent out to clean up after Leydon, he might well have talked to the patient Leydon had promised to represent. In which case, Jurgens would have known the patient's name. Which meant that Jana Shatka probably knew it as well.

If the police were still treating Jurgens's death as a suicide, they might not have bothered interviewing Shatka. My track record with her had been unimpressive so far, but perhaps I could frighten her into coughing up the inmate's name.

38. HOT ON A TRAIL— OR SOMETHING

"You're too late."

I had pulled up in what was beginning to feel like "my" parking place, across from Shatka's duplex. One of the women I'd seen on my first trip out saw me and pushed her baby over to talk to me.

"Too late?" I felt my stomach turn over: Shatka had been murdered in the night.

"She left yesterday afternoon. Five suitcases she had with her, and when the taxi came, she told him to take her to O'Hare."

"You heard her, did you?" I asked.

"Not me, but Anita Conseco happened to be out front when Jana left. She even helped her put her suitcases into the trunk, not that the *puta* had one word of thanks for her."

"So when she went out last week—the day I first came here—did Anita happen to hear where she told the cab to take her?"

The woman looked as though she was going to get on her dignity— she pulled herself up and took a breath—so I forestalled her. "No one around here has time to gossip or spy on each other, I know—not with kids and work and laundry—but if you're like me and my neighbors, you try to keep an eye out so you know if someone's in trouble."

"That's right, and that's what that bitch Jana never could appreciate. My brother shoveled her walk the first year she was living here, before Xavier moved in, and was there one word of thanks? Just swearing that if he thought he could squeeze a nickel out of her he was mistaken!"

"So did anyone hear where she went last week?"

My non-gossiping, non-spying informant shook her head regretfully. Jana had managed to depart in secrecy.

The woman's cell phone rang. She began an animated conversation in Spanish. I walked up the drive and let myself into the house. The lock wasn't much of a challenge, and even if the Burbank police came around again I didn't think they'd hassle me.

Jana had left in a hurry. She'd apparently dumped the contents of her closet and drawers on the unmade bed and abandoned what she didn't want to take with her. Xavier's clothes still hung in a corner of the closet, looking somehow shrunken and forlorn. I went through all his pockets, my flesh cringing, as if I were touching his dead body again. I found some spare change and a card from the Bevilacqua car dealership, but nothing else.

Jana's remaining clothes also held nothing more interesting than used tissues and an empty glasses case. I scrabbled through bureau drawers and kitchen cupboards, hoping for some damned thing or other, a computer, a thumb drive, a cell phone, but whatever else she'd left behind, she'd been careful to take all her electronic trails with her.

I moved the bed away from the wall but found only large gray mounds of dust. Not good for an asthmatic, if that was her complaint, but there was no point in telling her that now.

A couple of thin blue aerograms covered in Cyrillic script had fallen behind the dresser. I put them in my briefcase. It shouldn't be too hard to find someone who could translate them for me.

The landline sat between the microwave and the sink. I scrolled through the caller ID. Very few calls had come in over the last week, but I wrote down all the numbers and names; I could check them when I got back to my office.

The bathroom was in a state of complete disarray, with bottles of lotion and bath salts scattered on the floor amid used linens and Jurgens's dirty underwear and hospital clothes. I fished through more pockets, even took the top off the toilet tank and looked under the float, but didn't find as much as a parking receipt.

I scrubbed my hands at the kitchen sink, spraying them with Clorox and washing myself up to my elbows. I looked again at the landline. I had checked the incoming calls but not outgoing. The landline didn't give a long history, not like a cell phone, but it did let me see the last five numbers dialed. One was an 800 number, which turned out to be Polish Airlines. The most recent was a local cab company. I was about to try a third, in the 312 area, when I realized I knew that number. It belonged to the main switchboard at Crawford, Mead, my ex-husband's firm. They'd changed buildings, but the phone numbers were the same they'd been when he went to work there twenty-five years ago.

A plane made its final approach overhead, the noise drowning the hum of the refrigerator and a distant lawn mower. I sat down gingerly on one of the kitchen chairs and tried to think.

The sequence of calls Jana had made yesterday: she'd called 911 to report me to the police. She'd called Crawford, Mead. And then she'd booked a flight and fled town as fast as possible.

What had made her run? Me, with my news that her lover had been murdered, had that scared her into bolting? Or had it been her conversation with Crawford, Mead?

Miles Wuchnik had done occasional freelance work for the firm. Eloise Napier and her rodent-looking pal, Louis Ormond, had denied using Wuchnik recently, but this phone record made them look like a couple of liars. Wuchnik had gotten Xavier to let him into the locked wing, and somehow, Xavier had found out that Wuchnik was doing it for my ex's firm. On behalf of a mystery client.

If I called Crawford, Mead, I wanted to make sure I had a good escape route planned. Maybe I could hole up in the Umbrian hills, where my mother's father had hidden during the war.

I drove slowly back to the city, concentrating on the traffic, looking for anyone who might be staying close to me. I thought I was clean. I stayed south, returning to the University of Chicago. The closest parking was half a mile from campus, nothing when you're fresh and the air is, too, but a wilting walk in the muggy late-morning.

I found the Slavic languages and literature department. The young man working the reception desk reluctantly put aside the thick volume he was reading when I said hello for the third time. He unwrapped himself from his chair to see what I wanted, proving to be such a tall, thin stick of a guy that I wondered how blood made it from his feet to his brain. I showed him the Cyrillic aerograms, explaining I was hoping to get them translated. He brightened: he was a graduate student in Russian literature; he could do the work in an evening. We agreed on a hundred dollars, but he waved aside my offer to give him half up front.

"Send me a check when I've finished. Just write down your phone number and your e-mail for me."

He made copies of the letters for me on a machine behind him and was coiled back in his chair over his book—in Russian—before I'd left. It made me wistful to see someone so deeply in love with the written word that money seemed not to matter to him. So different from the world where I spend most of my time, filled with the dying or the lying.

Back in my office, I stared blankly at the database giving me the list of inmates in Ruhetal's forensic wing.

The Umbrian hills hadn't really kept my mother's father safe—there are always neighbors like the women on Jana Shatka's street who know what you're doing, and inevitably, one of them will betray you, in exchange for safety, or money, or, in wartime, for a little extra food. Perhaps that was Chaim Salanter's wartime secret—not the grand plots that Wade Lawlor wove around him but something he was too ashamed to admit now.

Salanter had encased himself in a vast fortune here in the New World, but it hadn't been enough to protect his granddaughter. I sat up abruptly. Whoever had doped her and put her in the trunk of the Camaro to suffocate would have no qualms about going into her hospital room and putting something nasty into her IV.

I called Lotty's clinic to see if her staff could work their hospital networks to get me an update on Arielle Zitter, explaining my fears about her security. "I don't need to know what hospital she's in, but the Salanters should have security professionals in place to inspect any meds or food she gets and any visitors who come."

Jewel Kim phoned back twenty minutes later to tell me that Arielle's mother was moving her to a private rehabilitation clinic in Israel, where the family felt her security could be guaranteed until she recovered. She'd flown out on the Salanters' private plane this morning. That was reassuring. If Arielle was fit enough for a ten-hour flight, she must be recovering fairly quickly.

Everyone was leaving Chicago. Maybe Lucy and Kira Dudek should, too—go to their *tata* in Poland. They didn't have the Salanters' private jet to whisk them behind Mossad's protective radar. If it was Kira's phone that had been used to summon Arielle to Mount Moriah two nights ago, the assailant might well think Kira knew something about him—or her, I added, conscientiously.

I called my cousin to make sure she and the girls were still all right. She'd left them with "Uncle Sal" while she went in to work.

"I just talked to him ten minutes ago, and he's getting kind of worn out. Anyway, the girls want to go home, and their mom doesn't like them being away, either, especially since you and Uncle Sal are strangers."

"I don't want them to go home if I can't guarantee their safety," I fretted. "Things are looking ugly and scary from where I'm sitting. If I could hire—" I broke off; the words gave me an idea. "Hold that thought: I'll get back to you in a minute."

I called Chaim Salanter's PA. "Ms. Balfour, I understand that Arielle is out of the country, in a safe place."

"How did you know that?" she said. "Only the family—"

"Don't worry about it; I'm not passing the word along. But there are two girls from Arielle's book group at the Malina Foundation whose safety has been compromised by Arielle's shenanigans. Their mother scrapes out a living cleaning hotel bathrooms. It would be an act of charity if Mr. Salanter would spring for a private guard for them so their mother can stop worrying about them while she's at work."

She dithered, she dickered, but I told her she had nothing to bargain with, since it was her boss's mania for secrecy that had put the Dudek girls at risk. Finally, she put me on hold while she conferred with Chaim. He came on the line himself, asked a few questions, such as how I knew where Arielle had gone: had I been spying on her?

"No, sir. I don't even know what hospital she was taken to. But nothing involving more than one human being can be kept secret forever."

"The Dudeks—is that their name?—have no claim on my generosity."

"Your granddaughter was the ringleader of the group that sucked them into her cemetery adventure. Arielle took advantage of Kira's mother working all night to use the Dudek apartment for her private meetings. If not for Arielle, Kira Dudek wouldn't have been in Mount Moriah cemetery two weeks ago. The loss of her cell phone was a financial blow to Kira and her mother, but if it had incriminating photos or texts on it, whoever attacked Arielle may well try to find Kira to silence her. I'd say that was a pretty large moral claim on your generosity."

I did my best to keep the bitterness out of my voice, but he wanted to know next whether I was threatening to disclose Arielle's location if he didn't help the Dudek girls.

"No, sir," I said. "Even if I wanted to dicker over their safety, which I don't, you could keep moving Arielle and I don't have the energy to follow her."

"How long will it be before the police discover who was behind the assault on my granddaughter?"

"I can't speak for the police, Mr. Salanter, but I am hard at it. With more information, of course, it would be easier."

"Nothing in my life story would illuminate these crimes, Ms. Warshawski, but I will ask Gabe Eycks to arrange a guard for the girls; he'll call you for the details."

I let out a breath I hadn't realized I was holding. "Thank you, sir. Perhaps you might worry a bit about Sophy Durango's daughter, too."

There was a pause on the other end, then an energetic agreement. Nia would enjoy a trip to Israel, to help Arielle with her recovery; he should have thought of that himself.

39. CHASING SHADOWS

"I'm going to have to start billing you, Vic, if you come around here all the time."

That was Dick's idea of a joke. I smiled and got to my feet. "That's okay. I'll just bill you for my waiting time."

I'd called Crawford, Mead as soon as I finished talking to Chaim Salanter, but Dick couldn't see me until the end of the day. He hadn't wanted to meet with me at all, but after I said I was investigating what his law firm was doing at a murder victim's home, he—or, really, his secretary, who was crisply relaying messages between us—said he'd fit me in at six-thirty, before dinner with clients. It was nearly seven before he stepped into the waiting area, a vision in pale gray summer suiting.

Since I'd had the afternoon free, I'd been able to go home and wait for Gabe Eycks to turn up with a bodyguard for the Dudek girls. Mr. Contreras was worn out, as my cousin had said, and was glad to turn the energetic sisters over to me. While they danced under the jet from the backyard sprinkler, I changed out of my wrinkled T-shirt into a tailored knit top in my favorite gold, with a light rayon jacket to cover my shoulder holster.

I joined them in the yard. As we threw tennis balls for the dogs, I casually asked Kira what she'd seen at the cemetery the night of the shape-shifting ritual.

She stiffened instantly and looked at the back door, as if ready to run to Mr. Contreras for shelter. "Just rain."

"Kira. You know why you're here with me and Mr. Contreras, right? And why we're getting a bodyguard to look after you and Lucy?"

"To keep us from getting hurt by the person who hurted Arielle," Lucy piped up.

"Do you know why he might want to hurt you?" I asked.

Lucy said, "Because he's a big mean stranger danger," but Kira turned her head away, glowering.

"It's not about you being illegal, or whether the Vina Fields girls act snobby to the Malina girls. It's about what you saw. You girls were all taking pictures with your cell phones, but you dropped yours. I think whoever picked it up saw that you'd gotten a perfect shot of the person who was hiding near your group."

"The vampire!" Lucy danced in her excitement. "You took a picture of a vampire, Kira. If you find your phone, we can sell the picture, we'll be rich, we can buy a horse!"

Kira turned to her sister and ordered her in Polish to shut up. Lucy fired back some insult of her own and marched off in a huff with Mitch to a far corner of the garden.

"There wasn't a vampire in the cemetery. It was a—a person." I bit off the word "murderer." Kira probably guessed that was who'd been near the Carmilla ritual, but putting it into words would make it seem real and terrifying.

"I need to know who or what you saw. The sooner I know, the sooner I can see that your life returns to normal."

"Tyler screamed that there was a vampire," Kira whispered after a minute. "I turned around and took a picture, and then, when I lost my phone, I thought it was the vampire's power that took it from me."

"What did he look like?"

"I don't know, it all happened so fast, and it was rainy. He had a black shiny hood over his head, and his face was white, I thought he was Death, that's what Death looks like in Lucy's and my picture Bible. When Arielle almost got dead I thought he cursed her, for seeing him, and now he'll curse me, too."

"You're sure it was a man? Could it have been a woman?"

"I don't know."

"Do you have a sense of how tall he was?"

Kira was starting to cry. "I don't know, I don't know, I don't know."

I pulled her to me. She stood stiffly in the circle of my arm, tears running down her face. When Lucy saw her sister was crying she rushed back over, her own sense of injury forgotten. She grabbed Kira's hand and tried to pull her from me, shrieking at us to say what was wrong, what had happened.

"Oh, just go away," Kira sobbed. "I want to go home, I want my mom, I want my *tata*, I want life to be like before he left us."

The dogs began twining around her, licking her legs. Their mewling made her relax inside my embrace. She leaned against my breast, her chest heaving with her sobs. Lucy clung to my other arm, frightened at seeing her big sister so vulnerable.

After a time, when Kira's tears had eased, I took the girls upstairs and filled the tub with lavender salts. Both sisters climbed in. When Mitch wanted to join them, I left Kira to deal with him. Fighting him would take her mind off her own fears.

From the shrieks and splashes I heard while I tidied the bedroom, it sounded as though Mitch had brought a sense of normality back to the girls. I fixed lunch on a tray so they could sit in bed like princesses, watching TV and eating peanut-butter sandwiches. Mitch, his black fur drenched, but smelling sweetly of lavender, bounded into bed with them.

As I mopped the bathroom floor and strained black hairs from the tub, I mulled over the skimpy information Kira had given me. No wonder the man in the black rain slicker looked like a vampire or death itself: he'd just murdered a man. It must have sent a shock through him to have that group of girls show up singing and dancing seconds after he'd stabbed Wuchnik.

Or had it? I went back to the question I'd been asking all along: had he chosen the cemetery, along with a vampire-style killing, because he knew the Carmilla girls would be there already?

But then, how had he known? Wuchnik was the blackmailer, the eavesdropper. I was assuming he was the person the Ashfords had sent out to Ruhetal to put a stop to Leydon's work on behalf of her mentally incompetent client, but what was the connection between the Ashford family and the Carmilla club in the cemetery?

I called Petra over at the Malina Foundation: it was just possible that Trina Ashford—Leydon's niece—belonged to one of the Malina book groups. Petra clicked through computer screens while I waited but came up empty.

"I don't want to cause any more panic than the parents in your program already feel, but they need to know there's a possibility the vampire killer may attack other kids in the group. He may worry that they have his face on their phone screens."

The doorbell rang as she was hesitating—she was afraid calls like that would further jeopardize her job.

I assumed it would be Gabe Eycks at the door with a bodyguard for the girls, but it turned out to be Terry Finchley from Area Six. I buzzed him in and told my cousin that I would bring the matter up with the police.

While Finchley climbed the stairs, I dashed to the bedroom to tell Kira and Lucy they needed to stay there until I came for them. However far beyond corruption the Finch was, if he knew one of the girls he was trying to trace was with me, he'd jump on her—and me—with both feet.

Peppy remained in bed with the girls, soulfully looking at their crusts of bread. Mitch felt that a knock on my apartment door was his call to action, but I forced him to stay in the bedroom—I didn't think he'd add anything to a conversation with the police.

"Detective!" I opened my front door with a flourish.

Elizabeth Milkova followed Finchley into my living room, her white shirt limp with sweat under her bulletproof vest. Finchley, as always, looked freshly cleaned and pressed, but his mouth was set in a hard line.

"Victoria Iphigenia—did your mother name you that so the rest of us would always know how ignorant we are around you?"

My smile turned brittle: jokes that mention my mother rattle me. I needed to be careful not to let Finchley's angry ribbing cloud my judgment. "What is making you feel especially ignorant today, Lieutenant?"

"Bodies in my jurisdiction that no one tells me about." He sat on the arm of my couch, right leg dangling. Milkova stood next to him with parade-ground stiffness, hands clasped behind her back.

I gestured toward a chair, but she shook her head. I looked at Finchley. "Unless it's a job requirement that your underlings stand in your presence, please command your officer to sit. She's making me so uncomfortable that I doubt I can focus on your questions."

The frown lines in Finchley's face deepened, but he said, "Take a pew, Liz. And you, V.I., tell me about Xavier Jurgens."

"The techs were saying that all the evidence pointed to Jurgens having committed suicide. You don't agree?"

"That was before we looked at the vodka bottle: it had been wiped clean of prints. That made us ask Vishnikov to do a complete autopsy: Jurgens's hands had been bound before he passed out. It's looking like someone force-fed him a bottle of pill-laden booze, then untied him. So talk to me about Salanter's granddaughter and the hospital orderly."

"What—the FBI isn't sharing?"

"Oh, the feds, they never share with us CPD lowlifes. But if you'd called me yesterday to report Jurgens's death, I might have had a crack at questioning Jana Shatka."

"What happened to her?" My mouth was unpleasantly dry: I'd been assuming Shatka had run away, but maybe the death-dealing vampire had reached her first.

"She was on the five-twenty-five to Warsaw last night. She landed in Kiev at six-thirty this morning, Chicago time. Who knows what time it is there."

"She's from Lithuania," I said. "Is she moving to Ukraine?"

"I don't care where she goes in Foreignland, but for what it's worth, the consulate told me Shatka's mother moved to Kiev last month. They said anti-Russian feeling is running high in the Baltic states."

"Can you extradite her?"

Finchley's mouth was a thin bitter line. "No treaty with Ukraine. That's why the Ukrainian mob sits over there, happily hacking into our bank accounts. Why in God's name couldn't you call me yesterday when you found Jurgens?"

I felt my eyes turn hot. "I am thoroughly sick of every cop in the six-county area blaming me for their problems. *I* found Jurgens, *I* saved Arielle Zitter's life, *I* got Leydon Ashford to the hospital after she was pushed off the Rockefeller Chapel balcony. I did all this even though I'm a one-woman shop and you have a team of thirteen thousand. Go yell at the evidence techs who went over Jurgens's Camaro. Scream at the patrol team that responded to my 911 call, but get off my back!"

Finchley frowned at me for a moment, then gave a reluctant nod. "Point taken. Tell me everything you learned from Shatka. I know you talked to her—Burbank let me interview the neighbors."

I told him everything I knew, everything except the aerograms I'd dropped off at the university. I couldn't see the point of adding to Terry's workload by sending him after the translator—for all I knew, those were letters from Shatka's mother, telling her the cabbage crop had failed and she'd better stay on in Chicago, collecting disability checks. I also didn't tell him about finding the Crawford, Mead phone number on Shatka's landline—he could discover that for himself, after all.

"How'd you get involved with Shatka, anyway?" Finchley said.

"My friend Leydon Ashford. She was a patient at Ruhetal, where Xavier Jurgens worked. Jurgens took Miles Wuchnik into the locked ward, and Leydon was convinced Wuchnik was there, spying on her. Which may not have been a paranoid delusion. Someone at Ruhetal called the family to report that Leydon was stirring up the inmates.

"Sewall Ashford and his mother sent a minion out to the hospital to stop Leydon. They didn't tell the therapists they were intervening, or interfering, whichever it looks like to you, so the therapists don't know who the family sent. You could talk to Vernon Mulliner, the head of security at the hospital. Or maybe Leydon's mom, or her brother, Sewall, will be more forthcoming with you than they are with me."

"Sewall Ashford? Oh, great, Warshawski. You couldn't have a connection to someone a little more accessible, could you?"

Meaning someone who would respond to police threats. "I wish! I've been banging my head against inaccessible people all week. Dick Yarborough, Eloise Napier and Louis Ormond at Crawford, Mead. Harold Weekes and Wade Lawlor at Global. Chaim Salanter. Maybe you can come up with a more subtle approach."

Finchley gave a sharkish grin. "Anything I do would be more subtle than you, Warshawski. What else about Shatka?"

"If you look at Jana Shatka and Xavier Jurgens, she was the strong-minded member of the couple. Whatever Jurgens knew, if Shatka thought it was valuable, she bullied it out of him. Someone paid Jurgens a bundle, and I'm betting Shatka knew who that was. If you pull her phone records, you should be able to find who she talked to without needing to extradite her or anything."

"Pull her phone records!" Terry snarled. "You're like all the juries in Cook County, you think we have the time and resources to gather evidence on every case the way they do in *CSI*. We searched the premises, but there wasn't a piece of paper in the place. She was smart."

"She was scared: her lover had been murdered. And she was pretty sure she knew who did it, pretty sure it was the same person who killed Miles Wuchnik two weeks ago."

"You can't know that," Finchley objected.

"Please, Finch—both of them at the same cemetery? Have you interviewed Jurgens's coworkers at Ruhetal? Do they know where he got the money for the car?"

Finchley shook his head. "He just showed up with it one day, bragging about it. Perhaps what his girlfriend told you is right. Maybe the Camaro has nothing to do with his death—maybe he bought it with money he saved skipping lunch. It was how my grandfather bought his first Continental, after all."

I bowed my head briefly, acknowledging his grandfather's frugality. "Have you talked to the kids in Arielle Zitter's book club?"

Finchley stared at me. "Why should I do that?"

"The feds really have kept you in the dark." I told him about the text message Arielle had received. "Arielle wants to uncover Chaim Salanter's history, which somehow plays a role in this story. For all I know, the kid hired Wuchnik to investigate her grandfather, and Salanter killed him for his pains."

"Yeah, I can see my watch commander's face when I tell him that cute theory. We don't interrogate people in Salanter's income bracket, let alone their granddaughter or her friends. Not unless we've found their DNA smeared an inch thick on a piece of rebar. Which, before you ask, was free of any evidence except Wuchnik's blood. And skin tissue and so on."

"Terry, the kids saw something, or the killer thinks they saw something. Otherwise, he wouldn't have targeted Arielle, using a cell phone from one of the girls in her group. I heard that Sophy Durango's daughter is leaving the country today or tomorrow, but—"

"How did you hear that?" Finchley demanded.

"By listening to what people tell me," I snapped. "I am an investigator, Terry, and every now and then I stumble on a fact. I can't track down every girl who was in that cemetery two weeks ago, or make their parents talk to me, but you can. And you can get a warrant allowing you to look at the pix on their cell phones, to see if one of them got a good shot of the killer. And you can warn the parents to keep their kids close to home until we get this maniac. We owe it to these children."

"I don't need you to tell me how to do my job," Finchley said.

"You know you would've done this two weeks ago if you hadn't gotten that directive to minimize your investigation into Wuchnik's murder. I've been spinning in circles, trying to follow up on Wuchnik's sister, his missing electronics, and these girls. I don't think they were involved in killing him, but I do believe someone went to a lot of trouble to get Wuchnik and them to the same place at the same time. You have the resources to find what was on their phones—including any spyware Wuchnik might have uploaded."

Finchley glared at me, but he was a good cop, and he knew I was right. "Liz, make a note. Make it a priority when we're back in the car."

Officer Milkova nodded stiffly and pulled a pad from a pocket beneath her vest. Finchley got to his feet; Milkova rose as if on remote-controlled marionette strings.

"If you think of anything, or if you find another corpse, you call me, Warshawski," Finchley said. "I don't care if it's two in the morning and the body is on Mars. If you find it I want to know about it."

"Copy that, Lieutenant. Officer Milkova, a glass of water before you leave? It's a miserable hot day out there."

She flushed but spoke her first words of the afternoon. "No, thank you, Ms. Warshawski. We've got water in the car."

I followed them down the stairs to make sure they really left the building. As I climbed back to the third floor, I felt a grudging respect for Jana Shatka. Maybe Terry would have gotten something from her if he'd been able to interrogate her with the might of the law behind him, but I didn't think so. Instead, she'd be dead, because whoever killed Jurgens and Wuchnik would think she'd ratted him—her?—out to the cops.

I went back into my apartment. "Prosper in Kiev, Ms. Shatka. Stay away from Ukrainian mobsters; they're easily as ruthless, or more so, than their American counterparts."

I parodied a toast with my coffee cup, but saying the words aloud made me think again that the case might revolve around drugs. I should have suggested that to Finchley. Perhaps Shatka had a connection to a Ukrainian mob, or perhaps she was tied to a South American cartel.

That flight of fancy didn't take into account a possible connection to Salanter, though. Nor had Shatka seemed much like a mobster in our two encounters. She had seemed like what she was: a two-bit con artist milking Social Security for a disability check, but smart enough to run from murder.

It was hard to believe Chaim Salanter had ever given in to blackmail. I could see those remote eyes looking unflinchingly on murder if he thought Wuchnik and Jurgens were big enough threats. But these had been strenuous murders, or at least Wuchnik's had been. Salanter would have required help to get Wuchnik's body onto a slab, and I couldn't picture him leaving himself vulnerable to further blackmail by letting Gabe Eycks in on his secrets. And would he have put his own grand-daughter in the trunk of a car? Despite what Dean Knaub had said earlier, about the impenetrability of the human heart, I didn't believe it.

I went to my bedroom to tell the Dudek girls they could come out. They'd used the time to dress the dogs again, putting a straw hat and scarf on Peppy and one of my silk blouses on Mitch. They'd also painted his toenails red. He looked at me, and then dropped to his belly in mortification. I was about to protest their raiding of my wardrobe, but Mitch's face was too much for me. I was laughing so hard my sides hurt when Gabe Eycks showed up with his bodyguard.

Eycks's years with Arielle had given him a good sense of what kids respond to: the guard, Teodoro (*everyone calls me Teddy*) Martinez, was young, peppy, nice-looking without being in love with himself. Mr. Contreras, who came out to inspect him when the doorbell rang, had a rare moment of bonding with another man. I didn't know if that should be a warning sign, since he's bristled at every guy I've ever dated.

I quietly searched my databases for Teodoro while Kira and Lucy conferred in Polish. By the time I'd rejoined the group, confident that Teodoro was the guard he claimed to be, without any noticeable criminal record, the girls had apparently decided he was a status symbol; they would love showing him off in their neighborhood. They got into his Jeep, after some snively farewells to Peppy and Mitch.

When the Jeep was out of sight, Mitch pawed at me to undress him. "I don't know, boy. If putting clothes and makeup on you calms you down, maybe we should keep you gussied up."

"Come on, doll," Mr. Contreras began. "Oh, you're teasing. I was glad to have those girls here, they livened up the place, but you take that dress off Mitch. I'm going down to watch the last race at Arlington."

I got Mitch out of my flowered blouse without tearing more than one armpit seam and losing a button. And still had time to drop in on Nia Durango before my six-thirty appointment with Dick.

40. LAWYER FEES: IMPRESSIVE!

NIA WAS PACKING FOR A MONTH IN ISRAEL, SO EXCITED AT HER pending adventure that she didn't bristle at my questions in a way that she might have if I'd asked them while Arielle was still missing. Diane Ovech, the Durangos' housekeeper, sat in on our interview in the Durangos' living room, since Sophy was campaigning in Rockford this afternoon.

"Nia, you and Arielle laughed at the thought that Miles Wuchnik might have been a genie. Did that mean you thought he was interested in Arielle's genealogy search?"

Nia sucked in a breath. "How do you know about that?"

"The websites Arielle visited," I said. "She was trying to learn something about her grandfather's boyhood during the Second World War. Did she ever actually meet Miles Wuchnik?"

Nia was a tall girl, almost my height, but she looked very small and vulnerable right now. She started drawing a circle in the living room rug with her big toe.

"If Arielle confided in you, you're carrying a load you need to share with us," I said.

"You must answer, Nia." Diane's voice was calm but carried an authoritative weight.

"I wasn't trying to make a joke about a dead person," Nia said miserably. "I know that's rude and mean-spirited. We were nervous, that's all, but, see, one day Ari got this text message, it was from this guy who said he worked at Global News. He said he was really fed up with how the network talked about Grandpapa Chaim, and if we'd get him the truth about what happened during the war, then he'd put it on the teleprompter in the middle of one of Wade Lawlor's rants, and Wade would find himself reading the truth to the whole world!"

I felt the hair stand up on my neck. "That must have seemed like an exciting idea" was the only response I could come up with.

"We thought it was awesome," Nia said, her face flushed. "You know the kind of horrible garbage he says about my mom and Ari's grandpapa, we wanted to pay him back!"

"Why didn't you tell me?" Diane said. "Or talk to your mother?"

"We knew you'd say not to do it, and we wanted Wade Lawlor to look totally stupid and wasted on TV!"

"Is that when Arielle started doing all that genealogy research?" I said.

"First we tried to ask Grandpapa Chaim, because that was the simplest way to find out. We talked to him at the cottage one night—in Michigan, you know, where he's the most relaxed he ever gets. We said, like, he was our age in the war, and how did he make it without his folks, because we couldn't imagine it, it's hard enough for Ari and me, not having our fathers, but if our moms disappeared—and he just got really quiet, and looked at us, like—I can't even say what his face looked like."

She looked up at me, her eyes big in her narrow face. "We were so frightened; we thought we'd be in horrible trouble if we ever told another soul. And then, when Ari disappeared, I was really scared, because I thought it was something about Grandpapa Chaim, about what he did in Europe during the war, you know. But when you found

Ari in the trunk of the car, I knew Grandpapa Chaim would never hurt her, I mean, he might've gotten cross about her asking too many questions, but he wouldn't leave her to die in the trunk of a car."

I wondered again about the human heart, Chaim's heart.

"Did the person who texted Arielle give her a way of checking on whether he really worked at Global?"

"He had to write us anonymously," Nia said earnestly. "We couldn't check on him because he was afraid he'd get fired."

"Nia, these are the typical things that con artists say. If anyone approaches you, or Arielle, again, talk to me, or talk to Diane here. If Arielle had come up with real information about Chaim—about her grandfather—your texter would have used it to hurt him."

"How do you know?" Nia tried to speak forcefully, but the misery in her eyes told me she knew I was telling the truth.

"Did you ever meet him in person?" I asked.

Nia took a deep breath. "Who we met was the vampire's victim."

I took a breath of my own, counting slowly, not wanting to shriek. "Tell me about it."

"He came up to Ari after school one day. We gave him the brush-off, we looked for the school guard. Maybe we don't know about con artists, but we've been taught since we were two years old about stranger danger, especially Ari, because, you know, how rich her grandpapa is, kidnappers could steal her for ransom.

"But, anyway, the vampire guy, he called out, 'I know you're looking for Chaim Salanter's history,' so we thought it was the person texting Ari, so we went up to talk to him, and then he said he really needed us to work harder, because they were starting to get suspicious of him at work, and we were like, we're doing all we can but we don't know anything, and he said, maybe we should go look in Grandpapa Chaim's computer. Then Ari said she couldn't possibly do that, and he said, well, if we gave him Grandpapa Chaim's passwords, he could do it for us from a remote location."

"And did you?" My mouth was dry as I asked the question.

"We couldn't; Ari doesn't know them. And he said if we loved Grand-papa Chaim we'd be more cooperative." Nia looked up. "When he said that, we got scared, we just took off and ran home."

"Why didn't you tell your mother or Aunt Julia, or even me?" Diane burst out.

"We couldn't!" Nia said. "You'd tell Grandpapa Chaim and we were scareder of him than anyone."

I thought of Julia, frantic about her daughter, worried about her father. If Arielle had confided in her mother, Julia might have enlisted Gabe Eycks in helping her dispose of a blackmailer.

"Did he come back again?"

"No, but every day until school ended in June, we were, like, totally scared, we'd leave by a side door, we'd run around with girls we usually didn't talk to just so we were in a group. And then when he got killed, all we thought was how Carmilla had protected us!"

I didn't know if I felt more like screaming or smiling at the needle-point poise between childhood and adulthood that made girls caught up in a murder imagine that Carmilla might be real.

"You knew when you saw him in the cemetery that he was the man who tried to blackmail you?"

"We didn't see his face at the cemetery, it was the next day, when you said his name, and we were so happy we didn't think about the rest of it."

"How did you know his name?" I asked.

"I told him he couldn't talk to us if he didn't tell us. First he gave this stupid made-up name, like we were so stupid we never heard of Sam Spade, and then he said his name, and we told him we had to see a business card."

The benefits of having a mother in a high-profile position. I hadn't known what a business card was when I was twelve.

"But why did you choose the cemetery at all?" I asked.

"Arielle suggested it." Nia picked at a cuticle. "I mean, I'm not trying to get her in trouble, but we knew if we went to a park, we could get busted for being out after curfew, and the cemetery, it's abandoned, so no one would see us. It's where her mom's grandmother is buried, so we'd been there before, we knew about that tomb that's built like an old temple, you know, falling down in ruins like in our history books."

Neither Diane nor I spoke for a minute, then the housekeeper gently told Nia to go finish packing, because the car to the airport would be arriving in less than an hour. As soon as her charge was out of the room, though, she turned to me in worry: the police had to know, Sophy had to know, but did it have to be today?

I looked at her unhappily. "I know that making this public will be another blow to Dr. Durango's campaign. But we can't sit on it any longer."

"Do you think Nia was truthful, about not having seen the man again, I mean? I hate having to ask this, she's always been a very truthful child, but—" Diane clipped her sentence off without finishing it.

I nodded; I'd been turning the question over in my own mind. "Miles Wuchnik was a blackmailer. He had some kind of device for listening in on people's calls; he might even have loaded something in the girls' cell phones so that their texts would pop up on his own phone. The technology exists; I just don't know how to use it.

"The bigger question to me is how he learned enough about Salanter or Arielle to eavesdrop on her in the first place. But I'm beginning to see that his eavesdropping might have led him to the cemetery—he would have known that the girls were going to hold their ritual there. And the biggest question of all is which of his victims was so threatened that he or she needed Wuchnik dead. I hope Carmilla's protection extends to Julia and Chaim—I don't want to think either of them was responsible."

"Maybe I'll borrow Nia's Carmilla amulet while she's in Israel." Diane smiled weakly. "When will you tell the police?"

"Probably tomorrow." I got up. "Unless I learn something at my next meeting that will let me keep the girls out of the picture altogether. Are you staying in Chicago when Nia flies out? I'll call you in the morning, give you enough advance notice that Dr. Durango's PR team can be ready, if worse comes to worst."

The housekeeper walked me to the door. "I've worked for Sophy ever since Nia was two, when her husband was first diagnosed with lymphoma. She—you know the saying, that no man is a hero to his valet? I've seen Sophy in situations that would tax any of us to the limit, but I've never seen her take it out on me, students, or staff. She really is a great candidate for any office in this country. I don't want this murder to derail her. And maybe, like Nia said, that's heartless, but what if the killer did all this just to embarrass her, to guarantee that that right-wing creep Kendrick gets to the Senate?"

Her words echoed some conspiracy fears of my own; they shaped my conversation with my ex-husband, when he finally descended from his forty-eighth-floor office to Crawford, Mead's reception area. After our barbed banter about who got to bill whom, he took me to the same conference room where we'd spoken last week.

He looked at his Journe watch: I'm important, don't forget it. "I've got fifteen minutes, Vic, then I'm due at the Pottawatomie Club."

I was supposed to be impressed: the Pottawatomie is one of a handful of social clubs around the country where who gets to do what to America is decided. "I've eaten there, Dick—I don't think you'll regret skipping the appetizer."

"Was there some reason you wanted to see me other than to taunt me?" Dick demanded.

I helped myself to the red grapefruit juice on the drinks cart. "You know, this is the only place in town I ever see this juice, and it's the perfect hot-weather refresher. You told me last week that Crawford, Mead doesn't take political positions, but of course everyone knows that Eloise Napier is one of Helen Kendrick's lawyers."

"You know I can't comment on our client list."

"I'm not asking you to, I'm telling you. When Eloise Napier flaunts Kendrick's jewel-crusted gold corncob flag, I know that she, if not the firm itself, is working for Helen Kendrick. So I'm picturing a dinner party in Lake Bluff with the Reapers, I think that's what they're called, the people who bundle together quarter-million contributions to the Kendrick campaign."

"Gleaners," Dick corrected me without thinking, then glared when he realized I'd gotten him to betray his involvement in the campaign.

"Right. So we're at a dinner party with the Gleaners. Sewall Ashford and his mom are there, among others, and so is Kendrick's lawyer, Napier. Or was it you?"

I paused, but Dick wasn't going to betray himself any further.

"And word comes in that Leydon Ashford, the dirty laundry or the blazing light of the family, depending on your viewpoint, is acting as a lawyer for a guy in Ruhetal's forensic wing. Sewall and his mom want it stopped, and Eloise tells them she has a PI she uses for odd jobs, and what could be odder than this one? So she says she'll send her PI out to Ruhetal to find out what Leydon's up to and he'll make her stop."

Dick shrugged. "Could be. We do a lot of things for our clients that they don't cover in Introduction to Client Relations courses."

"So when Miles Wuchnik was found dead, Eloise must have raised those perfectly painted eyebrows of hers. Despite her pretense of not knowing what Wuchnik had been doing for months and months."

"Vic, that smacks of cattiness." Dick pretended to be shocked.

"You're right: meow. Now, here's an interesting thing that Eloise may or may not have shared with her managing partner. Wuchnik's contact at the hospital was killed this past Tuesday. Suffocated in the front seat of a shiny new Camaro that he'd plunked down fifteen thousand for in cash. Yesterday, the dead man's girlfriend phoned Crawford, Mead. Whatever she learned from that phone call made her flee the country. I'm assuming she wasn't seeking green-card advice."

Dick frowned, drumming his long fingers on the table. It was those hands that must have attracted me twenty-five years ago—surely I'd never been drawn to that petulant mouth.

"What's the name?" he said.

"Jana Shatka. Her dead partner was Xavier Jurgens."

"Spell," he demanded.

I printed the names on one of the pads of paper laid out helpfully for clients. Dick used the phone in the middle of the table to call into the bowels of the firm. He identified himself, gave a number that I presumed was his secret password, and then asked about Shatka and Jurgens.

When he hung up he frowned some more. "We don't have any record of a call from Shatka. She might not have identified herself, of course. She wasn't a client."

He paused.

"But Jurgens was?" I asked.

"No." He paused again. "Can I count on your discretion?"

"Not if it's a lead in a murder case, you know that, Dick."

He bit his lower lip. "Oh, damn you, anyway, Vic. Ten days ago, we got a packet of money. Sixteen thousand two hundred dollars in cash, to be exact. A typed note asked us to deliver the money to Jurgens, less twelve hundred as our fee for ninety minutes of work."

41. A STEP AHEAD

That was all Dick could, or maybe would, tell me. He didn't know if the money had been delivered by messenger, FedEx, or dropped by Carmilla's beak from the clouds, and he refused to call his mail-processing center to see if they had a record of the sender's address.

"Dick, we're talking about a guy who's been murdered, not someone who provided evidence in a money-laundering scheme."

"You can't prove that the money has anything to do with his murder. It sounds as though it's the cash he used to buy the Camaro, am I right?"

I had to agree with that. "But which lawyer got the commission? Eloise?"

"I'm not going to reveal our in-house secrets to you, let alone breach confidentiality laws. And now, if you don't mind *very* much, I'm already late for dinner with the Chinese trade consul."

Waiting with him for the elevator, I asked if the note had revealed the client who was providing the cash.

"Even if I knew, it can't possibly be any of your business."

"It is my business, Dick. It's connected to how Leydon Ashford ended up in a terrible heap on the Rockefeller Chapel floor." Dick and Vic. Leydon used to tease us about our rhyming relationship. "Was the client Sewall Ashford? Or Helen Kendrick?"

"Don't jump to conclusions, Vic. You might outjump your shadow."

The elevator arrived just then. Late though it was in the workday, two of Dick's colleagues were on board. They eyed me curiously but didn't ask for introductions. Instead, the three discussed their upcoming vacation plans. Dick and his wife were off to Martha's Vineyard with their three children. One of the colleagues was heading to Thailand, the other to Ethiopia with his church to help build affordable housing.

"I'll be spending my summer in South Chicago, waiting for someone to build affordable housing there," I said chirpily.

Dick rolled his eyes while the colleagues backed away from me. Conversation froze for the rest of the journey.

At street level we all separated, Dick into a waiting limo, the colleagues moving toward the suburban rail station, me heading east to pick up the Blue Line. If Dick and I were still married, I could get door-to-door limo service instead of making my tired legs carry me down the grimy stairs to the L platform. Of course, I'd have to wear high heels and makeup instead of my cushioned sandals.

The dim lights in the stairwell made my shadow waver and bounce in front of me. I'd have a hard time outjumping that. But Dick had given me a clue, I realized, as I stuck my CTA card into the magnetic reader. I was assuming the wrong client, or the wrong partner, or both. If Eloise hadn't been the go-between for Xavier's cash, then it was likely her gray, self-effacing colleague, Louis whoever. If the client wasn't Ashford or Kendrick, then—was it Chaim Salanter?

It was like one of those Rubik's Cubes, where you had to keep turning the sides to fit all those colors together. I'd never been able to line the blocks up right, and this story was the same: I kept finding leftover pieces every time I tried to put them together.

When I got to my office and typed in the code at the street door, fire was pulsing in the windows on the north side. Not a cause for alarm, just a sign that Tessa Reynolds was working late with her blowtorch. She had a commission from a Chinese municipal council to provide them with some enormous metal abstract for their main plaza, and she was working overtime to finish it. Perhaps she was the beneficiary of Dick's work with the Chinese trade consul.

I resolutely put aside thoughts of vampires and Camaros and put in a couple of hours for my real clients. I was nearing the end of a complex search when my cell phone rang.

"Uh, Ms. Warshawski? This is Ted Austin, I'm the, uh, graduate student you gave those Russian letters to this morning."

"Have you finished already?"

"They only took me a couple of hours. They're both to a woman named Jana from her mother. I, uh, I'm e-mailing the translations to you, but they seem like maybe they should go to the Wiesenthal Center or something like that."

I sat up straight in my chair. "They deal with Nazi war crimes?"

"Not in so many words. They're mostly just the kind of thing a mother might write, but—well, when you've read them, you'll see what I mean. The translations aren't super-polished, but after I'd roughed them out, I thought you might want them now. I'll do a better version in a day or two."

I opened the e-mail before he'd finished speaking.

Dear Janushka,

So, this is a very strange idea [or perhaps better word choice: request], to find out information about this Jew who lived with your grandmother's brother during the War. I looked at the ad you found and discussed it with your auntie, and she agrees, you want to be careful: ask who is wanting this information. Is it the Jew Salanter himself, wanting to do additional hurt to our family? Or is it truly someone who is seeking to expose the Jew?

He certainly betrayed the great generosity your great-uncle showed him. How strange that he [*the Jew, she means*] and you both ended up in Chicago together—it is as if the Fates had willed that you be there to balance the scales. If there really is money to be had from him maybe it will make up for your hardships in America.

Your brother is still not able to find work, but he comes every day to help me with my injection for the diabetes. Even though he complains greatly, still, he knows I will not give him any money unless he helps me here.

The rest of the letter went on in the same vein, with complaints about a granddaughter who couldn't be bothered to visit her grandmother. How rude local people were in the shops when you spoke to them in Russian (*Maybe there were difficulties under the Soviet Union, but at least a Russian was treated with respect. Your auntie writes from Kiev that it is much different there, although still many people are without jobs.*)

The second letter began with another litany of complaints about the writer's swollen legs and the disrespect of her son, her granddaughter, and the concierge in her apartment building, before moving on to the subject of Chaim Salanter.

I don't know what this detective you found thinks we can give him in the way of proof. In the Second War, you were lucky to find a cabbage leaf to eat; you didn't look for a piece of paper to write down every event that happened.

I took your letter to my cousin, hoping perhaps your great-uncle confided something more detailed to him, but your cousin's mind is not stable [*or perhaps reliable*] these days. I mentioned the possibility that we could finally recover some money and live like kings, that my cousin could move out of that terrible room he lives in and reclaim our family's farm, but he said the Jews have spies everywhere and he believes the man his father befriended is just trying to track us down to do us further damage.

Your great-uncle suffered because of his wartime work. You know this, you know he was sent to a Soviet forced labor camp, and he came back broken in spirit and more bitter than ever that he was betrayed by the Jewish boy he tried to protect. "I should have just sent him to Ponar with his mother," he used to say. "There is no gratitude anywhere, especially not with the Jews, they're only out for themselves." And it is true that we were made to suffer after the war for our service to the Lithuanian Army, I was just a child, but I remember the bitter disgrace we all suffered, and all because of the Jews, really.

Of course, as my mother always said, your uncle was infatuated with the Jewess Salanter. They had enormous sexual powers, those Jewish women, and he fell under her spell, and when he heard of her death he was so infatuated, he took the boy and protected him. My mother and your grandmother both pleaded with him, the danger was enormous, even though your uncle was with the Police Battalion—if his comrades found out he was harboring the boy, the Commandant would not have protected him, but your uncle wouldn't listen, the boy resembled his mother and Uncle never recovered from his infatuation with her. (Even when he married a Christian woman he would drool with longing for the dead Jewess). But despite all his care for the Jewess's son, the boy stole Uncle's savings and ran away. Which shows why we have always believed there are two sides to the story of the Nazi occupation of Lithuania.

Of course, as for proof—you will have to use this information and see what kind of bargain you can create. I will continue to talk vigorously to your cousin [*she means her cousin, the son of the great-uncle—in Russian there's a specific word that clarifies the relationship*] and explain how our happiness lies in his hand—or in his mouth!

We have not had rain for three weeks and the parks look like dead lands, but I am leaving for Kiev next week to stay with your auntie. What can we do, after all? It's in God's hands.

At the end, Ted Austin had included a note about the Lithuanian Police Battalions:

Ms. Warshawski, maybe you already know this, but "police battalions" was the sanitized name given to Lithuanian units that supported the Germans in their extermination campaign against the Lithuanian Jews. They were at least as cruel and ruthless as the German Einsatzkommandos and made it possible for the Nazis to murder the Lithuanian Jews quite rapidly.

I printed out the e-mails and read and reread them. The language made my skin crawl, the whining over how ungrateful everyone was to the writer, how ungrateful the boy Chaim had been to his protector. The story sounded appalling, however you looked at it: Salanter's mother was murdered, and then he went to live with a member of one of the commando units that had been involved in killing the Jews of Vilna.

I tried to put my emotional reaction aside, tried to figure out the chain that had linked together Wuchnik and Shatka.

My guess was that Helen Kendrick had asked her lawyer to find an investigator to dig up dirt on Salanter, as a way of undermining the Durango campaign. Wuchnik was someone Eloise Napier had worked with before from time to time, and he must have been happy every time an affluent client like Crawford, Mead called for help. He pulled out all the stops, approached the granddaughter, tried to get her to break into Chaim's computer.

And then Wuchnik had been inspired to place an ad—where? In some publication, or meeting place for Lithuanian immigrants—looking for information about Chaim Salanter's war experiences. It had been a good strategy. Lithuania is a small country, after all, and it wouldn't be a stretch to imagine some Lithuanian immigrant might have known him all those years ago.

Shatka had seen the ad and remembered family stories about Salanter, "the Jew." She'd gotten in touch with Wuchnik. Perhaps she'd used Xavier as a middleman: that would explain why Wuchnik had gone to Ruhetal in the first place.

If Shatka's great-uncle had taken in the boy Chaim Salanter, then the uncle had done a good deed in a dangerous time and place. What I couldn't figure out is why Salanter should be trying to hide that history. Was he ashamed of having sought refuge with a member of the ruthless Police Battalions?

Salanter might feel that he'd been a collaborator, even though he'd been too vulnerable to have other choices in such a poisonous situation. But when Lawlor accused him of collaborating with the Nazis in those rants on GEN, perhaps it brought such painful memories back that Salanter couldn't bear for his daughter or granddaughter to know anything about them. *His face was so scary,* Nia Durango said, the night she and Arielle asked him about his mother. *We were scareder of him than anyone.*

I gave up on it. It was past ten by now, and I hadn't even made a start on the Ruhetal patient database I'd opened twelve hours ago. I was too tired to look at it now, and anyway, I was hungry. I'd pick up a pizza at Aubigné's on Damen and see how abysmally the Cubs were doing against the Giants.

When I got home and saw the Mercedes sedan parked in front of the building, I pulled up behind it. Pennies from heaven, or something like that. I wanted to talk to Chaim Salanter, and here he was. Of course, I would have liked some time to think through how or what to ask him, but this was a gift. I got out of my car and walked over to the driver's door.

Gabe Eycks opened the window just far enough that I could see his head. "Mr. Salanter needs to talk to you."

In the dark, with the Mercedes's tinted windows, I could see that the car was full, but not who was in it. "Hey, Gabe, you're right, this is the Twenty-four/seven Detective Agency. Our licensed ops never need to sleep, so you can barge in any hour of the day or night and find them bright, chipper, and ready to detect. All major credit cards accepted."

Just because I wanted to talk to Salanter didn't mean I needed to be enthusiastic about yet another imperious summons.

Gabe frowned at me. "We're all tired, but we wouldn't have come if it weren't essential to talk to you. Since you betrayed Mr. Salanter's trust, it would be better if you dropped your facetious tone."

A surge of anger rode through me. I turned and marched up the walk to my front door, fed up with the way the Salanters and their team began all our conversations. I heard the thunk of the heavy sedan door closing, and footsteps behind me on the walk, but I didn't turn, just found my keys in the bottom of my bag and undid the lock.

Eycks said, "Nia Durango and Arielle Zitter's safety is in question here, and you'll stay up until we get a reliable promise from you not to jeopardize them further."

"Yeah, well, I promise. On my cousin Boom-Boom's jersey, and I don't get more sacred than that. Now I'm going to bed and you're going home." I went on through the door.

Eycks grabbed my arm. "Not so fast, not until you talk to Mr. Salanter."

I dropped the pizza, turned into his body, and chopped his wrist with my left hand. He gasped in shock more than pain but dropped my arm.

I glared at him. "If you want to talk to me about this, ask politely. Every conversation I've had with someone from your Schiller Street protectorate has begun with the assumption that I'm a lead-footed cretin out to harm you. So if you want to talk to me, you need to give me a reliable promise to have a civilized conversation."

I picked up the box and looked inside. The crust had broken into a dozen jagged pieces and goat cheese and spinach were mushed together in the bottom of the box. It didn't look at all appetizing anymore. I sighed and started up the stairs.

42. OLD NEWS

Eycks didn't follow me up the stairs, but he did stay inside our entryway, cell phone in his ear. In my own apartment, with all the locks in place, I looked out the front windows and saw Chaim Salanter get out of the back of the Mercedes. Lotty and Max climbed out the other side; Sophy Durango stepped from the front seat.

"*Merda!*" I said under my breath: I couldn't shut Lotty out of my home.

I took the pizza to the kitchen, washed my face, took off my shoes and socks, collected a whisky bottle and some glasses. By the time I'd done all that, Eycks was leaning on the bell outside my third-floor door, the rest of his entourage in tow. When I opened the door, I heard a couple of barks from the bottom of the stairwell, and then a shout from Mr. Contreras, wondering if everything was all right.

"Not the dogs, Victoria," Lotty said. "Make him keep the damned dogs downstairs."

"We're absolutely splendid," I shouted down to Mr. Contreras. "Dr. Herschel's allergies are acting up—she wants you to hang on to Mitch and Peppy."

My five visitors entered my living room, looking like a jury in a capital case. I poured myself a few fingers of Johnnie Walker and offered the bottle to my executioners.

Max and Lotty gave me polite negatives, but the other three stared at me glassily. Sophy Durango took the lead.

"In Wade Lawlor's attack on me this evening, he mentioned that Nia was joining Arielle overseas. How did he learn that? Our two families are the only people who know this!"

"Along with Gabe, Diane Ovech, the flight attendants on El Al, anyone at O'Hare who recognized Nia—"

"Who did you tell?" Gabe interrupted me.

"I'm not going to answer that one, Mr. Eycks. Since you think I'm capable of betraying my word, then you won't believe anything I say."

Lotty addressed me gravely. "I know you well, Victoria, and I know you would never put children in danger, but is there any possibility you mentioned this to Murray, thinking you could trust him to keep it confidential?"

Max chipped in with an equally mixed message, whose gist seemed to be that I was wonderful but impulsive. Durango and Salanter were more passionate—I had put their precious girls at risk.

When they'd all finished their differently calibrated pitches, I said to Eycks, "Arielle's cell phone wasn't with her when I found her yesterday morning. Did it ever turn up?"

He shook his head. "Julia bought a new one to give to her on the plane."

I turned to Durango, "Did you and Julia Salanter lift the text-message block on your daughters' cell phones?"

She looked disdainful. "I assume that question is relevant, or that you are trying to shift attention away from yourself to the girls."

"Something like that," I agreed. "I told you yesterday that it was possible someone was monitoring their texts to each other. If Nia and Arielle were telling the truth—"

"Don't start suggesting that our children are liars just to excul-
pate your—"

"My involvement in this business began because your children lied
about where they were spending the night. Each claimed a sleepover at
the other's home as a cover for going to a midnight rendezvous in a
cemetery. So let's stop pretending the girls are above reproach and con-
centrate on what we know, okay?"

"What do you think you know?" Max asked, before Durango could
leap to a further defense of her daughter.

"Miles Wuchnik apparently was hired to dig up dirt on Chaim
Salanter: Nia told me this afternoon that he approached her and Arielle
outside Vina Fields earlier this spring."

Salanter and Durango both gasped in alarm and looked at Eycks,
who shook his head—this was the first he'd heard of it.

"I don't know who hired Wuchnik," I continued, "but I learned this
evening that he was doing dirty work on a different project, and that
he'd been hired for that by one of the attorneys at Crawford, Mead.
So I'm assuming a Crawford, Mead client was trying to find out Mr.
Salanter's deeply held secrets, maybe as a way to derail your campaign,
Dr. Durango. That means it could have been Helen Kendrick herself,
or one of her Gleaners. Perhaps Sewall Ashford."

I stopped. If that was the case, Ashford was how Salanter and Ruhetal
and Leydon all hooked up. Could Sewall have murdered Wuchnik? He
was strong enough physically, but was he strong enough mentally? If
Wuchnik had found out some vile secret of Sewall's and was holding
him up for more money—

"Victoria!" It was Max who brought me back to the present. Chaim
Salanter sat unmoving, as if we were discussing the weather in Kam-
chatka rather than attempts to dig up his carefully guarded past.

"Right," I said. "After Wuchnik's death, his apartment was stripped
bare, but from what his ex-wife said, he used high-tech spy equipment
to dig up dirt on people. Wuchnik approached Arielle and Nia. He

spun them a line about wanting background on Mr. Salanter so that he could embarrass Wade Lawlor on national TV. This inspired Arielle to try to learn something of her grandfather's history. She approached the Holocaust Museum, and went to genealogy websites, but she apparently came up empty."

Salanter's hands came up in an involuntary gesture, trying to push something away from himself.

"Yes, Nia said they talked to you, Mr. Salanter, but you shut them down in such a frightening way that they never approached you again. Wuchnik got hold of their cell-phone numbers, either directly from the girls or through one of the databases that provide people's private information."

Lotty was shocked. "That can't be right, Victoria! If you pay to have an unlisted number, how can someone find it and sell it?"

I smiled sadly. "I'm sorry, Lotty, it's not that hard and I have to confess I use those same databases. But Wuchnik took it a step further; at least, I'm guessing that he did. Once he had the girls' cell-phone numbers, he used a program to install a remote transmitter into their phones. Any messages they sent or received would be bounced to his phone without their knowing it. This is just a guess, mind you, but I'm assuming it's how he knew they were going to Mount Moriah that Saturday night he was murdered. It was how he tried to keep track of Arielle's searches into her grandfather's history, and how he realized she wasn't making any progress. When Wuchnik died, I think whoever killed him knew what he'd been doing and picked up on the eavesdropping where Wuchnik had left off."

"How do you know that?" Gabe Eycks demanded.

"It's just an assumption, of course. But it's a pretty good bet that Wuchnik was blackmailing someone who killed him for his pains. And that his killer would have figured out how Wuchnik got some of his information."

I rolled my whisky glass between my hands, watching the liquid slosh—little ocean waves created in my living room. I was more than tired; I was depressed and anxious about confronting Chaim Salanter over his past. *Swallow it, get it over with,* one of my mother's frequent admonitions. *The poison builds the longer you hold it in your mouth.*

"Jana Shatka," I said. "She saw an ad that Wuchnik placed where Lithuanian immigrants might find it. He wanted information on—on a refugee from Vilna, and the name rang a bell with Shatka. Her great-uncle had known the man as a youth during the war. Shatka wrote her mother, who was still in Lithuania, for information, hoping to collect a big payout. Shatka lived with a guy named Xavier Jurgens."

Gabe Eycks made a strangled sound and glanced at Salanter, who shook his head.

"Yes, Jurgens, the same man who was dead in the car where I found Arielle. Jurgens was an orderly at Ruhetal State Hospital. One of Wuchnik's clients had sent him to Ruhetal, where he persuaded Jurgens to let him into the locked wing. So there is a connection between the two men, but I don't know that it has anything to do with the Salanter family."

I paused, looked invitingly at Salanter, but he only shrugged.

"A lawyer gave Jurgens fifteen grand a few weeks ago, a cash gift from a client. It wasn't from Wuchnik, that's all I know. Jurgens used the money to buy a new Camaro, and someone with access to and knowledge of pharmaceuticals used a powerful antipsychotic to kill him. The knowledge of his murder terrified Jana Shatka—she knew everything Jurgens had known and she realized his knowledge cost him his life. So last night she hopped on a plane to Kiev."

Durango made an impatient gesture. "This is completely irrelevant to Nia and Arielle, and how the news of their flying to Israel leaked out."

"Perhaps." I swallowed some of the whisky—the alcohol, or maybe the sugar, gives a jolt of wakefulness before it numbs you. "But going back to the ad Shatka responded to, the ad for information about a Jewish refugee from Lithuania whose name Shatka recognized. She wrote her mother, her mother wrote back. I don't know what Shatka said, but I found two aerograms from her mother to her. A Chicago graduate student translated the Russian for me earlier this evening. Shatka's mother can't give chapter and verse, but she does talk about the man's history in a believable way."

Everyone was staring at Salanter, who continued to sit like a small Buddha in the corner of my couch.

I pulled the printout of Ted Austin's e-mail from my bag and held the pages out to Salanter. "I don't understand what's in this history that's so shameful you would forbid your granddaughter to discuss it. But you have put great energy into keeping your past to yourself. Did Jana Shatka come to you? Or Miles Wuchnik?"

"If you are asking whether they tried to buy my silence, you are correct. The man Wuchnik wanted to meet me, he wanted to give me the opportunity to bid on the information in here"—he took the printout from me and shook it—"against whoever his other buyer was. I didn't see the letters, but Wuchnik described their content. I never met him personally, of course, but he persuaded Wren Balfour to bring me to the phone. There isn't much in here, the half memories of a bitter woman who doesn't know anything firsthand."

"But when he died, and you learned I was involved, you tried to bribe me into *not* investigating his murder," I said. "Didn't you realize that would raise red flags, make me want to know what you were concealing?"

Salanter shrugged. "If Wuchnik had found information out about me, then I knew it was only a matter of time before it appeared on Wade Lawlor's TV show. Killing the detective would have solved no problems. I wasn't thinking broadly enough when I met with you—I was concerned about my daughter and granddaughter's peace of mind, and that made my approach to you narrow. And ill-advised, as it turns out, but my one experience of a private detective had been Wuchnik— I imagined all were like the one."

This sounded like a noble apology, an invitation to believe he thought I was his equal in broad thinking, but he was a master juggler; if I paid too much attention to the ball in the air I'd miss the two he was whipping into his pocket.

"You frightened Nia and Arielle when they asked about your past, so much so that they even concealed from their mothers the fact that they'd been approached to try to uncover the information," I said. "If you could react so vehemently to your own granddaughter, I don't believe you'd have just shrugged off an approach from an outsider."

"So you think I murdered Wuchnik. Even if that had been my impulse, I would have needed help, and getting help, even from Gabe, would have exposed me to a domino of potential blackmailers."

He crumpled the printout into a ball, saying with sudden savagery, "Let the whole damned world read these. Let them share the affronted outrage of this mealymouthed peasant woman: the Jew was ungrateful after all her uncle did for him. And after he fell under the spell of those sexually potent Jewesses, who were alluring even while they were starving to death in the ghetto. They were so wanton, so lacking in . . . in humanness that they were willing to lie with a pig at night so their children could get a little something to eat in a man-made famine."

He flung the balled-up paper at Max. "So the bastard spent time in a Soviet gulag—for the wrong reasons but, by God, it was a righteous judgment."

Max unfolded the printout and read it, then handed it to Lotty, with a murmured comment I couldn't hear, although it was probably a warning that she would find the material distressing. As she read it she took his hand and squeezed it tightly. When she'd finished with it, she didn't speak but passed the printout to Sophy Durango.

"Of course, there's nothing in there but the usual dreary stereotypes." Max made a face. And so this man Shatka was your mother's—" He broke off, fumbling for a word: *lover, rapist.*

"His name wasn't Shatka—that's the name of this woman Warshawski encountered, I suppose the married name of his niece. My *bene-factor's* name was Zudymas." Salanter's rage had subsided. He was lean-ing back in his corner of the couch, his face pale with exhaustion.

"When the Red Army retreated in the face of the German invasion, my parents had twenty-four hours to decide what to do before the German troops moved in." Salanter's eyes were shut, his voice dull. "Rumors abounded about German cruelty to Jews but we didn't have real information. My parents decided that the most bestial rumors couldn't be correct, that no one could really be throwing babies into lime pits and laughing at their agonized death screams. My parents believed adult men would be at risk but that the invaders wouldn't harm women and children.

"So my father and my older brother fled east, into the Soviet Union, where they fought with the partisans, only to perish in Stalin's gulags after the war—news I learned long after the war's end, news I learned only after years of seeking their fate. It was easier to recover my grand-father's paintings than to discover my father's grave, but in the end I found both." He broke off, panting.

Gabe left the room; I heard him in the kitchen, finding a glass, run-ning the tap, but, like the other three in the room, I couldn't move, couldn't take my eyes from Salanter. When Gabe returned, Salanter sat up to drink some water, then leaned back on the couch again.

"The rest of us, my mother, my sister, and I, stayed behind to be slaughtered, with the eager help of the local populace. In Poland, the ghettos existed for several years before final deportations, but in Lithu-ania, most Jews were murdered almost at once, before the end of that first summer of the occupation, prodded to their execution by Lithu-anian police auxiliaries."

He squeezed his eyes shut again. "My mother—I suppose every boy thinks his mother is beautiful, so I was like all boys. My mother and my sister were the most beautiful women in the world. In that single way I agree with the cretin Wade Lawlor, when he weeps on television about his beautiful murdered sister. My sister and my mother were beautiful and they, too, were murdered. Marched off to Ponar Forest and shot, on Yom Kippur, dumped into one of the oil storage tanks the fleeing Red Army had left behind.

"But for the three months of the summer, when we were crowded into a ghetto in Vilna, Zudymas helped himself to my mother. Sometimes at night, sometimes in broad daylight. She submitted, in exchange for extra food for me and my sister, or because she was powerless, or because we all heard the shots of the executions, all summer long, and she thought, sex with this pig will save my children's lives. And it did. Or, at least, it saved mine. Not my sister's."

The five of us had to lean forward to hear him, his voice had grown so low.

"The day of the Yom Kippur massacre—all was confusion. We were ordered to line up, to march, and Zudymas, with his fellow villagers in the Police Battalion, they swaggered along next to us. He had spent the previous night with my mother, but he whipped her along with the rest of the women. She flung herself at his feet, she begged him, if not to save her, then to save my sister and myself.

"I have always been small, and although I was thirteen then, I still looked like a child of nine or ten. When we reached the forest—not far, it was not far enough away—Zudymas suddenly snatched me from the line of marchers. I begged to stay with my sister and my mother, but she—that was the last I saw of her—go, save yourself, live to be a man, she called to me in Yiddish. It was over so fast I didn't have time to think. I tried to run but Zudymas caught me easily and carried me to his farm. Where he kept me, my benefactor, my savior. Missing my mother, he satisfied himself with me. Locked me in the basement when he reported for his duties, came home at night to my small body. Yes, this is a story that I long for my granddaughter to know."

His face was waxen. No one could speak, until, some minutes later, Sophy Durango said timidly, "But you managed to escape?"

"Oh, that. Yes." He brushed the air with his hands, as if the escape were of no importance. "The night came where he was so used to my small, compliant presence that he didn't lock me in again. While he slept, I took the money from his trousers and fled. He had helped keep me captive by depriving me of clothes, so I took his Sunday suit as well.

"I must have seemed a comical sight, scampering through the woods in clothes twice my size. But I found an old rag dealer on the outskirts of Vilna who was glad to trade me some children's clothes for his Sunday suit. I tried to join the partisans but they wouldn't have me, I was too small, so I started living by my wits on the streets of Vilna. I hoped I might come on Zudymas by stealth and kill him, but the opportunity never arrived. I made some money, the war ended, I bribed my way onto a freighter to Sweden. From there to Chicago."

He gave a laugh that wasn't completely bitter. "My whole life, eighty-three years, collapsed into a few sentences. Now you know. You know why I let Lawlor's chatter roll off me—it's not that I'm indifferent, but the worst has already happened to me. Until the harm to Arielle made me see that fate always has another card up her sleeve, another way to make you dance to someone else's melody. I would kill someone, yes, to protect Arielle. But not to preserve my own reputation."

He was quiet again but finally said, "I would take some of your whisky now, Ms. Warshawski."

I went to the dining room and brought my mother's red Venetian glasses out. Five remain whole of the eight she wrapped in her clothes to carry with her from Umbria to Cuba to Chicago. A sixth has been glued back together by expert hands. I drank from that, poured into the undamaged glasses for everyone else, including Lotty, who almost never drinks spirits.

Salanter drank, and some of the waxiness left his face. "So, Ms. Warshawski, we came to accuse you of betraying my family and instead you get the story of my life. You told me last week that anyone who wanted to dig it up could find it, and you were right, of course. Zudymas, his family have their own version that they doubtless tell everyone—the Jew betrayed our uncle, took a vast fortune from him; now he lives like a king in America. And you will create your own version to tell for your own ends—my history is in the open air now, I have no control over it."

"I'm not like King Midas's reeds," I said. "No one will hear your story from me, nor should they. Everyone in this room has some greater or lesser version of it, after all—my own mother—you're drinking from the wineglass she brought with her when she fled Italy in 1939. And, yes, she loved Mozart. But this is Handel."

I went to my stereo and put in the CD Jake Thibaut had made for me from my mother's old reel-to-reel tapes. *"Vieni, o figlio,"* we heard Gabriella's rich pure voice. *The child's eyes are closed. He is lost to me, lost forever.*

43. ALAS, POOR SISTER

We all sat in a numbed silence until Salanter, his nut-brown face still pale, pushed himself to his feet. "Gabe, I would return home. Loewenthal? Sophy? Dr. Herschel?"

He tried to speak with his usual authority, but his voice, for once, betrayed his age. He didn't fight off the protective arm Gabe offered as he walked slowly to the door.

Salanter paused briefly in the doorway to say to me, "My mother was a pianist. She, too, loved Mozart."

Sophy Durango left with Gabe and Salanter, but Lotty and Max stayed behind. They sat on the couch, not quite touching.

Lotty looked at her watch. "Thank God we do no surgery on Friday. I would not guarantee anyone's health if I had to cut into her tomorrow morning."

Her own voice was heavy with fatigue. We were all exhausted from the emotions of the past hour.

"How come you were with Salanter tonight?" I stirred myself to ask. "I didn't think you knew him well."

"We don't," Max agreed. "But I was at Lotty's when Salanter's minion Gabe arrived. He came up to explain that Salanter and Dr. Durango were on their way here to demand a reckoning from you about their girls. Salanter thought Lotty would have a better chance of talking you round than he would himself, or Dr. Durango—she was too distressed about her daughter to feel she could speak calmly. I came along because you and Lotty are both volatile compounds."

He grinned. "Salanter has pledged ten million to the hospital. I didn't want one of you blowing him up before he wrote the check."

I shadow-punched him, but we all laughed, and some of the strain went out of the room.

"I do apologize, Victoria," Lotty said. "It wasn't well done of us—of me—to assume the worst of you. I know you wouldn't deliberately put a child in harm's way, but sometimes you are so single-minded in your search for answers that you don't always think of the consequences.

"But when Chaim started to reveal his history—we were safe in London, while he was—enduring—Lithuania. It was hard not to think of my own mother, to wonder what she might—" Her face crumpled.

Max took her in his arms. After a moment he looked over her head at me. "Do you believe him? I mean, do you believe he didn't murder that detective, that Wuchnik?"

I grimaced. "I don't think he did, if for no other reason than the one he gave—that he'd have left himself open to an endless chain of blackmail, because he's not physically strong enough to have moved Wuchnik's body around. But if Salanter didn't commit the murders, then who did? And why?"

I wondered again about the two lawyers in Dick's firm. If Louis Ormond and Elaine Napier had worked together, perhaps they could have done it. I couldn't picture it, though. The murderer was more likely the person who'd sent sixteen thousand to the firm to pay off Xavier Jurgens, for—of course. I'd been an idiot not to see it sooner.

"Xavier killed Wuchnik," I said.

"What?" Max blinked at me. "I don't know what you are talking about, Victoria."

"Xavier Jurgens. He's the man who died in the Camaro where I found Salanter's granddaughter. Someone sent my ex-husband's law firm fifteen thousand in cash to deliver to Xavier. I think Xavier was hired to kill Wuchnik, or at least to play a role in the murder. Fifteen grand was a huge amount to Xavier, practically a year's pay after taxes. And then, I'm guessing, the killer became worried that Xavier would track him down, or maybe Xavier, or his lover, Jana, did track him down. It's all so murky."

"It's too complicated," Max complained. "X hires Y to murder Z and then Y blackmails X. This sounds like Agatha Christie, Victoria, which I can never follow even when I'm wide awake, and I'm very nearly in a coma right now."

"Does it matter? Do you have to know?" Lotty said. "The police, after all—"

"Yes, the police, after all," I interrupted. "Finchley may put it all together, but if he doesn't do it soon, I worry about the safety of the girls in the Carmilla club."

Lotty protested that she didn't know what I was talking about, so I tried to explain my belief that the murderer had found Kira Dudek's cell phone with his picture on it. "He used the phone to bring Arielle to the cemetery. I think he probably destroyed Arielle's phone, or the police or the FBI would have found it through GPS tracking. Unless they've stopped paying attention to the attack because they're assuming it was Xavier Jurgens who lured her there and then killed himself. I, however, think it was a third party."

"You don't always know better than the police," Lotty said crossly.

"I know, darling," I said gently. "Anyway, Max is right—it's way too late to try to think about this tortuous business now. If you want to spend the night, I'll let you into Jake's place—there are clean sheets on his bed."

Max and Lotty murmured to each other: toothbrushes, night clothes, all those things they wouldn't have here. They decided to return to Lotty's. I walked them down to the corner of Belmont to catch a cab, my gun loose in a belt holster, despite Lotty's protest: she cannot bear the sight of guns.

When I got back home, Mr. Contreras and the dogs were waiting on the stoop. I had to assuage his hurt feelings at being omitted from tonight's drama. The conversation took all my meager stock of patience. I knew he deserved some kind of answer—his loyalty and care are not qualities I dismiss lightly—but I also didn't want to violate Chaim Salanter's privacy any further.

"Salanter's granddaughter's life is at stake, so he isn't acting like the high-stakes options player—he's as scared and frantic as you would be if someone was threatening Petra."

That proved to be the wrong tack: if Petra was being threatened, Mr. Contreras would be out moving heaven and earth to save her, not jauntering around Chicago harassing private eyes. I agreed that he was twice, if not thrice, the man Salanter was, that Salanter might know how to manipulate the stock market but he couldn't begin to navigate a real fight with real pipe wrenches. Mr. Contreras let himself be persuaded and finally, long after one o'clock, I fell into bed.

As late as the night had been, I still forced myself out of bed at eight the next morning. If my late-night inspiration had been correct, that someone had hired Xavier to kill Wuchnik, and then killed Xavier in turn, I couldn't lie around in bed waiting for him to do more damage.

Before logging on to my machine, I called the Dudeks' apartment to check on Kira and Lucy. Their mother answered the phone; after a few linguistic gymnastics, she put Teodoro Martinez on the line. The girls were still asleep, he said. He was keeping a close eye on them wherever they went but couldn't shake the feeling that now and again, someone was watching them.

"I talked to Gabe Eycks and he agreed to send someone over today to put in a few surveillance cameras," he said. "You been in this building? It's a mugger's paradise. They'll put a camera on the fire escape outside Mom's window, one on the back door, and one in the hallway, and I hope that'll make me feel better about going to bed at night."

We were hanging up when he added, "Just so you know, Eycks contracted our firm for a week's work, which means that if you need me after next Wednesday, you'll have to talk to him."

Today was Friday. I wondered if I could possibly sort out this tangled business in five days. I felt panicky when I hung up. Not the best frame of mind for good detective work.

I did half an hour of stretches, trying to persuade my weary legs and arms that a good workout was the equivalent of ten hours' sleep. And that caffeine would make up any remaining deficit.

It didn't really work, but I resolutely settled myself at the dining room table with my laptop, looking at the list of inmates that the Department of Corrections had placed at Ruhetal. Most people in the forensic wing are there for a short time only; if they are psychotic, they are medicated until they are mentally stable enough to plead. I was assuming that anyone Leydon had wanted to talk to in the locked wing was there after a successful insanity or incompetency plea. And I was hoping I could find someone whose incarceration was linked to arson.

I'd pleaded incompetence or insanity only a few times in my stint as a public defender, even though a huge proportion of offenders are mentally ill, or addicted to drugs—the two often go together—or can't understand the crimes they'd allegedly committed. Anyone working in public-aid law has seen more than their share of perpetrators with competency issues, and if the system had worked well, I would have mounted that defense more often.

Unfortunately, incompetent inmates become stateless and defenseless. Letting your client be deemed unfit for trial is like condemning him to a horrible purgatory. If your client never stands trial, he's never sentenced. Doctors, not a court, decide whether he ever becomes fit enough to stand. If he's never tried, it's a tribunal, not a judge, that decides whether he can be released. And most of those judged mentally incompetent come from families without the education or resources to lobby for a tribunal hearing.

I opened the results file. No one was at Ruhetal because of arson-related crimes, but the DOC database gives information only at the highest level. There were plenty of murders, attempted murders, aggravated assaults, assaults with attempted murder—any of those could have been caused by arson.

I went slowly through the Ruhetal list but didn't find anyone I'd represented. Perhaps I could pick someone at random and see if they or their families would appoint me as a lawyer. The state says that a lawyer in good standing can call any inmate and offer to represent them, and the hospital has to let you in.

There were three inmates who'd been at Ruhetal so long that they predated the automation of case reports—the case-file system didn't include the crime they'd been arrested for. One of the names sounded vaguely familiar—Tommy Glover. Google gave back twelve million results when I asked it.

The court records didn't tell me what Glover had done, just that he'd been sent to Ruhetal twenty-seven years ago. I went into Lexis to do a news search but didn't turn up anything. There was no way to get access to arrest reports—even if the arresting force had kept them after all these years, they're not available to the public eye in any shape or form.

I'd been hunched over my laptop for more than two hours and my neck and shoulders were too sore to continue. I took the dogs to the lake, where the three of us swam a half mile between the buoys. When I got home, I needed a nap more than ever. *Sleep is just a craving, I told myself. Distract yourself and the craving will diminish.*

I drove to my office as a distraction so I could go through my complete case file on the vampire killing. I found the reference by accident, after sifting through all notes and documents I'd collected during the past two weeks.

In desperation, I pulled out the clippings I'd removed from Leydon's Hermès bag the day she fell at Rockefeller. Most were about the Fukushima reactor or on nutrition, but she'd also kept a story on the death of Netta Glover in a hit-and-run accident.

Two days before Wuchnik's murder, Netta Glover had been walking from her suburban bus stop to her home in Tampier Lake Township when she was struck by a car and killed. It was nine at night and no one had seen the incident, but a man walking his dog had come upon her, probably within minutes of the accident. He'd called 911 but by the time an ambulance arrived she was already dead. So far, no one had come forward to ID the car that had hit her.

When I looked up the story online, it didn't mention her family, just that she had been on her way home from her job as a nurse's aide in a neighboring suburb, that the road was badly lit, so a driver going too fast could well have swerved onto the sidewalk, and that services would be held at the Open Tabernacle Church in Tampier Lake Township, where Netta had worshipped for many years. The Net couldn't tell me anything else about her; people like Netta Glover don't leave a trail behind, not even on the World Wide Web.

Leydon had thought Netta's death was important enough that she'd cut out the story. I suppressed the thought that she'd also clipped stories about the goji berry. Maybe a trip to the Open Tabernacle Church was in order. I combed my hair and tried to smooth the wrinkles out of my cargo pants.

For once, I hit the tollways and expressways when everyone else was at work or the beach or something: the fifty miles out to Tampier Lake Township took just an hour. The Open Tabernacle Church, on Slough

Road, also proved easy to find. Even a tired, bewildered detective is lucky every now and then.

The message in the sign box in front of the modern brick building surprised me: "Wherever you are on life's journey, the Open Tabernacle community welcomes you. We learn from your journey as we hope you learn from ours."

My prejudices constantly catch me up: from the church's name, and Netta Glover's occupation, I'd assumed that this would be a storefront, fundamentalist church. Instead, as a list of principles posted inside the narthex door stated, they were an open and affirming community, embracing anyone, regardless of race, creed, sex, or sexual orientation. Beneath that earnest welcome was a staff listing: the pastor, Al Ordonez, a Christian ed director, a secretary, Doris Kaitano, and a music director.

The pastor wasn't in the building but a woman in her sixties, presumably Doris Kaitano, was in the parish office, creating the bulletins for Sunday's service. She wasn't happy at being interrupted—"I'm here on my own. Can you come back?"—but when I introduced myself, and explained that I was hoping to learn something about Netta Glover, her expression softened. Slightly.

"If you could wait for Pastor Ordonez it would be better. Her death was a sad one, but I don't really—"

"I'm sorry," I interrupted. "Can you answer one question for me? Is she related to anyone named Tommy?"

"Tommy? You honestly don't know? That's her son. Goodness! And what he will do—Al—Pastor Ordonez—has explained to Tommy that his mother is with Jesus, but we're not sure he understands."

"He's at Ruhetal, right?"

"Yes. It was all long before my time. People say he killed that poor girl, but he's mentally deficient and they finally decided he wasn't competent to plead and put him in the mental hospital. Netta says—used to say—it's why she joined our church—her old church, they told her

it was God's will, that she should accept the burdens that He was plac-
ing on her and not fight against them so hard. She always said Tommy
couldn't have killed the girl, and even though the evidence was against
him, of course a mother should stand up for her son."

"She tried to get a tribunal hearing for him?" I asked, trying to figure
out the narrative.

Ms. Kaitano was so caught up in her story that she'd forgotten how
harassed she was, there on her own and all. "Netta did hire a lawyer,
but the law fees just about ate her alive, she's still paying that old bill.
She worked two jobs, bad jobs, nurse's aide and clerking at Buy-Smart,
because she had to keep paying the damn—darned—lawyers, even
though they never did anything for her. She even had to sell her car to
pay those bills! Which is how she got killed, poor soul. Getting up to
Downers Grove to see Tommy, that was a public-transportation nightmare. We have people who volunteered to drive her once a month, but
they didn't always come through for her. It might have been easier if
she'd sold her place and moved up near to the hospital, but it's a little
bit of a house that she wouldn't get anything for, and even one bedroom
up in Downers Grove would've cost her a fortune."

"Did Netta talk to you about any of the other patients she met up
at the hospital?" I ventured. "A woman in the regular part of the complex, for instance, who was a lawyer."

Ms. Kaitano nodded slowly. "I forgot about that, but Netta did say
there was a lady who offered to talk to Tommy, maybe put together a
defense for him. A lawyer who offered to do it for nothing. I told Netta
not to trust her, because in the first place, what lawyer works for nothing, and in the second, if the lady was a patient, it could all be a delusion. But Netta was so glad to find someone interested after all this time
that she went ahead with it, at least, I think she did, but maybe nothing
came of it, because she never mentioned it afterwards."

"Leydon Ashford, was that the lawyer's name?"

Ms. Kaitano threw up her hands. "I sit here all day long listening to

a million stories. If Al—Pastor Ordonez—is out people think I'm or-
dained or something, with the time to let them chew my ear off. If
Netta said the name, I wouldn't remember anymore."

"Right," I smiled. "I know you're overworked and I'm sorry to take
up this much of your time, but one last thing: the murder Tommy was
accused of—did it have anything to do with arson?"

"Arson? Good grief, no. Completely the opposite—it was water,
drowning. You mean you don't know? They said Tommy killed Wade
Lawlor's sister. His older sister, Magda, that Tommy drowned her right
here in Tampier Lake."

44. NEIGHBORHOOD GOSSIP

"ARE YOU ALL RIGHT, DEAR?" DORIS KAITANO HAD GOTTEN up from her desk, was offering me water, wondering if I needed to lie down.

"I'm fine. Just an ignorant idiot." I heard myself laugh wildly but tried to control it when I saw how alarmed Ms. Kaitano was looking. "He trumpeted his sister's death in my face, but then he attacked my mother so that I paid attention to the attack, not to the rest of his text. It's his best technique, it's how he keeps people like Salanter or Sophy Durango off balance, isn't it?"

"I think I should call someone. Is there anyone who can come get you?" Ms. Kaitano backed away from me uneasily, her hand hovering over the phone.

"No, no. I'm gone, don't worry." I thanked her for her time, her trouble, her information, babbling like Leydon at her most manic, sliding out the church door to sit in my car.

In death they were not divided. Not Iva and Miles Wuchnik. Not even Leydon and Sewall Ashford. Magda and Wade Lawlor.

After a time, my head cleared. When Kaitano revealed that it was

Wade's sister's killer Leydon had been visiting, my brain had jumped off a cliff. I hated Lawlor so much that I'd assumed I'd found the thread that unraveled the whole tapestry, but it wasn't that simple. Lawlor didn't try to keep his sister's death a secret: he wept like a lachrymose walrus every time he mentioned her on his broadcasts. And he didn't keep Tommy Glover a secret, either. He'd referred to him obliquely as one of the "underdogs" I spent my time supporting. He would have killed Tommy himself if he'd known he wouldn't get the death penalty, Lawlor had said on-air.

But. But. Wuchnik and Leydon had both been in the locked wing where Tommy Glover was housed. What had they unearthed?

If I was right that someone had paid Jurgens fifteen grand to kill Wuchnik, well, Wade Lawlor could peel off those Ben Franklins as if he were scraping carrots and not notice he'd spent them. But why would he want Wuchnik dead? My big breakthrough was beginning to look like more of the same confusion I'd been feeling ever since I went into that abandoned cemetery for the first time.

I wanted to see Tommy Glover, but I needed to take this one step at a time. Leydon had come back from the locked wing obsessed by fire, not water. I needed the facts on Magda Lawlor's death before I did anything else.

The Tampier Lake Township Library lay a few blocks from the church. They had plenty of documents about the town and its history, with a special drawer devoted to their most illustrious native son, Wade, but nothing on the murder, just a few references to the tragic loss of his sister. Tampier Lake had never had its own newspaper. Their news was tucked into the larger *Southwest Gazette*. Between the *Gazette's* micro-form copies and some of the subscription databases I called up from my laptop, I got what information was available.

On July 6, twenty-seven years ago, Magda Lawlor's dead body had been found floating in Lake Tampier in the far western suburbs. There wasn't much beyond that. Twenty-seven years ago, Wade Lawlor had been fourteen, not a national television celebrity. The twenty-four-hour news cycle lay in the future, so a suburban teen's death didn't make many waves, even a beautiful suburban teen.

Two days later, Tommy Glover had been arrested. The day of the murder, Magda's boyfriend had found Tommy at the lake, watching her body from the shore. The boyfriend said Tommy had a history of trailing around after her. Nothing was said about a sexual assault, about whether Magda had tried to fight off Tommy. The one piece of forensic evidence the paper reported was that Magda had been strangled before she was put into the water.

I couldn't find out anything about the legal process that had landed Glover in Ruhetal's locked wing. There was no record of who had evaluated him, how his incompetency had been determined, or whether his mother had any reason other than her love to proclaim his innocence.

The time had come to abandon the World Wide Web and do some legwork. I started with the people next door to Wade Lawlor's childhood home, a run-down ranch whose current occupants were a few decades behind on painting and weeding. No one was home on one side, but on the other, a neighbor, now in her eighties, could tell me what she'd been barbecuing for dinner when her youngest son had raced home from a pickup baseball game with the news. After getting what I could from her, I tracked down the woman who'd been the high school librarian, who told me how the kids had put up a photomontage in Magda's memory when school started that year.

I spoke with the mother of Magda's boyfriend. Jackie Beringer was working in her garden, when I stopped by. She didn't question why I was coming around to ask about the old murder: it had loomed so large in the lives of the people in Tampier Lake Township that everyone I talked to assumed the whole world knew and cared about Magda Lawlor's death.

"Oh, her death hit Link—Lincoln, my boy—so hard, it scarred him for years. He joined the Army, but after that he couldn't settle down.

He finally married three years ago, a nice enough lady, but they live down in Texas and I don't know if they'll ever have kids, it's as if seeing Maggie—that's what we all called her, not Magda—get killed made him think it was too dangerous to bring a child into this world."

"He saw her get killed?" I asked.

"Oh, just a way of talking, miss. Link went to work that day at noon; he had a summer job in his uncle's box factory out by Wheaton, working the one-to-eight shift.

"The police went into all that at the time, could he have killed Maggie himself, but it was a small factory, everyone knew he'd been there all afternoon. We knew they had to ask those questions, but that was hard, too, for me and for Link's dad—he passed three years ago—the cops come and talk to your boy, and you're mad and righteous in standing up for him, but there's a little splinter of doubt that buries itself in your mind, wondering if your own son could have done such a cruel thing."

"It must have been hard on the Lawlors," I said. "Did you know them well?"

Her mouth pursed into a tight "o." "The dad, he took off when the kids were little. That was before we moved here, so we never met him. As for the mom, if Virginia Lawlor was ever sober after ten in the morning, I never saw it. Maggie pretty much raised Wade. Even when he got to be a teenager himself, he was still as close to her as when he'd been a little boy. She'd be so proud, if she'd lived, to see what he made of himself."

Lincoln's mother shook her head sadly. "Maggie was a beauty, but she was a sad lonely girl, living with Virginia, doing all the housework and raising Wade. That's what drew my boy to her. He felt she needed someone watching over her. Link used to say she'd make him bring Wade along when they went out sometimes because she hated to leave him home alone with Virginia. You can imagine how hard it hit Wade when she was killed."

"I guess Wade was a different kind of person than his sister—she doesn't sound like someone who'd have been comfortable in the kind of big public role he's taken on."

Jackie agreed heartily. "But it's good that he can bring his message to the country. We don't need any more liberals going to Washington messing in our business, and Wade is doing an important job, making sure people know what this Sophy *Duran-goo* is really like."

I dug my nails into my palms to keep the anger out of my voice. "The person who killed her, Tommy Glover . . ." I let my voice trail away.

"That was another sad story in the neighborhood," Jackie Beringer said. "He just was mentally—I don't know what word we're supposed to use now. But he could never learn his alphabet. He'd try to say it, and he'd get up to the letter 'g,' and then he'd forget. He'd be so upset, some days he cried. Back then, this was still like a little country town and folks looked out for him. He used to follow Maggie around some, but no one ever thought he meant any harm by it. He'd follow a dog for a day, or sometimes ride with the local volunteer fire crew or the sheriff's deputies—we were all so surprised when he killed Maggie, but the deputies said likely Tommy saw my Link kissing Maggie and got all excited and confused. His ma, she begged and pleaded, she said he never could have hurt a soul. But he was twenty or something like it, big guy, it was obvious he was plenty big and strong enough to kill a little bit of a thing like Maggie."

"Someone saw him do it?" I asked.

"No, but Maggie, she was crossing through the woods as a short-cut to get to her job—she worked as a cashier at the drugstore; back then it was a little local-owned place, not a Kendrick's, like we have now—and Wade said he saw Tommy go into the woods after her. Wade didn't think anything of it, of course, because Tommy was always wandering around. It wasn't until late in the afternoon, when they called from the drugstore wondering where Maggie was, that anyone went looking for her, and it wasn't until night, when he got off work, that my Link came on Tommy Glover staring at her where she was lying in the lake."

I got the same story in shorter and longer forms from everyone I talked to, along with praises for Netta Glover for standing by her boy. She'd been a good mother before he went and killed Magda, no one blamed her for one minute. She taught him at home, showed him how to do simple jobs like shovel snow or mow lawns and that was how he made a little money. But she'd been at work herself when Maggie was killed, so how could she possibly be a witness to his innocence? Everyone reckoned it was just as well for him to stay at Ruhetal until he died: what were you going to do, let a big man with no sense run around loose in the community?

It was past seven when I finished talking to people who had known the key players. I was about to head back into the city when something occurred to me. I called Murray; I heard bursts of laughter and glasses clinking in the background when he answered.

"How's the girl detective?" he said. "Any dazzling feats of investigation that make the rest of us look like chumps?"

"I detect that you're in a bar, and that you imagine you're being amusing and conciliatory at the same time, but that's more the result of my psychic powers than active investigating. Do you happen to remember the names of the long-term mental-health inmates you were proposing to look at it in the series you pitched to Weekes?"

"Why? You have proof that one of them is Weekes's love child?"

It is not fun talking to people who've been drinking, especially when they think they're being witty. "Murray, my psychic powers are seeing one of the names glowing green in my mind, but I can't quite call up the other two."

He was instantly serious. "What happened? Did one of them escape? Was he released?"

"You have the names on you in the bar or bleacher seats or wherever you are?"

"Hang on a second." He put his phone down; over the roar of laughter, talk, clinking glasses, a woman asked what was going on, didn't he know it was rude to take calls when you'd invited someone out for a drink?

"It is, it is, you're so right," I heard Murray's babble. "But this is V. I. Warshawski, and I think she's got something."

I smirked at myself in the rearview mirror: You are hot, V.I., and all the guys know it.

A scrabbling sound, Murray scraping his phone across the bar. "Hey, Warshawski. Yeah, I kept the e-mail in my inbox to spit on every now and then. The three guys at Ruhetal were Greg Robertson, Tommy Glover, and Sheldon Brookes. You want the names from Elgin, too?"

"Not tonight. Did you do any digging on them, find out what crimes sent them to Ruhetal?"

"No, I just pulled them out of the DOC database. Why?"

"I know you're on a date and it's Friday night and all, so I hate to interrupt."

I paused and waited until Murray practically screamed at me to deliver. "I believe I know why Harold Weekes canceled the series."

45. FIRE TRUCKS, FIRE TRUCKS

THE LAWYER-PATIENT VISITING ROOM AT RUHETAL WASN'T much different from rooms like it that I'd used in the state prison's. Scarred furniture, stained gray carpet, the smell a mix of disinfectant and urine. The main difference was that the guard who brought Tommy Glover down to see me didn't stay in the room with us and didn't manacle Tommy first.

I met with Tommy Glover on Sunday, during peak visitor hours. The whole hospital complex, including the forensic wing, was loud with noise—crying babies, anxious lovers, querulous spouses, sullen adolescents who'd been dragged against their will to visit a strange relative. I felt so fretful about the time slipping through my fingers that I hadn't wanted to wait for a weekday.

"Tommy, your visitor is here," the orderly who brought him to the lawyer-patient meeting room said. "It's great that you've come to see him, Ms. Warshawski. Since his mother died, he hasn't had any visitors and he misses company. Tommy, this is Ms. Warshawski. Can you say that?"

Tommy blinked at me. He was a big man, somewhere in his forties, with heavy jowls and close-cut iron-colored hair. He tried to say my name but it got strangled in his throat.

"How about 'Vic,'" I suggested. "Tommy, I'm Vic."

"Hi, Vic," he said, after a bit of prodding from the orderly.

"I have a lot of people to see to this afternoon," the orderly said. "You'll be fine with Tommy here, but when you're done, or when he gets tired and wants to quit, you push one of the buzzers." He showed them to me, in the table, by the door, on the floor. "He understands most things pretty good if you talk slowly enough and don't use real big words."

"Fred? Fred?" Tommy said as the orderly started through the door. "This lady, is she a friend of my mom?"

"She's a lawyer, Tommy," the orderly said. "She wants to see if you need help with the law."

"The other lady, she was a lawyer, my mom brought her to see me. She had hair that was so pretty I wanted to touch it and she said, fine, you can touch it, but then Xavier made me stop."

"That's too bad," I said, as Fred shut the door. "I think I know that lady lawyer, and you're right, her hair is very pretty. Let's see if we can find her picture in here."

I pulled some photographs out of my briefcase. Murray and I had spent Saturday putting together a portfolio of everyone I could think of who had a connection with the case: the Salanters, Gabe Eycks, Iva and Miles Wuchnik, the Carmilla club girls, my cousin from Chicago. I also included the lawyers from Dick's firm. I'd found a snapshot of Leydon and me in our law school robes, grinning like maniacs, another of Leydon at my wedding in a gauzy white hat.

Murray brought the pix we could find online, or in my old snapshots, to the photo director at the *Herald-Star*. The photo director, who'd worked with Murray for years, didn't try to probe into why we were getting headshots of Chaim Salanter or Wade Lawlor; he just grunted and cropped Leydon's graduation shot so that we had a close-up of her face, the eager smile, the red-gold hair curling around her like fine-spun threads.

While Murray worked with the *Star's* photographer, I'd gone back to Tampier Lake Township and found a couple of snapshots of Netta Glover at the Open Tabernacle Church. I'd also persuaded Jackie Beringer to lend me a photo she had of her son Link with Magda Lawlor; the man at the *Star* had worked his magic on these as well.

The town library had old high school yearbooks; I'd found pictures of an adolescent Wade, with his thick black hair worn like early Paul McCartney; getting contemporary photos was easy. I'd struck out with Virginia Lawlor, Wade and Magda's drunk mother, but the yearbooks gave me a couple of shots of Magda, looking solemn and fragile in the high school chorus.

This afternoon, in the lawyer-client room, I laid a quartet of pictures in front of Tommy: Leydon, Julia Salanter, Eloise Napier, and Lotty. I asked if the lady with the pretty hair was one of them.

"That's her," he crowed, picking up Leydon's picture and stroking her hair. "I liked her, I took her up to my room but then Xavier got mad, he made her leave, he said it was against the rules."

"Do you remember anything the lady said?"

Tommy sucked on his index finger. "She said it was sad and terrible to lock me up here like I was a dog, some kind of dog, not like Good Dog Trey but a sick dog."

"Rabid," I suggested.

He smiled again. "That was her word. You and her, you know the same words! She said she could help me leave, maybe, and go live with my mom, but my mom died and the lady, she never came back, so now I just keep staying here with Fred and all these other people. Anyway, when people leave they get put in handcuffs, I see them, they get put in handcuffs and chained up in this old white bus, I hate that, I hate handcuffs, they make your hands hurt and hurt and hurt. The police make you safe but then they take you away from your mom and Good Dog Trey and make you hurt!"

"What happened, Tommy? Do you know why the police took you away from your mom and put you in handcuffs?"

Tommy looked at his hands, big hands, white and flaccid from long years without much to do. He was quiet for several minutes and I let him take his time.

"Because I was watching Maggie in the water. I didn't know it was a bad thing, she liked me watching her, but she never woke up again, and the police took me away. First they put handcuffs on me and I didn't like it. Then they took the handcuffs away because I was good."

"Handcuffs are no fun, I know that. It's good that you don't need to wear them anymore."

I took some more pictures out of my briefcase and started laying them out slowly, beginning with Tommy's mother. His heavy face lit up.

"That's Mom. She died, she's in heaven with Jesus. Did she send you this picture? Is it from heaven?"

"No. The minister at her church let me have it. Mr. Ordonez."

The name didn't mean anything. "I miss Mom, she brought me clothes and trucks and jelly beans."

"You like jelly beans, Tommy?"

"Yum, jelly beans are good, good, good."

I hadn't been sure I could bring food, or if he might have allergies I needed to know about. "When I come next time, I'll bring jelly beans. Today, I only have pictures."

Tommy didn't recognize Salanter, or his daughter or Lotty. He thought he knew Sophy Durango but then wasn't sure, but he recognized Wade Lawlor's current photo at once, from seeing him on television.

He frowned over the old picture of Wade as a young teen for quite a long time, and then nodded decisively. "He lives next door. We don't like him."

"Who's 'we,' Tommy? You and—?"

"My mom. He hates Good Dog Trey, I seen him kick Trey, then when I told on him, he called me 'retard' and said I was too dumb to know anything, but when I see I know, he was a liar, and you can't call people bad names, like 'retard,' that is a very bad name."

So Lawlor had started his name-calling career young. "Your mom told you that?"

"Yep."

"She's right. It's a bad word and Wade was a bad boy to say it."

"Yeah, Colin called me that and I punched him, but they took my trucks away." His lips trembled in remembered injury.

"Who's Colin?"

"You know Colin. He has all this long yellow hair and he laughs like—like the wild animals on TV, like this!" Tommy gave an imitation of a hyena's laugh. "They gave him drugs and now he's in prison. That's what he gets for using bad words."

I was guessing that Colin had been a Ruhetal inmate with a treatable mental illness who'd stood trial, presumably for a worse crime than calling Tommy a 'retard,' although you never know.

I put Magda's yearbook photograph on the table. The *Star's* photographer had created a glossy out of it that made it look recent, modern. "Do you know this girl?"

"Of course I know her, silly. That's Maggie! She lives next door to me, so I know her. Her brother, he's the bad boy who kicked Good Dog Trey."

"Is Maggie the girl you were watching at the lake?"

He pouted, not wanting to answer. Perhaps he assumed I was there to criticize him.

"If I saw someone lying in the water, I'd go watch her, too," I said. "I don't think watching is a bad thing. Tell me what happened."

He inspected my face for any signs of anger, then blurted, "Maggie was lying in the water. I seen her, her hair was all floating around her head, like an angel. She floated, she didn't say anything, she was sleeping. I wanted to see her eyes open, like when she lies out over by the lake on a towel, she does that sometimes, trying to make her skin turn brown, I watch her and then she opens her eyes and says, 'That you, Tommy? I thought it was Prince Charming,' and I laugh and she laughs, but then the police came, they said I did a bad thing. She never said, 'Go away, Tommy, don't be watching me,' but it was very bad to watch her, that's why they put handcuffs on me."

He started to cry.

"It's okay, Tommy," I said quietly. "They took the handcuffs off, didn't they? So they must know you're a pretty good guy."

He brightened again. "I am a pretty good guy, and when I'm good, I get my fire engines."

He pulled a pair of red plastic fire trucks from his pocket and started running them across the table, making a little siren noise. I felt the hair prickle along the back of my neck. Leydon had come back from the locked ward, her speech incandescent with fire imagery. Was it from Tommy Glover's fire trucks?

"You like fire engines, huh?" I said. "Do you like fires, too?"

"The firemen let me ride with them. Before. Now I have to stay here. Now they took my picture."

I blinked. "The firemen took your picture?"

"No!" he shouted, pounding his trucks on the table. "Bad people stole my picture and now they won't give it back!"

Fred heard the shouts and popped his head in through the door. "Everything okay here?"

"He's upset about a picture he says someone took away," I said.

"Oh, that. He had some old photo in his room and it's disappeared.

It's not good to remind him about it. Come on, Tommy. No shouting, no getting upset, or we have to put your fire trucks in the garage for a week, remember?"

Tommy quickly stuck his fire engines back into his pocket. "Fire trucks are in the garage, Fred. They're staying in the garage."

"That's the spirit. Maybe half an hour is enough for today, Vic."

"You want me to go now, Tommy? I'm a lawyer. I'm here to make sure your rights are respected. If you want me to stay, I'll stay. If you tell me to go, I'll go. You get to choose."

Tommy looked uneasily from me to Fred. "Vic says she'll bring me jelly beans." His tone was defiant.

"Jelly beans, huh? Maybe five more minutes, Vic. But no talk about p-i-x, savvy? Sometimes Tommy acts out a bit too much. We put the trucks in the garage, and when he's behaved for a week, he gets them back."

We were all pals now, apparently—no more 'Ms. Warshawski.' I turned back to Tommy. "Let's see who else you know."

Tommy recognized Miles Wuchnik and his face darkened. "He was here, he fought with the lady because I showed her my picture. She was so pretty, she let me touch her hair. The man got super-mad but I told him, mind your own darn beeswax, I'm talking to the lady."

I sucked in a sharp breath. "So the lady with the gold hair saw your picture. What was in it?"

"Me. I'm in it. Me and the firemen!"

I leaned across the table. "Tommy, what firemen gave you the picture?"

"My friends, of course, silly. Good Dog Trey's friends. I ride with them. Not now, I can't because I live here. When I live with my mom, that's when I ride with them."

"Tommy. I'll talk to the firemen. If they have another picture, I'll bring it to you when I come next time. Ready for some more of these photographs?"

"No. I don't like them, I want my own picture!" He took the fire trucks out of his pocket and started running them over the photos, making extra-loud siren noises.

"Of course, your own picture is best," I agreed. "I'll come visit you again soon, okay?"

"If you bring the jelly beans. Bring beans, beans, beans, beans, they make you fart, they're good for the heart, fart fart fart." He started laughing loudly and began pounding the table with his trucks.

Fred came into the room again. "Time's up, huh, buddy?"

"I want to stay. My time's not up, you can't make me!" Tommy saw Fred eying the fire trucks and stuffed them into his pocket.

I stood. "Tommy, I'll come back very soon. I'm your lawyer. I'll come sometime this week, okay?"

"Don't get him excited, Vic," Fred said. "It's bad for him and then we have to medicate him. And if we medicate him he won't be able to talk to you."

"And if you keep him medicated so that he can't talk to me, then I'll go to a judge and we'll dance that dance." I smiled, the kind of smile that is really a mask for anger.

"The pretty girl, she danced that dance, she danced with the boy," Tommy said.

"Which boy was that, Tommy?" I knelt to pick up the pictures he'd flung about and spread them fanlike in front of him.

"That boy, they danced, they were in love." He picked out the photo of Link, Maggie's boyfriend. He started spinning slowly around on his heavy clumsy feet, dancing the dance.

"Why are you showing Tommy all these old photos?" Fred demanded.

"If I'm going to represent him in an appeal to the tribunal, I need to see how reliable his memory is." I continued smiling. "He certainly knows a hawk from a handsaw."

"What?" Fred scowled. "If you brought a saw in here, then you are in violation of the rules, and you could even be arrested yourself."

We'd been pals when the afternoon started, but now he didn't like me. "Relax, Fred—it's just a figure of speech. And who knows, the wind may change tomorrow and it'll be a different story."

Tommy had been watching us, frowning with worry as he tried to follow our conversation. "I like Vic, Fred. Don't be mad at her. Vic has curly hair, and it's short like a boy, but she's a girl and she's very pretty."

"I like you, too, Tommy," I assured him. "And Fred and I were just joking. Nobody's mad at anybody, are we, Fred?"

"No, I'm not mad. I just don't think you should joke about saws in a place like this," Fred growled. "Lot of unstable violent guys here. Some gals, too."

"You're right, you're right," I agreed quickly. "Sorry."

I lowered my voice. "Miles Wuchnik, the detective who was murdered two weeks ago—he got onto the patient floors, didn't he, and went into Tommy's bedroom."

Fred shifted uncomfortably. "Xavier let him in, way against regulations. I didn't say nothing at the time, but, man, if that had got out, we'd all be working extra shifts for a year."

"Miles did some work for my husband's law firm," I said. "But he never told anyone about the picture in Tommy's room. Did you ever see it?"

"Don't go bringing that up—gets him all wound up!" Fred jerked his head in Tommy's direction. "It was just an old photo of him with some firemen. He's been carrying on like it was the Last Supper or some damned thing!"

"And you don't have any idea who took it?"

"Why do you care so much?" Fred demanded.

I smiled blandly. "It's all part of my presentation to the tribunal, whether he's getting the kind of care here that's best for him. If the staff have enough time to protect him or not—as you said, there are a lot of violent offenders passing through here."

"We take damned good care of Tommy, as long as he behaves himself. Now why don't you leave so I can *protect* Tommy from predatory lawyers."

As I left, I saw Tommy uneasily holding his hands in his pockets, protecting his fire trucks.

46. WHAT'S IN A PICTURE?

VERNON MULLINER, THE DIRECTOR OF SECURITY, WAS AT THE locked wing's gate when I left. He recognized me at once and pulled me aside.

"What are you doing here?"

"Visiting one of the patients. How about you?"

"I thought I told you to keep clear of this hospital."

"Mr. Mulliner, I'm a lawyer, and I represent one of the patients here. You may not like it, and I'm not crazy about it, but so much of life is like that these days."

"You never said you were a lawyer. As I recall, you claimed you were a detective the last time I saw you."

"It's not impossible to be a member of two professions at the same time. As Mark Twain said, you can be an idiot and a congressman both at once. I do understand, though, after Xavier Jurgens's death, you can't be too careful here."

"Jurgens stole from the pharmacy. He died in Chicago, probably killed in a drug deal. Nothing to do with us here at Ruhetal."

"Except for lax security at the pharmacy, but you can't be everywhere at once. And speaking of lawyers, how did the Ashford family find out that Leydon Ashford had agreed to represent Tommy Glover?"

Mulliner did a narrow-eyed Clint Eastwood impersonation. "We keep track of who tries to stir up trouble in the forensic wing. Which means, of course, that I'll be keeping track of you."

"They give you a bonus for keeping track of people?"

He glanced at the guard, who quickly looked away. "What are you talking about?"

"That beautiful house you just moved into. Five million dollars on your and your wife's salaries—that's a lot of appreciation."

The look Mulliner gave me now was more in the Hannibal Lecter category. "Private eyes who snoop into people's private lives don't last long out here. If you come around here again, I'll take steps."

My hand went involuntarily to my chest, to the place where the stake had entered Miles Wuchnik. "Mr. Mulliner, I've agreed to represent a patient in the forensic unit, so any steps that get taken will be in front of a judge. And I don't imagine you want that kind of spotlight on your security operation here at the hospital, because then we'd have to talk to the Ashford family, and find out why they got to send their own PI out here. And whether they paid you for that privilege."

He took a hasty step toward me, then realized that not only the guard but visiting families were staring at him. The tendons in his neck strained, but he managed to master his fury enough to say, "You'd better really be a lawyer. Do you have any proof?"

I pulled out the laminated copy of my PI license and the card that declared I was a member of the Illinois bar in good standing. Meaning I paid my dues every year.

Danced the dance, as Link and Magda had done, watched over by my client, Tommy Glover. I'd been surprised that Tommy remembered Magda so clearly. He didn't have a good sense of the passage of time, but he remembered people. I pictured him in the shrubbery between his mother's house and the Lawlor place, spying on Lincoln Beringer and Magda Lawlor, and shivered.

I felt sickened, too, by my own behavior. Vernon Mulliner wasn't that far wrong: I was pretending to be a lawyer, pretending to care about Tommy's interests, when all I really wanted to know was what went on in the locked wing that had interested Miles Wuchnik and Leydon Ashford both. The photograph, apparently, but what was so arresting about the picture of Tommy Glover with his local fire department? Why would that make Leydon return to her therapist overflowing with language about fire?

The social workers weren't in on Sunday, of course; I'd have to talk to Tania Metzger tomorrow, to see if Leydon had said anything about Tommy's photograph.

I'd hit a nerve with Mulliner, bringing up his mansion and his brokerage account. I hadn't wanted to accuse him of dealing drugs in a public space, so I'd blurted out the idea of someone paying him a bonus to report on visitors to the locked wing. It had been meant as a wild guess, but now I was wondering if there was some truth to it. Maybe Wade Lawlor wanted to make sure his sister's killer stayed permanently behind bars.

I needed to do more digging, to see if I could find out a way to learn who was bulking up Mulliner's account. Maybe Murray could do some of the heavy lifting on that. In the meantime, since I was out this far anyway, I drove back south to Tampier Lake Township.

Twenty-seven years ago, when Tommy lived there, they'd had a volunteer fire department, but the town had grown, become incorporated, had a full-fledged department with two station houses. I struck it lucky at the first, where one of the men on duty directed me to an Eddie Chez.

"He's an old-timer, he was here when it was just a bunch of volunteers who worked day jobs. He never lets us forget how easy we have it, not having to fight fires after teaching high school all day, which is what he did. Mind, Sunday afternoons, Eddie is likely to be on the golf course, but you can take a chance, see if he's home."

My informant called Chez for me. My luck held: Chez didn't mind if I stopped by, although I should know that the grandchildren were visiting, too.

"Hope you've got time to burn, miss," one of the other firefighters called as I left. "Eddie can talk the hind leg off a donkey. When that falls off, he moves on to the front leg."

The other men laughed, but not unkindly.

Chez's home was in a cul-de-sac that backed onto a big public course, perfect for a golfing man. No one answered the door, but I could hear kids screaming and laughing behind the house, so I followed the noise and arrived at what looked like a small amusement park. Chez had one of those big aboveground pools, and it was filled with kids, some sliding on a plastic slide into the pool, some trying to play with a beach ball, others shouting that so-and-so was hogging the space. There were swings, bikes, and even a volleyball net tucked into a corner. A dog, barking madly, climbed a ramp on the pool's far side and jumped in.

The pool and the kids were so overwhelming that at first I didn't see the adults on the patio. Seven or eight were drinking from pitchers of iced tea or lemonade, but beer seemed to be on tap, too. One of the women nudged a stocky guy whose hair was bleached white from the sun; he got up from his lawn chair and walked over to me, limping a bit.

"You the lady who's writing up the history of our fire department? The boys told me you'd be stopping by. Eddie Chez." He held out a meaty hand, wet from holding a glass of iced tea.

"V. I. Warshawski. I'm not a writer; I'm a lawyer, and I'm a long time after the fair, but I've agreed to represent a guy at Ruhetal. Tommy Glover. Do you remember him?"

"Tommy Glover?" Chez's jolly red face clouded over. "Oh, my. That was a sad story if ever there was one. His poor ma, and getting killed that way—hit-and-run, I talked to Damon Guerdon, he's our police chief, told him if they track the SOB down I want first kick at him. Netta, she always said Tommy never killed Maggie, but of course she would do—my wife would say the same if, God forbid, it was one of our kids."

"So there wasn't any question that Tommy killed Magda Lawlor?"

"The boyfriend, Link Beringer, that was his name, found Tommy there at the lake, staring at Maggie. All Tommy would say was that he was waiting for her to wake up. It was like some cat who kills a mouse and brings it to you, thinking you can make it start running around and squeaking again."

"They're sure it was Tommy who killed her, not the boyfriend?"

He nodded, grunted. "You'd have to go to the police, look up the file, but what I recollect, the autopsy showed she'd been dead for four or five hours by then, and the boy had some kind of job—Mavis!" He hollered over to the women on the patio. "What kind of work did Link Beringer do? Before he joined the Army, I mean?"

A merry-looking woman who didn't mind spilling her thirty extra pounds around the sides of a swimsuit came over, carrying a glass of lemonade for me. "You're interested in all that ancient history? My word. Link, he worked at his uncle's box factory, over in, now, I don't remember, was it Lyle? No, I think Wheaton. What I do remember is how worried Jackie Beringer was, although of course she didn't put it into words, until they had the whole timetable worked out from when poor Maggie died and it was clear Link hadn't killed her."

"This lady's a lawyer," Eddie explained. "She's trying to see what she can do for Tommy."

Mavis shook her head. "He seems happy enough over there at Ruhetal, from what I hear, and I don't know where he could live if you got him out, not now that Netta's dead. No offense, miss, but no one here in Tampier would ever be really sure he wouldn't do it again, and where would a big man with no more sense than a five-year-old go to live, anyway? We all liked Netta, and he was a sweet-natured boy; no one wanted to see him get the death penalty, although I guess Wade Lawlor still holds a grudge—he sometimes carries on about his sis on that show of his as if it was yesterday, not a quarter century back."

"Tommy talked about Good Dog Trey," I ventured.

Gilcrhist laughed. "Gosh, he can't be as stupid as they say if he remembers Trey. That dog was our mascot—he belonged to one of the other volunteers. Trey always rode in the truck with us when there was a fire. Tommy loved Trey, and a lot of times the guy who owned him left him with Tommy during the day—guy worked in a bank and couldn't be bringing the dog to work with him."

"Tommy said Wade kicked the dog, then tried to blame Tommy for it."

"Could be, could be, I wouldn't remember that. But the Lawlor boy, he could be a handful. Losing his sis like that straightened him out. She carried the can for him, you see, those times he got caught shoplifting, or when he was in trouble at school. But I guess when Maggie died Wade saw he was going to have to fly solo. Not to speak ill of the dead, but his ma was never going to look out for him. He started going to his classes regular, earned that scholarship to Northwestern to study broadcast journalism—everyone here is pretty proud of what he made of himself."

A little boy whose bathing suit was drifting to his knees ran up. "Gramma, Gramma, a butterfly drownded in the pool, can you fix it?"

Mavis Chez bent over to look at the bedraggled butterfly. She tugged at the boy's trunks and suggested they make a little nest for the butterfly. The two disappeared into the house.

"Tommy talked about a picture the firemen took of him. Would you remember that?"

Chez shook his head. "I expect we took his picture when we posed for our annual calendar or something, but I couldn't tell you anything more specific. He liked to go to fires with us, loved the excitement. He was real proud of having his own fire hat. Netta got a scanner so she could keep track of when we were called out, and she'd drive him over to the fire, if she wasn't at work. We'd let him help hold the hose if we needed an extra pair of hands—he could remember how to do a job if it was simple and you explained it to him careful. And he was a strong boy, so those hands came in useful on a fire hose—they're heavy, they're tricky if you don't know what you're doing."

Heavy boy with strong hands. I thought of those big white hands I'd seen this afternoon, around Magda's neck, or maybe even my own.

Two granddaughters came over, needing Chez to tighten the chains in their bicycles. I spent another half hour with the lively family, but neither Eddie nor his wife could add anything to the story.

I took a slow route back to Chicago, avoiding the expressways, turning the afternoon's conversations over in my mind. Tommy had been obsessed with Magda Lawlor, used to stand watching her as she sunbathed, as she danced with Link Beringer. Maybe he'd imagined dancing with her himself and she had told him no, or laughed at him. He was prone to sudden rages; he had poor impulse control. He might have shaken her until her neck broke and then laid her in the lake.

I didn't think he thought in such a complicated way that he'd say, oh, no, she's dead, better make it look as though she drowned. More likely, he'd followed her to the lake. He'd followed her to the lake and somehow broken her neck, and then watched her, waiting for her eyes to open, for her to say, 'That you, Tommy? I thought it was Prince Charming.'"

I shuddered. But twenty-seven years in the locked ward had calmed him down. It seemed mean of Fred to threaten to take his trucks, but maybe that was kinder than using restraints.

While I was with the Chezes, Murray had been texting me and leaving ever more urgent voice messages, wanting to know what I'd learned from Tommy Glover. Murray so much wanted to prove it was Wade

Lawlor who had pressed Weekes into canceling his *Madness in the Mid-west* series that he was ignoring all the other ramifications of the case. He'd even wanted to come with me to Ruhetal, but only licensed members of the bar could go cold-calling on Ruhetal inmates, and it's easier for camels to make their proverbial journey than for journalists to get into a forensic wing unannounced.

Still, he was entitled to some information; he'd paid his dues by getting the *Star* to make me professional-quality photos to show to Tommy. When I reached my office, I gave Murray a report.

"The key to the situation may be in an old photograph of Tommy with the local volunteer fire department. He showed it to Leydon, and Wuchnik saw it, too, but it's gone now. If Leydon took it—I don't know—I've been through her apartment and her car, and didn't come on anything with a fire department in it. And Wuchnik's and Jurgens's places were swept bare. If any of them removed it from Ruhetal, it's probably in the CID landfill now."

I also went over my conversation with Eddie Chez, and Chez's suggestion that it might have been one of their old volunteer-fire-department calendars. Murray said he'd take care of that angle. He could go out to Tampier tomorrow and track down some of the other people who used to be part of the volunteer squad. Somewhere, one of them would have a copy of the picture with Tommy in it.

I locked the photos in my office safe. When I drove home, I found that my cousin had shown up at Mr. Contreras's place. Petra had spent the weekend in Kansas City with her mother and sisters; tomorrow she'd go back to the Malina Foundation, where they were trying to rekindle enthusiasm for the book club program among the families who'd fled the mayhem of the past month.

"What are you doing?" Petra asked.

"Trying to find an old picture of a suburban fire department."

"Well, gosh, Vic, that will help Arielle and the Dudek girls come out of hiding, won't it!"

"I don't know." I ignored her sarcasm. "It seems to be a picture that meant a lot to Miles Wuchnik and Leydon both, but it isn't in her apartment. If I can find it, maybe it will tell me the whole story."

I went up to my own place to wash and to change clothes. I was meeting Max and Lotty for dinner at Max's home in Evanston. He and Lotty were taking off for Cape Cod at the end of the week, and would drive from there to Marlboro.

"You've created a situation for yourself, haven't you, Victoria?" Max said, as we sat on his patio, discussing Wade Lawlor, the Salanters, and my meeting with Tommy Glover. "Getting this man's hopes up when you think he's guilty."

I grinned. "It's Murray whose hopes are riding high. Poor Tommy Glover—his biggest expectation is that I'll get his picture back. I wonder if he'd settle for a calendar of firefighters—I ought to be able to find one of those easily enough."

Lotty shook her head. "He wants something specific. It will make you seem untrustworthy if you offer him a substitute. You're sure that this photograph matters that much?"

"Xavier Jurgens took Wuchnik up to Tommy's room, completely against the rules. I learned that this afternoon. And from Tommy's account, Wuchnik and Leydon fought over the photograph. Whatever it showed to Leydon, to Wuchnik it opened a door on blackmail. I guess I'll go back to Leydon's apartment in the morning and give it another sweep, but—"

"What about the sister?" Lotty asked. "That is, as you pointed out, the situation is filled with sisters. I mean the blackmailing detective's sister down in Danville."

"Yes," I said slowly. "If Wuchnik stole the photo, he might have sent it to Iva inside a hollowed-out book, although I didn't see it in the books I inspected. I suppose she could have put it in a bank vault.

"Your comment about sisters: Leydon told Wuchnik that if he understood the Bible verse *In death they were not divided,* he would understand everything. I can see her in Tommy's room, laughing at Wuchnik, spinning words around him, getting him furious."

I toyed with the stem of the wineglass. "Her saying that means the picture may have something to do with Magda and Wade Lawlor's relationship. If it showed brother and sister in some compromising situation, everyone who saw it in Tommy's room for the last twenty-odd years would have recognized it, too. And I cannot for the life of me imagine a photograph that would involve Tommy, the firefighters, and the Lawlors."

Max and Lotty played around with the idea, too, but neither of them could come up with any believable possibilities, either. I left soon after. At home, I prowled restlessly around my apartment. Miles Wuchnik had worried that Leydon would muscle in on his blackmailing turf. Of course, that was ludicrous. She'd seen the picture, and it had agitated her, but its full significance hadn't dawned on her until after Wuchnik's death, or she would have tried to call me sooner.

Maybe Fred had stolen the picture. If it was valuable enough that Xavier Jurgens could get the price of a Camaro from blackmailing someone in it, then perhaps Fred was trying to cash in on it himself. In which case, he was probably as good as dead.

At eleven, Jake called from Marlboro; he'd finished an exhilarating day of music-making and he missed me. That cheered me. He might be surrounded by young violinists or bassists who had no white in their hair or spider veins in their legs, but he still missed me.

"Come out next week with Max and Lotty," he coaxed.

"I miss you, too," I said. "If I can clear up this problem—"

"Oh, don't put conditions on it, V.I. Just come. If you haven't solved it by then, a break from it will do you good. At least it will do me good."

I felt better after the call and went straight to bed. The thrumming of the air conditioner, the laughter from the drunks straying away from the bars on Belmont, the honking, all blended into an urban lullaby that rocked me into an easy sleep.

47. CLEANING UP FOR A CHANGE

IN MY DREAMS, FIRE TRUCKS WERE CHASING LEYDON AND ME across the University of Chicago campus. Leydon's red-gold hair was streaming behind her in the moonlight; she was throwing jelly beans onto the quads, shouting, "They took my picture, they took my picture."

I sat up, waking myself so abruptly that I almost fell out of bed. It was five-thirty, but the sky was a dull lead: more rain was coming.

If Leydon had taken Tommy's photo, I might find it in the landfill in her condo. I pulled on cutoffs and a T-shirt, collected the dogs from Mr. Contreras's place for a short walk, and then drove up to Leydon's Edgewater apartment. The rain had just started to fall, heavy, greasy drops, when I found a parking space around the corner from her building.

Early though it was, Rafe, the doorman, was on duty. He remembered me from last week and asked after Leydon.

"She's still in a coma," I told him. "The prognosis isn't very good, but they're moving her from the hospital to a nursing home this week."

While he made commiserating noises, I added, "She mislaid something in her papers that I'd like to try to find."

Rafe accepted the ten I slipped him with the dignity of a man for whom money is unimportant. He called down to the night super to relieve him and took me up to Leydon's apartment. He flinched, as I did, at the sight of the mess, which looked worse than I remembered it.

"Maybe she has her problems, but she's unusual—unordinary, if you know what I mean. She made me think of moonlight on the lake, the way she talked." He laughed, embarrassed at his own poetic flight. "You let me know when you're done so I can double-lock the doors."

While lightning forked and writhed across the lake and rain made the floor-to-ceiling windows shudder, I sifted through the papers in Leydon's living room and bedroom. I made no attempt to organize them; I simply looked for a picture that included firemen. All the clippings, all those articles about diet or conspiracies involving oil or water, I put into blue recycling bags.

Around ten, when I'd been at it for three hours, it occurred to me to call Leydon's sister-in-law. No, Faith said, Leydon hadn't shown or mailed any pictures to her, of firemen or of anything else.

"I talked to Sewall," she said quickly, as I was hanging up. "We'll move her to a place in Skokie, probably next Monday. They have a good reputation, and maybe she'll get back to—" She broke off, as she remembered what normal was for Leydon.

"That's good, Faith," I said with a hollow heartiness.

I was glad that Faith had taken a stand with Sewall on his sister's care, but Leydon's depressing condition, combined with the mess I was sorting, made it impossible to be optimistic. The weather dragged my spirits down as well. At noon, when the rain paused, I went out for food.

The little indie bar I'd found before made me up a vegetable sandwich and two cappuccinos. I brought them back with me—I was afraid if I took a long break I'd never summon the energy to get back to the Augean stables.

At two, I was pretty sure I had handled every paper in the apartment, gone through mattresses, couch cushions, books, looked under appliances and inside CD covers. I lay on the Navajo rug in the living area and stretched my sore shoulders and hamstrings. After a time, I remembered my other obligations. Still lying on the floor, I called various clients, and then checked in with Murray.

He'd found five members of the old volunteer fire department. They'd all been glad to show him their group photos; he'd even seen one with Tommy holding Good Dog Trey's leash, grinning like he'd just won the lottery, but the pictures didn't shed any light on the Lawlors.

·"Tommy's photo has to be a red herring," Murray announced. "It has to be something Tommy said that Wuchnik and Leydon both pounced on. You'd better go talk to him again."

"You could be right," I agreed dispiritedly.

If the photo had meant something, the person who attacked Leydon probably found it when he rifled through her handbag. Or cleaned out Wuchnik's apartment. I'd buy some jelly beans and go see Tommy tomorrow afternoon. I needed to do some real work in the morning for my most important client.

I lay back down on the Navajo rug. A spider had put up a three-dimensional web in a corner by the windows. A literary detective like Spenser or Marlowe would have a good time drawing an analogy to my confused brain, but I thought it just showed that the cleaning service wasn't doing much of a job for Leydon. It was hard to blame them, given the level of chaos in here.

My mind wandered off to other places where Leydon might have put Tommy's picture, which made me realize that only my conscious mind agreed with Murray. I called down to Dean Knaub at Rockefeller, but he said the housekeeping crews hadn't turned in anything else that might have belonged to Leydon, either pictures or news clippings or pill bottles. He even trundled up to the balcony to see if she might have stuck something in a hymnal, but came back empty-handed.

I called Tania Metzger. She didn't have much time to spare, so I tried to speak fast. I explained to her that I had become Tommy Glover's legal representative, and had spoken to him yesterday about the day that Leydon showed up in the forensic wing. I gave her as concise a history as I could about Glover's situation.

"Leydon told him she was a lawyer," I added, "which of course she was. I know you said she didn't tell you the name of the person she visited, but did she talk about his story in a general way? I'm wondering how she got to him to begin with. If it was through his mother, how did Netta find her?"

Metzger mulled over what she could say without violating Leydon's confidentiality rights. "She talked a lot about the law and mental illness, and she used the Internet here to look up Illinois case law on mental incompetence. I thought she was preparing some defense of her own, because she'd also started talking about people spying on her."

Her voice became tinged with anger. "I thought she was being delusional. Now I see she thought she couldn't trust me—she thought I knew that her family, or the hospital, had sent this investigator to the hospital! How could I—well, never mind that now. This person, Glover, did you say his name is? I don't know much about the people in the forensic wing, but if Leydon had encountered his mother, that wouldn't have been hard, given what a warren this place is, and how easy it is for patients to move around, despite the watch that the staff try to keep on them. On top of which, Leydon is a skilled escape artist; she's so articulate that she could fool unwary staff members into thinking she had some official role in the hospital. What does Glover's mother say?"

"She died. Killed by a hit-and-run driver a few days after Leydon was released from Ruhetal."

"Oh my God, not another death! You don't think—"

"What, that it had something to do with Leydon talking to her son? I know that life throws up a lot of coincidences, but that's not one I believe in. I think Netta Glover's death and Leydon's fall had everything to do with each other, and probably something to do with Wuchnik's and Jurgens's deaths as well."

"I'm keeping a patient waiting," Metzger said. "Unless there's something else—something quick?"

"The photograph that went missing from Tommy Glover's room. Did Leydon describe it, or describe arguing with Miles Wuchnik about it? Or even bring it back and give it to you? It's missing and I think it's a crucial item in sorting out what went on with Glover and Leydon and a whole bunch of other people."

"I told you she came back speaking about fires, but she didn't say anything about a picture, at least not that I can remember. She talks— talked—so much that I didn't always catch everything. I tried to listen for the subtext, since I couldn't follow her across the surface. She was always showing me newspaper articles, either online or things she'd cut out of the daily paper. She managed to get hold of some paper every day, even though I tried to stop that; I thought reading the news over-excited her."

She hung up on that note. I took one of Leydon's printouts and tried to construct a chronology on the back.

The first thing that happened was that Leydon met Netta Glover— somehow—wandering around, the escape artist leaving the ward and roaming the halls at Ruhetal. Leydon heard Netta's sad story and introduced herself as a lawyer; Netta got permission for Leydon to meet Tommy.

Miles Wuchnik showed up in the same bat cave at the same time. Because he was following Leydon, on her mother's orders? Or a coincidence? How had Wuchnik become aware of Tommy Glover? If he'd been spying on Leydon, then he knew she was talking to Glover, but what made him bribe Jurgens into taking him to Tommy's room?

Lawlor did not want anyone looking at Tommy Glover. Because memories of his sister were so painful that they made him cry on-air, or because, like Netta Glover, he knew Tommy was innocent? Which meant he was protecting his sister's killer.

I felt queasy. Could Lawlor have killed Magda himself? But why? He adored her, and he needed her—that wasn't just his on-air story but what everyone said who'd known the two as children.

A lot of deaths around Leydon, her social worker had pointed out. But there was also a lot of death around Tommy Glover. Despite what Murray thought, I had to find that damned picture.

I'd looked through Leydon's car after I'd been to her apartment the first time; I would have remembered a photograph of a group of firemen. I smacked my forehead in annoyance: Leydon's had been in the shop. It was Sewall's car she'd driven down to the University of Chicago. His BMW, which he kept in the garage at the building on North Franklin, where Ashford Holdings had their offices.

Rafe knocked on the door as I was getting to my feet; he was ready to leave for the day; was I finished? When he stuck his head into the room and looked around, he was dazzled by the order I'd created, the stack of some dozen recycling bags.

"Leave them there. I'll get Clarence—the super—to take them out tomorrow."

We rode down in the elevator together. Rafe was heading up to Rosemont with his two girls to catch a game by the Bandits, Chicago's women's pro softball team. The sky was still a heavy gray; more rain was forecast, but perhaps it would hold off for their outing.

I drove down to the Loop and found a street space not too far from Ashford Holdings. In my cutoffs and T-shirt, I didn't look very professional, but I told the garage attendant I was Faith Ashford's assistant; she'd sent me down to see if she'd left a document in her husband's car. The attendant, no doubt remembering the furor over Leydon's making off with the Beemer two weeks ago, tried calling Sewall to get permission, but fortunately for me, Sewall was in a meeting.

As a compromise, the attendant stood over me while I looked under floor mats and seats and lifted the felt lining in the trunk. Nothing except the usual detritus of human life: parking slips, ticket stubs, seven quarters, which I put in the coin holder. A packet of condoms. Well, Sewall, you naughty Ashford.

Does Faith know you travel with these? I couldn't stop myself from scrawling on the back of a parking slip to place on the dashboard next to the packet.

I gave the attendant a five and took off. I'd better wrap this case up soon—the tips I was spreading around town were eating a hole in my bank account.

I got back to my car within seconds of the city tow truck. I'd forgotten to check the rush-hour no-parking sign. Cops were writing tickets and a phalanx of tow trucks was hauling off the guilty, all in one smooth movement; I backed up as the truck operator was about to attach the chains, ignored the goose-honk from the squad car, and darted into traffic, heading for the Dan Ryan Expressway. They wouldn't bother to chase me in this traffic. V.I., you're so cool.

I was so cool that I didn't notice where I was going until I saw the I-57 sign overhead. I was heading south, not north: my unconscious mind had decided to go to Danville, where Iva Wuchnik lived.

48. THE PURLOINED PHOTO

It was past eight when I pulled up in front of the shabby building near the Vermilion River. I let myself into the lobby; I didn't want to try to have a conversation with Iva through her intercom.

I ran quickly up the three flights of stairs and rapped sharply on her front door. A young man in running clothes, coming out of the apartment across the hall, stopped to stare at me. Perhaps I was the first visitor he'd ever seen at Iva's place.

"Who's there?" The door muffled her flat voice so that I could barely make it out.

"V. I. Warshawski, Ms. Wuchnik."

"I don't want to talk to you. Go away."

"I have some exciting news for you: I know who killed your brother."

The man in the running shorts couldn't help being interested. Iva opened her door the length of the chain bolt. Her skin looked muddy in the bad light.

"So it is you. Who killed him?"

"Do you want me to bellow it through the door here, where all your neighbors can hear?"

She scowled but began scraping back her array of bolts and chains. As I walked into the musty apartment, the runner reluctantly made his way down the stairs.

Iva shut the door with a bang and faced me just inside the furniture-packed living room. I looked over to the scarred teak cabinet. The books Miles had used for sending her cash were gone. She had moved his photograph in its heavy silver frame to the middle of the cabinet top.

"All right. Who killed Miles?"

"Xavier Jurgens." I smiled at her brightly.

"Who is that?" she demanded.

"Xavier was the guy who paid cash for the brand-new Camaro. When I was here before, I thought Miles had given him the money for it, but I realized that someone else paid off Xavier for killing your brother."

Her face puckered in misery, and when she spoke, her voice had thickened with unshed tears. "Why didn't the police tell me they made an arrest? They said they would tell me if they learned anything, they knew I was Miles's only close relative."

I felt ashamed for treating the conversation as a game. "I'm sorry, Ms. Wuchnik, but someone else killed Xavier before the police could get to him."

"What?" She shook her head, trying to make sense of what I was saying. "Why did you drive down here to tell me this? Why would a complete stranger kill my brother? You've made this up, haven't you?"

"I don't have any proof, or I'd have taken this story to the police. But Xavier Jurgens is the person who let your brother into Tommy Glover's room at Ruhetal. Tommy had a picture on his wall, of himself with some firemen. Your brother removed that picture, and it's because of what it showed that Miles was killed."

Iva's eyes turned to her brother's photograph on the teak cabinet.

"Yes. I've come to collect it. He sent it to you, didn't he, and asked you to hide it for him?"

I walked over to the photograph and undid the clasps at the back of the frame. I had expected Iva to fight me, but she watched me passively, shoulders slumped. When I pulled off the cardboard backing, I didn't find the photograph I was expecting but a newspaper clipping, yellow and brittle with age.

I unfolded it carefully and saw the faded color shot that had been the pride of Tommy Glover's life: the Tampier Lake Township volunteer brigade, dirty from a fire they'd just put out, clustered around their truck. The caption read, "Tommy Glover joins Eddie Chez and the rest of the boys for a celebratory photo after battling a blaze at Reinhold's Garage yesterday afternoon."

I stared at it. I could just make out a much younger Tommy, arms around a big mongrel dog, both of them grinning ear to ear. I could understand why it mattered so much to Tommy, but not why Leydon or Miles Wuchnik would have cared about it.

There was a small paragraph about the fire, which had started in a pile of oily rags and gotten out of control. I looked at the top line, for the name of the paper. The story had run in the *Southwest Gazette* on July 7, twenty-seven years ago.

"Did Miles say anything when he sent you this picture? I don't understand why—" I broke off in the middle of my own sentence, my spine turning cold.

The story had run a day after the fire. On July 6, when he was supposedly murdering Magda Lawlor, Tommy Glover had been with Eddie Chez and Good Dog Trey at Reinhold's Garage. It had been a small story in a small suburban paper, but for Tommy, it was a treasure, his time in the limelight.

After the fire, Tommy had left his buddies and wandered through the woods to see if Magda was lying by the lake "to turn her skin brown." Perhaps he wanted to brag to her about how he and Good Dog Trey put out the fire. He found her floating in the water and stared, hoping she'd look up and say, "That you, Tommy?"

And then Link, the boyfriend, came on Tommy, watching Magda lying dead in the water. I could almost hear the shouts, the hysterical accusations, *What have you done, you damned retarded bastard?* and Tommy's bewildered *I'm waiting for her to open her eyes.*

"Miles told me to keep that for him," Iva Wuchnik whispered. "What are you doing with it?"

"It's private property, Ms. Wuchnik; it belongs to the man from whose room your brother took it. And it's also evidence in a murder case. I'm taking it back to Chicago with me."

Using my cell phone, I photographed the back of Miles's picture where the clipping had rested, photographed as much of the ambient space as I could, and then took several shots of the clipping itself before carefully putting it into a file folder in my briefcase.

"You said your brother never mentioned anyone named Leydon Ashford," I said, "but did he ever talk about a lawyer who was with Tommy Glover when he went into Glover's room to take the picture?"

"He said there was some crazy lady pretending to be a lawyer who wanted the picture. He was lucky to get it away from her without tearing it."

"She is a lawyer," I snapped, "and one of the brightest who ever passed the bar. I want to know what she and Miles said to each other when they fought about the picture."

"I don't know," she suddenly shouted. "I wasn't there! You think you're so special, coming in here, ripping up my property; well, you're not. If that smart lawyer thinks she's going to muscle in and make the money Miles promised—"

"Miles died because he thought he could turn this clipping into cash," I said coldly. "You are an incredibly lucky woman that I am the person who figured out he'd sent it to you. If the people who organized his death knew you had it, you would be dead now yourself. If you take my advice, you'll forget you ever saw this piece of newsprint."

I turned on my heel and left. Behind me I heard her cry out that I could at least have put her brother's picture back together.

I'd been on the go since five this morning, but I ran down the three flights of stairs to the lobby, propelled by a nervous energy, a need to get back to Chicago as fast as possible and get this clipping into my safe.

I tried to phone Murray: I didn't want to be the only person who knew about this. When his phone rolled over to voicemail, I left a message about what I'd found, urging him to go into the *Southwest Gazette* archives to get the details on the July 6 fire all those years back.

The photo was crucial, because the story didn't say anything about Tommy. The photo was the only proof that Tommy had been elsewhere when Magda Lawlor was being murdered, and pictures often didn't show up in microforms, especially not from small suburban newspapers. We needed more print copies, I told Murray's voicemail, along with the log of the fire department, if it even still existed after all this time.

All the way back to Chicago, I kept an uneasy eye in my rearview mirror. I remembered the call Iva Wuchnik had gotten when I left her place the first time. She was angry with me; she would report me in a heartbeat to whoever she'd spoken to before. I didn't think it would have been Lawlor, showing his hand in person. Maybe Vernon Mulliner, earning his mansion. Or one of the Crawford, Mead lawyers.

Even this late at night, traffic was heavy. Bouncing around amid the long-haul truckers and the SUVs, I was having a hard time telling whether any particular set of brights in my mirror was tailing me or just tailgating. When I-57 finally fed me into the Ryan around eleven o'clock, I got off and took side streets until I was sure I was clean.

I drove to my office: I wanted to get the newspaper into my big office safe, more secure than the little one in my closet at home. I could crash on the daybed in the back, even wash off in my leasemate's little shower stall.

Our little parking area was empty. I surveyed the street, gun in hand. The coffee shop across from my office was closed, but the bar five doors up was still in full gear. Despite signs urging customers to respect the neighbors, the band noise spilled out onto the street, and the smokers, leaning against cars or girders, were creating their own field of noise.

Briefcase under my arm, I kept my gun in my hand while I typed in the code on my front door. One last look around the street, and I slipped into my building.

49. IN THE AQUARIUM

THEY WERE WAITING FOR ME JUST INSIDE MY OFFICE. I smelled the sweat just after I turned on the lights. I had my gun out, but one of them hit me from behind, a chop to the back of the head. I fired wildly as the assailant's arms locked around my neck.

I collapsed in his grasp, falling back against him, legs locked around his so that he had to go down under me. His head hit the cement floor and he grunted. I rolled over, but the blow to my head had dazed me and a heavy foot stepped on my gun hand before I could fire again.

I pulled my knees to me and kicked hard at the shin. Heavy-foot yelped and backed away, and I fired again, trying to roll over and get to my feet.

The man on the floor recovered and put an arm around my throat. "Sit on her chest," he panted, and a third man was suddenly straddling me.

I tried to bite him but got a mouthful of vinyl. There were three of them, all wearing black hooded rain jackets. The faces of death, Kira had said. The faces of death looking down at me.

"Get a needle into her fast, before she does any more damage. That last shot, she clipped Lou."

"Mulliner!" I recognized the Ruhetal security director's voice. "This is how you earned your mansion, isn't it?"

I made myself relax, deflated my chest, twisted to my side, was almost free, when I felt the sting of a needle through my cutoffs into my hip. I got a knee up and into the groin of the sitter, tried to stand as he fell away with a scream of pain, but then I fell myself, my head and arms as heavy as if a thousand pounds of sand had landed on my head.

"Ten milligrams. I thought that would get to her fast." Mulliner speaking, proud of himself.

"Where's the clipping?" I was sure I knew that voice, too, that fruity baritone.

I had to protect the clipping, I knew that. I could see my briefcase by the front door and I tried to crawl to it, but I was so dizzy and heavy-headed that I could barely move. One of the death dealers walked over easily, picked it up, dumped the contents on the floor, found the clipping.

"We'll take care of this now," Fruity said. He pulled a cigarette lighter from his pocket.

"No smoking in here," I tried to say, but that wasn't the point, the point was he was setting fire to the newspaper story, which I needed to save, it was so important, it was the story of Leydon's life. No, that wasn't right, but it didn't matter, he was rubbing the charred fragments between his fingers and laughing.

"And now let's get this overeager snooper to bed. She needs to sleep with the fishes tonight," Fruity said.

"Not Marlon Brando," I muttered. "Know you."

"Yeah, bitch, and I know you, too. So up you get." He laughed again and tried to pick me up. "Jeez, bitch weighs a ton! Give me a hand here, guys."

"She got Lou in the nuts," Mulliner said. "And my head isn't too good, but hers won't be worth shit in the morning."

Mulliner put an arm between my legs, seized my arms, and tried to lift me, but a hundred fifty pounds of dead weight is hard to move.

"Why do you want to go all the way out to the country with her? Leave her here. Smother her or something and let's get going."

"Chicago cops won't let it rest if they find her here," Fruity said. "Anyway, it's poetic justice."

Together, Fruity and Mulliner got me up, slung me over Mulliner's back. The motion made me seasick. I threw up and Mulliner swore, but he wobbled along, bouncing, making me sicker.

"Lou, you nutless wonder, stop crying, hold the doors," Fruity said.

We bounced down the hall. Out the back door. Something hit my back. Pellets? Was Boom-Boom firing his air gun at me? Gabriella would be furious. No, *idiota*. Water. Water from the sky. Rain, rain, I made myself remember the word. Death dealers wear slickers, I get hit by rain.

Over Mulliner's shoulder I saw the alley door to my building swinging loose. It opens from the inside only. How they got in, they blew out the lock. Noise, whole street full of noise. Sky noise, too. Thunder.

"I'm going home from here," Lou said. "You don't need me for anything else, and I need to get to a doctor; I'm bleeding all down my arm."

"I always need you, Lou: I'm your client, and a good lawyer sticks with his client."

Lou walked away. I wanted to cry; that was my only friend, he was leaving me with the death dealers. That wasn't right, he was a killer, too.

"Everything all right here?" A male voice, sharp, concerned.

"It's okay, buddy. We try to keep her out of the booze but she sneaked over here with a bottle."

"Not drunk. Drugs, they drugged me, get a cop." My mouth couldn't shape words, nothing came out but my raspy breath.

Buddy was solicitous—did Fruity and Mulliner need help getting me to the car? Nope, not as long as I hadn't thrown the damn keys away; I'd done that once and he'd had to call AAA in the middle of the night. I tried again to move my arms, but the punch I wanted to land drifted through the heavy night air like the tentacles on a jellyfish.

"We're okay here," Fruity said. "It's embarrassing to have you watch—can you move along?"

"Buddy, don't go." My tongue had become thick and furry, a dog tongue that wouldn't produce human speech.

Fruity opened a car door. Black SUV. Mulliner dumped me onto the backseat and I threw up again.

"Bitch threw up on my leather upholstery!" Fruity cried. "You should have warned me, damn it, Mulliner, I could have put some towels down."

A whiner would complain if God poured gold from the sky onto his head, that's what my mother said when our neighbor won a new Chevy in a contest at the mill and complained because he wanted a four-door. *Oro dal cielo,* of course, she said it in Italian and ever after that's what Boom-Boom and I called him, Signor Oro, which made him mad because he knew we were making fun of him but he didn't know what it meant.

"I'll follow you in my car," Mulliner said, slamming the door shut.

My head was spinning like a ride at the street fair. I begged and begged to go, all the other kids get to go, why can't I? My mother said they weren't safe, the company was unreliable, but Boom-Boom and I ducked under the fence and climbed onto the Spin Out and we both threw up the cotton candy we'd shared beforehand.

My eyes were still unfocused; I didn't see my father standing by the gate, grabbing me as Boom-Boom and I staggered out.

"We never strike you, Tori," my father said. "We think it's brutal to hit a child, but what can we do to get you to listen? The companies that run these street fairs don't bolt down their rides properly. If there's an accident, do you know what that would do to your mother and me?"

He threw me down onto my bed. I was too big for it, maybe he was punishing me by making me sleep in my baby crib. He stuck his hand into my pants and took my keys, I couldn't leave the house, but then he had pushed me onto the Spin Out and was whirling me around. "Stop, I'm sorry, stop, please," but the bouncing and the whirling kept on and on.

I threw up again, but my mother didn't wipe my face. She was too angry with me, I'd broken her heart for good and she was leaving me to rock and bounce in this horrible unsafe ride while the thunder rumbled and lightning bolted and a mean man with a voice from television laughed about me.

My head was filled with gravel. Signor Oro was so angry, he'd poured gravel into my ear. First he filled and filled my head with it. I couldn't think, I couldn't move. I was asleep, in the middle of a terrible nightmare, but I couldn't wake up.

The ride stopped but my head was still spinning, too many circles, too much gravel, we were at a gravel pit, mean Signor Oro was going to fill me to the bottom of my feet. Where was my papa, even if he was mad at me he should save me.

Signor Oro leaned into the Spin Out. "Now how am I going to get you out of here? Where's Mulliner? He's supposed to be behind me, and he fucking disappeared on me."

He pulled me to a sitting position. "I need a fucking crowbar to move you. Should have put that in my commentary, bleeding hearts add thickness to the belly. Maybe I will tomorrow when they put out the sad news you drowned. Snooping around Ruhetal, talking to the retard. But you got the clipping for me, thank you very much indeed."

Clipping. My brain moved feebly, as weak as my heavy arms and legs. The story about Tommy. Not Signor Oro leaning over me. Wade. Wade Lawlor. He'd killed his sister, and now he was going to kill me.

"Why? Why you kill Mag?"

I slurred the words into Lawlor's shoulder, barely intelligible, but they goaded him into fury. He flung me back onto the SUV's narrow backseat.

"Why did I kill Maggie, you fucking useless bitch? Because she had sex with that loser Link. Me. I was the one who loved her. I was who she loved best, she told me that, then I saw them, saw them by the lake. And that idiot retard Tommy saw them, too. Dancing. He said they were dancing, he didn't know what he was looking at. They were *screwing.*"

He was leaning over me, covering me with spittle. Bad to spit on people, but he wouldn't stop. "I ran off, but I came back later, came back when Link had gone to work and the retard was getting his rocks off at a fire. Maggie was sitting by the lake, smiling—smiling over Link, not me.

"'How could you.' I was crying, sobbing real tears, can you believe that, over a stupid bitch who lied to me. 'Oh, Wade, I'm in love with him,'" Lawlor mimicked her in a savage falsetto.

"In love with him? She was in love with that stupid loser? And look what's become of him, never held a job for more than six months, needed the Army just to get him out of bed in the morning. She could have had *me*. I'm the success, I make fifty million a year, she chose the wrong person to play games with.

"I choked her, my God, that felt good, and she made it easy, putting her hands on my arm, 'Oh, Wade, don't take it so hard, you'll find the right girl for you, you'll see.'

"'But what about me? You always said, you and me against the world, I'll always love you, Wade, but you were lying, you're just the whore of Babylon.'"

He grabbed my shoulders and shook me in his rage. He could strangle me right now and I couldn't lift my arms to save myself. I tried kicking but my feet moved clumsily. My slack hand bumped against my pocket. My phone. I had just enough strength to turn it on, but I couldn't speak loudly enough for anyone who answered to hear a cry for help.

"Tommy," I managed to croak.

"Don't cry over him." Lawlor let me go and dusted his hands. "He's lucky they didn't give him a lethal injection back then. I called the cops, I told them they'd find Tommy up to no good at Tampier Lake, and sure enough, there he was, crouched over Maggie's body, looking at her the way he did, like some useless dreary spectator at the show of life."

"Wuchik?" I slurred.

"Oh, him. You PIs, you think you're so smart, you watch too many TV shows. Vern Mulliner knows the pain I feel over my sister's death, the fact that the state lets that retard live on. He lets me know if anyone like a reporter or a fucking stupid lawyer goes talking to him, like the Ashford bitch did! We were already using Wuchnik to dig up crap on Salanter; when we learned that Ashford's crazy sister was talking to Tommy, we sent Wuchnik out to put a stop to it. And then he saw the clipping and thought he could put the bite on me. Bite me! The vampire bit back. And you thought you could outsmart me! No one can, you socialist liberals, you've been after me for years but you can't touch me."

He gave a hyena laugh, the way Tommy had, then suddenly bent and picked me up. I still couldn't fight, couldn't move my arms except to pat him, a touch like love, not rage. My head spun, swooped, as he hoisted me, raindrops on my face, he staggered, cursed, wobbled along a path in the dark. Frogs, I could hear them, and crickets, night noises. Water lapping.

He shoved me and I fell hard. Metal across my chest and legs, rocking underneath me. Nothing in my stomach, dry heaves, and then a laugh, metal rocking harder, the world upside down, metal on top, water below.

Hold tight to the rail, Boom-Boom said, *we go upside down here, cool, it's the coolest thing ever.*

I grabbed the rail, metal cutting into my hands, we were floating through space, so cool, don't be mad, Mama, we floated like fish in the Aquarium.

50. GONE FISHING

Stan Chalmers drove to Tampier Lake just as the sky was turning pink. A morning on the lake with a rod and line usually cured most of the ills he'd ever suffered, and he badly needed a cure today. Too much unpaid overtime, too many unpaid bills. He'd call in sick at seven, when his shift started.

He walked down to the quay, but didn't see his boat. When he realized the dock line had been cut, he tried to dial back the rage that swept through him; that was bad for his blood pressure, already high. A day at the lake was supposed to relax you, not give you a stroke.

He started the long hike around the shore, slapping at mosquitoes, swearing under his breath at the garbage-brained, meth-snorting, beer-guzzling jerk who'd done this on the one perfect fishing morning of the month. He caught a bit of luck: he spotted the boat a mere half hour after setting out. It had come aground upside down in a mesh of reeds and high grasses. Stan fought his way through the reeds and lifted the boat up. His plan to row quietly back to where he'd left his gear evaporated when he saw the body of a woman underneath.

51. V.I.'S LAST CASE

"I WANT TO THANK MR. WEEKES FOR MAKING THIS STUDIO available for today's taping of *Chicago Beat*. I want to thank the friends and family of V.I. Warshawski for being present, as well. We know this was a difficult decision for them."

A woman with a clipboard, who'd identified herself as Deirdre Zhou, paused while the audience turned to gape at the friends and family. Petra Warshawski shrank into her chair as the cameras panned them, but Lotty Herschel held herself upright, looking straight ahead, as if she weren't there. Max, on Lotty's left, could feel her trembling, and gently squeezed her hand.

Deirdre Zhou thanked the audience for understanding why the studio inspected their cell phones on their way in. "We tape this, but the show goes out live. We don't want you tempted to make that one ultra-important call in the middle of the show."

A little ripple of laughter greeted that.

"We'll be starting in about five minutes. We debated whether to call the show, 'V.I.'s Last Case' or 'Chicago's Own Nancy Drew.' We chose the second title because even though V. I. Warshawski is well known in our city, the show goes out to many other locations where they won't have heard of her, and we in the production team decided she was very much Chicago's own girl detective."

"Vic would just hate that," Petra burst out. "She can't—couldn't stand it when people call grown-up women 'girls.'"

The cameras swung around again to focus on her. Mr. Contreras, sitting next to her, shielded her face with his straw boater. "They're acting like we're some kind of zoo exhibit or something," he said to Lotty and Max. "That Beth Blacksin, the reporter who Cookie gave a million leads to, she even tried to come up to us with a mike when we got here, like we're a movie or something, not people with real feelings."

Jake Thibaut, who'd driven him and Petra to the event, patted Mr. Contreras comfortingly on the shoulder, and the older man subsided. His voice had carried through the small space, though, and a number of people turned to look at him, including Wade Lawlor. Lawlor, in his signature checked shirt, had smirked at Lotty when she and Max arrived. She had withdrawn into what Max called her "Princess of Austria" hauteur: Lawlor was vermin whose existence she didn't acknowledge.

Murray had never before rated Global One's premier studio space, where Wade Lawlor taped *Wade's World* in front of a live audience. Lawlor was unhappy at Weekes's decision to let Murray use the studio, but the head of the news division was adamant: *Chicago's Own Nancy Drew* was generating ad revenues almost as big as a *Wade's World* taping. Tickets to the show were gone within five minutes of appearing online.

Weekes stayed on the forty-eighth floor for the show, but most of Global's other big guns arrived, including their pet Senate candidate and commentator, Helen Kendrick. After looking at Kendrick, resplendent in red, Lotty noticed a pudgy, balding man sitting next to her. Although his round cheeks and turned-up nose made him look like a surprised baby, he had cold, shrewd eyes that Lotty found unnerving. She nudged Max, who—unlike Lotty—followed local news.

"Les Strangwell," Max scribbled on a piece of paper. "Right-wing kingmaker, Kendrick's campaign adviser."

Lawlor's and Kendrick's excited supporters leaned across Max and Lotty, hoping for autographs from their stars. Max tried to keep people from stepping on Lotty, but two small older people apparently didn't exist for the excited fans. Lotty shrank from the fawning fans. She wished she hadn't agreed to attend. *This is not my method, to make a display, a pretense of feeling. Everything I hate about the current world is present in this vulgarity.* She looked at her watch, wishing the program would start, end, be done.

Murray Ryerson had moved onto the set while she'd looked away. The brashness that usually annoyed her had left him; he seemed withdrawn, uneasy, and while he was going over some details with Zhou, he ran a finger behind his collar button, as if his shirt felt too tight.

Zhou said, "Thirty seconds to live, people."

The theater lights went down. Zhou stood in the wings, looking into a monitor. She held up a hand, lowering her fingers one at a time, and then the *Chicago Beat* theme song began and Murray half danced to stand in front of a city map. As the opening credits rolled, he touched parts of the map and the city beneath came alive, ballparks, suburban forests, the malls, the beaches along Lake Michigan.

When the music stopped, he put a finger on South Chicago and everyone saw the mills in full operation.

"V. I. Warshawski was born down here amid the fire and water where the country's great steel mills used to stand. The life and death of the mills, the life and death of her parents, of her beloved cousin, Boom-Boom"—and the Black Hawks hero, grinning, appeared on screen, holding up the Stanley Cup while V.I. joined the team on the ice to pour champagne on his head—"above all, the life and death of communities, of justice, made her who she was. Boom-Boom helped shape her as a street fighter—a pit bull, some called her—but her demand for justice for the least of those among us brought her first to the law, and then to her life's work as a private detective.

"Her successes were legendary. She and I first worked together twenty years ago; I was part of the famous, now defunct City News Bureau, which used to turn news wannabes into real reporters."

The audience laughed, then murmured appreciation or gasped as Murray went on to recount some of V.I.'s death-defying escapades: the time she jumped from a crane into the Sanitary Canal, the time she crawled through a burning building to rescue her aunt Elena, the night she was slashed by street gangs, the day she was trapped in the tunnels underneath the Loop, where she'd gone to bring a homeless family to safety.

"Her last case began as so many of her others did, with a call for help from family and friends. It ended in Tampier Lake ten days ago. We may never know what caused a strong swimmer like Warshawski to drown in those waters, but after a break, we'll uncover the events that led her to that suburban lake in the middle of the night."

While the commercials ran, the audience noise rose, until Zhou once more called time.

"Brothers and sisters," Murray said. "We love each other, hate each other, fight, but no one else understands our lives and our histories the way those people we grew up with do. And this is a story of brothers and sisters, of a sister whose mental illness led her from a brilliant legal career to a state mental hospital and the brother who thought she'd disgraced a famous family."

The camera picked out Sewall Ashford, who frowned ferociously. Lotty recognized his wife sitting next to him—Victoria had introduced them at the opera one night. Lotty knew that Murray had invited them today but was surprised that they'd shown up.

"A different brother and sister were devoted to each other. Miles Wuchnik was a private eye in Chicago. Like V. I. Warshawski, he had a solo practice. Unlike V.I., he supplemented his income with a little blackmail on the side. People hired him to uncover dirty secrets, and then he ferreted out the secrets of his clients. And charged extra to keep those secrets to himself.

"An Illinois politician's campaign hired Miles to dig up dirt on one of Chicago's richest men. The candidate's team hoped they could find some way to pressure Chaim Salanter into dropping his support for Sophy Durango's Senate campaign."

A shocked gasp went through the audience. Helen Kendrick looked as though she was going to get to her feet in protest, but Les Strangwell apparently cautioned her to silence. The studio camera left them alone— the crew knew Strangwell appeared on-screen rarely, and only when he had complete control over the situation.

Murray went on to explain how Miles tried to approach Salanter's granddaughter, and how he started eavesdropping on her text messages by planting a bug in her cell phone.

"There is yet another brother and sister in this story: a lonely pair of suburban teens. The sister took care of a brother three years younger than herself, because their drunk single mother wasn't up to the job of raising him. When the sister was seventeen, she was murdered, leaving her brother desolate. The killer, a man named Tommy Glover, was judged mentally incompetent and has been spending his days in the Ruhetal State Mental Hospital's forensic wing.

"The brother went on to have a successful career, but he's always been bitter that Glover wasn't executed. He paid a handsome fee to the hospital's security director to let him know if anyone ever approached Glover: the brother didn't want a lawyer or a reporter trying to drum up sympathy for a mentally incompetent man who'd spent nearly thirty years behind bars."

Murray nodded to Zhou, and the big TV screens showed Ruhetal Hospital, and then a stern-looking Vernon Mulliner, locking an Audi convertible and walking up to the front door of a mansion.

"Yes, the state of Illinois pays Mr. Mulliner two hundred thousand dollars a year to look after security at this hospital, but this summer, he bought the house he's walking into here for five million dollars. He also acquired that beautiful German sports car. And when we looked at his brokerage statements, we saw some amazing activity in them."

When Murray showed Mulliner's brokerage statements—obtained in ways that she didn't want to know—Lotty sat rigid. She didn't dare look at the men from Global Entertainment behind her, but she heard a sharp whisper—Lawlor to Strangwell? *Where did those come from?* The statements showed pay-ins of hundreds of thousand dollars' worth of shares in high-flying companies.

"By one of those coincidences that occasionally happen in life," Murray continued, "the mentally ill sister—the brilliant lawyer Leydon Ashford—met Tommy Glover's mother when Netta Glover came on one of her frequent visits to her son. Netta claimed that her boy was innocent, but that he'd never had proper legal representation. Leydon, who was still a member of the bar, agreed to take on his case. Two weeks later, Netta Glover was killed in a hit-and-run accident. Coincidence?

"The day Netta died, Leydon was released from Ruhetal; she was desperately trying to get in touch with her old law school buddy V. I. Warshawski to tell her about Tommy, when someone pushed her from the balcony in Rockefeller Chapel.

"In the last few days, Leydon recovered enough from her injuries to tell me what she learned in the locked wing; I'll share that with you when we come back."

The murmur through the audience this time was one of shock but also expectation; Lotty heard Lawlor say, "Sewall told me she'd never recover! Why doesn't someone pull the plug on this damned farce of a show?" and Strangwell reply, "Calm down, Lawlor. Don't turn a match into a forest fire. I'll just make sure Harold is watching upstairs."

As the show broke for another five minutes of commercials, Lotty saw Strangwell hurry from the studio. She didn't know if Murray also saw him go—he spent the break going over notes with Zhou. When the cameras started rolling again, Murray continued.

"When Leydon Ashford went to see Tommy Glover, Mulliner moved smoothly into action. He let the grieving brother know a lawyer was calling on his sister's killer. The brother complained to Leydon Ashford's family and they said, 'We're already working with a private investigator who's digging up dirt on Chaim Salanter for us; we'll get him to go out to Ruhetal and put a stop to Leydon. She doesn't listen to us, but a PI can be ruthless if he has to.'"

Lotty heard Faith Ashford's shocked outcry, quickly suppressed by her husband.

"And lo and behold, when Miles Wuchnik went into that locked wing, he found a picture, a photograph, that had also interested Leydon. Because this photograph suggested that maybe Tommy Glover hadn't been a killer after all." Murray made a suitable dramatic pause.

"And now Miles made a huge mistake. He stole the photograph from Tommy and mailed it to his own beloved sister, and then he tried to blackmail the man who he thought might be the real killer. Well, a guy who can strangle a woman and dump her body into a lake, and then let a mentally deficient man go to prison for it—a man like that knows how to deal with blackmailers.

"Our killer knew from Miles Wuchnik that Chaim Salanter's granddaughter was a big fan of that popular series of fantasy books, *Carmilla, Queen of the Night*. Wuchnik, eavesdropping on the girls through the bugs he'd planted in their cell phones, knew they were going to an abandoned cemetery for a late-night ritual to act out the lives of their favorite characters."

Murray paused while footage ran on the screens of the initiation ceremony. One of the girls, possibly Nia Durango, had been persuaded to turn over her cell phone, with its shaky video of the ceremony. The audience was able to laugh at the girls dancing in the rain, and tension in the studio eased a bit.

"Our killer thought he could kill two birds with one stone: murder Miles Wuchnik, and throw dirt onto Chaim Salanter, whom he seemed to hate for no particular reason. Our killer worked with one of the orderlies out at Ruhetal. He gave Xavier Jurgens the price of a new Camaro for going to the cemetery and murdering Miles Wuchnik.

"Our killer was a mile away at a lavish fund-raiser in his honor, but he couldn't resist slipping away to the cemetery to make sure the foul deed had been done. He called the police himself, hoping that Chaim Salanter's granddaughter and Sophy Durango's daughter would be trapped at the cemetery next to Miles Wuchnik's dead body."

The screens showed Miles Wuchnik with the rebar sticking out of his chest, police evidence photos that the public had never seen. Again, there were oohs and ahhs of horror and titillation.

"Imagine how annoyed our killer was—cranky, to use one of V.I.'s own favorite understatements—to discover that she had found the girls and was shepherding them to safety."

Murray paused to drink a glass of water. When he spoke again, his voice was dry, sunk at the back of his throat.

"V. I. Warshawski was a dogged and intrepid investigator. She followed Miles Wuchnik's trail and she discovered Xavier Jurgens. When V.I. started talking to Xavier, Xavier's girlfriend panicked and went to see the killer's lawyer. This lawyer was the man they'd worked with, the man who'd actually given Xavier the cash for the Camaro in exchange for killing Miles Wuchnik.

"When the lawyer reported the girlfriend's panicked visit to the killer, our man was cool. He laughed—he was riding on the big roller coaster, the one where you play God and decide who shall live and who shall die.

"The killer told Xavier he needed some antipsychotic drugs from the

Ruhetal pharmacy, and Xavier, in exchange for a bonus, agreed to meet him near the cemetery with the drugs.

"One of the Carmilla club girls had dropped her cell phone the night of Wuchnik's murder. The killer had picked it up that night, but it didn't have any way for him to identify its owner. However, he was alarmed when he saw that whoever owned it, she'd photographed him. He decided on a bold throw of the dice: he would get rid of Salanter's granddaughter. She was the girls' ringleader; if the others realized Arielle Salanter had been murdered, well, they'd be very circumspect about anything they said or published about their night in the cemetery. So he lured Arielle to the cemetery with a bogus text message, got Xavier there, filled them both with antipsychotic drugs, and left them to die in the shiny new Camaro Xavier had bought."

The monitors again showed police evidence photos, this time of Xavier Jurgens in his Camaro.

"But all this time, the killer worried about Tommy Glover's photo. Remember that? The evidence that Miles Wuchnik had taken from Tommy's room? The killer ransacked Wuchnik's home and car, he stole Leydon Ashford's computer and went through her papers, but the photo was nowhere to be found. After another break—who found the picture? And what did it prove?"

"What a crock of shit," Lawlor snapped. "And why are you in my studio space? A retard has a photo on his wall and this gets a lawyer and a private eye bent out of shape? Come on, Ryerson, you can do better."

"I'll try, Wade, I'll try." Murray waved from the set.

After the commercials, Murray brought out Iva Wuchnik. She was belligerent; she thought V. I. Warshawski had behaved like a common thug, coming into her home, taking apart her precious photo of her dead brother.

"If she got killed, I'm not surprised. She probably got someone else really steamed, someone big enough to teach her a lesson."

"Yes, it looks as though she did get someone else thoroughly steamed. But when she took your brother's photo apart, what did she find, Ms. Wuchnik?"

"A newspaper, an old newspaper that my brother had sent me for safekeeping. He said it was dynamite and that it would make our fortunes, but he died before he could explain why. And I wouldn't be surprised if the Warshawski woman was behind—"

"Take a look at the monitor to your right, Ms. Wuchnik," Murray interrupted. "Does that look like the same clipping your brother gave you to keep safe?"

Everyone craned their necks to look at Tommy Glover, grinning in the midst of the Tampier Lake volunteer fire department, with his arms around Good Dog Trey.

Iva Wuchnik grudgingly allowed as how it was the same photo, as far as she could recollect.

"And what did the article say?" Murray said.

"I don't know—it was something about a fire they put out. What difference does it make?"

Murray gave an odd smile. "We have an expert here in the studio who can explain that."

Everyone watched a white-haired man limp onto the set, heard him introduce himself as Eddie Chez, heard him explain that the picture was taken of his volunteer firefighters after they'd put out a garage fire in Tampier Lake Township on July 6, twenty-seven years ago.

"And what's so special about that fire? Or really about that date? For that, we'll turn to our final guest."

A woman emerged from the wings. She moved slowly, as if walking were not easy for her. A large hat shrouded her eyes and nose, but when she spoke, her voice was strong and clear.

"The photo shows that Tommy Glover was with Mr. Chez, putting out a fire, at the same time that Wade Lawlor was strangling his sister, Magda."

The murmur in the audience grew to an uproar: "What did she say?" "The fireman killed Wade's sister?" "*Wade* killed his sister? No way!" "Gosh, whoever that is, I hope she's got a lot of money, he's going to sue, for sure."

Murray let the noise build for a moment or two, then brought the room back to silence. "How do you know that, ma'am?"

"He told me. After he'd shot me full of haloperidol, so that I couldn't move, but before he dumped me into Tampier Lake to die. He killed his sister because she was in love with someone besides his own precious self."

"No!" Lawlor shouted. "That's a lie, it's a lie, whoever you are, whatever casting service Ryerson got you from! It was on the news feed, you said it yourself in the huddle, Ryerson! You saw her body, you went with the foreign doctor, you identified it, everyone in Chicago knows V. I. Warshawski is dead."

Lotty let out a breath she hadn't known she'd been holding. Murray pushed a stool forward, and the detective sat.

"Greatly exaggerated, that news," she said.

52. RAISING THE DEAD

I CAME TO WHEN THE BOAT BUMPED INTO THE REEDS. I WAS thirsty, feverish, my arms suspended above me on a metal bar. I thought my parents had wrapped me in a shroud and were burying me alive. Water was seeping into the coffin. I was going to drown before they realized what they'd done. Mama! Papa! I tried to shout, but I couldn't get out anything except a hoarse cry. The birds were singing, they were covering up any noise I could make.

Someone lifted the coffin away. I couldn't open my eyes; the sunlight was too sudden, too intense.

"Jesus H. Christ." It was a stranger's voice above me.

I tried to cry out again. A jumble of images, of my mother, the Spin Out, a black SUV. I couldn't make sense of it; my mother was dead, but maybe she had sent for me?

"Oh my God, she's breathing." The stranger was talking to himself.

I felt him cutting the shroud away from me. "It's a hell of a way to try to kill yourself. Next time, steal someone else's boat!"

"I don't steal," I tried to say, but it was too much effort; I drifted back to sleep.

I was being shaken, pulled, the shroud came off a bit at a time, I was wet. Had I peed all over myself? "Sorry," I slurred.

"Yeah, you should be sorry. You want to drown yourself, don't involve other people."

I didn't want to drown myself; I felt indignant that anyone would think that, but then the shroud was off, I was slung across a man's back. That had happened before, the man put me on his back and threw me into the lake. But now we were in a forest. Was I at camp in Wisconsin? That wasn't right somehow, but I couldn't figure it out and went back to sleep.

When I woke again, I was in the front seat of a pickup. The driver was a sunburned man who I'd never seen before.

"Are we in Wisconsin." I managed to ask.

"Is that where you're from? I'm taking you to the nearest hospital, not to goddamn Wisconsin. What got into you, stealing a boat in the middle of the night to do away with yourself?"

My childhood kept blurring into the present, but I knew that I had a photograph I had to protect.

"Lotty will help," I said, the name coming to me out of the blue. "My phone, my phone too wet, use yours, call Lotty."

The driver was happy to offload his problem onto someone else. Lotty's phone number, I'd dialed it so many times it popped into my head before I had time to worry about whether I could remember it.

"Ma'am? You don't know me, but I got a half-drowned lady in my truck who says you can help her."

Lotty spoke to me, realized how little able I was to respond, talked to the Good Samaritan, who gave her directions to a motel near Palos Heights. He waited for her to arrive—more because he didn't want to be stuck with the motel bill than out of kindliness, but I was thankful not to be left on my own.

Lotty probably broke every speed law in the four-state area, racing to the southwest suburbs. As soon as she saw me, she realized how badly drugged I was.

"You need to be hospitalized, at once, to get this junk pumped out of you, get fluids into you. But—the nearest hospital—I wouldn't be able to keep an eye on you. Can you hold on until we get back to Chicago? Drink this."

She somehow came up with a glass of orange juice. I was so feeble that most of it went down my damp and smelly T-shirt, but she brought another glass, put a straw in my mouth, held it steady while I swallowed.

"Call the police?" she said to the Samaritan. "I'll take care of that for you: I'm a physician, they know me."

He was glad to let Lotty do the rest of the work. "Ma'am, no offense, but—if I hadn't decided to take the day off to go fishing, no telling what this gal would have got up to. She stole my boat, see, and I went off looking for it. When I come to pick it up and get going, well, there she was, trying to drown herself. If she's a patient of yours, you'd best get her into a hospital."

"Yes, don't worry, you've been more than kind. We will of course reimburse you for damage to your boat. And your name, if the police need to talk to you?"

"Don't worry about that. Can't have my boss finding out I wasn't home with flu. Even though it's too hot now for the fish to be biting, I need a day on the water to recover from finding your patient."

On the drive back into Chicago, I tried to explain to Lotty what had happened, but I was having trouble with my memory at that point. Besides, it was still hard for me to talk.

Lotty stopped at a fast-food place and ordered a giant lemonade; she kept shaking me awake and demanding that I drink. The traffic was heavy, and the way she darted around tractor-trailers would have made me fear for my life if I hadn't been so doped.

Despite my incoherence, Lotty grasped enough of the story that she decided not to take me to the hospital: if Wade found out that I was still alive, protecting me would be a security nightmare. She took me instead to her own home. Jewel Kim agreed to tend to me personally; Lotty found a temporary advanced practice nurse to look after the clinic.

It was a good three days before I was well enough to sit up on my own. My memory came back slowly, too, but somewhere deep in my unconscious mind, I must have already decided on a strategy for exposing Lawlor: Lotty said that even while I was still delirious, I was crying, "Don't tell him I'm alive."

When I began speaking, and thinking, clearly again, Lotty reluctantly gave in to my demands to see Murray. It was Murray who said he would announce my death in the huddle.

"Wade's been mighty strange in the mornings," Murray said. "He hovers around, wanting to know if anyone's heard about unusual deaths in the area. I asked him point-blank if he thought the vampire was sucking children's blood, and he went off in a tirade. Hearing that you're dead should lull him."

Lotty and Max had spoken to Jake, who took a leave from his Marlboro fellowship to see me: every afternoon he played a private concert for me, a medley of my favorites from the bass repertoire.

Petra and Mr. Contreras had to be told the truth, too. I was afraid my cousin might not be able to keep the secret, but she handled it by taking a leave of absence from the foundation and hunkering down with the old man and the dogs.

Petra drove Mr. Contreras over to see me every afternoon. He annoyed Lotty by making spaghetti and meatballs for me in her kitchen, but she didn't have the heart to send him away, except on the day he thought it would be a good idea to bring Mitch and Peppy with him. Jake, his arms around me in the guest bed, laughed with me as Lotty ordered the dogs away so fiercely that Mitch's voice was strangled mid-bark.

It was after I'd made my first solo walk from Lotty's guest room to the balcony and back that Lotty let me start working with Murray on the program. Murray's first hurdle was to clear the topic with his management.

Murray's producer, Deirdre Zhou, didn't know I was still alive; she'd been told that Murray's final guest was someone with a special insight into the death of Wade Lawlor's sister. Part of what kept Murray up several nights running was writing two scripts: one for Deirdre Zhou, which showed me following leads to nowhere in the so-called vampire murder. That was the one that made it up and down Murray's chain of command, getting approval from Weekes himself.

The second script was the one that Murray memorized, going off the teleprompter, leading Wade to his frenzied outburst.

Once his producers had gotten permission from Weekes to do the show, Murray worked like a demon. He turned up another copy of the *Southwest Gazette* with Tommy Glover's picture in it. Wade apparently had gone into the paper's archives when he first learned about the photo and pulled their old paper copy, but Murray put out a bid on eBay, and paid five hundred dollars to someone in Utah who had kept a copy of that issue. Murray persuaded Iva Wuchnik to come on the show, telling her that this would be her chance to vindicate her brother. He went to Eddie Chez, from the Tampier Lake Township Fire Department, and said they wanted to go over a story that went back to the department's volunteer days.

We all wondered why Chez hadn't come forward when Tommy was first arrested. When we spoke to him after the show, the old fireman scratched his head in embarrassment.

"I didn't connect the dots. Tommy, when he was arrested, it was two days after the fact, and, well, even though he hung around our crew, a lot of times we didn't really notice him special. And then Wade, well, he told everyone he'd seen Tommy follow Maggie into the woods. It's terrible that we all believed him without even thinking about it.

"And even though Netta kept saying Tommy was innocent, well, she'd been at work when Tommy was at the Reinhold Garage fire, and even she was so rattled she didn't connect the picture in the *Gazette* to the murder. Wade must've been like a cat on hot coals when that come out, but nobody put two and two together. It's like my wife says, we all had this unconscious idea about what a retarded guy might do— we all were just prejudiced, plain and simple."

53. VAMPIRES DON'T KILL EASY

IF MY STORY CAUGHT MEDIA ATTENTION AS FAR AWAY AS MY mother's hometown in Umbria, the results were more complicated here at home. Max, who has more organizational savvy than I, knew that we couldn't blindside Detective Finchley. Right before we left for the Global studios, Max called Finchley to warn him that a major balloon was going up involving me, Lawlor, and the deaths of Miles Wuchnik and Xavier Jurgens.

Even so, Finchley was angry that we'd kept him in the dark. "If you'd come to me straight off, instead of playing your cute game on television, I could have gotten a warrant to search Lawlor's SUV. He got rid of the car, says it was stolen and he doesn't know where it is, but the trail Liz Milkova followed suggests he sent it to a junkyard. Which means, as you know very well, that we'll never find the backseat where you threw up, or the front fender that probably killed Tommy Glover's mom. Lawlor bought a nice new Land Rover with his insurance money."

"Terry, he confessed it all to me, and he tried to kill me!"

"I don't doubt your word, but we can't get the state's attorney to agree that a confession you heard while you were heavily drugged carries weight."

"But he also confessed right there on television," Max said.

Finchley shook his head. "He said something wild on television, but he's getting beaucoup e-mails and phone calls crying out for his vindication: his fans believe he's the victim of a frame-up by Chaim Salanter and the so-called liberal media. The state's attorneys from Cook and DuPage are very aware that they're up for reelection—they don't want to antagonize his massive fan base. And Global is exerting its own pressure on the state's attorneys and the CPD, believe me. I'm doing my best, V.I., but, man, it would be so much easier if you'd brought me in on day one."

Even so, Finchley was able to get Mulliner and Louis Ormond to strike deals. Ormond admitted that he had delivered money to Xavier Jurgens on behalf of his client, but insisted he knew nothing about any murders, or attempted murders: yes, he'd been in my office when Mulliner and Lawlor jumped me, but he'd been trying to persuade his client to use the law, not brute force, to restrain me.

Mulliner was on shakier ground: a search of hospital records proved that he'd removed ten milligrams of injectable haloperidol from the pharmacy on the day I'd been assaulted. Lawlor had paid him so much money for reporting on visits to Tommy Glover that he'd felt compelled to do whatever the cable star wanted; each demand he acceded to sank him deeper in Lawlor's mire.

Our biggest breakthrough came from finding the owner of the rowboat. Murray haunted the fishing quay at Lake Tampier, offering rewards to anyone who could ID the rowboat Lawlor had stolen. Stan Chalmers finally came forward. He'd been afraid that his boss would fire him if he learned that Chalmers had been playing hooky, but Murray's money, coupled with the drama of my story, got him to change his mind. Chalmers let Finchley take the boat; the evidence techs found Lawlor's fingerprints on the prow.

The Internet gave us another break. When Les Strangwell, Helen Kendrick's campaign guru, had gone up to the forty-eighth floor to alert Weekes to what Murray was actually saying, Weekes pulled the plug. Weekes also tried to kill any footage of the "Nancy Drew" episode of *Chicago Beat,* but by then the show had gone viral across the Web.

The blogosphere was filled with screams over the story. Wade's detractors thought it was such a chilling story that he should be banned from the airwaves. When advertisers began backing away from *Wade's World* as fast as fleas jumping from a dead plague victim, Harold Weekes gave Lawlor a leave of absence. This caused Wade's hardcore supporters to picket Global One for a good ten days, demanding his reinstatement, but GEN's senior staff noted that the pickets weren't just a small group, but one that was decidedly unmediagenic.

All the time we'd been putting together the script for the show, Murray had worried that he'd lose his job. I'd scoffed: it just didn't seem possible that a great scoop, one that gave Global the best viewer rating they'd ever had, would boomerang on him, but that's what happened. A week after the Nancy Drew segment, Weekes fired Murray. By e-mail, not even giving him the courtesy of a phone call, let alone a personal meeting. He might agree in private that Lawlor had been a criminal, but he couldn't forgive Murray for killing his golden-egg layer.

Once the axe had actually fallen, Murray seemed more relaxed. He took a job with Sophy Durango, as her campaign's media adviser. They exploited the Kendrick campaign's hiring of Miles Wuchnik to dig up dirt that didn't exist on Chaim Salanter, and Durango's poll numbers going into the end of summer kept climbing. Sometimes class wins.

Murray and I both put as much muscle as we could into getting Tommy Glover released. Murray framed the copy of the *Southwest Gazette* story he'd bought for the show; I delivered it to Tommy Glover in person.

Tania Metzger at Ruhetal agreed to act as Tommy's advocate. She got the Open Tabernacle Church to rally around him—they were, after all, an open community, embracing people wherever they might be on life's journey. The church was able to get his arrest voided, although that took an amazing amount of work. And they found a place for him in a group home. The Tampier Lake Township Fire Department made him their honorary mascot, so that was one happy ending.

Dick came to see me one night. I was back in my office part-time, trying to assure my clients that I hadn't become such a media hound that I'd forgotten my professional commitments. Dick wouldn't apologize for his partners, but he did say that the "incident" had caused them to draw up strict guidelines for the use of outside investigators, and what those investigators could do.

"Louis has agreed to take early retirement. We believe him when he says he didn't know he was giving Xavier Jurgens money to kill Miles Wuchnik, but we're a little concerned about the ethical lines he may have crossed."

I didn't argue with him about it—he'd done more than many in his position might have. He left behind a case of Barolo. I was touched that he'd remembered my favorite wine after all these years, although I couldn't help wondering if I was letting myself be bribed into silence by accepting it.

Right before Labor Day, Chaim Salanter sent his private jet to fly me to Marlboro with Max and Lotty so we could attend Jake's end-of-the-season concerts. The pilot had just brought Arielle Zitter and Nia Durango back from Israel in time to start the school year. Arielle, like me, had fully recovered from her drug overdose.

When we boarded Salanter's plane, the flight attendant gave us each an envelope, with information about the jet's amenities, how to make phone calls on board, and the sanitized, public version of Chaim Salanter's life. My envelope also included a check, for fifty thousand dollars, drawn on Salanter Enterprises, labeled "for professional ser-vices." Which covers a lot of ground indeed.

Chaim's gratitude spread in several directions. He persuaded Boadi-cea Jones to come to Chicago to give a private reading from her new *Carmilla* book for the girls in the Malina Foundation's book groups. That event brought girls and parents back to Malina in record numbers. He also hired Kira and Lucy's mother to work as the resident house-keeper at his fifteen-room Michigan cottage—another happy ending, especially since he had a couple of horses out there.

My own happiness during the flight to Marlboro was muted: Leydon had died the week before. Murray's on-air claim that she had regained consciousness was never true—just an effort to get Wade to expose himself.

I went to the funeral with Faith and her daughter, Trina. Neither Sewall nor his mother attended. Leydon's will specified that she wanted to be cremated, and her ashes spread in Forest Park's Waldheim Cem-etery, where the anarchists Lucy Parsons and Emma Goldman lay. Sewall threatened to go to court to block the burial, claiming that Leydon was not in her right mind or she wouldn't have chosen a post-humous way to embarrass her family further.

Faith told Sewall that by the time he got an injunction, he'd have to get a rake to collect his sister's ashes, and that he would look pretty darned stupid. I don't know who was more impressed, Trina or me.

Jake's High Plainsong group played the funeral service at Rockefeller Chapel. They let me dust off my rusty alto to take part in singing the Stravinsky setting of Psalm 39, which Leydon had liked all those years ago. Dean Knaub conducted the service and delivered the eulogy.

"We know that Leydon did not believe in God, or the Resurrection of the Body, but there is an immortality to love, to the love within Leydon that made her lay down her life for a stranger, to the love of her friend, Victoria, who risked her own life to see justice done to that same stranger.

"Perfect love casts out fear, we are told. None of us is capable of perfect love, but as we help each other along this difficult journey which is life, the love we bear for one another does ease our burdens. And even in death, that love binds us together; truly, in death, we are not divided."